Loveless in the Nam

by

Jim Boersema

DORRANCE PUBLISHING CO., INC.
PITTSBURGH, PENNSYLVANIA 15222

Many of the events and locations in Loveless in the Nam are real and a matter of history and public record. Many of the scenes were created around historical incidents for the purpose of fiction.

There may be persons alive who took part in similar events or in the historical actions that occur in this book. It is possible therefore that someone may be mistaken for a character in this book. However, all individuals and persons who appear in Loveless in the Nam are the complete creation of the author and entirely fictional. Any similarity by a character in this book to a real person, living or dead, is entirely coincidental.

The exception is the one public figure mentioned by name, President Richard Nixon. The scene in which he appears was an actual event, although it did not transpire exactly as described in this book.

To My Parents, Munroe and Waneeta

Dorrance Publishing Co., Inc.
701 Smithfield Street
Pittsburgh, PA 15222
Visit our website at www.dorrancebookstore.com

ISBN: 978-1-4349-1176-6
eISBN: 978-1-4349-3885-5

Prologue

The following composition was provided for publication to the editor by the family of Colonel Frank J. Loveless. Colonel Loveless served in the army for more than twenty years and disappeared in China in the summer of 1992. He was apparently on temporary assignment for an intelligence operation at the time, although his exact mission has not been revealed.

After waiting a number of years, his family decided to publish the memoirs of Colonel Loveless. This manuscript is but the first of several that detail his career. It will—as he himself stated—shock and embarrass a number of individuals. There will likely be some people who will come forward in the coming months to denounce the validity of Loveless's writings. Yet, these memoirs are even more damaging to the reputation of Loveless himself. They reveal him to be at times cowardly, dishonest, and treacherous—quite the opposite of his public persona. This critical self-assessment lends an air of truth to the documents.

Frank J. Loveless was the son of a military officer who traveled extensively during his childhood. Drafted into the army in 1968, he had served a total of twenty-three years before vanishing in China. During that time, he fought in major conflicts like Vietnam and the Gulf War, as well as some smaller engagements in places like Panama and Iran. He was decorated for valor a number of times and, if these memoirs are accurate, was a prisoner of war on several occasions. Here is his story of Vietnam, warts and all.

CHAPTER ONE

I may be the only soldier in American history to be nearly killed in combat by a can of beans and franks. It may sound strange for someone to admit to such a thing, but the night it happened in the brush country of South Vietnam was a major turning point in my life. It kicked off an unplanned military career that has seen more than its share of fame and fortune over the past two decades.

Those who really know the truth about me—that I'm a fraud and perhaps the world's biggest coward—are mostly dead now, thank God. The few others who suspect the truth won't speak out for fear of being thought jealous of someone who's been decorated by no less than two US presidents. Besides, it would be their word against mine and, while I've never received much public recognition, Colonel Frank Loveless is a legend in the army—praised by the brass, envied by his peers, and admired by the uninformed. I may be the luckiest man alive, and the beans and franks were the start of it all.

It happened in the spring of '69. I was a second lieutenant, newly commissioned in the US Army, and assigned as the Third Platoon leader with Bravo Company, an infantry unit operating in the northern part of South Vietnam. I'd only been in the field a short time and was still learning how to take malaria pills and the names of the twenty plus soldiers assigned to my unit when our company commander, a Captain Prion, convened a late-night conference. There were about a dozen of us, hunched over in the dark, a sliver of moon glistening above, our only light, and the wind blowing through trees off to one side as he issued his instructions in a low voice.

"Intel says the VC have a staging area near the ocean where they've been recruiting and training," Captain Prion said. "They think there could be up to a hundred gooks there, probably well armed and well rested 'cause the Division hasn't had anyone up there in months. Our job," he added, pausing deliberately for effect, "is to go in tomorrow morning and clean out the whole mess of 'em. If Intel's got it right, we can expect plenty of trouble. Nothing we can't handle, but it won't be easy and we'll probably have some losses. So tell your men to get a good night's rest 'cause tomorrow could be a long day. And make sure they're ready for an early morning pick up. Aviation will be here at 0600."

Someone had sense enough to ask if we would have any support from other friendly units, and Prion said something about artillery and another infantry company that would be nearby. But he made it clear that he didn't want any help, and wouldn't ask for it unless things really got out of control, which he promised would not happen so long as he was in command. That wasn't a comforting thought, especially for someone like me who had yet to come under enemy fire. But no one else spoke up, so I kept my mouth shut.

It didn't surprise me that no one challenged Prion. In the short time that I'd known him, I never saw anyone question his decisions. Of course, he was our commander, but, at about six and a half feet tall and what must have been 300 pounds in weight, Prion was more than that. He was an imposing, domineering soldier who I found to be short-tempered, foulmouthed, and vindictive to those who weren't his favorites. I don't think I ever saw pleasure on his square, flat face except when he was barking out orders to some poor soldier. He was the type of thug I had avoided in high school. But in the 'Nam, I had no choice: he was my boss. So, despite what I felt were obvious reservations on the faces of others in that meeting, we all just accepted Prion's words and then split up to get our separate platoons ready for the next day.

I hardly slept that night. I just laid there on the ground, my head propped on my rucksack and staring up at the night sky while imagining the worse that could happen the following day. I didn't think about it at the time, but I have since read somewhere that mental stress can cause a person to have physical problems. I believe that to be true, having now experienced such reactions numerous times over the years. That night, my stomach was definitely tied in a knot which surely, in turn, contributed to my problem the following evening.

The sun had barely peeked over the horizon when Prion had us assemble in small groups along both sides of a large clearing near a highway. We sat for nearly half an hour as the sun rose steadily in a clear sky. I had already started to break out in a full sweat when we heard the "*thump-thump-thump*" of helicopters headed our way. At the sound of them, someone popped smoke grenades to signal our location, and within seconds, a pack of Hueys appeared on the horizon, coming from the direction of the Chu Lai military camp down south. Before long, they swarmed down on us like so many angry hornets and then hovered in place just a few feet off the ground. We ran, ducking down to avoid winds and dust kicked up by the bird's swirling blades, and clambered aboard. Then with a whoosh we were airborne, streaming towards our target, miles away to the east.

It took only a few gut-churning minutes to get there. It was a typical army chopper ride, bumping along in mid-air, the wind blowing through open side doors, until the one I was in suddenly tipped forward and plunged straight down at the ground, nearly throwing me forward against the wall that separated us passengers from the pilots. I grabbed hold of something on the ceiling to steady myself and looked sideways to see a Cobra gunship, flying past and spewing rockets and mini-guns at something to our front. Farther out there was a Loach skimming along a line of trees, laying out a smoke screen, which I assumed was meant to cover our arrival. Seconds later, the explosions from the Cobra's rockets echoed back and I felt myself trembling, fearful of what was coming. I closed my eyes, took deep breaths, and tried to calm myself.

Then abruptly we were down, landing with a jolt in an open field. I tumbled out of the chopper, ran for ten or twenty seconds, and then hit the dirt hard on my stomach when I saw other soldiers around me going to the ground. I stayed facedown, flat in the dirt, until I realized there were no shots being fired, either by us or an enemy force. At that, I carefully raised my head and glanced around to see what lay ahead. What I saw was a long line of trees about a hundred feet to our front, with smoke rising from within at several locations, probably caused by the Cobra's rockets. To my left and right, the rest of my platoon lay on the ground, with everyone looking to their front or over to me, as if expecting instructions; behind, the choppers were already going airborne, leaving the scene. Other than that, there was nothing. No gunfire. No apparent movement of anyone in our vicinity, much less enemy combatants. There was nothing except the sounds of chatter coming from my RTO's radio, as Prion's voice barked out instructions.

I didn't catch his exact words, but soon after, several soldiers from the First Platoon, off to my right, cautiously stood up and then, crouching down, made a few hesitant steps towards the tree line. *Better you than me*, I thought, watching them slowly walk towards possible death. But nothing happened so they slowly advanced towards the wood line. By the time they were halfway there, more soldiers rose to their feet to trail along, and then slowly each of us followed in turn, until the entire company was headed in the same direction.

We entered the tree line, with me walking directly behind my RTO, a soldier from the Midwest named Smyth, and went only a short distance into the woods before the command came to halt in place. I crouched down against a tree, with Smyth unknowingly shielding me off to one side, and peered around the lightly wooded area. It wasn't nearly as thick with growth as other places we'd been in earlier that week and it didn't look to me like anyone, certainly no large group of soldiers, had been there recently. The only sign of life I saw were the ever-present bugs that seemed to infest everything in Vietnam.

Of course, with the choppers and all, we'd made enough noise to wake the dead on our way in there. If there had been any dinks, they probably di-di-maued the moment they heard us coming over the horizon. Smyth looked over at me and said something like: "Well, this was a wild goose chase." I smiled weakly and nodded in the affirmative, while silently taking in a deep breath of relief. I was absolutely thrilled that no one had been waiting for us.

But Prion wasn't so complacent. We had been sent there to find the enemy, and since they weren't in that location, he decided to look for them. He assembled us platoon leaders for a short pep talk and said, "They must have left here on the last day, which means they haven't had time to go too far. The ocean's over there," he said, pointing east, "and down south it's more open country, where they would be easily observed and caught. The most logical place for them to have gone is up north, so that's where we'll go. Get your men ready to move out. We'll go company on line and head in that direction. If they're around here someplace, we'll find 'em."

I wanted to shoot the idiot. To me, if the gooks didn't want to wait around for us, so much the better. But no one else spoke up, so I took a deep breath and bravely said, "Sir, don't you think we should wait here for further orders? I mean, if the enemy has moved to a new location, G-2 will find them and then take us wherever they are. This is an easy place for pickup."

Prion looked at me like I were something stuck on the bottom of his boot and said disdainfully, "You can wait here if you want, Lieutenant, but the rest of us are headed north. Our orders are to come here and fight the enemy. Since the enemy isn't here, we'll go find where they are, if that's all right with you!"

I assured him it was, since any other response would have been at my own peril, and off we went, more than a hundred of us stretched out a city block wide, trudging our way towards God knew what. I was certain we were headed straight for an ambush and had visions of John Wayne dying on the slopes of Iwo Jima, surrounded by people who didn't care. Each man went forward slowly, staying just far enough away from the person on their left or right, in case anyone stepped on a booby trap. As an officer, I walked behind the platoon with Smyth by my side and made sure to step in the exact footsteps of the man in front of me, reasoning that whatever he had just walked on was safe from land mines.

The area we went through was desolate, filled with scrub bushes, scraggly trees, and ground baked hard by a sun that beat down on us mercilessly. The only thing that seemed to live there were plenty of insects, and they were apparently sorry for it, since they took every opportunity to land on me. I remember the place even smelled bad, but then I was still new to Vietnam. The longer I stayed in that infernal country, the more I got used to strange smells.

We trudged forward for most of the day and, except for a few signs that said someone might have been there recently, never saw a living soul. By midafternoon, even Prion was willing to admit that there weren't any VC in the area. He finally issued orders to stop near a small wooded area, where we set up a perimeter defense and began to dig ourselves in for the night.

Every soldier there was relieved, except possibly our beloved commander. The day that started out so fearfully had ended up much like the other four or five I'd already spent since joining the unit—just another walk in the country. Instead of being in my first real battle, I'd made it through the day with nothing worse than an upset stomach, which must have been caused by a combination of stress and my lunch meal of warm Carling Black Label beer and C-ration beans and franks.

I'd already spread out my sleeping mattress on the ground and was prepared for some shut-eye when, just before dark, Prion called up on the PRC-25 and said, "Loveless, I still think the dinks are out there someplace close. After the sun goes down, you take a squad about 50 yards north and set up an ambush site. If they're around here, that's the most likely way they'll come. But keep it quiet and don't engage unless you have to. If you hear anything, just signal back. Understand?"

"Yes, Sir, I understand," I answered, hanging up the receiver. And I did. I understood that whoever went out there in the dark, fifty yards away from the rest of the company, would be sitting ducks if the VC showed up. Yet, I didn't dare disobey Prion's orders. So I did the best thing under the circumstances. I pulled aside my platoon sergeant, a tough veteran named Mann, and relayed the commander's orders, saying I would rather go myself, but asked that he instead take the lead because I was feeling really sick just then, which was true since my stomach was in turmoil. Mann was a soldier's solder. He'd been in-country for more than six months but acted like he'd been there his entire life. As tall as me at a little over six feet and very physical, Mann was always alert to his surroundings, could speak some Vietnamese, and took no bullshit from the troops. He was as good a soldier as Prion, but without Prion's arrogance and obsession with control. I was glad Mann was my platoon sergeant, but figured we would clash sooner or later once he realized my true nature—that I really didn't give a damn about that stupid war and just wanted to go home alive. Fortunately, that night was still early in our relationship.

Mann gave me a strange look but never said a word, just went around and selected his men and then led them quietly out of the encampment. I watched them disappear in the dark and then lay down on my flattened air mattress to get some sleep. It wasn't to be. My mind was too alert, filled with fear of the unknown, and my stomach was, if anything, getting worse by the hour, even though I'd had nothing to eat since the can of beans and franks hours earlier. I just lay there, unable to doze off, staring up at the night sky. Then the dinks came.

It was sometime after midnight when Smyth woke me up to say the ambush site had signaled us—two flashlight beams of light. That meant they had heard noises—human noises. I had no choice but to radio Prion and tell him about the signal. I hardly got the words from my mouth when he snapped back. "Loveless," he screeched, "what the hell are you doing with a radio on ambush? Are you crazy? They can hear you!"

"It's okay, Sir," I pleaded, "I'm in the perimeter. Sergeant Mann wanted to take the ambush team out, so I stayed behind with the platoon. They signaled us by light."

I heard some muttering over the radio, including the words "Mother F—," and then Prion was back on, saying, "Loveless, now listen up, you chickenshit! When I tell you to send out a squad that means *you* lead it, not someone else! You're the goddamn platoon leader. Now I'm coming down your way. When I arrive, you better be out on that patrol or I'm gonna shoot you myself! Is that clear enough, Soldier?"

"But, Sir," I cried, "they signaled that there's movement in the area. I can't go out there now!"

"Suit yourself, but you're a dead man if you're there when I arrive," said he, hanging up.

The logic of his argument was convincing. So, ignoring the pain in my stomach, I grabbed Private Bobby Bryson, a black GI from Chicago who had joined the unit with me just days earlier, and the two of us began crawling out to the ambush site. It wasn't far, maybe one hundred feet, but the beans and beer had my stomach churning something terrible by this time, so it felt like we were crawling across Kansas. What worried me more than my stomach was the thought that our own people would shoot us in the dark as we inched towards them. But I needn't have worried. They were so focused on sounds coming from their front that we could have had bells on our boots and still come up on them unseen. As it was, we got right up to the edge of their site and then I whispered out Mann's name as loud as I dared. A muffled reply came back and we crawled forward again, taking less than a minute before dropping down into a small ditch, almost on top of one of our guys. In the dimness, I could make out Mann and several others leaning against the far side of the small depression, which looked about eight feet square and up to three feet deep. They were staring out into the dark with a starlight scope.

"Sergeant Mann," I asked, sliding up beside him, "what's up?"

"Movement, Sir," he replied quietly. "They're in front of us and on the right side, too, slowly headed for the unit."

"Right! Okay, let's get back to the company lines," I answered, starting to move to the rear of the little pit.

"Can't do that, Sir," said the sergeant, grabbing my arm and holding me in place.

"And why not, for Christ's sake?" I wailed quietly. "We'll be killed if we stay here!"

"Maybe, Sir," said Mann calmly, as though he didn't care about dying. "But the dinks are headed in that direction. They don't know we're here, and if we're lucky they'll bypass us. Being out in the open will be worse than here. We didn't expect anyone from our rear, so you guys snuck up on us, but eight of us trying to crawl back to the company will be a lot harder. Our own people will think we're Charlie and we'll be caught out in the open between both sides. We're safer staying right here and keeping quiet."

He was right and I knew it. We were trapped like rats on a sinking ship. Leave or stay, it didn't matter. Either way, we were in a hell of a spot. So I muttered something, slunk to one side of that little hole, and peered out into the dark, my heart pounding and my hands in a sweat despite the coolness of the night.

I've noticed many times since that my senses are heightened when face-to-face with death. It was certainly true that night. At first, I couldn't make out a thing in the blackness. Then I gradually became aware of small sounds and the slightest movement in bushes to the front of our hole, as Charlie slowly inched his way towards the main camp. One particular bush caught my attention. I was mesmerized watching it alternately sit stationary for a bit of time, and then inch forward again. It was damned eerie, I tell you, hiding there, knowing there were men just a short distance away who would kill me if they had the chance. I kept perfectly still and said a prayer to God for help, *"Oh God, let them go away. Let them go away. Let them go away...."*

That was a mistake, as God must have been listening to this hypocrite. I no sooner finished the prayer than I felt a sharp rumbling pain in my stomach. The beans and the stress I was feeling finally came to the fore, and against my own will I broke the stillness of the night with a loud, long fart. The movement in the bush stopped instantly, one of my group said "shit" in a low voice, and I doubled over at my knees, releasing yet more gas and certain that I would soon be dead. But nothing happened. For ten, maybe fifteen, seconds, there was dead silence as we all froze in place. *No one heard*, I thought briefly and sighed with relief.

Then some idiot back at the company broke the spell by laughing out loud, followed quickly by several others, who probably thought it was one of the dinks who had farted. That did it. Almost immediately, there was a "boom" directly in front of me, followed by a flash screaming through the dark as an RPG exploded near the unit's position. Then all hell broke loose. I heard three or four loud explosions in the company area, probably grenades, followed by the popping of M60s and 16s opening up and the return sound of AK-47s crackling from the dark all around us. For the next five minutes, an eternity if you're in the middle of it, the onslaught continued, as both sides tried to outdo the other with sheer firepower. Then suddenly it quieted down somewhat, with each side becoming more deliberate in targeting their shots.

That's when I heard the screaming. It came from the company lines and was the most hideous and frightening sound I had ever heard. Even now, after more than twenty years, I can hear those terrifying screams echoing through the night. I later learned that one of our troops had taken grenade shrapnel in his mid-section, and no amount of painkiller or medical care would stop his agony. He must have known he was dying, so he lay there screaming in the dark, getting the last full measure of life. It unnerved me, I can tell you that.

Throughout it all, our small group just stayed as quiet as possible, not joining in on the fight. As for me, I just buried my head in the ground, curled up my body, and mumbled over and over, "Just don't let them find us...just don't let them find us...just don't let them find us..." Amazingly, no one did, even though I'd given away our position with my gas release. Several times I heard footsteps running close by, but no one stumbled on our little hideout. As I crouched in my corner, Mann stayed on the opposite side of the depression and had our small group arranged so that someone was covering every avenue of approach. Each of them was leaning against the short dirt wall, peering into the dark, and fortunately holding their fire, which probably kept us from being discovered.

More time went by with both sides still trading sporadic gunfire. Then, from out of nowhere, a head-numbing explosion literally bounced me off the ground. A second one quickly followed, only louder and closer. It was artillery!

Prion had called in artillery from a nearby firebase and was deliberately marching it back towards his position, trying to catch the gooks in a trap. The only way they could avoid it was to flee the area running through the artillery fire or move towards the company lines, where our troops waited. It was a smart move by Prion, but he'd either forgotten or didn't care that our ambush team was in that trap, too! If he pulled the artillery in close enough, we could be blown to kingdom come! I sprung up and started to clamber out of the ditch when I felt a tug on my ankle that pulled me back. It was Mann. "You fool," I yelled, "that's artillery! If we stay here, we're dead! Prion's forgotten us! He's trying to save the company, not this goddammed squad!"

"Maybe so, Lieutenant," said Mann, cool as can be, "but we're still safer in this hole than out there. Shrapnel explodes up and out. If we're standing up outside, it can hit fifty feet away and still kill us. We can't get hurt in this hole unless it comes straight in on top of us. Plus, there ain't no gooks in here. Go out if you want! You're the officer! But the rest of us are stayin' here where it's safe!"

Well, how would you like to stay here with a couple of M16 rounds up your ass, you stupid jerk, I thought. But I restrained myself and just said, "Yeah, I guess you're right. We'll just have to keep down and ride it out," and I crawled back to my corner of the hole, shaking uncontrollably each time another round exploded nearby.

It was about then that I noticed my pants were wet. To my surprise, it just came out; I couldn't stop myself. It has since become routine for me in near-death situations. First, I feel the exhilaration of combat, with my senses totally alert, followed by mind-numbing fear as my brain analyzed the situation and concluded that death was on its way, and then the cool refreshment of urine running down my leg as my body just lets go. I think a lot of guys under fire wet their pants, but few ever admit it. In the 'Nam it was so muggy, we could hide it by just saying our pants were wet from sweat. I did once.

Turned out Mann was right about staying in the crevice. The artillery came in close but stopped short of our position. I did feel some small bits of metal tinkle down from above several times, but those, having lost their explosive stream, were harmless. And the big guns did stop the VC attack. When the explosions finally stopped, the night turned quiet again, with the enemy having slunk away. The only notable sounds were screams that still came from the company area, and those didn't end until half an hour later, when a dust-off chopper landed in the unit perimeter to retrieve our dead and wounded. At the time, I thought the pilot was crazy, landing a helicopter in the dark, knowing an enemy force was probably still in the area. When the chopper did come down, the guys back at the unit did their part by blasting away in all directions in a mad minute of sustained fire. If Charlie had still been there, he most likely would have kept his head down. But by that time, having lost the element of surprise, I don't think there were any VC hanging around still looking for a fight. Those of us in the ditch were the only ones outside the perimeter, and we sure weren't about to stick our heads up.

At sunrise the next morning, the eight of us straggled back into camp, exhausted from a night of anxiety and no sleep, but relieved to be alive. Although isolated and in the midst of the action, we didn't have a scratch on us. The main camp hadn't been as fortunate. Two had been killed and three wounded, including the screamer. Even though I had survived my first firefight, the memory of that night has remained etched in my mind. At quiet times, relaxed and with my eyes shut, I can drift back to again feel the explosion of artillery rounds and hear the terrifying screams of men wounded and dying in the dark, far from their homes. Even though I've since been through a number of even more terrifying situations, somehow, that night still lingers.

Within minutes of our return to the camp, I learned that one of the KIAs the night before was my RTO, Smyth, who had taken a bullet through the chest. It was a big loss for me. Even though I'd known him less than a week, I'd taken a liking to Smyth. He was an excellent radioman and one of the few guys in the platoon whose conversation wasn't limited to women, sports, and beer. More than that, his death also caused a problem because it meant I needed a new RTO. When I told this to Prion, he took a very sarcastic stance and said he couldn't spare anyone experienced and then he ordered me to not give the task to anyone else in my platoon, but to carry the PRC-25 myself. Even though all officers were trained on the big field radio, it was unusual for a platoon leader to carry his own. Prion was just trying to show me who was boss. At first, I was angry, and somewhat embarrassed, but by the end of the day, I thanked God for that radio.

We spent most of the morning licking our wounds and cleaning gear before heading in the direction Prion figured the gooks had fled. Mann told me it was a waste of time because the Cong always disappeared during the day, when they were working as farmers or fishermen, or maybe custodians on US military bases. For sure, he said, the VC would avoid American infantry units in the daylight because of their superior firepower. Mann felt that the only enemy forces who would fight in daylight were regular NVA units, and they were always up by the DMZ or next to the Cambodian and Laotian borders, not in our location, close to the ocean. But with no choice and nothing better to do that day anyway, we followed Prion and trudged on in pursuit of an invisible foe.

Like the day before, it was hot and dry and miserable. Down nearer the water, we were in lowlands, so most of where we walked on was flat, with small sagebrushes, little shade, and no place to rest. After a while, the ground turned to soft, white sand, which meant we were approaching the South China Sea. By early afternoon, with nearly everyone dried up from the heat, Prion ordered a rest stop. Still tired from the night before, I laid down in the shade of a small tree, hoping to get a few minutes sleep. I should have known better. A kick to the side of my boot caused me to pop up and find Prion and two other soldiers looking down at me.

"Grab your radio and tag along, Lieutenant," said Prion in a demeaning manner, before turning on his heels and striding off towards the ocean with the other two following behind. "Yes, Sir," I answered, throwing on my rucksack, which had the radio attached, and scampered after them. I quickly realized it wasn't easy to catch up to them. The ground was very loose, like sand along a beach, which made sense as we weren't that far from the ocean, and the added weight of the radio made it a struggle to keep up with the pace of the other three. But I persisted, pushing myself extra hard, and asked, "What's up, Sir?" as I drew near to Prion.

"Nothing special. We're just going to check out that elevation while the guys are resting," said he, pointing at a small dirt mound that looked to be several hundred yards away. "We needed a radio, so that's why you're coming along, too."

I wanted to ask "why me?" since he had a regular RTO who was always at his side. But I kept my mouth shut and just tagged along for a short pace, until it struck me that being treated like dirt shouldn't have been my main concern. "Sir, don't we need more men?" I asked, looking back at the unit receding in the distance.

"Naw, we're not going that far. Anyway, you know how to use the prick," he answered, meaning my radio. His words only made me more concerned, but there was no sense arguing with him so I plodded on, glancing back every few seconds to see if the company was still in sight.

We had gone about halfway to the dirt elevation when suddenly we were stopped in our tracks by an unexpected sight—a man walking straight across our path not more than a hundred feet away. He wore what could have been described as a dark-green uniform, had a weapon slung over his shoulder, and looked so unconcerned, you'd have thought he was out for a Sunday stroll. We had only a second to stand there and stare at him before the gook turned, saw us, and took off running full speed in the opposite direction. "Come on," yelled Prion as he popped off his rucksack and took off chasing after the guy. The other two soldiers also pulled their snaps to drop their backpacks and sprinted after Prion.

If I'd been thinking straight, I would have immediately radioed back to the unit for help. But as usual in such situations, I panicked. When the other three took off, I instantly ran after them, not wanting to be left alone. But unlike them, the radio was attached to my rucksack, so I couldn't drop the heavy thing from my back. While they only had a few bandoliers of ammo tied around their bodies, I had to carry an extra fifty to sixty pounds while trying to run on loose, sandy ground. Given the fast pace they set, it was an impossible task and, in short order, I was gasping for breath and falling farther and farther behind.

We must have run for no more than three or four minutes, with me nearly out of breath, when Prion and the others went up a small dirt embankment about thirty feet to my front and disappeared over the top. Almost immediately, I heard the distinctive crack of multiple AK-47s break out, along with what sounded like a lone M16 returning fire. *Ambush*, I thought to myself as I hit the ground at the bottom of the mound they'd just gone over seconds earlier. I pulled on the receiver of the PRC-25 and yelled, "B Company, B Company, answer up, we're under fire!"

"Dragon Three, where are you?" came back a frantic reply in seconds.

"I don't know! Run in the direction of the fire!" I shouted. "We're getting hit up here! Hurry! Hurry!"

"Is Six with you Dragon Three?" the voice asked.

"Yes! Yes! He's here! Just hurry! Hurry!" I bawled, pulling the radio and rucksack off my back and looking frantically for someplace to get under cover. But no sooner had I got to my feet than the shooting stopped and the other side of the dirt pile became suddenly quiet.

I felt a lump of terror rise to my throat. Running away from the mound of sand suddenly seemed crazy. There were a few short bushes back where I'd just come from, but going for them meant running over open terrain with my back to the enemy if they happened to come over the mound looking for anyone else. Trying to get back to the unit, which was surely coming my way by then, was the same, only more open ground. There was no good option except to pray that the company would find me before the gooks did, so I threw myself flat back on the ground, faced up to the top of the mound, and listened intently for any sounds coming my way.

There was nothing. No sounds at all, except a bird that flew over, flapping its wings and gliding past towards the sea. Then, from far behind me I heard something, just a murmur, but a sound nonetheless. I turned on my side to see the bare outline of men, B Company, running furiously towards my location, but still a ways off. I flopped back onto my stomach and watched the hilltop, praying they would get there fast. But then another frightening thought ran through my mind. What would the unit think if they found me lying in the sand, while on the other side of the mound the other three were in God knows what kind of shape? After all, I was an officer. Everyone would expect me to be in the thick of things, not lying on my stomach on the opposite side of the fight. So I took a deep breath, glanced back once more, and then did one of the most courageous things in my life.

I crawled slowly up to the rim of the mound of sand. Once near the top, I halted and listened again for a sound, any sound. Hearing none, I inched up to the top and peered down at a sight I would never forget. The embankment I lay on was like a big horseshoe, stretching out maybe a thirty or forty feet to both my left and right before turning towards the ocean, while directly across from my position were a series of small patches of vegetation several feet high. But my view quickly moved from the topography and fixed on the bodies inside the triangle. There I saw the two GIs, sprawled on the ground close together, with their feet towards me. One was moving, but only slightly, while the other lay motionless. On their right was Prion, curled up on his side, facing my direction, and blood oozing from either his chest or stomach. Behind them, walking deliberately towards the prone Americans, were three Vietcong dressed in what looked like dark pajamas, all carrying rifles.

For a second, I thought about opening fire on them—after all, they were in the open, easy targets coming straight towards me. *But what if I didn't kill them all?* I thought. I would be outnumbered until the unit arrived, long minutes to stand alone. Besides, I reasoned, Prion and the others couldn't be helped now. They were already dead. So I lay low to the ground and waited for the unit to come up.

As I did, a macabre scene unfolded before me. The Vietnamese walked up to the first American lying on the ground, the one I'd seen moving slightly. One of them pulled out a handgun and then, at point blank range, shot the prone GI through the head; then he turned and did the same to the second American. It was deliberate and gruesome. He was making sure they were dead. As he shot them, the other dinks stooped down and began to strip the bodies of ammo and guns and even started taking the shirt off one of the GIs.

I should have turned and fled down the hill, but I was so terrified that I could only watch the dreadful scene as the shooter turned and walked towards Prion. Instinctively, I glanced at Prion and realized with horror that he was staring straight at me. I thought it was my imagination, but then his mouth opened and closed and I saw his hand move towards his pistol belt. Prion was alive! It wasn't possible, but he was still alive and trying to talk and looking at me for help!

The scene completely unnerved me. I had leaned backward on one elbow to turn and run back down the mound, but instead lost my balance. My elbow slipped on the dirt and I fell, face first, into the ground, causing my M16, which I'd been holding in one hand, to hit the ground hard and fire off a quick burst of automatic fire.

Those rounds might still be traveling somewhere because they sure didn't hit anything. But they had a sudden effect on the Vietnamese, who hadn't expected more Americans. If it'd been me, I would have run like hell out of that hole. After all, the gooks were in the same trap they'd just pulled on Prion. But these were real soldiers. I raised my head to see what my volley had caused, and saw all three of them had knelt down and were turning their weapons in my direction. Instinctively, I threw myself back to the ground, half expecting bullets to rip through my body. Instead, I heard and felt a loud explosion echo out of the pit.

I flinched at the blast and covered my face. Seconds later, when I opened my eyes and looked down, I saw all of the VC sprawled out on the ground, one twitching and moaning, obviously badly hurt, while the other two were motionless. Prion had changed position, too. He now lay on his back a few feet from his previous spot and motionless. With no other explanation, I guessed he must have detonated a grenade, killing them and himself, too. I paused for a deep breath, took a look around to see if there were anymore VC, and, when I was certain there weren't any, walked cautiously down into the ambush site.

I went first to the lone Vietnamese who was still alive. He had one hand on his neck with blood oozing out from between his fingers. He was bleeding badly, making strange gurgling sounds and obviously dying in great agony.

"See how you like it," I said, aiming my M16 and putting a shot through his chest, knocking him several feet away. I checked the other gooks to make sure they were dead and then went over and knelt down in the sand next to Prion, more from curiosity than anything else. He lie there, eyes closed and blood coming out of multiple places, including an obviously critical wound in his stomach. Except for a growing pool of blood all around him, he looked like he was just asleep.

"You poor son of a bitch," I mumbled, looking down into his face. At which he opened his eyes and looked right at me! I hollered and jumped up with a start, bouncing backward onto my butt. He was still alive! With blood coming out from a half-dozen places, he was still alive!

I bounced back forward and saw that he was gasping for air, his chest heaving and eyes blinking rapidly with the effort. So I crawled back to him on all fours, wondering what in the hell to do. As I drew near, he saw my face and rolled his head in my direction and tried to move his mouth. He wanted to say something, so I drew closer and knelt down to listen. He could barely utter a sound. I cradled his head in one hand and put my ear next to his mouth. "Pis...tol," he said in a barely audible sound.

Pistol? I thought. *Did he say pistol?* Then I noticed his left hand tapping on his holster. "Do you want your pistol?" What must have been a smile crossed his face and I thought to myself, *He's in such pain he's going to shoot himself.* So I took the .45 from his holster and placed it in his hand as his fingers wrapped around it with effort. "Do you need help?" I asked, not sure what else to say. He looked at me and again tried to say something. Once more, I put my ear down close and listened. His mouth moved and he whispered something, but it was so faint I could only make out what sounded like the word "itch," and then he shot me!

I screamed and fell away, rolling in the dirt and coming up holding my left leg. It felt like it was on fire, with my blood pumping out and already wetting the ground. I hollered in pain, squeezing my hands over where I'd been shot to try and stop the bleeding. Then I looked back towards Prion. I saw him trying to lift the gun up above his body. "No! No! I'm on your side," I bawled, turning to pull myself away from that madman as fast as possible. I crawled along the ground, leaning to my right and dragging my bleeding leg behind me. As I did so, I yanked out my own pistol from its holster and turned to shoot Prion before he could get me again.

I took aim straight at his midsection and then stopped. His hand, still cradling the gun, was on the ground to his side, while he lay fully on his back, motionless, with his face pointed straight up at the sky. I held my fire and watched for just a bit before deciding he must be dead, finally done in by the gook's bullets. I pushed my pistol back in its holster and crawled to his side, trying to ignore the pain oozing from my leg; I had to make certain he was really finished. He was. I stared down at him and saw that his eyes were closed and his chest still from no more breaths, although it did seem to me there was a smile on his face. I sat back, emotionally and physically drained. The egotistical maniac had given his last order, but in dying he'd done his dirty work. I thought, *He had the strength to stay alive just long enough to shoot me when I was trying to be of help*. With that thought, I came back to my senses and I finally took a good look at my injured leg. The bullet had creased just inside the outer edge of the leg, causing blood to ooze out in a slow, but steady, stream. It hurt like hell and I had nothing to stop the bleeding except my own hands, so I yelled out, "B Company! Where are you?" hoping they were getting close.

"We're here, Sir," said a voice, and I spun my head around to see Corporal Alan Baker, another soldier who had come to the unit with me and Bryson just days earlier, striding towards me. Several other soldiers followed close behind him and the rest of the unit was coming over the embankment, strung out in a wide line. In fast order, while most of them flanked out in all directions, just in case there were more dinks, Baker and another soldier carefully laid me out and propped my head up on something. Soon after, the company medic came up, did a quick look-see, had them pull off my pants, and then turned me over so he could get a better look at the exit wound on the back of my leg. "Don't cut it off, Doc," I pleaded, "they can fix it in the rear!" Truth was, of course, I had no idea how badly I was hurt, but I didn't want some novice taking away my leg.

"No chance of that, Sir," he said, pushing something sharp and painful into the leg. I let out a grunt and he said, "I know it hurts, but this is just a flesh wound. You won't lose your leg. It'll be fine. Just hold still so I can stop the bleeding. I've numbed it. You won't feel the pain much longer."

That was good to hear. My main concern had been the leg, but then another thought came to mind. "Baker," I called out, "Captain Prion, don't let him—"

"The captain's dead, Frank," said another voice from behind.

"What? Are you sure?" I said, rising slightly and twisting my head to see the talker. I tried to sound depressed but actually was relieved that they'd confirmed what I had thought.

"Stay down, Sir," said the medic, pushing me gently back to the ground.

"Yeah, you can't help him now. You did all you could," said the other voice, who I now recognized as Terry Kitchen, the First Platoon leader.

"Did he...did he say...anything?" I asked, sure that he hadn't, but slightly concerned nonetheless.

"No. We were too late. He was already dead...the others, too. Three of ours. Three of theirs. You're the only one left. Just relax and let Doc fix that wound," Kitchen said. "We'll take care of this."

At that, my emotions gave way. I felt actual tears come to my eyes and I wiped them away, while taking very heavy breaths. I was alive! Alive! And Prion, who'd tried to kill me, was himself dead!

The sight of my tears brought a response from the people around me. "It's all right, Lieutenant," said Baker. "You did all you could. You're lucky to be alive."

"Yeah, just take it easy LT," said another. "There's nothing else you coulda done, Sir."

It was dumbfounding. The morons actually thought I was crying for Prion and the others. "Yes, yes…." I blurted out, my body slightly shaking with emotion.

It must have been a convincing performance because over the next few minutes, one after another, the men of my unit came up to ask how I was doing and to offer me their condolences. At first I was surprised by their reaction, but then I realized my stock has risen considerably in their eyes. Not only had I survived a fierce firefight, but to them, my first concern, even though wounded myself, was for my fellow soldiers. I was no longer just the guy who farted in combat. I had proven myself, you see, in the only arena that counted with them. And from then on, even the most hardened of the bunch treated me with respect.

Once Doc finished bandaging me up, the pain did go down considerably as he'd said, so they put me under a big tropical tree to rest until a medevac chopper arrived. The rest of the company, after placing the bodies of Prion and the others under some ponchos, spread out in a wide arc to wait for the helicopter. We left the gooks laying in the open where they died, after some of our guys stripped them for souvenirs.

It was a strange feeling, as I sat there facing the ponchos, to reflect back on the past twenty-four hours. I'd gone through my first real combat battle and then miraculously survived an encounter that had taken the lives of three fellow soldiers. Sure, I'd been shot, but I'd been assured it was nothing permanent and, once the medevac arrived, I would be on my way out of the hellish place and back to the Americal Division headquarters at Chu Lai, some thirty to forty miles south. Once there, I would have a warm bed, warm food, and no one trying to kill me.

As I lay there contemplating fate, there was a commotion off to one side and then a half dozen of my troops came into sight, led by Baker, who was pushing in front of them a Vietnamese dressed in grey pajama-type clothes. I could tell right off it wasn't just any Vietcong soldier. It was a woman, or perhaps a young girl; I wasn't sure which at first since it was always hard for me to tell the age of Vietnamese females. All of them looked like teenagers until they got into their early thirties, after which they aged rapidly. I met women over there in their forties who could easily pass for elderly grandmas back in the States. I think it was just the hard life they lived, taking care of their men and working as farmers or laborers all their years. But as that one drew nearer, I saw she was no teenager.

They led her up in front of me and then Baker pushed her from behind and she fell to the ground a few feet away. She quickly propped herself up by her hands and gave a look back at Baker and the others before turning to stare into my face. She was pretty, that was for sure, at least for a Vietnamese dressed in little more than ragged pants and shirt. Her face was round, like a lot of her countrymen, and there was color in her cheeks, although that might have been from fright. Her chest was heaving up and down from rapid breathing, and I could feel the fear in her eyes as she looked from me to the others and then back again to me, her eyes pleading for help.

I stared back, wondering how such a small woman could carry around a chest like that, and was about to ask when Baker spoke up and said, "We found her hiding nearby, Sir. She claims to have been a prisoner of the VC, says they've been dragging her around since taking her from her family a couple weeks ago. But Tran thinks she's lying. He says she's a VC nurse." Tran was our Kit Carson Scout, a former Vietcong turned to our side. He came with us everywhere and, for some reason we never learned, seemed to hate the Vietcong more than any of us.

"Its bullshit," said Tex, a short, stocky soldier in the group. I'd met him earlier in the week and had already mentally put him down as a psycho. He was right at home as an infantryman in Vietnam, always angry and cursing at nearly everyone and everything. "She ain't no prisoner," he said. "She's their goddammed whore, and now she's ours," and he stepped forward, grabbing her right arm to pull her up, while several others shouted out, echoing similar thoughts.

"Hold it," I commanded, looking at Tex and raising my open hand. He stopped pulling on her but kept his grip and waited. "What do you propose to do with her after you're finished?" I calmly asked, looking at him directly and silencing the rest. I wouldn't have challenged him the day before, but I felt emboldened by my wound. I sensed even a brute like him wouldn't give me grief after what I'd just gone through.

"Put her with the others," he answered, pointing at the three dead dinks in the distance. "She's one of them, ain't she?" And again there was a chorus of approval, although somewhat quieter this time.

I couldn't blame them; this was the first woman some of them had seen in weeks, and her comrades, if they were that, had just killed three of their friends. But it just wouldn't do. Word could too easily get back to division headquarters that we'd raped and killed a woman prisoner. I knew, as the officer on the spot, that I'd be the one to answer for it. The other two platoon leaders weren't that far away with their own troops, but it was my platoon that stood there with the girl. I looked at her and she stared back with that frightened look and chattered out something in Vietnamese, grabbing at my trousers. She knew we were discussing her fate and had figured out I was the one who could save her.

"I understand how you feel, Tex," I said calmly, looking up at him. "But this woman's more valuable to us alive. I want to get the people who caused this as much as you do, probably more," I continued, pointing at the ponchos covering Prion and the others. "She might be able to lead us to more of 'em, but not if she's dead. And if she's telling the truth, she can give us lots of info about the VC in this area. Let's let G-2 decide her fate." It wasn't what they wanted to hear. They didn't really care if she was a dink prisoner or Mother Teresa; they were young, horny males and they had a woman.

"Well, I say we use her anyway, and then give her to G-2 if you want," snorted Tex, looking about at the others. I was about to tell him to address me as "Sir" when there was the sound of some jerk pulling back the bolt on his rifle, which meant a round had been loaded.

At that, Baker, who was standing just behind the girl, whirled and faced the others with his M16 held high. "She ain't worth someone getting killed over, Boys," said he as he backed up next to my side, holding his weapon at the ready.

It was a tense moment, with them struggling between carnal lust and the fear of killing their own. I wouldn't have bet on how they'd have gone, but just then, a voice from behind the group spoke up and asked, "Is there trouble here?"

The group swirled around and then parted down the center as Sergeant Mann, his weapon loosely held to his side, walked through the middle of them. That decided it. We all knew Mann was too honorable in the old school ways to harm a prisoner, especially a woman, and there wasn't a man there who would take him on.

Tex let go of the prisoner's arm, kicked the ground, and muttered, "No trouble, Sarge. Just talking about the prisoner," and then he slunk away, followed by most of the others.

Mann watched them go, then turned, looked at the girl, and, before walking away himself, said to Baker, "Make sure she gets on the chopper."

Some might think me heroic, standing up to them like that. But, truth be told, I was sure they wouldn't harm an officer in such an open place, and it had already crossed my mind that, if she really was a nurse and since I was wounded, she might come in handy on the flight back to Chu Lai.

As Mann walked off, Tran said something to the girl and then both he and Baker joined her and me on the ground to wait for the chopper. She pulled her knees up to her chest, wrapped her arms around her legs, and just stared at me with a little grin on her face. I was about to ask Tran her name when we heard the familiar *thump-thump-thump*, and then watched as a Huey came in low over the trees and landed in the field nearby. Once the blades slowed down, two people from the helicopter put our three KIAs in body bags and carefully placed them in the back of the chopper. After that, I climbed gingerly aboard, my leg still a bit sore but feeling much better, and then I watched as Baker and Tran brought the girl. The rear seat had been folded up to make room for the body bags, so the girl and I ended up sitting on the floor next to each other. As the others walked away from the helicopter, Mann remained for a bit longer, so I called out to him, saying, "Sergeant Mann, I guess this is good-bye. I'm sorry we didn't get to work together longer."

"Oh, don't worry, Sir," he replied. "I'll still be here when you return."

"Return!" I exclaimed. "I'm wounded! They won't send me back here!"

"Yes, Sir, you're wounded, and you'll get a Purple Heart and all. But your wound isn't bad. Out here you'd get infected with ringworm or rot, but back in the rear, with real food and a roof over your head, you'll be as good as new real soon. Oh, you'll be back! And don't worry, I'll take care of things till you return!"

"Right," I answered, much subdued. It had never occurred to me that I would have to come back to the field. I had assumed wounded soldiers got shipped back home, or, at the worse, were reassigned to one of the big base camps where it was fairly safe. Mann's words stung and he knew it. The last sight I saw, as they slammed shut the chopper doors, was him grinning at me.

As depressing as his words were, they were forgotten as soon as the chopper lifted off and my attention turned to the girl. To keep Prion and the other KIAs from sliding around, the crew had lashed the body bags down and closed the passenger doors, which were normally kept open in flight. The door gunners, who had helped store the bodies, were outside hanging in their harnesses, while the pilot and his partner were up front facing away. They had left the girl and me alone in the dark interior of the Huey.

I smiled over at her and she returned a long look that was a mixture of both gratitude and interest. Then she said something to me in Vietnamese. I had absolutely no idea what it was, but I replied, "Why not?" and dragged myself across a few feet to where she sat. After all, given my short time in-country, I hadn't had many opportunities to improve American-Vietnamese relations and didn't want to pass up the chance. Besides, we were alone in the chopper except for the three corpses, and they wouldn't be talking.

The movement across the metal floor caused me to twist my wounded leg and I winced in pain. That got a response from the girl. She moved forward on the floor and, with a few soothing words, began to gently rub my wound. *Son of a bitch, she is a nurse*, I thought as the pain in my leg calmed down and began to be replaced by a physical sensation I hadn't felt since coming to the field days earlier.

I reached over and slid my hand beneath her shirt to find, as I expected, a firm, good-sized breast. She gave a little gasp and looked up into my face, but made no move to stop me, so I pulled her closer by the back of her head and kissed her full on the lips.

It must have been her first experience with a kiss, because when I pulled back she just sat there with a dumb look on her face. That was a surprise to me. Every woman I'd ever known was either pleased at being kissed or angry I'd done it, while she didn't seem to know what had happened or what to do about it. I figured either Vietnam was an uncultured country or she was just stupid; whatever the reason, I quit fooling around and gently pushed her down on her back. That she understood.

She smiled up at me, made herself as comfortable as possible, and then, with a few loosening of clothes, we were at it. It wasn't the best sex I'd had, far from it, what with me wincing in pain each time my leg moved. But, being up there in mid-air, bouncing along on a hard metal floor, it was certainly an experience to remember. I half expected the chopper crew to look in on us, given the sounds that girl made, and kept halting for a few seconds now and then to see if we were still alone. Maybe the roar of the chopper itself drowned her out or maybe they never imagined that we would be doing anything back there. Whatever the case, the chopper crew never let on that anything had happened aboard, even after we landed. By the time we got to the big base camp at Chu Lai, Miss Heavy Chest and I were probably the most satisfied passengers they'd ever carried aloft.

Once on the ground, my companion was handed over to the MPs, who took her away to wherever prisoners went. The last I saw of her she was walking away, looking back and waving good-bye. But a few weeks later, at the Chu Lai Officer's Club, I heard that a female who had been caught sometime earlier had been sent back to her family because it had been decided she wasn't a danger. That's how much they knew.

I saw the last of Prion that day, too. A detail was waiting at the helipad to take away him and the others for shipment back home. I silently watched them load the body bags on a truck, knowing that I could just as easily have been making that last ride. It's an eerie feeling to watch the dead bodies of men you'd been talking to just hours earlier be taken away in the back of a deuce and a half.

Thinking back, I have to give Prion some credit. He was a hell of a soldier, the kind who makes our army the best in the world. We will always need plenty more like him, if we are to maintain our position as the Free World's leader. But it was his own fault he got shot; we should never have gone out on that patrol with just four men, and he should never have run into the ambush with the other two guys. In the 'Nam, as in all wars, it sometimes took only one mistake to result in death. Prion's had caused three deaths. Six, if you count the gooks.

Mann was right, of course. I did go back to the field to rejoin him and B Company a few weeks later. If I'd known then what lay ahead, he would never have seen my face again. I would somehow have found some way to stay back in Chu Lai or return stateside. But I didn't know what the future would bring and had no idea that my experience in Vietnam would become even more horrible in the weeks and months to come.

CHAPTER TWO

I should never have gone to Vietnam. I'm sure there are thousands, if not hundreds of thousands, of 'Nam veterans who wish they'd not gone to that accursed place, including plenty of folks who felt at the time we had good reason to be over there fighting the commies. In my case, I probably could have stayed out of that miserable country if I'd just played it a bit smarter. I was safe at Michigan State University, with a student deferment from the military draft and an ace in the hole—an uncle who worked for the military draft board back home in Hawaii.

Of course, the war was in the news every day, but it was far away and, while many of my classmates were out demonstrating against Vietnam, I gave it little thought. My daytimes were spent listening to boring classroom lectures, while at night I hung out at the Coral Gables nightclub, located a few blocks east of the MSU campus, and tried to communicate with the fairer sex. Truth be told, I was quite content and enjoying life. My parents were paying the tab, classes were simple, and there were plenty of women. I had no plans for after graduation anyway, so was in no rush to finish my degree.

This was 1968, mind you—a year of well-publicized disasters that included the Tet Offensive in Vietnam, the Kennedy and King assassinations, and Nixon's first election. Protests against the war had been growing on campuses across America for several years, but in '68, they grew dramatically in both size and scope. Before then, most of the antiwar protestors had been college students, but after Tet, it seemed like people at all levels of society, even some of the well-to-do, had decided it was time to end that conflict. I didn't disagree. The only things I knew about Vietnam was that it was somewhere in Asia and I didn't want to go there. Life was so comfortable; it just never dawned on me that I would end up in that cursed place.

My road to Vietnam began in a most unlikely manner—with a phone call from a policeman in Miami, Florida, to my father, who lived then in the town of Kailua, Hawaii, on the main island of Oahu. I well recall sitting on a hard wooden bench, leaning against the wall, and staring around a huge room with police officers coming and going every few minutes. I was there with a bunch of other young men, each of us waiting our turn and dreading the time when the cops would get our folks on the phone.

There were nearly a dozen of us, all college students, groggy from lack of sleep and hungry for sure, but mostly annoyed with our situation. We'd come down south for the annual college spring break, but instead of being out at some bar entertaining women, there we were lined up like a bunch of common criminals waiting for sentence. The police had taken us from a plane that had landed in Miami a few hours earlier, hauled us down to their building, and then began calling our parents one at a time. I watched about half a dozen of my compatriots go through the motions of their call back home and then being escorted from the building by the cops. When they finally got around to me, I had to stand by like some schoolboy waiting for his teacher while they got my Dad on the phone. I only took part on the tail end of the call, but I've heard my father describe the conversation often enough to have it etched in my mind. It went something like this: "Good morning, Mr. Loveless, this is Officer Kaley from the Miami Police Department in Florida. I'm sorry to bother you so early in the day, Sir, but we have your son in custody and need your assistance." He was a middle-aged, regular-looking guy except for his uniform and spoke in a flat tone of voice like the call was no big deal.

"My son! That's impossible," said Dad. "Taylor just left for work. Alan's asleep upstairs and Frank and Bob are both at Michigan State. They can't be in Miami!"

"Yes, Sir. Frank's the one. He's standing here with me," said the cop. "He was delivered to us this morning by US Customs. Your son and some other young men were tossed out of the Bahamas last night and turned over to us as the closest US police force. We've already told them if they go back to the Bahamas, they could be arrested and they seem to get that. Most of them, like your son, are under twenty-one, so we thought it best to contact their parents before we just let them go."

"What! Frank was in the Bahamas? Just lock him up," responded my compassionate, loving father.

"We can't do that, Sir. He hasn't broken any laws here. We can't hold him for more than an hour or two," answered the cop.

"What is my son accused of anyway?" asked Dad, probably thinking the worst.

"Like I said, he's not accused of anything here in Florida. He and a bunch of other young people were deported from the Bahamas because of disorderly conduct. Apparently, they were involved in some kind of big fight that destroyed public property. The Bahamian police didn't jail them, bad publicity for their tourist trade, I guess. But they definitely want your son and the others to stay away. If you could, just talk to him. Make sure he doesn't go back to Nassau. Then we'll let him go," said Officer Kaley.

Now, at that time, I was already twenty years old and fully grown, and like most people that age, hated having anyone lecture me on how to behave. If it had been anyone but my father on the phone, I would have just told him to shove off. But Dad was the one person I didn't dare go against. He'd lived a strict, regimented life, having survived the Great Depression and World War II, before serving in the US Air Force for a number of years. In the early 60s, he retired from the military and moved the family to Hawaii where he operated a successful clothing business making aloha shirts and muumuu dresses. My entire life he'd been telling me and my brothers what to do, and how to do it. As the oldest of the brothers, it seemed I was always the one who received the brunt of his lectures and criticisms, although looking back, I was sure he always meant well for me. All of us boys had worked for him through high school, and he was still my main source of income in '68, paying all my college bills and sending me just enough cash each month for living expenses. I never felt comfortable expressing my opinion on anything for fear of pissing him off, and in truth, I avoided talking to him as much as possible. But there was no choice then, as the cop handed me the phone.

"Dad," I cried out before he had a chance to say anything, "thank God it's you! You won't believe the horrible experience I just had—"

"Shut up, Frank," he interrupted. "Don't even bother to explain! I just want to know one thing for your mother's sake—are you physically okay?"

"Yes! Sure! Dad, I'm okay!" I said. "But really! Nothing happened! I didn't do anything," I continued, noticing that Officer Haley had a very puzzled look on his face.

"Of course," Dad replied in a now clam, but sarcastic, voice. "Police departments around the world have nothing better to do than spend their days on the likes of you." He didn't say it, but I knew he was referring to a time in my high school days when I was locked up by the cops on the North Shore of Oahu and another time when the Lansing, Michigan police had found me unconscious in the street and contacted him. Both instances were over little things like underage drinking, but my father made a big deal out of them, like I was the operator of a white-slaver ring or something. "Listen carefully, Frank," he continued calmly, which only made me more worried. "I'm only going to say this once. In forty-eight hours I'm going to call your dormitory room at Michigan State. You better be there to answer the phone. I don't want to talk to your roommate! I don't want to talk to Bob! I don't want to talk to someone pretending to be a doctor and telling me you've lost the ability to speak! I want to talk to *you*! You got it?"

"Yes, Sir," I answered, knowing from experience that it was best to keep my mouth shut when he was in that kind of mood. He wasn't going to listen anyway.

"If you're there, then I'll do you a favor, Frank," he continued. "I'll let you finish out this school year. You're one semester from graduating. I would hate to waste all the money that we've already spent on your education. Just understand this: if you're not there, my next call is to your Uncle Burt! You got it?"

"Yes, Sir," I answered meekly, taking in a deep breath. I had got it very well. Uncle Burt was my father's younger brother, the one who served on the

Hawaii draft board. We both knew Burt didn't like me much, preferring my second brother, Taylor, a whiny little jerk who's never known his place. I knew for sure Uncle Burt would do anything my father asked, including moving my name to the top of the list of people being drafted.

"One more thing," said the Old Man. "I'd hoped by going away to college you might get an education and maybe, just maybe, learn a little bit about being a responsible adult. It's become increasingly obvious that a college degree is wasted on you. First that idiot thing in Africa that almost got you killed, and now this! You don't have the guts to grow up and make a man out of yourself! Left to your own devices, you'll end up either dead or in jail! So I'm going to do you one more favor," he said in a tone that I knew forecast trouble. "The week you graduate," he continued, "I'm still going to make that call to Burt. You'll never be a man on your own! Maybe the military can make one out of you. At least you'll have your degree."

"But, Dad," I cried, "I have plans for after college! Amy and I are going to get married! I'm going to graduate school! I plan to—"

"Frank," he said, cutting me off, "you have forty-eight hours! Don't waste them," and he hung up.

My father, you see, knew me well, and wasn't about to waste time talking. He knew I wasn't the marrying type, even if I were lucky enough to meet a decent woman who would have me. And he was well aware that my grades weren't good enough for graduate school. Hell, I'd already dragged out college an extra year just to avoid the draft anyway! No, he wasn't fooled. And I'm sure he was doing what he thought best for my future. Of course, nowadays, he likes to take credit for my success and tells anyone who will listen how he started my military career with that phone call. I don't think he's ever really believed all the press reports and army citations, but my success in the military made him look good with old war buddy friends and that's all he really cares about anyway.

The call from the Miami police would never have taken place if I had stayed at school that March. But like many other students enrolled in colleges up north, I was sick of winter weather, and being from Hawaii, with its year-round warm weather, just made it that much worse. I've never understood why anyone would choose to live in a place that has snow six months a year. I only went to Michigan State because my father grew up in western Michigan and had yet another relative, this time his uncle, who worked at State. MSU was all right for a college, a big party school with a good sports program, classes that weren't that hard to pass, and plenty of women, but I always hated the cold weather from October to March.

Spring break, with its two weeks of vacation, offered the chance to get away from the cold. Florida, with its year-round warm weather and a promise of loose women, beckoned on TV. So, along with thousands of other college students up north, I went south that spring, searching for sex, adventure, and the sun—but mostly for sex. It wasn't my first time. The year before, my brother, Bob, and I had gone to Ft. Lauderdale for the same purpose, but that trip had been an abortion. We'd been fine the first few days, staying in some rundown motel and cruising the bars in Ft. Lauderdale. Then, hungry for something more exciting, we went to some dog racing place and lost almost every dollar we had. The rest of the trip was spent sleeping in the car with Bob, stealing food from orange groves to the west of the city for our dinner, and working several days at a gas station to earn enough money to get back up to Michigan. It was definitely not a fun trip.

But I won't linger on the pleasures of spring break. There have been enough movies and books over the years describing the hordes of young people who descend down south to partake in wild, unending orgies that take place on Florida's eastern coast. For me, I just wanted to get out of the cold, have some fun, and not have a repeat of the prior year's trip. The opportunity to do just that, while avoiding the crowds in Miami and Fort Lauderdale, presented itself when I heard about five other guys in the dorm who planned to go over to the town of Nassau, in the Bahamian islands. They had learned that Nassau was only a cheap half-hour flight from Miami, had warm tropical weather, plenty of beaches, and, with so many Americans going there, did not require a passport. Plus, even though it was a foreign country, English was the main language of the Bahamas.

Of the five, only Ron Halson and Jim Denis were actually friends. Ron, who was my dormitory roommate that year, was a real Michigander, born and raised on the state's upper peninsula. I had known Jim much longer, as we had been roommates our freshman year and had also shared one summer in Kansas as apprentice painters, plus spent hundreds of hours at school, analyzing and studying women. He came to Michigan State from his parent's home near Buffalo, New York, and if anything, he was a calming influence on me. While I was in college mostly to enjoy myself and, hopefully, find a high-paying, non-stressful job after graduation, Jim was an actual scholar who enjoyed learning new things. We would have been roommates that year, too, except for the fact that he had met some girl the summer before and was shacking up with her. The other three travelers with us were just guys I'd seen around our dormitory, McDonald Hall, but they weren't anyone special, and with the exception of Bobby Kohler, I've long since forgotten their names. I do recall that one of them was killed in Vietnam within two years, but none of us were thinking about the war on that trip.

We drove south in two cars, taking turns behind the wheel and everyone chipping in to buy gas. No one wanted to waste time; we only had sixteen days before school began again, so we drove straight through from Lansing to Miami in about thirty-six hours. I don't remember much about that trip except it was long and boring and Ron needed better mouthwash. The only excitement was when we hit a dog along a mountain curve in the Appalachians. But we made it to Miami safe enough, and almost immediately boarded our plane for the Bahamas.

I read not long ago that Nassau has become quite a resort destination today, with big, luxurious hotels and golf courses dotting the island, fed by a steady stream of tourists from all along the east coast. In those days though, the Bahamas were mostly the domain of well-heeled travelers, primarily Europeans, who stayed in a couple of high-brow hotels. The only exceptional times, we were told, were a few weeks each spring when American college students came over, and then late summer, just before the school year began, when families flew in from Florida for a change of pace.

We were actually quite surprised when we discovered that the streets of Nassau were overrun with American students. We had expected to find some of them, what with a James Bond movie having been made down there the year before and the Beach Boys new "Sloop John B" song playing on the radio every half hour. But none of us thought there would be thousands of young Americans loitering on street corners, hogging the stools in bars, and lying on the beach. They were everywhere, and while that meant there would be more women to choose from, it also created a housing problem. Unlike Miami or Ft. Lauderdale, Nassau didn't have limitless hotel rooms.

All the cheap places, which we highly desired, were already packed with clientele and had no rooms available. The better establishments, which actually had bathrooms attached to the bedrooms, recognized right off that we couldn't afford their rates and treated us like something you'd hose down the driveway. One snazzy hotel wouldn't even let us in the door, as a security guard was turning away anyone not wearing a necktie. Coming from a tropical destination myself, I couldn't believe that attitude. There were hundreds of hotels back in Honolulu and I never heard of anyone having to wear a tie to enter one of them. Hell, some places in Waikiki barely required clothing. But of course, I was still young then and didn't realize that Nassau was still very much a British crown colony. The requiring of ties was probably just their way to segregate vacationing European aristocracy from college riffraff flying over from the USA. Mind you, I'd have the same attitude nowadays, given the depths to which young people have fallen.

As it was, we spent the first night down near the beach, sleeping on a wooden sidewalk. I should say "tried to sleep" because there were several loud, noisy bars nearby, and every few minutes, some drunk or two would stagger by, heading down to take a piss in the ocean. It was miserable and kept me on edge all night.

By the next morning, all of us had pretty much decided to forget Nassau and go back to the mainland, and we would have, if Bobby Kohler hadn't met up with an old friend. Bobby, a tall, blond-haired fellow who was probably the most self-centered one in our group, had gone down the beach towards some small wooden shacks to buy some food. He was supposed to return in a few minutes, but instead came back an hour later, bringing with him a thuggish-looking guy he introduced as Tom Van Horn, a high school buddy of his who had gone on to Ohio State. Van Horn struck me right away as one of those guys who always think they had to be tough to get any respect. He wore a black T-shirt with the sleeves rolled all the way up his arm, obviously trying to show off his arm muscles, which I admit were considerable, and walked with a purposeful menacing swagger. I mentally put him down as someone to avoid, but paid attention when he said he'd been on the island several days and knew a hotel that was offering a special package to college students. Since we had nothing to lose, we tagged along after him and soon found ourselves at the Royal Victoria Hotel, a big, pink, stucco building on the edge of town, with a pier sticking out into the ocean.

In my grandfather's day, it must have been one of the better hotels in Nassau, as it had an elegant entrance and was located on the water across from idyllic-looking Paradise Island, an atoll about half a mile away. By 1968 though, the Royal Victoria was definitely on the skids. Sure, it was still an attractive building and the staff were all very cordial. Maybe the rooms were good, too, but I couldn't testify to that because we never got into one. The "special" they were offering at the Royal Victoria seemed to me to be nothing more than a desperate move to make money. The hotel had opened up an unused former nightclub in the basement of the building and was allowing American college students to stay there at a low rate of four dollars per night.

When we moved in, there were already dozens of American college students, men and women, who had staked out positions in the room. There were bathrooms for men and women, but there weren't any showers, privacy, or a place to store your belongings. There weren't even any beds, just pool deck chairs that folded out for sleeping. But we didn't complain. It was indoors and cheap and we hadn't traveled to the Bahamas to find privacy and security. We wanted warm weather and attractive women, and it looked like there were plenty of them in the Royal Victoria. So we dumped our stuff on some empty deck chairs in the middle of the room, since all the better places were taken along the edge of the room, and went out to enjoy the town.

Even though I didn't spend that much time there, I have a good memory of Nassau as a hot, crowded, and smelly place where it was nearly impossible to get a drink of water. Our breakfast that morning was some donuts and fruit we bought at a roadside stand, and then we spent most of the next hour just trying to find a water fountain. Those were the days, before bottled water made an appearance, and for some reason, we couldn't even find canned soda on sale. Other than that minor inconvenience, I found Nassau to be a quiet, laid-back resort town. It was much like West Maui in the early 70s, with tall palm trees lining the streets, a turquoise-blue ocean that matched the sky above, and lots of small specialty shops and stores.

Most of the commercial properties were brightly painted two- or three-storey buildings that came right up to the street, with only a small sidewalk separating them from rows of cars parked in front. There were plenty of people hawking their wares, mostly snack food or island souvenirs, from small push-carts or right off their back. It was quite similar to what I remembered from my younger school days in Seoul, Korea, where there were a myriad of small retail stores. I noticed tourists were everywhere on the streets of Nassau, a few looking for bargains, but most just trying to buy something to prove they'd been to the Bahamas on vacation. Our group of six, having virtually no cash, bought little, although I did invest in a two-foot-wide brimmed straw hat from a street vendor to keep the sun off my face. It wasn't much, but then, shopping and sightseeing weren't really on our agenda.

That afternoon, while the others took some kind of bus tour to the far side of the main island, Ron Halson and I caught a ferry from the city over to Paradise Island. We'd heard Paradise Island was where the Bond film (I've forgotten which one, probably *Thunderball*) had been made, and that the beaches were better and more crowded than on the main island. So over we went to check out the place that had recently become famous and, hopefully, find some women. We did. There were hundreds of the fairer sex, most wearing less than an eyeful, sunning on a wide, white sandy beach that stretched on as far as we could see. Being from Hawaii, I was used to crowded beaches and babes in bikinis, but nothing back home had caught my attention like Paradise Island. While there were always lots of people on the beach in Waikiki and other places on Oahu, many of them were older people or families with kids on vacation. There were young women on vacation in Hawaii, too, but not like in numbers like I saw on Paradise Island that day. Almost everyone on that Bahamian beach looked like they were in their twenties.

The weather was also like back home—warm sunshine, a few white clouds above, and a mild breeze that helped reduce the sun's effect. It was a perfect place for being outdoors. As it was, Halson and I strolled about a bit, checking out the place before settling on a shady spot close to several refreshment stands. Figuring that's where the women would eventually migrate to, we spent the mid-part of the day leaning back against a short brick wall, drinking beer, and checking out the stock. We wandered down to the water's edge a few times, too, but didn't go in the ocean. I knew from experience back home, despite what movies might feature, that it's near impossible to pick up women when they're splashing in the surf. You might get a little feel now and then, but that's about all. The girls are having too much fun in the water to pay attention to men. Besides, I'd learned there was another reason to keep out of the water at Paradise Island.

On one of our initial strolls down the beach, we came upon a uniformed man planting a small red flag about ten feet from the shore. Noticing several more of the little red flags farther down the beach, I went up to him and asked, "What's that for?"

He didn't bother to look up, just focused on getting his flag firmly stuck in the sand, but replied, "It's a warning to keep people out of the water. Spiny urchins have been spotted in this area and we don't want anyone to get hurt."

"What are spiny urchins?" I asked. Back home in Hawaii, on nights with full moons, we sometimes had infusions of jellyfish that could cause painful burns to swimmers they touched, but I'd not heard of spiny urchins.

"Small shell-like sea animals," he replied. "They can't kill you, but if you step on one, you'll know it right off. They have stingers that are like knives and hurt like hell if they get in you. Once in a while, they come in near shore." Finally looking up at me, he continued, saying, "When that happens, we post these signs to warn tourists off. We wouldn't want anyone to get hurt." He said those last words in a tone that sounded like only someone really stupid would step on the critters.

I got his point and left him alone with his flags, although, being a typical young man, I did venture a few feet into the water while walking off, just to show him I was neither afraid nor stupid. I didn't go in above my ankles though because, sure enough, there were about half a dozen brown shapes on the sea bottom less than twenty feet out. I stopped to watch them for a bit, lost interest when they didn't move, and then waded out of the water. Since I hadn't gone to Paradise Island for swimming anyway, I really didn't care about the critters. But later that day, the caretaker's warning came back to me. It happened like this: Shortly after noon, Halson and I were sitting at a small table outside one of the walk-up refreshment stands when two women came up. They were the kind of women most men would trade their brother for—long legs, full figures, tight-fitting swimsuits, and gorgeous faces (actually, I'd trade one of my brothers for a lot less). From their dress and the way they moved, it was obvious they hadn't come to the Bahamas looking for a religious experience.

While the taller of the two was ordering drinks, her friend, a strawberry blond with long, dangling hair and an inviting smile, gave me a lingering glance that clearly said, "What are you waiting for, Stupid?" I'd recognized such a look since high school. Being slightly over six feet tall and well proportioned, as I was in those days, women often found me attractive at first glance. Later, when they got to know me better, they often formed a different, more permanent opinion. But I wasn't planning on a long relationship in Nassau, so I smiled back, and seeing there were no more empty tables, motioned for she and her friend to come over and join us.

I didn't have to ask twice. She tugged on her friend's arm, pointed in our direction, and then the two of them, drinks in hand, sauntered over to our table and she asked, "Got room for two more?" We did, of course, and before long, the four of us were wrapped up in serious negotiations over beer and hot dogs. Her name was Judy and she was more than eager to make my acquaintance while leaning chest first over the table. Her friend had a name, too, I'm sure, but I couldn't even remember the color of her hair, much less her name. Ron and I exchanged the usual dribble and mixture of lies men give women, and before too long found ourselves down by the water, sitting on their beach towels, soaking up the sun and enjoying the scenery. Like us, the girls were Midwest college students who'd come south to find adventure and a suntan. As destiny would have it, they were staying at the Royal Victoria. We were roommates, so to speak.

After a few minutes of sunshine and mandatory small talk, Ron got up some courage and talked the other girl into some swimming lessons, leaving me along with Judy. They hadn't even hit the water when Judy decided to make a move on her own. "It's really hot here," she said, rubbing her hand down her very shapely leg. "Can you give me some help with my back side?"

she asked and, without waiting for an answer, handed me some lotion and rolled over on her stomach. The view wasn't as good as the front side, but it was marvelous nonetheless, and denying her would have been rude since I was, after all, a guest on her beach mat. So I lathered up my hands with the slippery gook, positioned myself above her rear, and set to work in earnest—rubbing and squeezing to my heart's delight.

I'd just finished moving up her legs when a heavy force suddenly struck me from behind, pushing my face down violently into the beach. I came up spitting out sand and rubbing my eyes and turned over on my backside to find Tom Van Horn, Kohler's high school friend, standing over me. "What the f... do you think you're doing with my woman?" he shouted down as I stared wide-eyed up into his face.

"Van Horn?" I quailed while staying flat down on the ground. "Your woman? Hey! Relax! We're not doing anything! I was just helping with her suntan lotion! That's all! I didn't know she was your girlfriend." Given the wild look in his face and his domineering size, there was no way I was going to provoke him further. It takes an exceptional brute (and I've met a few) to hit someone lying on the ground and, fortunately, Van Horn proved no exception.

"Find your own woman!" he said, turning to glare over at Judy, who had gone to her feet and was standing about five feet away facing him, with a frightened look and her arms crossed in front. It seemed to me she was as afraid of him as I was.

I lied in a panic. "I already have a woman. I'm engaged to a girl back in Michigan! I was just doing her a favor," I said, pointing to Judy, who gave me a wide-eyed return look!

"Yeah right," said he, looking menacingly at her and then back to me. "Well, from now on, I'll do any favors she needs! You got it?"

"Sure, Tom, sure," I answered, still scared, but becoming a bit more confident of not getting pounded. "Sure. Anyway, I'll be going out in the water and join Ron." I gestured out towards the ocean, secretly hoping that Halson had seen what was happening and might be coming to my aid.

The reference to the ocean seemed to calm Van Horn down, but it also brought out a more ominous nature. He glanced out at the Caribbean and then, in a menacing tone, said, "Oh, that's right. You're a Hawaii boy, aren't ya? So you must be big time in the ocean," he added. "I suppose you're a surfer?"

"Sure," I answered, coming up to my knees, "back home, everyone surfs." Truth was, I'd always been afraid of the water and could swim just enough to keep afloat. My brothers rode surfboards like they were glued to them, but the one time I'd tried it, I ended up in the water after hitting my head on the board. There was no way Van Horn would know that, and since I'd never heard of anyone surfing on the Atlantic side, I figured it was okay to tell him whatever I wanted. I should have known better.

"Why don't you and I have a little race then," said Van Horn, pointing at a floating object way out to sea, "say… out to that buoy and back? I'd like to see how well I can do against a real Hawaii boy."

He spat out his words, making it clear where he was headed—he wanted to show me up in front of Judy, who was still standing apart from us, watching the exchange with interest. It would have been easy for him, since I was a poor swimmer. He didn't know that, of course, but I had to assume he was good in the water or he wouldn't have made the challenge. There was nothing to gain by playing his game, I thought, staring out at the ocean, especially since it would fast become obvious that he was the better person in the water. But I knew just backing down would probably not stop his intimidation. My mind was racing for a reply to his challenge, and then I had it.

"Sure, why not?" I said, coming to my feet with a flash of inspiration and digging my toes into the sand. Facing him full on, but still keeping my distance from the maniac, I said, "But if you want a real test in the water, let's try knee-surfing. Anyone can swim or stand on a board and float!"

"Knee-surfing! What's that?" said Van Horn, skeptical, but rising to the bait.

"A test of Hawaiian manhood," I lied as my mind quickly devised the sport. Trying to goad him just a bit more, I added, "In old Hawaii, almost everyone could swim, so they came up with a sport that was more difficult—sort of a way to separate the men from the boys."

"A test of manhood, huh," he said, looking over at Judy, who had kept quiet the whole time. "What do ya do?"

"It's easy," I answered. "Two guys go out into the ocean side by side, about knee-deep, and then race about a hundred yards along the shoreline without raising their knees out of the water." And then hoping he would dwell on the "lower body" thought, I said with emphasis, "It's a real test of lower body strength and much more difficult than swimming."

"How come I never heard about this sport before?" he asked, which made me worry he was catching on to my bluff.

"Have you ever been to Hawaii?" I inquired, silently praying that he hadn't. "Knee-surfing was originally just for the ancient Hawaiian royalty. Nowadays, lots of local guys do it back home, but it's not that popular with outsiders. The tourists mostly go to the safe, calm beaches, like Waikiki. Besides, knee-surfing is a lot of work and most guys can't make it that far without falling down." Then pointing to the buoy and shrugging my shoulders as though I didn't care, I added, "'Course, if you'd rather just swim out there…"

That got him.

"I'm not gonna fall down," said he, pointing his finger at my face. "Let's go." And off he went for the shoreline. Judy gave me a look like I was a stupid idiot, but fell in behind when I followed Van Horn.

The two of us edged into the water and pushed out till it came up just above our knees. I positioned myself to his left, nearer the beach, which made sense since he was several inches taller than me, and besides, I wanted him to be farther away from the shore. The water felt warmer than the ocean back home and I thought to myself that maybe I could even beat Van Horn since he was heavier and the water might slow him down more. But winning a stupid race wasn't my plan.

I looked down the shoreline at the fairly still water, with only a few small waves breaking ashore, and pointed at some small specks stuck in the sand far down the beach. "See those red flags down there? Let's race to the third one. It's about the right distance."

"Okay. What are the rules?" he asked.

"None, really," I replied. "Just don't lift your knees up out of the water. If you fall down, get up and continue. Don't push or trip the other guy, and if other people are in the way, you run around them. First one past that red flag wins," I said, with a look over at Judy, who was standing nearby.

My glance wasn't lost on Van Horn. We both knew the other one was trying to impress her. "Okay," he grunted. "Judy, you count to three, then we go."

She did, and at the sound of "three," we took off sloshing through the water. It was dammed hard. I hadn't gone more than a few feet before I was breathing heavy from the physical exertion. But Van Horn was having a time of it, too, and despite his greater size, we stayed nearly dead even most of the way. I might actually have won if we'd continued all the way to where the red flag were. But, like I said, winning a race in the water wasn't my plan.

I kept my eyes focused ahead at the red flags, and when we were a minute or so away from them, I pretended to slip, falling face-first into the water. My timing was good. I heard Van Horn laugh and, as I rose up in the water, saw him glance over his shoulder at me as he burst ahead. I waited till he drew a short distance ahead, then struggled to my feet and started forward again as though continuing to race. I stopped after only taking a few steps when Van Horn, who had just gone past the first red flag, let out a scream and pitched face forward into the water. I stayed still and watched as he popped up chest high out of the water with another high-pitched scream. I could see him yanking at a brown shape attached to his right arm and then, off balance, he fell backwards into the water and let out yet a third piercing screech. I smiled with satisfaction, as it was wonderful, much better than I had imagined.

"Aahhh! Aahhh! Help me!" he wailed as he lay sideways with just his head above the waterline and began clawing his way towards the shore! Knowing the danger, I wasn't about to go anywhere near where he'd been. But I had to make it look good, so I sloshed out of the water onto the shore and then fell in behind Judy, as we went waded in a short distance ahead, to help drag Van Horn up on the beach. I managed to take hold around his waist, while she grabbed his good arm, and between us we pulled him onto dry land.

"What's wrong, Tom? What happened?" I hollered as we laid him on his back. He didn't answer because it was obvious why he was in pain. Just as I'd hoped, he'd found the spiny urchins and had big, nasty looking, needle-shaped things sticking out of his right arm and foot. He was trying to hold the foot up in the air to keep the needles from sticking in deeper, while using his right hand to yank more of the prickly things from his left hand and wrist.

"Pull them out! Pull them out!" he bawled in agony, his face a crimson red, as Judy took his head in her lap and I knelt by his side. Being the Good Samaritan, I was only too happy to help, but I wasn't about to get one of them stuck in me. So I carefully raised his right arm up, took hold of one of the spiny things that was protruding out, and then yanked sideways as hard as I could. It came out all right, drawing blood, and, to my satisfaction, caused him to wince with pain. Then I grabbed a second one, while Judy just sat there with her mouth open, watching it all take place.

By this time, other people on the beach who had heard his screams came running and joined us at Van Horn's side. Some guy with a strange accent took hold of my arm just in time to stop me from yanking out another thorn or needle, or whatever they were. "Don't pull no more! You make it worse! Help me get him there," he said, pointing up towards what looked like some concession stand seating with an overhead cover.

I'd much rather have kept yanking them from his body and watched his reaction, but realized that wouldn't have been accepted well just then, what with probably more than twenty people then surrounding us. So I put personal pleasure aside and joined with three others to carry Van Horn across the sand and into the shade of a little hut along the back side of the beach. It was no more than four stout sticks holding up a grass roof with a dirt floor beneath, but at least it was in the shade. We gently placed him back on the ground and someone tried to make him comfortable with a rolled-up towel under his head, while the know-it-all guy ran off to get help from somewhere. Van Horn just lay there with his eyes closed, whimpering like a puppy dog and trying to keep his right side elevated. One guy even tried to help by holding up his leg.

Deciding there was nothing more that I could do, I backed away to the edge of the little hut and up close to Judy, who was standing there with an anxious look on her face. I put my arm around her shoulder, gave her my best smile, and told her not to worry because his wounds weren't serious, just painful. She responded by placing her arm around my back, looked me straight in the eye, and then squeezed my side with her hand. I wanted to cheer! Here I had thought she was worried about Van Horn, and instead she was reassuring me! Even though her eyes kept returning to Van Horn, I realized she wasn't that worried about him. She was thinking about me!

For a few minutes, while the guys on the ground continued to minister to Van Horn, Judy and I just made small talk. Then a small white truck drove up and out popped someone, who I took to be a medic, carrying a satchel. He went straight to Van Horn's side, took a quick look, and then ordered the others to hold him still as he pulled out a bottle from his bag. Before long, he was slowly pouring what looked like hot wax over the needles protruding from Van Horn's body. The waxy stuff caused Van Horn to groan and flinch, and each time it went on, it probably burned him a bit. Soon after, the medic pulled out what looked like an unusual pair of pliers and then proceeded to methodically pull the thorns out of Van Horn's body, one by one. They seemed to come out easily under his guidance, and when the last of them was removed, the medic had us carry Van Horn to the back of his truck, which was open and flat.

After making sure his patient was comfortable in the truck, the medic turned and asked if anyone knew Van Horn, at which time Judy and I introduced ourselves. We explained that we were tourists and all staying at the Royal Victoria, to which he replied, "Okay. Well, he probably should spend the night in the hospital, just to make sure. I think he'll be okay in a few hours, except for some minor pain. That's almost always the case in these things. But what was he doing out there anyway? Didn't he see the warning flags?"

"We didn't know about those things," I lied. "We're just visiting here and were, you know, enjoying the water."

He gave me a look that said I was really stupid, then he said, "Yeah, well, be careful from now on when you're someplace new." And then he got into the driver's seat.

As he did so, I couldn't resist the temptation and bent down over the truck's open side, where I could see Van Horn lying on his back. "Tough luck, Tom," I said. "You had me beat, too. Don't worry. You'll be okay and I'll make sure Judy gets back to the hotel safe. We'll see you tomorrow."

He gave me a nasty look and, ignoring me, stuck his hand over the side of the truck and motioned for Judy who was standing just to my rear. When she came up, he grabbed her hand and said, "Judy, you go back with Sheila and wait for me at the hotel! I'll be back today! Don't do anything with this jerk, you hear?" At that, I shrugged and grimaced, as though stung by his words, and backed away.

"It's okay," said Judy, as she released his hand. "Don't worry, I'll be all right. Just get well." He looked at her hard and then gave me a death stare as the truck started up and pulled away. Not trusting his own woman, he was clearly trying to frighten me.

Perhaps I would have been frightened, if lust hadn't been a more powerful emotion. Oh sure, I knew better than to mess with the woman of someone much larger than I. But when it came to females, I've never had too much sense. Over the years, I've been stabbed, shot, poisoned, imprisoned, and tortured because of women. They'd given me the most exquisite pleasure but also caused me the most grief. Nassau was to prove no exception.

I did take Judy back to the hotel. But not before we spent the rest of the day enjoying ourselves, including some time alone behind some sand dunes on the other side of the island. Turned out, she'd seen the James Bond movie and wanted to reenact a scene that she swore was in the film. I didn't remember that scene but was more than willing to play the male role. As it was, we lingered on Paradise Island until near sundown and then took our good old time getting back to the Royal Victoria. It was well past midnight when we finally walked into the sleeping lounge, laughing and touching each other like a couple of lovebirds. Despite the late hour, the room was a chatterbox, packed with people talking, listening to their radios, and drinking beer. Only a few were trying to sleep on their lounge chairs.

I escorted Judy to her corner of the room, gave her a final squeeze, and started away to my own sleeping space when I felt a crushing blow to the side of my head that sent me spinning across the floor. I've been hit in the head a number of times over the years since then and always have the same reaction—at first a sharp painful sensation accompanied by a bright light, then a black darkness rushes in and takes hold as my body collapses. My hearing always comes back first, I think after just a few seconds, as my head tries to regain normal operations. My vision stays blurred in those first moments and my head numb to almost all sensations except pain. Later, when my body begins to heal itself, the real headaches come and can linger for hours.

That's what happened then. Everything was a blur as I fell to the floor, my head reeling in pain. Yet, somehow, I was aware of being down and injured, having fallen over both furniture and people. Then, loud and clear, I heard the words: "You f—ing shit!" screeched into my ear, and abruptly, my chest exploded from a second blow that was probably a kick. As I rolled to one side and held my chest, I heard other people shouting and stuff falling down around me, followed swiftly by "Having a good time now," and I recognized the screamer as Van Horn. Somehow, he had been released early from the hospital and must have seen Judy and me as we entered the room.

Normally, when faced with danger, my natural instinct is to either surrender or flee, if that is possible. Neither was a choice then, but instinctively, I turned my head away from his voice, curling my body into a ball and moaning loudly, hoping for mercy from my assailant. Instead, there was a loud, crashing noise as I felt several bodies fall across my legs, followed by sounds of grunting and thrashing around as they moved away. With my eyes mostly closed, I could only feel what was happening, but it sounded like someone had come to my aid and was struggling with Van Horn. I only knew for sure there was a tussle going on nearby, that lots of people were moving about and yelling, and that I wasn't being hit anymore.

I stayed curled on my side for just a bit as the combatants moved away from my location. Then I rolled onto my stomach and slowly crawled away from the fray, going under and around the deck chairs, people, and anything else in my way. Only when I was safely across the room, hiding under a table and with my head clearing, but still in pain, did I look back to see Van Horn locked in battle with my friend, Jim Denis.

I could barely see them, as they were ringed by a crowd of spectators who moved with the flow of the fight, staying just out of reach, and, instead of trying to stop it, encouraging them on with cheers and yells. The two of them had knocked over tables, chairs, and luggage as they struggled across the room and were clenched in an ugly embrace. Then suddenly the fight was decided, as Van Horn got a hand free and let loose with a fierce punch that sent Jim sprawling. That would have ended the brawl, except no sooner had Jim hit the floor than someone else smashed Van Horn over the head with one of the lounge chairs. I only got a glimpse of the chair thrower, who looked like one of our group, because he was quickly punched by someone else and then the whole room exploded.

It was like one of those saloon brawls in old western movies! One instant there were just two people struggling with each other; the next there was total pandemonium as dozens joined in—men and women alike—yelling, swinging, and throwing things at each other in the close quarters of the room. Those who weren't involved were making a mad scramble for the room's few doors, trying to escape from the melee.

I stayed down, ignoring my own painful head and chest, transfixed by the brawl unfolding before me. It was insane! No one seemed concerned about getting hurt or that property was being destroyed. I saw a lawn chair come flying through the air to smash against the wall behind me, and then a man ran past, clutching his face, with blood running down his hands. Someone hollered close by and I turned to see a girl trying to fight off an attacker who had ripped her blouse away and was looking to do more.

I would have watched that particular action longer, but something big crashed off the table above me, snapping one of its legs, and I knew it was time for Frank Loveless to vacate the premises. I backed out from beneath the table and went on my hands and knees as fast as I could towards the nearest exit. I came to my feet as I got there, but halted in place when I heard a piercing scream that was somehow different from the surrounding commotion.

I looked back and saw the reason—a fire had started on the far side of the room and was already lighting up the back wall area. Stupidly, I stopped for a second to watch and got pushed hard against the wall by someone rushing out the door, causing me to painfully bang my head again. It only took seconds for me to grab the back of my head and clear my eyes, but in that short time things got worse. The fire had burst into huge flames and was fast going out of control. What had been left of the brawl was done as the mob inside the room were yelling in fear and stampeding for the doors, with fire alarms adding to the discord.

That was enough for me. Forgetting my pain, I burst through the door with dozens of other people, ran down a corridor already starting to fill with smoke, and then past startled hotel guests in a large lobby, before emerging into an outdoor parking lot. Only when I was across the street, safely away from the building, did I pause to catch my breath and look back. Behind me people were streaming out of the Royal Victoria from all sides, trying to get away from the blaze that looked as if it had already moved out of the vacant nightclub space. The parking lot and road in front were packed with people from the hotel, who were soon joined by the police, the fire department, and a large crowd of onlookers.

I found Ron in the confusion and together we watched as the firemen hooked up their hoses and fought to control the blaze. They did a pretty good job considering they had to drag hoses into a big building while going around dozens of people who were too stupid to voluntarily get out of the way. In less than an hour the firemen had the main blaze under control, although smoke continued to drift out from windows and doors. The frame of the building, being made of stone, while somewhat scorched, had seemed to withstand the conflagration pretty well. The insides, I was told, were not so fortunate. The fire had spread upwards from the old bar and burned portions of another floor, plus part of the main lobby, before it was put out.

As the fire raged, the police, concerned with safety, spent their time rounding up the hotel guests and staff and keeping the curious away from the building. After a while though, with the flames going down, they started to ask questions from the onlookers about how the fire had begun. An older and wiser Frank Loveless would have disappeared quietly into the night. But I was young then and stayed on the scene, hoping my belongings hadn't been destroyed and I might be able to retrieve them. I was sitting on the curb with Ron and two of our traveling partners when one of the cops came by and asked if we'd been customers of the hotel. I answered right up as my companions kept mostly quiet, telling the officer that we'd been part of the big college group staying in the old nightclub and we were hoping to go back in and find our stuff once it was safe. I was alert enough to act innocent and not say too much though, even questioning the policeman about how the fire got started.

It didn't help. Before long, the police herded nearly fifty residents of that room, including five of our group from Michigan State, into a couple of buses that took us from the scene to what must have been the Nassau town police station. Although I never saw any cells, it was a big multilevel building that looked very much like a government facility or community meeting place. The bunch of us ended up sleeping on the floor of a big auditorium, complete with a stage and lots of folding chairs, under the watchful eyes of several policemen.

During that night though, each of us was individually taken from the big room to a small office, questioned again by the police and made to fill out papers describing what we'd observed at the hotel. It was obvious that the cops had figured out that the fire had started in the lower lounge as a result of a fight, but they hadn't been able to gather any facts on how the brawl began. Van Horn and Judy weren't anywhere to be seen, having somehow escaped arrest, and outside of my friends who wouldn't say much, the other people being questioned that night probably had no idea what had happened. When my turn came to be questioned, I continued to play innocent, telling them I was asleep when the fight started and had just run out the door to escape the flames. I pretended to be angry because my vacation had been ruined and my stuff probably destroyed in the fire.

The next morning, an older officer in a white uniform informed us the hotel was not going to press charges. They knew where the fire had started, he said, but without someone specific to blame, the hotel either had to sue all of us or write it off as a bad accident. The first choice could take years and be expensive, he said, so the hotel planned to just repair the damage through their insurance company. Still, even though no charges were being pressed against anyone, the police made it clear we were all somehow responsible for the damage and no longer welcome in their country. We spent the rest of that morning filling out yet more paperwork and then sat around until mid-afternoon. At that point, we were hauled down to the airport and flown to Miami, where we were turned over to the local police. The phone call to Dad soon followed.

I've not been back to the Bahamas since. The only proof I've got that I was ever there are a few faded photos of me on the beach and at the Royal Victoria…and a copy of my deportation papers. But that's enough

CHAPTER THREE

My draft notice came in the mail about three weeks before my final class at Michigan State. It was the standard "Greetings from the President" letter that thousands of young men got in those days, written in a way to make me feel fortunate I had been chosen to serve the nation. Even though I was a legal resident of Hawaii, the notice had me reporting sometime in July to the Detroit Replacement Detachment, rather than Honolulu. I guessed that was Uncle Burt's doing.

My father had been good to his word, which didn't surprise me. He really believed serving in the military would make me a better citizen and more responsible adult. That's what had happened to him. He'd been a young man pumping gas in the Midwest for a living when the nation served him with a draft notice in 1942, subsequently sending him to Europe to fight the Nazis in World War II. With little formal education and no real career opportunities, not an unusual thing for his generation, he elected to remain in the military after the war. He spent the next twenty years as an air force officer, fighting in the Korean War and dragging his family around the world from assignment to assignment, before hanging it up and retiring to the islands. And he wasn't the first in our family to serve in the military. His father had been a naval officer in the Spanish-American War and most of my uncles had spent time in the army during World War II or Korea. So for my family, and many others in those days, military service was an American tradition and, on top of that, an honorable profession.

It wasn't the same for most of us who grew up in the 60s. When I first went to State in 1963, America was the most powerful country in the world and our economy was undergoing a two-decade expansion. Sure, the Russians were acknowledged as an enemy and trying to expand their ideology around the world, and nearly everyone accepted the fact that we needed a strong army and navy in case we ever had to fight the communists. But unless someone like Elvis got drafted, or a rare event like the Cuban Missile Crisis happened, few people under the age of twenty ever gave a second thought about our military forces. Life was good, what with the middle class expanding and all of us more connected than ever because of radio and television. We all knew there was a possibility of nuclear war, but it just wasn't that believable to the vast majority of young Americans. Not that many people even interacted with the armed forces, unless they lived near a military base.

All of that changed with Vietnam. Because of television and the ability of journalists to actually report live from a battlefield, it was the first war in our history that most people were able to see, on a daily basis, the full horror of combat, with its bloody casualties and property destruction. It became personal to many American families because the draft was still in force in those days. Unless a young man was attending college, had children, or was employed in some special skill, which usually meant working for the government, he stood a good chance of being drafted.

Before the 1960s most Americans had never heard of Vietnam, much less know how to find it on a map. But by the time I graduated from college in '68, Vietnam was the country's hottest topic of conversation, with most of the media and average middle-class people thinking it was a senseless conflict for us to fight. Antiwar protests expanded across the country in the mid to late 60s, with college campuses often the hotbed of antiwar fever. Only the most courageous or most foolish spoke in favor of the Vietnam War at any school in the later years of that decade, and I was neither.

Unlike many of my peers at MSU though, I didn't detest or fear the armed services. Because of my father's career, I'd lived around military uniforms all my life. My brothers and I were all born and raised on air force bases and had attended school in six different states and three foreign countries thanks to the nomadic life we lived. I knew firsthand that few military people are gung ho about going to war and that after a day of work, they take off their uniforms and live just like regular civilian people.

I'd tried army ROTC during my freshman year at State, partly to please Dad who was after all paying the bill, but also because first year male students were often encouraged to sign up for military training at many universities in those days. I continued the army classes until the end of my junior year and then quit the program. It was becoming very uncomfortable to wear a military uniform on campus by that time, and I more and more felt certain of ending up in Vietnam if I completed ROTC and was commissioned an officer. It was well known that many graduates of the two preceding classes had ended up there. Besides, I figured to avoid the draft by going on to graduate school or, in the worst case, getting married for a few years. I was overconfident, as young men tend to be, and never dreamed that my own father would be working to get me drafted within two years' time.

So, even though receiving my draft notice wasn't a total surprise, it still came as a shock. Life as I knew it was definitely ending and I briefly considered running off to Canada. A lot of others did in those days rather than go to war, and Canada was only a few hours' drive from East Lansing, where I lived. If I'd known what lay ahead the following year, my next phone call home would definitely have been from Ottawa. But I couldn't see the future, and besides, there were also financial reasons for not running off to Canada.

More than sixty years earlier, my grandfather on Dad's side and a few of his friends were among the first to realize that Americans would spend money on food created just for babies, much as they already did for their pets. Together, four of them invested what they could, started up a processing center and distribution channels for baby food and grew rich on the idea.

For reasons never revealed to me, Grandpa was forced out of the company management after a few years, but was allowed to keep his shares in the business. When he passed away in the late 50s, the family inherited millions, with my Dad and Uncle Burt splitting the bulk of it and then settling down in Hawaii. It was just a matter of time before some of that money came to me and I wasn't eager to blow such a grand inheritance by running off to Canada. There was no doubt that my father, urged on by my three greedy brothers, would have cut me off quick from any future financial reward if I'd fled the draft. Besides, I was sure Dad would come looking for me no matter where I ran and, once he found me, would have forced me back to the US.

As it was, in early July I caught a bus from Lansing and reported to the army's reception station in Detroit. I joined what seemed to be a thousand other guys waiting in line for hours to undergo a five-minute physical exam. When my turn came, nothing much happened except someone took my temperature, my pulse and a blood sample, and then an obviously bored doctor drilled me with questions. He took notes while asking, among other things, whether I had ever experienced a heart attack, was allergic to anything, or had homosexual thoughts. Figuring it made no difference what I said and anxious to just get it over with, I affirmed that I was in good health.

With the medical exam out of the way, I was then passed on to another place in the building to sit for several hours at a desk in a stuffy, windowless room with dozens of other draftees, as we waited to take a battery of boring mental tests. I say boring because I was able to complete all the questions in my packet in mere minutes and then spent what seemed like another hour waiting for the less-gifted people to finish their tests. At the end of the day, after our mental exams were graded and our physical results reviewed, we each got a paper letting us know whether or not we had passed and were qualified for army life. Earlier that day, upon arrival, we had been told by some sergeant that any man who wasn't physically or mentally fit to handle the rigors of army life would be screened out by the process and sent home as ineligible to serve. But from my observation that day, anyone who could walk and breathe at the same time made it through the process. I certainly did.

Afterwards, I took a bus back to Lansing and moped about in Michigan State for several weeks, doing nothing much except drink beer down by the Red Cedar River. Eventually, a letter came in the mail congratulating me for having passed my exams and instructing me to bring my bags and check in at a recruiting station there in Lansing. I again contemplated the nearness of

Canada, but in the end did report to the local army office, from whence I soon found myself on a flight headed to Fort Dix, New Jersey.

For many years, Fort Dix had been one of the army's main training posts for new recruits along the East Coast. Draftees from all across the Midwest and northeast were sent there for an initial eight-week basic training course designed to transition them from civilians into soldiers. Having never been in that part of the country before except as a very young child, when my Dad was assigned to a base in Virginia, I had always thought of New Jersey as a very congested place, overgrown with cities and towns. Indeed there are a number of large cities and towns in New Jersey, but Fort Dix was definitely countryside. While there was a small town outside the main gate, and what looked like more than a hundred buildings on post, the army base was mostly miles upon miles of open space with long, empty highways running through fields and pine tree forests. I got to know those roads well during my time there because we marched or ran down all of them multiple times on daily trips between the barracks and the rifle ranges.

I arrived at Dix on a bus with about twenty other new soldiers. We were greeted by a sign at the front gate that read: THE HOME OF THE ULTIMATE WEAPON. I initially assumed it referred to us soldiers. Later on, after several days of eating in the appropriately named "mess halls," I decided the sign applied to army food.

Our first day at Dix was spent getting assigned and processing in with our military units and moving into our living quarters. The barracks were, in fact, large rectangular brick buildings, with living space for several hundred soldiers, as well as storage areas for military equipment and offices for the officers and NCOs who had full control over every aspect of our lives. There were dozens of the huge buildings at Dix, with each separated from the others by big green lawns where we soldiers stood in formation three or four times a day. The barracks were definitely well maintained, but not very accommodating to someone who'd had his own room since childhood. We slept in bunk beds in open bays, with about thirty people to a room. Not counting my short time in Nassau, it was the first time in my life I'd slept in one room with so many people, most of whom smelled bad or kept me awake with their snoring.

At least the sleeping quarters were better than the bathrooms, or latrines, as they're called in the military. The bunch of us who lived in our sleeping bay all shared one large latrine with about ten toilets and a similar number of showers. Even though the latrines were fairly clean because of daily inspections by the full-time cadre, there are few things more repulsive than sharing a bathroom with dozens of young men. I decided then, and still feel, that most men under the age of thirty are filthy creatures with no sense of shame. Without going into details, I'll just state that I've done my best ever since to minimize my use of military latrines.

I found the army's mess halls to be as appealing as their sleeping quarters. We almost always ate hundreds of people at a time, going down a chow line as poorly trained cooks piled mystery food on our trays and drill sergeants rushed us into shoveling the chow down our throats, with little time to chew or swallow. It was all very much like dining hall scenes I'd seen in prison films.

Over the years, I've heard lots of guys talk about how much they value the memories of their first days in the army—the camaraderie of working with new friends towards a common goal, the excitement of new adventure, being able to train with real weapons, and so forth. Of course, I've noticed that it's always older soldiers who speak favorably of Basic Training, not the young ones who were actually enduring it. As for me, I can honestly say I hated every minute of the sixteen weeks I spent at Fort Dix doing Basic Training and Advanced Individual Training. My memories of those early army days include having the hair shaved off my head, hours and hours of standing in formations, my arm poked full of needles with every imaginable kind of vaccination, cleaning latrines, forced long-distance marches, having to wake up at 4:30 in the morning, and endless hours of running, jumping, and crawling through dirt—not the kind of stuff rationale people look forward to experiencing.

Of course, I was also taught how to fire and clean M16 rifles, M60 machine guns, and antitank weapons. Plus, I had excellent instruction on how to march in formation, give emergency medical care, and fight hand-to-hand combat with another unwilling combatant. For someone who had never before even considered owning a gun, much less shooting one at someone, each day was more dreadful than the one before. Every time I met a new weapon, I had nightmares of accidently killing someone, or worse, possibly hurting myself. Yet, I somehow survived and the credit must go to the people who spent their time training me and the others. Those four months at Fort Dix in 1968 were a dreadful memory, but during that time, I truly became a professional soldier.

Probably my most impressionable memory from those days at Fort Dix was First Sergeant Sidney Andrews, the top noncommissioned officer who oversaw our unit's daily regimen during Basic Training. He was a tall, lanky Black from somewhere down south who just loved his job, which, as best I could figure out, was to inflict on us recruits, as often as possible, the most devious abuse he could conceive. Everyone who dealt with us recruits screamed orders and pushed us to our physical limit. That's standard military training. But Andrews often went over the line. He was petty, vindictive, and cruel (I'm inclined to be of the same nature, so I know these traits when I see them). He took pleasure in denying us simple things—like sleep, food, and clean clothes. I'm still not sure he didn't want to kill a few of us, just to impress the rest with his power.

Andrews especially seemed to enjoy lording over those of us who were college graduates, which many new recruits were in those days, thanks to the draft. The best educated among our class always seemed to get the filthiest KP duty and the worst guard duty shifts. I always thought Andrews had a complex around smarter people and felt none of us would have given him a second thought if it weren't for his position as our army superior. He was right in that.

Conversations with Sergeant Andrews were memorable, in that no one dared to disagree with him. I still recall the time he first spoke to me.

Andrews: "Hey, Dickhead."

Me: "Yes, First Sergeant."

Andrews: "You a college boy ain't you, Troop?"

Me: "Yes, First Sergeant."

Andrews: "That means you like things nice and clean, don't it?"

Me: "Yes, First Sergeant."

Andrews: "So, why don't you go over there and clean out the inside of that Dempsey Dumpster, Boy? Take out that trash and shine up them walls! You'd like that, wouldn't you?"

Me: "Yes, First Sergeant."

Andrews: "And after that, why don't you spend the night cleaning our latrines? You'd be happy doing that, wouldn't you Lovelessssss (he enjoyed dragging out my last name)?"

Me: "Yes, First Sergeant."

Andrews: "Are you eyeballing me, Recruit?"

Me: "Yes, First Sergeant. No. No. I mean, no, First Sergeant."

And so on. It was all quite inspirational and made me much better appreciate the importance of being a higher-rank soldier. I have to admit though, Andrews did improve my vocabulary. Before him, I'd never heard the word "dickhead."

While training and the people I put up with were difficult, for me, the worst part about my time at Fort Dix was the women. There weren't any. This was years before women were allowed to train alongside men, so the only females we saw were wives and daughters of soldiers permanently stationed at Dix, who had little use for recruits and were off-limits for us anyway. Even if there had been women available, there was no time for them. Our typical day, which was basically the same seven days a week, began before sunup and went until well after dark, when we fell exhausted into our bunks.

I only got off post one time during my sixteen weeks at Fort Dix—when our unit was given a weekend pass near the end of Advanced Individual Training. About three hundred of us flooded the small local town of Wrightstown, our pockets full of money we'd not spent during the past four months and hoping to find some female action. What we found were pawnshops, a few drive-in restaurants, lots of small, seedy bars, and not much else. There were some women in the bars and walking the streets, but nearly all of them were obviously hookers and swamped with requests. I still had standards in those days, however slight, and wasn't about to stand in line for some shabby whore, so I spent my time just hanging around a couple of small bars, watching TV and drinking beer. By the time I graduated from AIT and left Dix the following week, I was really living up to my last name.

When I did leave New Jersey, the army gave me five days before I had to report to my next assignment at Fort Benning, Georgia. That was more than enough time to get down south, so I decided, since New York City was only a few hours away, that I would take a look at the Big Apple. Having never been to New York before, my plan was to see the sights, especially the Statue of Liberty and the Empire State Building. And I did see them, but only from a distance. That very first night, after checking into a cheap hotel, I met a nice and plump Latino girl at a bar close by and then spent the next three days making her acquaintance. We only left the hotel twice during that time, once for a fancy restaurant and another time to see a movie, so I have no proof I was ever in New York back then. No souvenirs, no photos, nothing. I don't even remember the girl's name, which was probably just as well, although I did promise to write.

Several days later, after a very long and boring bus ride, I arrived at Fort Benning, Georgia, and signed in with the US Army's 95th Infantry Brigade to begin Officer's Candidate School. I'd done well on those mental exams in Detroit, and since I had a college degree to boot, the army gave me a choice of either going to Officer's Candidate School or just remaining an enlisted soldier and taking my chances with a regular assignment. Figuring officers had better jobs, made more money, and lived in nicer quarters, I chose OCS. Besides, while many of my fellow Basic and AIT graduates went directly from Fort Dix to Vietnam, I knew the four months spent learning how to be an officer would keep me away from any possible assignment to Vietnam that much longer. Naively, I thought the war might be over by the time I got out of OCS. After all, Nixon had just been elected president and said he had a plan for getting us out of the war.

The first thing they had me do at Officer's Candidate School, while still wearing my dress uniform, was to crawl up four flights of stairs with a mattress on my back, dragging along my duffel bag. "Make your own bed, Candidate," said the friendly TAC officer who welcomed me, "but don't walk! Crawl! Crawl on your hands and knees! You can walk when you're an officer!"

So, along with other soldiers reporting in for OCS, I crawled from the ground level up to the top floor of the OCS barracks, carrying the mattress and my gear. It struck me as strange that they would make a young soldier undergo such a degrading and physically demanding exercise, when there didn't seem to be any point to it. Why wasn't the mattress already on my bed, like it had been at Fort Dix and probably at every other army post? When I got up the courage to ask a TAC officer that question some days later, he said it was because we were helping to replace old mattresses with new ones. But even if that were the case, which I doubted, why hadn't we been allowed to just carry them to our beds, instead of having to crawl up the stairs? I thought then, and still do, that it was just the army's way of making sure we knew our place, as "Officer Candidates," and not as "Officers."

I soon realized that my training at Fort Dix had been no more than a prelude to what would happen at Fort Benning. OCS was a challenging, formidable regiment that allowed for little sleep, frugal meals, and absolutely no entertainment, unless you enjoyed watching other people suffer. The daily routine for my classmates and I consisted of a two-mile run before breakfast, an in-ranks inspection, eight hours of instruction in the various arts of war, about thirty to forty minutes for meals (all three of them), a two-hour study session in the evening, several hours of deliberate mental and physical harassment by the TACs, and another four or five hours cleaning our rooms and equipment. Somewhere in there we also slept. It was not a fun experience, but again I give the army credit—the things I learned at Fort Benning had saved me on a number of occasions over the years.

The post swarmed with soldiers, as Benning was not only home to the army's Officer's Candidate School but also the Infantry Training Center for pathfinders, rangers, and other people who leapt out of airplanes, ate bugs, and were of a masochistic nature. I heard there were also soldiers hardening themselves to be Green Berets at Fort Benning in those days; I just never ran into any of them.

The living accommodations at Benning were somewhat better than those at Fort Dix, but that was probably because fewer soldiers used them during a training year. Our barracks were located across from a mammoth green field that had a tall tower at one end, which supposedly had something to do with the army's parachute jump school program. I never saw the tower used during my time there, but I saw plenty of the large green field, as that was where we did our morning calisthenics.

Instead of sleeping in big open bays, officer candidates lived in two-person rooms. Each of us had our own bed, a footlocker, a wall locker and a dresser, plus a desk that we shared. The footlockers were our only place of privacy. We were allowed to place personal items, like photos of our family, and unauthorized snack food in them and they remained locked except at night, when the TAC officers weren't around. Our dressers and wall lockers were just for show. They held our uniforms and other military gear, much of which we never touched; every piece of underwear or pair of socks was folded just so, every uniform hung in a proper order, and every bar of soap or toothbrush faced in exactly the same direction as every other bar of soap or toothbrush belonging to any other candidate in any other room. The only way to distinguish one room from another was by the names on each door or by the contents of the footlockers, which only the owner could open.

I soon noticed that a major difference between OCS and my earlier training was a propensity for cleanliness at Fort Benning that bordered on fanaticism. While we'd spent plenty of time at Fort Dix keeping our quarters clean, it was nothing like what I saw at Benning, where every inch of our living space was more sanitary than a hospital ward. Within days of our arrival, all of us candidates stopped wearing shoes in the rooms or hallways; instead, we wore socks and slid along the floor, buffing the wood as we went to keep it shiny. Only the TAC officers who supervised us were allowed to wear shoes, and I noticed they seemed to enjoy scuffing their feet along the ground as they walked. The latrines were exceptionally sparkling, with toilets so clean I sometimes felt guilty sitting on them. Even the steam pipes running along our ceilings shined; mine certainly did, thanks mostly to my roommate.

His name was Charles Deeds. He was shorter than I by a few inches, but more stocky and certainly more of a mama's boy, which meant he was a whiner. A graduate of Princeton, he had voluntarily joined the army and was in many ways the perfect Officer's Candidate. He actually studied army doctrines during his scant free time, insisted that our room be the cleanest on the floor, and looked for every chance to make himself noticed by the TACs. That was all fine with me because he did most of the work that caused our room to almost always pass daily inspection.

Each morning, while we were in class or on the rifle range, a TAC officer came through the unit area, looked through our rooms, and made notations on a demerit sheet that we were required to keep posted on our desk. If the inspecting TAC found anything amiss—dust on the floor, a uniform button out of place, too much sunlight on the wall—we found demerits listed on the paper when we returned to the room at the end of the day. Any Candidate who got too many demerits in a given week, usually anything over three, got extra duty to perform on Sunday afternoons, which was the only time not officially scheduled for training. We all soon learned that demerits were to be avoided, and that they could be awarded for the most bizarre reasons.

One morning, the TACs found a dead bug in our room and gave Deeds and I five demerits each for having an "unauthorized pet" on the premises. It was ridiculous, of course, but we were resigned to our fate until a fellow Candidate told us we could challenge demerits before a panel of TAC officers if we felt they were given unfairly. Although he was initially opposed, I convinced Deeds that we had nothing to lose by appealing, and besides, it would show that we were real officer material because we could not be pushed around so easily. So, wearing our best uniforms, we appeared before the appeals court several days later and argued that there was no way the bug could have been a pet, because the army's Code of Conduct was quite clear about never leaving a fallen comrade alone. I did most of the talking, while Deeds just stood there nodding his head and wringing his hands. It was a pretty ingenious argument, and I could tell the TACs were impressed with our ridiculous logic. But they weren't about to lose so easily. They listened to my speech, adjourned to another room for a few minutes, and then came back with their decision.

They admitted to making a mistake, agreeing that no good soldier would allow a beloved pet to die by itself in such a manner. So, they agreed, the dead bug could not have been our pet. However, we would still be charged five demerits each for having "unauthorized food in the room." I can still remember a smug-faced Captain smiling at us when he announced their decision, and asking if we've like to challenge that ruling also. I was tempted, but Deeds was in panic mode by then and would never have gone along, so I just gave it up and we ended up washing down motor pool trucks the following Sunday instead of having the day off.

That wasn't the only time Deeds and I disagreed. In fact, I decided early on that the two of us had very little in common. He really enjoyed playing soldier, often being the loudest voice in formation and the first to volunteer for extra duty. I volunteered for nothing and did only as much work as necessary to remain in the OCS program. In one of our first talks, the idiot told me he actually wished for an assignment to Vietnam after graduation, saying how glorious it would be to go and fight the Communists. I just listened and wrote him off as a fool. I didn't care at all about the Communists, since I'd never met one and they weren't bothering me. The TAC officers worried me more than Communists, although I strongly suspected they were of the same control mind-set.

Deeds and I somehow made it through several weeks together before our personalities clashed. One night, after a minor disagreement, he said I had a careless attitude and disregard for military protocol, and that I was a disgrace to the uniform. I stared at him for a second and then went back to reading the comic book I'd snuck into the room. I really didn't care what he said, and besides, in my mind, I thought what really rankled him, and what really set us apart, was that he knew I was the better soldier. Whether directing artillery fire, setting up a defensive perimeter, or analyzing large-scale maneuver tactics—I was always near the top of our class and Deeds was always near the middle. He never openly spoke of it, and never asked for my assistance, but he clearly was envious of my natural abilities.

Still, we lived in relative peace with each other until our first scheduled physical test, which came about six weeks into the course. The test was like a mini-pentathlon, with five events, which were supposed to measure our physical endurance and strength. Each event was scored separately, with a perfect score on each worth one hundred points. We were told that anyone scoring 450 points or better would get a one-day pass to leave post the following weekend, which was a huge incentive for soldiers who had been cooped up for weeks. I would have kissed my brother to get a full day off from that routine, so when the test came around, instead of doing just enough to get by, I actually pushed myself hard to get a high score. After the first four events, I had a combined total of 370 points and only needed to complete the final one, a one-mile run, in a little over eight minutes to qualify for the one-day vacation. I'd never been good at long-distance running but was determined to give it my best.

I ran so fast my lungs felt like exploding and was within twenty yards of the end when I heard the timekeeper announcing: "Eight minutes ten seconds, eight minutes eleven seconds, eight minutes twelve seconds." From somewhere I found a burst of energy and lunged past the finish line, collapsing on the side of the dirt track. I lay on the ground, gasping for breath, cursing my luck. I had near killed myself, but realized I'd finished the mile run just a few seconds too slow. I was utterly dejected. I'd come so close, but all my work had been in vain—and then I saw my scorekeeper walking towards me. It was Deeds.

"'Nice time, Frank," he said, handing me my scorecard. Sure enough, it read: "Eight minutes, thirteen seconds."

"Charlie," I said quietly, pulling him aside. "I'm three seconds over what I need for 450 points. How about putting my time down at eight minutes, ten seconds? I'd really appreciate it and I'll owe you one."

"But you ran it in eight minutes, thirteen seconds, Frank! I can't change it! That would be cheating," said the sanctimonious jerk.

"So what? No one knows what my real score was except you and me! No one even cares!" I exclaimed, dumbfounded that anyone could be so righteous.

"Sorry, Frank. It wouldn't be right."

"But we're roommates, Charlie, we have to stick together."

"It's because we're roommates that I'll forget this conversation ever took place," he said, turning his back and walking away.

I couldn't believe the pious SOB. He knew no one else could possibly know my exact time on the run! There was no chance of us getting caught! I was sure it was just his way of putting me in my place and I swore then to get even in a way that would cause him grief.

So, the next morning, instead of helping Deeds clean the common areas of our room, I pretended he didn't exist and just took care of my own bed and personal stuff. He, in turn, pretended not to notice and did the common area work on his own. I followed the same pattern the rest of the week, sticking to myself and acting as though everything was just fine while he quietly continued to do most of the maintenance. But I could tell it was starting to bother him and sure enough, on the fifth day, he couldn't contain himself any longer.

"Frank," he said abruptly, "we need to shine the ceiling pipes. I can clearly see dust on them."

"Shine them if you want," I replied, not looking in his direction. "They look fine to me."

"You know they're not and if we don't shine ours, we'll be different from everyone else. The TACs will notice it fast!" he whined.

"Who cares? They don't have to live in this room," I said, as though it were the least important thing in the world.

"We'll get demerits," he pleaded. "We have to be the same as every other room!"

"Why should we?" I countered, this time looking straight at him. "We always get demerits, no matter how much work we do. There's no way to win, so why try? Anyway, maybe the TACs will credit us for being independent."

"Look," he said, "I'm going to clean them, and we're roommates, so you can just help."

"Oh! So now we're roommates!" I said, my voice dripping with sarcasm.

That got him. He gave me a look that would have killed someone with a conscience, but didn't say a word; just went to work polishing those pipes. That was okay with me. I sure didn't want any more demerits.

From then on, we had an unspoken agreement. I cleaned my own stuff, and Deeds cleaned everything else. I believe at first he thought I would eventually be shamed into helping him, as that's probably how the other candidates in our class would have reacted. Well, he was wrong there. It's a rare day when Frankie Loveless felt shame about anything, much less trying to win the "Clean Room of the Year Award." I just let him do the common area work alone, sure that he wouldn't complain to anyone, and he didn't, not even to the other candidates. Still, it was damned unpleasant living in that room with him.

Our cozy little arrangement ended after a few weeks because I got hungry one night. It was one of those days that our battalion had stayed out late on the weapons ranges; we got back to the barracks as the sun was going down and the mess hall was closing for the night. A few desperate soldiers rushed into the dining facility, grabbing their food and gulping it down as they moved along the chow line, but most of my classmates just figured "the hell with it" and headed for their rooms, deciding not to eat. Not me. While riding back from the range that day, several of us had realized we would arrive back late, so we devised an alternative dinner plan.

We were already familiar with several take-out restaurants in the central part of Fort Benning that we'd visited on our Sunday off time and knew stayed open after the sun went down, including a hamburger joint, a pizza place, and several snack shops. So that night we decided, rather than go hungry, that we would get takeout pizza for dinner.

It was against the rules to bring food up to our rooms, so we devised a strategy to smuggle in the pizza without the TACs knowing about it. The first part of our plan was simple. We phoned in an order and had about a dozen pizzas delivered across the street to an office building, where two of our group waited and paid for it. Then we got a bit more creative. Each night a six-man work detail carried the battalion's rubbish out to the street in large metal trash cans where it was emptied into a dumpster. Afterwards, the trash cans were cleaned out and brought back into the barracks for use the following day. But our garbage cans were not like those found in ordinary homes across the country. Like everything else we touched, they sparkled with cleanliness. One of them was especially clean because it had never been used for anything other than discarded pieces of paper.

So that night, once the pizzas were received, we carefully placed them, still in their boxes, in the unspoiled garbage can and hauled them up to our company storage room. Anyone watching would have thought we were just returning empty garbage cans to the area. Once we were confident the pizzas had been safely smuggled in, our group indulged themselves until our stomachs were full and then sold leftover slices to our classmates, who paid a premium for our daring. It was the best meal I'd had in weeks, and on top of that, it fast became a profitable venture, as lots of our classmates came by to partake. As one of the ringleaders, I was thoroughly satisfied that we'd beaten the system through our daring. TAC officers hardly ever visited our floor after hours; they were probably home sleeping in comfort, so we didn't even bother to keep an eye out for them.

I can recall sitting on the floor, leaning comfortably against the wall, munching on pizza, and listening to three other candidates singing "ninety-nine pieces of pizza to eat..." Then the storage room door quietly pushed inward. I looked over, expecting to find yet another soldier who had come to buy pizza, and then nearly gagged when I saw Captain Brackens, one of the most feared TACs, standing there with a malicious smile on his face.

"Having a good time, Boys?" he asked, chuckling. If my mouth hadn't been full, I might have thought of something witty to say. As it was, I just sat there with food dribbling from my chin, but only for a second. Then, along with my three companions, I jumped to attention, arms straight down at my side, choking down cheese and pepperoni. We all stared straight ahead, not knowing what to say or do. We'd been caught and caught badly.

Brackens knew what to do. He had us drag what was left of the can of pizzas, and there were still several of them not eaten, out into the hallway. Then he shouted a command and within seconds the entire floor was lined with soldiers along both sides of the corridor, our heels and heads pressed back against the wall.

Brackens waited until every soldier in the unit, at least sixty of us, were standing ramrod straight at attention, eyes to the front and mouths closed. Then he began slowly pacing up and down the hallway, like a panther stalking its prey. When he was about fifteen feet away from me and sure he had the attention of everyone there, he began to speak in a clam, subdued voice.

"It seems," he said, "that some of us don't want to play by the rules! They're special people! They have their own idea of what is permitted and what is not. Fortunately," and he paused for emphasis before raising his voice several decibels, "there was one candidate in this group who didn't take part in this orgy and had the courage and honesty to report this infraction. For his sake, and his sake only, I won't report this *gross violation of the rules*!"

"But," and he wheeled and moved quickly down the hallway to come within two inches of my face and then bellowed, obviously expecting an answer, "*I would like to know whose idea was it to bring this into the barracks, Candidate!*"

"Sir! Yes, Sir! I don't know sir!" I said with pepperoni breath.

"Of course, you wouldn't know," he replied sarcastically, with a lower yet more frightening voice. "But," he said, as he pried open the garbage can and revealed the remaining stack of pizzas still in their boxes, "you are aware that this is unauthorized, aren't you?"

I glanced at the pizzas, and then at his face, as a smirk came over it.

Before I could answer, he turned and shouted down the hallway so everyone could hear. "Oh, wait! Maybe I've made a mistake! Maybe this isn't food! Maybe these are brushes for the floor buffer! Let's find out!" He turned to me and yelled, "Go get the buffer, Candidate!"

Well, I jumped to it, yes sirred him, and quickly dragged a floor buffer out of the cleaning closet down the hallway. I brought it to him and then jumped back into formation along the wall.

"Let's see how good these brushes are," said Brackens as he placed one of the pizzas, still in its box, upside down on the hallway floor! Then he plugged in the buffer, put it on top of the pizza, and then pushed the ON button. The results were predictable: chunks of cheese, crust, pepperoni, and cardboard flew in all directions, splattering everything and everyone in sight. "That one wasn't too good. We'd better try another." So he did, with the same results, and then another, and another, until the pizzas were all demolished and the hallway was a mess, with pieces of food sticking on walls, ceiling, and soldiers. Throughout the whole thing, no one had moved. He turned back into my face and screamed, "Well! I guess we won't be buying any more of those brushes, *will we, Candidate?*"

"No, Sir," I sheepishly replied, wondering why he was only picking on me when there had been four of us caught in the room.

"Good! I hope *everyone* has learned a lesson here tonight," he said, facing back down the hall. "And I hope you enjoy cleaning up this mess! I'll be back in an hour to see how well you've done!"

Of course, we jumped right to it and had the hallway cleaned in an hour. But that didn't end it for many of our class. Brackens had said someone, one of us, had reported the pizzas, and we wanted to know the name of that turn-coat. Without evidence, we could only guess, so we started eliminating one person after another until we had narrowed it down to only a few who could have been the culprits. Of that group, one person stood out from the rest— my roommate, Deeds. He had been sitting near our group on the bus when we were talking about ordering the pizza, and, while he had been in the hallway during Bracken's ranting, Deeds had been observed earlier that night leaving the company floor shortly after we brought the pizza upstairs. I added to the suspicion of him by reporting that Deeds sometimes seemed to resent my better standing in the unit training and that he often complained about the cleaning of our room, leaving out the fact that I didn't do my share of the work. Besides, I asked the others, why had Brackens directed his anger to-wards only me? It didn't make sense, unless someone... and I left it at that. My classmates needed no more convincing. We all knew Deeds was our man and there would be a payback for what he'd done. It came four weeks later.

We planned it for a Sunday, the one day each week we were allowed to leave post. That afternoon, one of my classmates and I went into Phoenix City, a town just to the west of Fort Benning, to find an accomplice for our scheme. We found her in a pool hall called the Alibi Bar. A long-haired brunette, she was young and cute and dressed like a schoolgirl, but a whore if I ever saw one. We bought her a few drinks and explained the plan we'd devised, making it sound like we needed her help to play a practical joke on a friend. At first, she was worried about getting into trouble with the military police, but when we told her how much we were willing to pay, she eagerly joined in.

It was just past dusk when the three of us got back to the barracks. While my partner made sure there weren't any TACs in the area, the girl, whose name was Kathy, and I went straight to my room. Deeds was there, sitting on the floor polishing his boots, when we entered.

"What are you doing?" he said, jumping to his feet. "Are you crazy? Get her out of here! We can get thrown out if they catch us with a girl in the room!"

"Relax, Charlie," I said, almost whispering. "Keep your voice down. She's going to stay for just a little while. You can have her next."

"I don't want her!" he stammered. "Just get her out of this room, or I'm going straight to the OD!"

His reaction was what I'd anticipated. "Okay, okay, have it your way," I said, sounding exasperated. "Just give me a minute to go to the bathroom. Then I'll take her somewhere else." I passed quickly out through the door, leaving Charlie and the girl together in the room, before he could react. I walked down the hallway, but instead of going to the latrine, I ducked into a room shared by two fellow plotters. From there, we slightly cracked open the door to observe the hallway.

As soon as I left, Kathy must have gone into the act we'd arranged— telling Deeds that I had tricked her into the barracks and that she was a good girl and scared and wanted to get away. I was certain Deeds would fall for her story and would do what he could to save the innocent maiden. Sure enough, within minutes, through the cracked doorway, I saw Deeds lead her out of the room and down the stairwell at the far end of the corridor. Our hero was rescuing the damsel in distress from that nasty Frankie Loveless!

They were halfway down the stairs when they met Brackens and Lieutenant Johnson coming up, led by Jerry Kappler, the officer candidate on CQ duty that night and another member of our little conspiracy. I wish I could have part of the greeting party, but the moment Deeds and Kathy went down the stairs, I was already speeding back to my room.

I was sitting there at our desk, with my back to the door, writing notes in my OCS journal, when I heard the door open behind me a few minutes later. Without turning around, I said, "Did ya have fun?" as though addressing someone returning to the room. The only response was someone clearing his throat, so I turned to look and then jumped to my feet and offered a "Good evening, Sir" to Captain Brackens. I must have done an excellent job of looking startled. He stared at me a few seconds, looked at the desk with my journal, and then left without a word. When Deeds returned an hour later, I was already in bed pretending to sleep.

The next morning we ignored each other, except one of us let slip the "F" word while the other just quietly chuckled. Nothing happened throughout most of the day as we went through our regular training routine with the unit. Then, in mid-afternoon, one of the TACs came up and told me to report to the company commander's office. I went straight there, trying to imagine in my head what might transpire. All day, I'd been thinking about what Deeds would explain about what had happened and how I would respond.

When I arrived at the commander's office, a sergeant greeted me in an outer room and then escorted me to a fairly small room where he announced my presence. I went in as the sergeant gestured for me to enter; then he closed the door and remained outside. Directly in front of me, I found Captain Daydif, our unit commander, sitting in the center of the room behind a desk, with a wall full of citations and military plaques behind him. A middle-aged Caucasian man with a small moustache, I'd only seen Daydif on rare occasions when he addressed the entire company. To his left, on a sofa below an open window, were two more familiar people, TAC officers Brackens and Johnson, while off to the other side sat Deeds in a ramrod position, watching me intently. I saluted Daydif briskly and said, "Sir, Candidate Loveless reporting."

"Stand at ease, Loveless," Daydif responded in an unemotional voice. "We'd like to ask you a few questions. Can you start by telling us where you were yesterday afternoon?"

"Yesterday, Sir? Yes, Sir," I said calmly as I spread my feet and folded my arms behind me. "I was in Phoenix City with Candidates Weekley and Ryan, Sir. We spent the day just hanging out, mostly at a couple of bars. But we didn't drink too much," I added fast, as though that was my concern.

"Did this hanging out include meeting any, ah, shall we say…women of ill repute?" he questioned.

I looked down at the floor and paused briefly before answering. "Well…ah, Sir," I stammered, "I don't want to get anyone else in trouble."

"I appreciate that," he replied, leaning forward and his voice becoming sterner. "But there has been a breach of protocol here and we will learn the truth about what happened one way or the other. Now, did you or did you not meet any women in town?"

"Yes, Sir, we did," I said. "I mean, we're men, Sir. If you know what I mean, Sir."

"Yes, I'm sure," he replied, leaning back but continuing to focus on my face. "The question is," he continued, staring at me hard, "did you bring any of these women back to the barracks? And remember, before you answer, a lie is a violation of the code of ethics. That could mean severe punishment, including possible expulsion from the course."

I was ready for that question, having thought about it for the past several days. "No, Sir," I said emphatically, standing straight and looking directly at Daydif. "We didn't bring anyone back on post! That's against regulations! Ask Candidates Ryan and Weekley. I came back with them, just the three of us. They can verify that!" I couldn't see him, but I could feel Deeds shifting uncomfortably on my left.

"They already have," said Daydif, shaking his head up and down. "We did a bit of checking on our own today. It seems some of your fellow candidates can't keep their mouths shut. So, you didn't bring a woman on post and you didn't take her to your room last night?"

"My room? No, Sir! That would be crazy," I answered, turning my head to look at Deeds with a question on my face, as though accused of child molestation or something worse. It was an accomplished piece of acting, but nothing new for me as I'd gone through a number of similar episodes with my parents growing up. Deeds just sat there staring at me with his mouth clenched, and I could feel his hate engulf me.

"Yes, it would be," Daydif replied in a somewhat calmer tone, I thought. "And I don't suppose you can you tell us anything about the woman found with Candidate Deeds, can you?"

"Sir," I said, pausing for effect, "even if I knew something—which I don't—I would not speak out against a fellow soldier."

"Of course, you wouldn't," said Daydif in a tone that seemed somewhat doubtful. I worried he knew something of my character, especially since he'd obviously been talking to Deeds before I arrived. He looked at me for a few long seconds and then turned and said, "Candidate Deeds, do you have anything to say about Candidate Loveless's testimony?"

"Yes I do, Sir," said Deeds, rising from his seat. "Candidate Loveless is lying. The truth is exactly as I have told you. He brought the girl to the room against her will. I was just trying to get her out of the barracks."

"Unfortunately, Candidate," said Daydif to Deeds, "Miss Leslie (*So that was her name*, I thought) says that she never met Candidate Loveless and that she spent an hour alone with you in your room. And all three of your fellow classmates' stories corroborate each other in that they went out on the town, came back without any females, and were down the hall talking about the war."

"Yes, Sir," said Deeds, "but they're not telling the truth. They're all in this together and Loveless put them up to it. He's a liar, Sir, and should never have been allowed in OCS!" His description was pretty accurate, but I wasn't about to speak just then, especially since the TACs didn't know me nearly as well as he did.

"The problem," said Daydif, ignoring the slander about me, "is we're left with believing either you or three other candidates. And while your record here has been good, so has theirs. We have no evidence and no reason to believe three other candidates would make up this story." Turning back towards me, he said, "Although I am curious, Candidate Loveless, about how you were found studying in your room just moments after Candidate Deeds left. What can you say about that?"

"I don't know when Candidate Deeds left the room, Sir," I replied innocently. "I was talking with Candidates Ryan and Weekley in their room and then just went back to my own room because I had work to do. Candidate Deeds was already gone when I got there."

"He's lying, Sir," said Deeds angrily. "My record is spotless. I would never lie or break any rule here."

I could sense he was getting desperate.

"You also claim that Candidate Loveless does not help maintain your common area," said Daydif, going back to Deeds. At this, I turned again in Deeds's direction and looked as shocked as possible.

"Yes, Sir. He makes me do it all alone. I have to clean the floor, the pipes, the windows, everything. He just sits and watches!" Deeds chimed.

"Candidate Loveless, do you have anything to say to this allegation?" Daydif asked.

I briefly turned my gaze to the two officers sitting on my right to see how they were reacting, but they appeared noncommittal, so I then turned to Daydif and deliberately said, "Sir, I can't believe what I'm hearing. Charlie— Candidate Deeds—has been my roommate and," and here I stammered a bit, "and until now, I thought my friend. I do my share in the room, Sir. I always try my best." And then I turned to face Deeds and said, "Charlie, just tell them the truth. It's the best thing now."

That got him. Deeds rose from his chair and started towards me but stopped immediately when Daydif barked out, "Candidate, you are at attention."

"But sir—" Deeds began.

Daydif cut him off with a wave of his hand. "That will be all, Candidate Loveless. You are dismissed. Candidate Deeds, you will remain here."

I left the room pleased as punch with my performance, but spent the next few hours worried about how Deeds would react when I saw him again. There was no question that he would be my enemy from that time on and I wasn't comfortable with the idea of sleeping in the same room with him anymore. But I needn't have worried. When I finally went to the room that evening, Deeds had already cleared out his stuff. The next day, we were told that he had been recycled, which meant he would start OCS all over again with another class. The three months he had already put in were for naught, although I'm sure the experience helped him the second time around. In a way, he was lucky. Instead of throwing him out of the school, he was given a second chance. Anyway, I didn't care what happened to him, except it meant I had to clean the room by myself.

A month later, the rest of us graduated in a ceremony attended by family and friends. Of the original two hundred forty soldiers who had started the class months earlier, only about one hundred ninety finished the course. We all marched across an open parade field near the company area in our best uniforms and stood there for upwards of an hour while going through the required military honors and salutes and then listened to some general and Captain Daydif drone on about what wonderful soldiers we were. I knew such ceremonies were army tradition, but it all seemed to me to be just a show for the crowd of people who were in attendance and not so much for us graduates. After standing in the sun for so long, I think the candidates were glad just to get the ceremony over.

Most of my classmates had family in the stands that day, as did I. My father and brother, Bob, had come to watch as my second lieutenant bars were pinned on. I'm sure Dad was proud, having had a long military career himself, but he didn't show much emotion. Truth be told, I think he was a bit surprised I'd made it through OCS. But I had made it, and so there he was, even wearing his old uniform.

There was one other person attending the ceremony, who I didn't expect. As I was walking off the parade grounds with my family, a young woman approached from behind and grabbed my arm. At first, I thought Bob might have arranged a "graduation present," but from the look on his face, I realized that wasn't the case. Then she spoke. I knew her…Kathy Leslie, the girl who had helped set up Deeds.

"Hi, Frankie, remember me?" she said.

"Of course, there's no way I could forget you," I replied, pulling her gently to one side and motioning for my brother to keep on walking with Dad, who hadn't noticed her. It was a bit of a lie because she looked very different from the night I'd first met her in Phoenix City. That time, she'd looked like your typical street walker with a short shirt, tight blouse, and lots of makeup. But out there on the parade field she was all dressed up proper, like someone you'd meet at a church social.

"That's good," she said, smiling sweetly, taking my hand in hers, "because I'm ready to collect the rest of my payment."

"Uh, the rest of your payment?" I asked, not knowing what she meant.

"Yeah! Remember? You promised me a trip to Hawaii when you graduated if I helped you and your friends. Well, I helped, you graduated, and now here I am for that trip."

I stammered. "Oh yeah, that…sure, sure, that's right. We owe you a trip…" I said, thinking fast about how I could talk my way out of there. "Why, just this morning I was telling my brother about you—"

"Good. Then there's no problem," she interrupted, grasping my hand tighter.

"Yeah, there's no problem. But you know, Kathy, right now I'm kind of busy with graduation and family here and all… If you can give me your address and a phone number then—"

"Look, Buster, I already gave you my number and you guys, you in particular, promised a trip to Hawaii at graduation. This is graduation. So come across with the plane tickets. Or maybe you prefer that I have another talk with those nice soldiers?" she calmly threatened while looking in the direction of some officers still hanging around the reviewing stand.

"No. No. There's no problem, Kathy. Don't worry. It's all right. We were talking last night about how to get you a ticket. I just can't do it right now, you know, what with my family here and all this happening," and I motioned towards my father and brother, who were now standing a bit off in the distance watching us talk. "But listen. You helped us out. We haven't forgotten that. We got the money and we'll be sure to get your ticket right after dinner today."

"Okay, Frankie. You've got till tomorrow morning. I'll be at the Alibi. After that, if I haven't heard from you, I'll be making a call to that nice

Lieutenant Backets (She meant Captain Brackens, of course). Here's my number again," she said, taking out a pen from her purse and writing on a number of a small slip of paper. "Don't lose it this time!"

I didn't. Before the day was done, I had collected money from both Ryan and Weekley and then gone to the post transportation office and made a plane reservation to Hawaii for the little blackmailer. Early the next morning, I went into Phoenix City and handed over an envelope containing both her airline ticket and, to her surprise, a hotel reservation in Honolulu.

"I know it wasn't part of the deal, but you'll need a place to stay when you get there," I said. "The Paradise Inn is right in the middle of everything, and it wasn't that much money."

She hadn't expected the free room; I don't think she was used to being treated kindly. For a minute she seemed lost for words, but then a smile spread across her face; she managed a weak "thanks" and asked if I'd like a beer before going back to Benning. I was in a hurry, but when she mentioned we'd have the drink up in her room, I rearranged my day. We walked about two blocks to a two-storey brick apartment building in a rather bland neighborhood. There wasn't much to look at in her apartment, but I wasn't there to invest money, just time and energy. Once inside her little place, as I'd hoped, I saw a different side of Kathy. Actually, I saw all sides of Kathy, some of which were substantial.

Two days later, Bob and I met her at the airport, helped checked her bags through, and then escorted Kathy to the plane. We bid her aloha in our best Hawaiian style and I promised to look her up when I got back to Honolulu. I would have, too, except I didn't think she would ever want to see me again, especially once she found out the Paradise Inn was a hangout for pimps and whores, and that the Honolulu police, including my old high school classmate, Rob Pilgrim, were planning to raid it while she was there. Bob and I laughed about it on the way back to Benning that day. I didn't realize then that mistakes in your youth could come back many years later, and this was one that surely did.

As for me, I had two weeks leave before reporting in for my next assignment. My dad, Bob, and I spent a few days visiting my mom's relatives in Alabama and then flew back home to Hawaii, where I spent my time hanging around with old high school friends and doing my best to not think about the army. Before I knew it, the two weeks were gone, my mother was giving me a tearful farewell at the airport, and I was off for my next assignment— Vietnam.

CHAPTER FOUR

The flight to Vietnam was short and uneventful. The plane, a chartered Pan Am DC-10, was packed with soldiers headed for the war zone, each of us wearing our army fatigues. I was one of only three who boarded the plane in Hawaii. The rest boarded the plane at Travis Air Force Base in California, where the flight originated and which was the main processing station for soldiers going to the 'Nam in those days. I watched from the Honolulu air terminal as several hundred fellow soldiers flooded off the plane when it arrived and then fanned out to shop for Hawaii souvenirs during their layover. One of them must have gone shopping for something more, because our departure from Honolulu was delayed for more than an hour when he went missing. But, eventually, he was found and brought back to the plane; then off we went across the Pacific, to our destiny.

Considering that nearly everyone on board was in their twenties or younger, it was a very subdued flight—very little conversation or joking around. Like most of my fellow passengers, I sat quietly, staring out the windows, thinking of home and wondering about what lay ahead. There was no movie, the food seemed sterile, and the stewardesses were old, already in their forties and fifties (that seemed old to me at the time). They did their best to try and cheer us up, always asking where we were from and about our families back home, but it definitely wasn't a cheery flight.

From Hawaii we went first to Yokota Air Base in Japan for refueling and then flew another five hours down to the 'Nam. While I'd lived in Korea as a teenager with my military parents, that was my first trip to southern Asia and I must admit it was interesting to see that part of the world. I recall passing by the island state of Taiwan and, towards the end of the flight, even getting a view at what I thought were the Philippine Islands far off in the distance. Most of the time, I was just looking out at the ocean below, trying not to think about where we were headed.

My first view of Vietnam from the window of the DC-10 came just as the sun went down in the west. I saw a long, strung-out coastline curving off to the south, with just a few open spaces between miles of forest that seemed to come down almost to the sea. Every once in a while there were a few scattered lights here and there, but I saw few signs of life, just a quiet, simple countryside. That changed soon after when, far below, the lights of a large city came into view. Suddenly, there were millions of small white dots of light arranged in rows along the ground and sprawling into the distance as far as the eye could see.

It was Saigon, Vietnam's capital city and home to several million people. I had expected to find some metropolitan areas in Vietnam, but nothing that large, so I sat transfixed to the window, watching a massive city unfold, as we coasted down towards the ground. As we came closer to the ground, I became aware of bright spotlights swaying back and forth in the night sky, while other small red lights—which I later learned were helicopters escorting us into Bien Hoa military airport—darted along beneath us. It was all very fascinating and looked so surreal that I told myself to relax; Vietnam would be just another adventure.

Our descent was faster than any landing I'd experienced in the past; from the time we were told to lock in our seat belts, it felt like less than ten minutes passed before we hit the ground and taxied up to a terminal building. Once there, we practiced an ancient army custom—we sat and waited for instructions. As we did, I kept my face cupped to the plane's window, anxious about what lay ahead and curious about the movement all around us. Even though it was already night, Bien Hoa was bustling with activity.

Across the runway we'd just arrive on, I could see what looked like a score of men, driving small flat vehicles, upon which large wooden crates were stacked on top of each other, while closer by there were dozens of pieces of large mechanical equipment, all waiting, I assumed, to be transported elsewhere. In the distance, a line of fighter jets sat parked in a long column with men scurrying back and forth between them, while overhead, helicopters darted past every few minutes. It was all very visible because, despite being in a war zone, the airport was bathed in the glare of bright lights. Years later, I read that Bien Hoa was the busiest airport in the world in the late 60s; from my observations, that certainly seemed to be true that night.

We sat fidgeting in our seats for nearly an hour, before a large and burly sergeant came on board and gave the official "Welcome to Vietnam" speech. "I know you're all worried some," he said in a deep southern accent, "and Vietnam can be a dangerous country. But remember this, ninety-five percent of the people who come here go home at the end of their year. Most of us are assigned to big base camps like this one, and we hardly ever hear gunfire. Almost all the fighting takes place out in the countryside, and you're not going there tonight. For the next few days, you're going to be here at Bien Hoa, getting acclimated to the 'Nam and going through some initial processing. After that, you'll move on to your permanent assignment. So there's nothing to worry about right now. Just gather up your gear and follow me." After that, he turned away and headed for the front exit. We rose from our seats to do just that, but stopped when he suddenly turned and added, "Oh, one more thing!

In case of mortar fire, there are bunkers on both sides of the terminal. If we get hit, keep your head down and run for them as fast as you can." With that reassuring thought, he led us out of the plane and into Vietnam.

The first thing I noticed was the heat. It was like standing with my face in an open oven door. By the time I'd hit the ground and gone ten feet, my uniform felt soaked and I was wiping sweat off my brow. I rolled my sleeves up and unhooked the top button on my uniform blouse as I walked, but it seemed to make little difference. Vietnam was just hot and muggy, even in the middle of the night. In time, like most Americans who served there, I got used to days of ninety degree temperature and ninety percent humidity and didn't even notice it, except on those few occasions when water ran low.

The big sergeant led us across the tarmac and through a wide door into a large open hangar where we found hundreds of other GIs, most of them lying on the floor or lounging about in chairs as though taking naps. As we entered, they came to life, standing up and bursting into applause and cheers. Some of them even formed a corridor, which we passed through on our way out the rear of the building. I was impressed and thought it quite a welcome, until someone mentioned that those guys were probably headed home, going back to the States on the plane we came in on. Basically, they were cheering for themselves, not us.

As we left the hangar and boarded buses that were waiting for us on the far side, I glanced back and saw a large sign hanging above the main door we'd just passed through. It read: WHEN I DIE, I'LL GO TO HEAVEN, 'CAUSE I'VE SPENT MY TIME IN HELL." For a second, I wondered what kind of idiot would let that greet new arrivals, but realized it was the same idiots who got us there in the first place, and then gave it no more thought.

The buses took us from Bien Hoa to Long Binh, a nearby army base where most newly assigned soldiers in Vietnam were initially assigned. The ride took less than half an hour from the airbase to Long Bien, down what appeared to be mostly deserted roads that were narrow and lined with trees and buildings that rarely rose above two to three stories. It was my first real look at Vietnam and it didn't appear frightening at all. If it hadn't been for the fact that we had armed guards on our buses, I wouldn't have even guessed there was a war going on. Everything just looked quiet and peaceful, which was fine with me.

At Long Binh, newly arrived soldiers like me were assigned to the 90th Replacement Detachment, where they went through some basic orientation on their new home before being assigned permanently to army units farther out in the country. Although I saw very little of Long Binh, I could tell even at night that it was a huge military base. We were put up in a typical two-storey army barracks and kept there for the next two days as we made the change from stateside soldier to Vietnam vet. For me, the memoires of those first few days include acclimating myself to the heat and going through a series of briefings in which we were instructed about the history and status of the war and taught a few of the local customs.

We also stood in line for hours to exchange our stateside uniforms for jungle gear (including new nylon boots and olive green underwear), and to trade in our American money for Military Payment Certificates. It was explained to us at the time that GIs weren't allowed to use real dollar bills or even coins in Vietnam because American money often ended up on the black market, and then, eventually, in the hands of the Vietcong. So instead, when shopping on post, we used MPCs, paper money in various denominations with pictures of pilots and submarines and such. There were no coins. Nickels, dimes, and quarters were made of paper, too, just smaller in size than the MPC dollars.

On the morning of my third day in-country, I was issued orders to report to the 23rd Infantry Division, better known as the Americal Division, headquartered on a peninsula up north, near the seaside town of Chu Lai. Even though the Division had been around during World War II, I'd never heard of the Americal before, and I suspect most other Americans hadn't either.

The notoriety of the Americal changed within months of my arrival though, primarily thanks to some highly publicized national news stories. The most infamous was an incident in the Vietnamese village of My Lai, where a group of Americal soldiers overreacted to combat fatigue and apparently killed several hundred defenseless women and children. It was a big story for months and helped to strengthen public opinion back home against the war and accelerate our withdrawal from the 'Nam. After My Lai, veterans of the Division were sometimes called "baby killers" by people opposed to the war and even by some troops from other units. It was embarrassing to many of the Americal's soldiers, especially since the vast majority of them had served honorably. Back in the 70s, there were some Americal veterans who would not even wear the unit patch after completing their tour because of the shame they felt. I wore mine though, and still do, on the right shoulder, where combat unit patches are worn. That patch, a blue field with four stars, became famous during the Gulf War, what with both Generals Powell and Swartzkopf wearing it on their uniforms.

As it was, with my orientation done at Long Binh, I was placed on a C-130 and flown from Saigon to Chu Lai, arriving around noon on May 21. I remember the date well because, while on the flight, I passed the time reading the *Stars and Stripes*, the American military newspaper in Asia that brought us all the latest news from around the world. The main article that day reported on the biggest battle in Vietnam since the Tet Offensive the year before. It happened at a place they were calling Hamburger Hill, where our 101st Airborne Division had just fought a week-long battle against a regiment of the NVA.

The "Screaming Eagles," as the 101st is traditionally called, had captured the hill, but only after sustaining high casualties in a number of brutal ground assaults. It was reportedly very fierce combat and, upon reflection, probably senseless. To be sure, the enemy lost more men than we did during the battle. But many of the NVA soldiers just retreated across the border to safety, in

Laos, where our side would not follow because Laos was a separate country. A month later, after destroying a maze of tunnels and warehouses that were found, we abandoned Hamburger Hill and, before long, it was reported that the North Vietnamese moved back to regain the same ground without a fight.

That's was probably one of the factors that made Vietnam so frustrating. Time after time, American military forces and their South Vietnamese allies inflicted heavy damage on the enemy and drove them from the field. But final victory was always out of reach because we could never finish the job. Sure, we bombed North Vietnam on a regular basis, and occasionally sent troops into Cambodia or Laos, which were regular conduits for North Vietnamese soldiers and weapons headed south, but we never really secured any area for very long. As a result, the Vietcong or NVA always seemed to just reappear in the same town or region some months later. I'm sure that's one of the reasons the American public finally tired of the whole bloody thing. Not only did most people not understand why we were even fighting over there, it seemed like our guys were just slowly getting killed off, with no end in sight of the conflict.

Interesting as it was, I soon relegated the news about Hamburger Hill to the back of my mind when the plane's crew announced our impending arrival at Chu Lai. From the air, it was an impressive camp and looked to me like a seaside town in one of our Southern states. There were hundreds of buildings, all connected by roads, stretching out along the South China Sea shoreline and then spreading inland for more than a mile. I had expected to find a big base since infantry divisions always have about twenty thousand military and civilian personnel assigned to them. Still, Chu Lai was larger than I had envisioned. It was in many ways like a small town with offices, warehouses, repair facilities, Quonset huts for housing soldiers, and motor pools with row after row of vehicles and stores, which I later learned were stocked with the stuff brought in from the States. There were even clubs and outdoor movie theaters for entertainment and, of course, a runway and helipad for helicopters and transport planes. And at Chu Lai, while most of the personnel were part of the army, there were also smaller air force and marine units working out of the big base. Of course, as it was an army post, almost everything, it seemed, was painted green.

All along its land-side perimeter, Chu Lai was protected by fences with doubled-layered concertina wire and thirty-foot tall towers every fifty feet or so that were manned day and night by sentries armed with machine guns and claymore mines. The side that faced the ocean had no wired fences, but there were more armed guard towers, and at night, bright searchlights flowed across the water. All that security was reassuring because it was virtually impossible for the enemy to infiltrate the base. In fact, Chu Lai, like all our main outposts in the 'Nam, was just too big for the enemy to attack, except for an occasional long-range rocket barrage. Such assaults were rare and short lived, as our artillery could fast pinpoint the origin of the attack and retaliate in much greater force.

By the end of my first day there, I'd made up my mind that Chu Lai was where I was going to spend the war. During my short time in the army, I'd discovered that there were two basic types of soldiers—the fighters and the support staff. The real frontline soldiers, those actually doing the fighting and mostly the ones dying, worked primarily out of smaller base camps, away from main Division headquarters. In the case of the Americal, that was certainly the case, as there were a number of smaller camps to the north, south, and west of Chu Lai, all of them connected by roads and helipads, but nonetheless isolated. For every soldier on the front lines, there were five or six working in support roles at the big base camps. These were the administration people, cooks, drivers, mechanics, people who handled supplies, and the like.

I'd heard it said that only losers, careerists looking for promotions, and psychos who liked combat ended up on the front lines face-to-face with the enemy. Clever folks—and I counted myself as one—usually found a way to be assigned to a rear echelon job. When my orders for the 'Nam came thorough after graduation from OCS, I made up my mind to do whatever possible to stay out of combat. Just to make sure, while on leave in Hawaii the prior month, I spent time reading up on army regulations that dealt with administrative stuff and I even paid an army clerk at Fort Shafter in Honolulu to tutor me on how a military personnel shop worked. Armed with that knowledge, and the fact that I had a college degree, I felt confident of getting a job in the rear and not out in the jungle when I was evaluated for my next assignment.

But, before being assigned to a full-time job, I and other newly arrived soldiers at Chu Lai had to attend the so-called "actuality classes," where we learned basic survival techniques that might come in handy during our time in Vietnam. Over a week's time, in addition to being reacquainted with various weapon systems, we also learned about such exotic things as how to handle snake bites, spot hidden land mines, or survive and find our way home if ever lost in the jungle. While I didn't plan on ever getting in those situations, I paid close attention and learned a few things that proved invaluable later on.

After completion of that specialized training, our group was sent to the Division Personnel Office where every newly assigned soldier went through a series of administrative steps before being permanently put in a specific place and job. This included having their medical records analyzed, making sure their pay was deposited in the right bank account, and preparing next-of-kin instructions just in case the worst happened. Most importantly though, even though we all had an MOS, or military occupational skill, before arriving in the 'Nam, each of us was interviewed and evaluated on our knowledge and work skills.

The Personnel Office was large enough to park a bus company. The ceiling was thirty feet above our heads and the place was filled with row upon row of desks and file cabinets, and very noisy because of the large number of people working there. Behind each desk sat an army clerk or a hired civilian technician clacking away on manual typewriters, while soldiers who were in-processing sat nearby and patiently waited. All of the military folks working there were enlisted soldiers, which I thought was unusual. But, at the far end of the auditorium, I could make out several private offices with small glass windows that the clerks entered every once in a while with their papers. That was where I assumed the brass sat and observed the goings-on.

As for me, I spent almost the entire day, along with other newly arrived troops, standing around waiting my turn to be processed. If I'd have been a high ranking officer, they probably would have processed me right away, but second lieutenants weren't that privileged, so I sat and waited with the regular soldiers. When my turn finally came, I wasted little time in displaying my administrative skills as I moved from station to station. At each step along the way, I volunteered to help the processing clerks by doing my own typing and, as often as possible, let them know I was familiar with army regulations and practices. It took more than three hours to go through the various stations, but I was confident that I'd made enough of an impression to land a great job there at Chu Lai when I got to the final processing desk. That's when I met Sergeant Bowers.

He was short, probably not more than five-seven, and appeared to be in his late thirties. Both his desk and uniform were well kept, and he had an air about him of command, even though he was little more than a mid-level sergeant. I tried to engage him in conversation, but other than a few one-word responses, he ignored me and quietly flipped through my papers, intently examining each sheet. Even though he said nothing, I began to get an uneasy feeling.

Finally, after what seemed like forever, he looked up and said, "Sir, Sergeant Wilton says you're familiar with army personnel actions and medical procedures. But I don't see in your records that you went to any admin schools."

"Oh that," I answered, trying to act nonchalant. "I took correspondence courses when I was at OCS, not for credit or anything, just to be as knowledgeable as possible. I've always had a good head for numbers and stuff and my goal is to eventually get into the AG Branch. You know, I studied business management in college." I lied.

"But it says here you studied journalism in college, Sir, not business," said Bowers, waving a piece of paper that must have had my educational history on it.

"Oh yes! Journalism! That was my major! I did study journalism. But there's little future in journalism nowadays, what with everyone trying to be a newspaper writer. So, I minored in business. Maybe it doesn't show it there," I said, leaning over to try and look at his document, figuring there were no journalism jobs at Chu Lai. "But I really prefer some kind of administrative work to journalism."

"That's too bad," said the sergeant unemotionally. "We need a new XO at the Public Affairs Office. We've been looking for someone with your education and background."

"Oh! Really! Well...I mean, yeah, I guess I could do that. It would be all right if I were a PAO. True, I'd rather work someplace like uh..., say, this office. But Public Affairs, that's okay. I'm quite good at writing, you know, even won an award in school. It's there somewhere in my records," I sputtered, leaning over again and pointing at the papers.

"I must have missed it, Sir," said the sergeant, this time, I thought, with a bit of cynicism. "Of course, we always need lieutenants in the field," he added, not looking up at me. "Lots of young officers want to be out where the action is."

That was a dangerous turn in the conversation, and I had to be careful how I replied. It wouldn't look good to be too eager to stay out of the field. "Well, I'll go where I'm needed, of course," I said, "but if you've got lots of others who want to go to the field, I'm just as happy being a PAO. I can probably contribute more back here anyway...especially since you're looking for someone in the PAO shop...."

"Are you sure, Sir? Promotions usually come faster in the infantry," he replied, and I was certain then that he was playing with me.

"Yes. I'm sure. The PAO job would be just fine," I said firmly without hesitation.

At that, he made a few notations on paper, ask me to wait, and then went off to one of the offices in the rear. When he returned a few minutes later, he said I should come back the next morning to pick up orders assigning me to the PAO shop. I was elated by the news, but maintained my composure. I politely thanked Sergeant Bowers and calmly walked away like nothing special had happened. Inside, I was ecstatic. All my prior preparation had paid off. Assignment to the PAO office meant I would be staying at Chu Lai for the rest of my tour, surrounded by thousands of Americans, doing a job that would see very little, if any, fighting. I was set and safe for the next twelve months until I made one quick stop on the way out of the building.

In those days, every American camp in Vietnam had a number of civilians working side by side with the military. Many of them were Americans who had volunteered to come to the 'Nam, but just as often, we hired Vietnamese contract employees. Usually, the Vietnamese were cooks or custodians, but sometimes they worked as interpreters or office assistants if their English was good enough. That was the case at Chu Lai, where it looked like about twenty Vietnamese worked in the personnel office. Most were your typical Southeast Asian, short with round faces, a medium build, and unglamorous clothing. But one had caught my eye.

She worked in the waiting room area and was anything but your typical dink. Taller than most female Vietnamese women, and with long dangling hair, there was a subtle beauty in her face that could have made her a film star in a different time and place. Like her countrymen and fellow workers, she wore loose-fitting pants and overshirts, but they couldn't hide the full figure hidden underneath. To top it off, while nearly all Vietnamese who worked with our troops spoke some English, hers was actually pretty good, despite her definite accent.

During the long morning wait, with nothing better to do, I had struck up a conversation and made my first Vietnamese friend. I learned her name, which I've long since forgotten, found out that she lived on post in a special building set aside for her kind, and that she was my age and single. By the time I began to actually in-process, she and I were already into the small talk and touching gestures that people do when flirting.

After hearing about my PAO assignment, I was so excited that it seemed only natural to press my luck a bit further. As I left the building I stopped at her desk, informed her about my new job, and ask if she would like to get together and celebrate my good fortune. She did, and a few hours later, as the sun went down, we met at the Chu Lai beach.

Coming from Hawaii, I was used to hanging out at beaches in the evening, but I found the one at Chu Lai to be a new experience. The army was taking no chances of a sapper coming ashore in the dark at the big camp. The tall bunkers with their armed guards took away any sense of privacy, while gunboats floated menacingly offshore against the blackness. Instead of moonlight bouncing off the waves like back home, there were army searchlights moving slowly up and down the sand and across the bay.

When my new friend and I wandered down to the water's edge, we were chased away by several armed security guards who came roaring out of a nearby bunker. A sergeant in charge got a good laugh at our discomfort, telling me the beach was off-limits at night, "even for officers." Rather than make an issue out of it, my lady friend and I wandered back across the street, sat on the steps of some office building, and drank beer while watching the ocean and pretending to be far away. I sat close behind her and told stories of Waikiki, cruise ships, hula dancers, and flower leis. When I said how nice it would be if she could visit me in Hawaii sometime, she began to warm up and leaned back against me. I wrapped my arms around her to maintain the warm attitude and continued with my tales of paradise. Her eyes glistened with excitement and I could tell that for her, Hawaii was a fairy land, a place far away that could only be a dream.

Soon I was massaging her shoulders, kissing her neck, and rubbing her stomach. It worked, and before long we were in a firm embrace as she rolled out of my arms and pulled me down next to her while yelling something in Vietnamese that probably woke the bunker guards across the street. I definitely didn't want to attract attention, so I put my hand over her mouth and gestured towards the guard posts. She understood and said, "Okay, we go my place," and before long, we ended up in the small room halfway across the post where she lived with another contract worker. Her roommate was away visiting relatives or something, which was fortunate, because for the next several hours, we were out of control. When I finally found my way back to my own sleeping quarters just before midnight, I was certain that my time in Vietnam would not be all wasted.

Early the following day, I returned to the Personnel Office to pick up my assignment orders and ended up spending another couple of hours just waiting for my name to be called. I looked for my little friend from the night before, but she wasn't at her station, which seemed strange. So, with nothing else to do, I just sat and read the *Stars & Stripes* and looked out the window to pass the time. Finally, my name was called out and a corporal handed me my assignment orders. I snapped them up and headed out the door, just by chance glancing at the paper to see the name of my new unit, where I would spend the next twelve months. But instead of a Public Affairs Office title, I found myself staring at the words "2nd Battalion, 1st Infantry, 196th Infantry Brigade."

That was wrong! I stopped and read the orders closely, and then reread them again. *It can't be true*, I thought. But there it was in black and white—"2nd Lieutenant Frank Loveless, 2nd Battalion, 1st Infantry, 196th Infantry Brigade." I'd been assigned to the infantry, not Public Affairs! I turned and ran back into the Center and up to the soldier who handed me the papers.

"Corporal, there's something wrong," I said. "I'm supposed to be going to the PAO shop here on post. These orders are for another unit."

"I don't know, Sir," he answered. "I just deliver them."

"Well, get me someone who does know," I said in desperation. "This is wrong. This is not where I'm going."

"Yes, Sir," he said, taking the papers from me and turning to walk back into the processing area. A minute later, he returned with someone I recognized.

"Sergeant Bowers, thank God it's you! Remember me from yesterday? I was supposed to go to the PAO office. Somehow my orders got mixed up," I blurted out. "These are assigning me someplace else."

"Yes, Sir, I know," he replied, cool as can be. "Your orders were changed. I guess they need you in the field more than in Public Affairs."

"The field!" I blurted out. "But why me? You said they need a Public Affairs Officer and I have a degree in journalism! There's plenty of other lieutenants here! Send one of them to the field!"

"It's not my decision, Sir," he answered. "Higher ups decided you should be out there. I just cut the orders."

"Well, let me talk to an officer," I demanded angrily. "This has to be changed!" I was desperate. Nothing would be more dangerous than a year in the infantry in the jungles of Vietnam.

"Yes, Sir," said Bowers, and off he went all the way to one of the offices at the rear of the auditorium. I could see him back there through the small window, gesturing and talking to someone seated behind a desk. That someone turned out to be a captain, who came out and, led by Bowers, walked across the room towards me.

"Sir," I began as he drew close, "there seems to be a mistake. My—"

"There's no mistake, Lieutenant! We're fighting a war here and you're needed in the infantry," the captain said abruptly, not letting me finish my sentence.

"But, Sir, I—"

"No buts, Lieutenant," he stated, staring directly in my face. "You may not like it, but those are your orders. You will report back here at 1400 for transportation out to your new unit."

There was no way out. I would have been on my knees in a flash if I thought begging would have made a difference. But that captain, for whatever reason, had made up his mind to send me to the field. I gave a meek "Yes, Sir" in reply and walked slowly from the building, feeling more depressed than at any time in my life.

The next several hours were mostly spent lying on my bunk in a fog of desperation. I tried thinking of any excuse that might keep me out of the field, such as going to the base hospital and claiming some kind of injury. But in the end, I knew any delaying tactic would just put off the inevitable and also bring a lot of attention to me. So, I resigned myself to my fate and went over to the PX, where I stocked up on candy bars and magazines, having heard that such things were hard to get in the field. Then, shortly after noon, I gathered up my gear and returned to the Personnel Office to sit and wait for transportation.

Right on time at two o'clock, along with some other soldiers headed for the 196th Infantry Brigade, I boarded a deuce and a half that would take us to our new home. Just as the truck's engine started up, something made me glance to the side where I saw a sight I have never forgotten. There stood Sergeant Bowers, a big smile on his face, not more than ten feet away, looking up at me. Standing next to him, with his left arm around her shoulders, was a Vietnamese girl, looking down at the ground. I couldn't see her face, but I knew that figure from the night before!

I jumped up and cursed at Bowers, shaking my fist! It was clear why my assignment had been changed! I'd picked up his woman and Bowers had pulled strings, sending me to the field! And now, as I rode off to hell, he was rubbing it in! The noise of the truck's engine surely drowned out my shouts, but he probably didn't care what I was yelling anyway. As we pulled away, I saw him laugh and turn back towards the personnel building, the girl meekly following behind. I watched until they went out of sight and then turned back to my seat, noticing for the first time that the other soldiers on the truck were all eyeing me. I sat back down and tried to appear calm, but I was furious on the inside, knowing that I'd screwed myself out of a safe job and there wasn't a damn thing I could do about it. I swore to myself that, if the chance ever came, I would pay Bowers back for what he'd done.

We traveled in a small convoy of army vehicles down a pretty good highway for slightly more than an hour from Chu Lai before arriving at a place called Landing Zone Baldy, which was located on a small hill not far from a small Vietnamese village. We had hundreds of such Landing Zones, or LZs as they were called, scattered about the countryside in Vietnam. Many of the LZs were little more than fortified hilltops, positioned away from main thorough-fares in strategic spots to support field operations. Many were connected to civilization by dirt roads, but some of them they were only accessible by foot or helicopter, which accounted for their Landing Zone title. Baldy, as the administrative center for the 196th Infantry Brigade, which included thousands of soldiers, was much larger than most LZs, nearly two miles in circumference. Even so, there wasn't much there except dirt bunkers, some low-rise wooden buildings, landing pads for choppers, and a few big 105 artillery pieces. The whole place was surrounded by concertina wire, with the ground outside the camp cleared of all vegetation for up to one hundred yards.

I later learned that, because it was a brigade headquarters, Baldy had been built adjacent to a main highway and close to a provincial capital, in this case the town of Tam Ky on Highway One. The LZ and town fed off each other with the soldiers from Baldy supposedly protecting the citizens of Tam Ky, while the town provided workers for the American base, mostly cooks and cleaners, as well as a flourishing black market complete with such staples as Coca-Cola and beer.

A number of rifle companies, an artillery battery, and small detachments of other units were stationed at Baldy. I say stationed because most of the time, the infantry units weren't physically at the LZ. Usually all but one of the combat units were in the field protecting local villages and looking for Charlie, while just a single infantry company took its turn pulling guard duty on Baldy's perimeter. Only the artillery battery guys, supply folks, and brigade administrative staff remained at Baldy on a regular basis.

I've long forgotten most of the men I served with in Vietnam. I can't even remember their faces, much less their names. But two stand out because we arrived at the 196th together that day and then went on to serve in the same field unit. One of them was Bobby Bryson, a Black from Chicago, and the other was Alan Baker, who could best be described as a white trash southern boy.

Back in the world, Bryson and Baker would probably have never met, much less become friends, and the chances of me interacting with either one of them would have been remote, unless they were selling something I wanted. But Vietnam was a different world. There were certainly cultural differences as soldiers, who had come from many different locations back home, had to live and work together. For sure there was also some racism, as Blacks and Whites often associated with just their own, especially when off duty. I still remember the Blacks with their "dap" hand salutes and the talk in those days of Vietnam being a "White man's war, not a Black man's war." But in many ways, our military was the leading edge of the civil rights movement that was going on across the country in the 60s. Vietnam was, in fact, the first war in which so many Black and White soldiers worked so closely together on a regular basis. From my experience, even though they may not have always understood or even liked each other, Black and White soldiers definitely supported each other on the job, especially in combat units.

That was certainly true for the three of us who arrived together at Baldy that day. While riding up from Chu Lai, we realized that the three of us were all going to the same unit in the 196th. So, we talked about who we were and shared stories about our homes and families. Bryson, Baker, and I each seemed to sense that our destiny and welfare was somehow linked to the other two, so we made an unspoken pledge to watch over the others in the coming months.

Bryson was smaller than me, about five-eight and weighing about one-fifty to one-sixty pounds. He was a nervous person, always fidgeting about his personal effects and endlessly cleaning his equipment. I don't think I ever saw him fully relaxed and don't think he trusted anyone in-country, except maybe Baker and me. The best thing about Bobby was his instincts. Although he grew up in a big city, Bryson seemed to be at home in the jungle and had excellent instincts when it came to such things as selecting ambush sites or finding places to bivouac at night. Often, when I wasn't sure about movement in the field, I would ask for his advice and, invariably, he would be right.

Baker was about my size, except stockier. He was a soldier's soldier, very knowledgeable about weapons, warfare tactics, and the history of Vietnam. He thought the 'Nam was a stupid place for America to be engaged in, but had decided to make the army a career, and so was determined to make the best of his assignment. Whenever we were in combat, there was no one I trusted more than Alan. He was born to be a soldier.

The three of us were at Baldy less than a day. Along with the other truck passengers, we reported in to the brigade office, got a short briefing on what to expect, had dinner at a mess hall, and then retired to a small wooden building with sleeping booths. After a fitful night's sleep, we spent the next morning being issued our combat gear, which included an M16 rifle, a ruck-sack, canteens, cooking utensils, entrenching tools, a steel pot, and ammo bands. We also got a supply of bandages, iodine pills for cleaning water that we might drink, about a hundred rounds of ammunition, C-ration food for several days, and a couple of grenades. Because I was an officer, I was issued a .45mm pistol in addition to my rifle. Altogether, my stuff weighed about fifty pounds, but when carrying it on my back in that heat, it felt like much more. Not content with that much weight, I also packed away four or five books in my rucksack that I'd bought at Chu Lai. I'd heard that most of the time in the field was actually boring, just sitting around with nothing to do but wait, and I figured the books might help to pass the time. They did, but like lots of new guys in the 'Nam, I put more stuff in my rucksack than I needed and then threw it away later on when I got tired of lugging it around.

Around noon on that second day, we ate lunch at the brigade mess hall, after which I and two other officers were taken to yet another small office and introduced to our battalion commander. While he gave us a short briefing on the surrounding countryside and enemy capabilities, Bryson and Baker got volunteered to burn shit, literally. I found them after my briefing, pulling large metal cans from underneath the camp's outdoor portable johns and then lighting fire to the human waste inside, before replacing the burned-out cans. It was a daily routine that apparently went to newly assigned soldiers, if any were available for the task. Newly assigned enlisted soldiers that is, not officers like me. After they finished, we sat around together for some more time, and then late that afternoon, the three of us gathered our gear and boarded a Huey that would take us out to join Company B in the field.

It was my first time in a helicopter, and with the side doors open and the wind blowing through, I found it exhilarating. Bryson and I sat on canvas strap benches, while Baker, surrounded by bags of mail and field supplies, rested on the metal floor across from us. Up front sat two pilots, while on both sides of the chopper, door gunners leaned out into space from some kind of metal seats equipped with M60 machine guns. All four of the crew members were strapped to their chairs, but not us. Every time we swerved left or right, Bryson, Baker, and I rolled in that direction. As much as I found the ride to be thrilling, I held on tight, fearful of sliding out one of the open side doors.

We bumped along about a thousand feet above the ground, high enough to be safe, yet low enough so that I got my first real view of the Vietnam countryside. It was lush green, with large open spaces separated by patches of brown and small clusters of trees. There were lots of thatched farmhouses clumped together in small villages alongside slow, winding rivers crossed by a few dirt roads that seemed to go nowhere, yet everywhere. I couldn't tell from up high, but learned later that most of the green open spaces were small farmlands, which provided rice, sweet potatoes, peanuts, and other products for both local residents and for export outside the 'Nam. In the far distance, the central highlands rose high against the sky, looking very much like the mountains back in Hawaii. It all looked very peaceful and I was becoming quite comfortable with the ride, then the door gunner to my left nudged me with his elbow and pointed towards the ground. I started to look down, but then had to quickly grasp tight to my seat as the chopper instantly fell downward into a steep dive.

In Vietnam, I learned, helicopters always took off and landed as fast as possible to avoid enemy gunfire. That flight was no exception. Before I could barely catch my breath, we were on the ground in a wide grassy area and the door gunner was yelling, "Hurry! Get out," and pulling me out the side door of the Huey. I vaulted out to the ground, dragging my rifle and rucksack along, and in the process nearly banged into a soldier who had come running up to the helicopter from somewhere. He pushed past me, grabbed one of the boxes on the chopper floor, threw it on his back, and started back towards a nearby wood line, yelling, "Come on," just as two other soldiers ran up to retrieve other boxes. I took off on a sprint following the soldier and nearly got to the tree line, when I heard footsteps from behind. I glanced back to see Bryson and Baker, who had exited out the other door, coming up fast and then, before I could face front again, felt myself flying through the air.

I had tripped on something while running and, already off balance with the heavy gear on my back, took a head-over-heels tumble, hitting the ground hard on my back. Momentarily stunned, I lay there gasping for breath, staring up at the sky. Then suddenly, the soldier I had been following was standing over me looking down at my face. "You must be the lieutenant," he said in a contemptuous tone.

I was about to say something back when Baker's face popped into view next to the insulter. "You all right, Sir?" asked Baker, sticking down his hand. I took hold and let him pull me to my feet, all the time staring hard at the other fellow. I might have said something not very nice to him but was distracted by laughter coming from the nearby woods. I had obviously made an impression on the battle-hardened veterans of B Company, who'd just seen a new lieutenant do a somersault onto his back while running across an open field. Fuming inside, mostly at myself for looking so stupid, I pretended to ignore the laughter as our small group made its way into the trees.

Once there, I was surprised to find dozens of soldiers lying about on the ground like they didn't have a care in the world. They were, in fact, quite different from what I had expected to find. All had filthy uniforms and many were unshaven or with long hair and moustaches; a number of them had towels around their necks, writing on their helmets, or wore floppy caps. They were definitely a marked contrast to the three of us new arrivals, with our clean uniforms and still shiny boots.

I walked over to the closest soldier who was actually on his feet and asked where I could find the company commander. He replied, without comment, by pointing off towards a thicker lump of trees not too far away. Followed by Bryson and Baker, I went in that direction, strolling past and trying to ignore the groups of soldiers lying about. As we passed by though, I heard low mutterings like "Stupid FNG" and "He's supposed to lead us?"

Baker must have overheard also because, from the side, I saw him start to move towards two of the lowlifes with a "What did you say?" look. Not wanting to challenge anyone just then, I grabbed his arm to hold him back, just as a gravelly voice to my rear said, "You Loveless?" I turned, letting go of Baker, and found myself face to chest with one of the biggest men I'd ever seen. He was well over six and a half feet tall and thick as a house. Although dressed sloppily like the others and wearing no visible military rank, he was clearly a commanding figure. The giant of a man was cradling an M16 in one arm and carried a pistol on the left side of his pants, which just happened to have a long tear going down nearly to his boot.

"Captain Prion," he said, looking down at my face, as I stood there momentarily speechless from his presence.

"Oh! Yes, Sir, I am. Pleased to meet you, Sir! I am Lieutenant Loveless. This is Privates Bryson and Baker," I said, referring to the two who were now standing just to my rear. "We came in together, Sir." Then I offered my hand.

"Yeah, I know. We've been expecting you," he said, ignoring my outstretched palm. "'Course, we didn't expect such a grand entrance."

"Yes, Sir. Sorry, I tripped on something out there."

"Well, out here, you've got to watch your step at all times. Don't run unless you have to, and then keep your eyes on the ground. We lose more men to dink booby traps than gunfire, so stay alert," he said in a manner that I felt was demeaning. I shook my head in the affirmative but, not knowing what to say, kept quiet.

"You'll be Third Platoon CO, Loveless. Check in with Sergeant Mann, down that trail," said Prion, pointing at a small path leading away from our location. "Bryson, you go with him. Baker, you'll be in the Second Platoon. You stay here. Loveless, get settled in fast, then you and Mann come back up here in an hour. We've got to talk about tomorrow."

"Yes, Sir," I answered, going into a salute.

"Don't do that!" he yelled. "Never salute in the field! The dinks could be watching us right now and would just love to know who the officers are. And take off that insignia. Out here, we're all just soldiers. No one wears rank."

I yessed sirred him again and then, feeling much the fool, began pulling the lieutenant's bars off my uniform as Bryson and I headed off down the trail. We found the Third Platoon a short distance away, resting comfortably around a small mangle of trees and bushes. Most of them just lay about talking, although a few were stretched out, sleeping on the ground, while one small group off to the side was huddled together playing cards. A few of the darkened faces viewed us curiously as we approached, but for the most part, no one seemed particularly concerned that we had arrived or that we were in a combat zone, for that matter.

We stood there for a few seconds, looking around, as I wondered what to do. Then an older soldier stepped forward from behind a bush and introduced himself. "I'm Sergeant Mann," he said, walking up to Bryson and me. "You must be the new platoon leader." The sight of him was reassuring. While somewhat scrubby like the other soldiers out there, he looked lean and fit, as I had always envisioned combat soldiers. Even though I'd gone through extensive combat training at OCS, I was still new to the field and definitely not confident of my ability to lead troops in battle. I had been secretly hoping the platoon would have a good first sergeant who could take charge, and Mann looked the part.

"Lieutenant Loveless," I replied, "and this is Private Bobby Bryson. He'll be with us, too."

Mann asked Bryson a few questions and then turned him over to someone before pulling me aside to brief me about the platoon. What he told me was not very reassuring. Bravo Company had been in almost constant combat for the past month. Casualties had been high in the Third Platoon, with three KIAs and nearly a dozen wounded in that time. As a result the platoon, which should have had about thirty or so men, was short five people, even with the addition of Bryson and me. The remaining troops were bone tired from the constant field duty, Mann said, and everyone was anxiously waiting for a three-day stand down at Chu Lai that had been promised but no one believed would happen soon.

Mann did assure me the people we had were good soldiers. They'd been through a lot and knew how to take care of themselves in a firefight, he said. That was personally important, as my first priority, actually my only priority, was to get out of the 'Nam alive. I knew that meant having good people around in case of trouble.

The two of us spent several hours that first day going over the personalities of soldiers in the platoon, talking about resupply issues and how we would handle command of our small number of troops. Basically, it was decided that because Mann had more than six month's experience in-country, he would make most of the operational decisions and, in turn, he would let me know what he had decided. It was understood that I, as the platoon's commander, could override him if I wanted, but we didn't discuss that option. That may sound like I was giving up actual command of the platoon, and in fact, I did. But my main concern was staying alive, not being the boss, and at the time, Mann seemed to be my ticket to survival.

We also spent time that day meeting with Prion and the other two platoon leaders in Bravo Company and learned that the unit really didn't have a mission just then, except to walk around the countryside and observe things. So the next few days were spent climbing up and down a lot of small hills, walking through farmlands, and camping out under the stars. We never saw any Vietnamese, much less the Vietcong, which was fine with me. I found the countryside of Vietnam to be as beautiful on the ground as it had been from the air, mostly flat with long lines of rice paddies, or small rolling knolls with a smattering of trees. Rice fields, I learned, were to be avoided if possible. They were impossible to walk through, difficult to walk around, and filled with mosquitoes. Even open fields could be a pain. Several times while walking in open turf, we traipsed through thick, lush foliage called "elephant grass," which grew as high as our waists. The first time I went through it, no one warned me and my arms were cut in a dozen places by the sharp-edged plant. After that, I wore my sleeves down whenever we ran across the stuff.

Most of my time, those first days was spent questioning Mann and a few others about Vietnamese customs and people and learning more about the twenty-seven men in my platoon. Most of them were young draftees from poor or middle-class families, with a few regular army volunteers thrown in. Only six were older than twenty-five and I was the only one with any education beyond high school, although Mann and another sergeant had attended some advanced army schools. Early on, I realized that despite their poor formal education, many of the platoon soldiers were sharp, tough people. Back home, most of them would have been construction workers, factory hands, or, in the case of a few who seemed to love their weapons, police officers. All of them seemed to be ready to fight and die if necessary, but everyone, when I asked them, said they wanted to get out of the 'Nam. By '69, the war had already become very political back home, and like me, none of them cared a bit about defending the South Vietnamese or fighting the spread of communism. I realized within days that they were a tight-fit group who would defend each other and who would follow me only so long as they felt I had their interest at heart.

Mann seemed to be the only exception. He was, I soon discovered, an exceptional combat soldier who actually believed in the war. In a platoon of tough guys, he was easily the toughest and the only person I met in Vietnam who seemed to enjoy firefights. He was crazy, but I never told him so, since it didn't pay to make enemies in the 'Nam, especially when you might need those same people when things got hot.

We all had nicknames—like Blackie, Little Big Man, or Tex. Most names came from where we'd lived back home, so Bryson became "Chicago." Sergeant Mann was simply "The Man," and he was, too. They called me LT, for my rank. There was one other guy from Hawaii, Roy Yoshimura, who went by "Pineapple." He was one of the few I got to know well, partly because we both hailed from the islands, but also because he was one of two soldiers who carried the M60 machine gun, or "Pig" as it was called. The Pig was our platoon's heavy weapon. The M60 was often decisive in firefights because it fired ammo fast and at greater range than the M16 rifles carried by most troops. Few soldiers wanted to carry the M60 though, because it was heavy and also because everyone knew Charlie concentrated on taking out the man with the Pig.

We even had our own medic, who went by "Doc." He made sure we took our daily malaria pills, patched up our jungle rot, and was often a lifesaver in case of battle injuries. Derek Smyth, nicknamed "DJ," was our commo guy, or RTO. He had possibly the worst job in the unit, carrying a heavy PRC-25 radio on his back. That radio, even more than the M60s, was our edge in combat. With it, we could coordinate actions with Prion and the other platoons and, if needed, could call in lethal air strikes or massive artillery support within minutes. The Vietcong, almost always outgunned on the ground, had virtually no chance in a fight once an RTO brought in jets or artillery. But few people wanted to be an RTO. Not only was the radio additional weight to be carried around at all times, in a firefight, the dinks always tried to shoot RTOs first, even ahead of us officers. That's because they knew the RTO could impose the most damage. Naturally, unit commanders relied heavily on their RTOs and I was no exception. Smyth was my shadow, always just a few feet away.

Finally, our platoon also had a mongrel dog called "Numb Nuts," who was actually a very good sentry at night and would run ahead with the point man when we were on patrol. He was clearly the most popular member of the Third Platoon.

Each day was pretty much the same. We rose at sunrise, got orders to move to some location, and then spent the day going there, stopping only for lunch or brief search parties. The three platoons marched in long, strung-out lines, each parallel to the other two. I was usually third or fourth in my line, following a point man and a guy with a grenade launcher. Smyth was on my tail and the rest followed him. Mann kept near the back where it was easier to control the platoon in case of a fight.

Although there were less than thirty people in our platoon, we carried enough firepower to obliterate a small town. In addition to the two "Pigs," we had several M79 grenade launchers for taking out bunkers or entrenched positions, and of course, each soldier had the standard M16. Everyone humped with hand grenades, smoke grenades, trip flares, medical pouches, and extra ammo for the M60s, as well as their own food and water rations.

Late each day, the company would stop and dig in for the evening. It was common knowledge that the night belonged to Charlie. So whenever possible, we set up next to natural terrain like mounds of dirt or close to the remains of buildings, anyplace it would be easy to hide behind. We also set out trip flares and claymores each night to cover any possible approaches and made sure we would have open fields of fire in case of an attack. On those days when we couldn't find easily fortified positions, we dug foxholes three of four feet into the ground, but that was rare.

I set myself apart from the others and made a name for myself early on by digging a hole each night that was one-foot deep and six-foot long. I slept in those long, shallow holes on a flattened air mattress, causing the others to joke that I was a "Gravedigger." That didn't bother me. Shoveling out a deep foxhole in which, at best, a person could only stand or sit, seemed like a lot of work to me. By contrast, the shallow hole I dug allowed me to lie down and sleep just below the plane of the ground. I knew in case of an attack, bullets and even shrapnel from RPGs (rocket-propelled grenades) or mortars would fly over my head so long as I stayed flat on the ground. The only danger would be if they landed directly in my hole, which I knew was highly unlikely.

Several times a week, resupply choppers came out to us, bringing mail, the latest Stars & Stripes newspaper, and a resupply of ammo and C-ration canned food. We often bartered over the C-rations, as each case had a dozen different meals. Some food selections were favorites with nearly everyone, while others were routinely fed to Numb Nuts. I wasn't too picky and ate everything. If I had a favorite, it was canned peaches mixed with pound cake for dessert. Since they came in different meal packets, I always had to trade for one or the other.

Once in a while, the choppers brought Carling Black Label beer and soft drinks and, if we weren't in a heavy combat zone, even a hot meal. Some guys traded their food for beer and then humped it around in their rucksacks for days as they slowly consumed it. Not me. Beer always got hot within a few hours in the field, which made the taste disgusting, although I sometimes held on to soda for up to a week. But at least the soft drinks kept their flavor.

I hardly ever got mail, except letters from my mother every week, telling me how much she worried and how nice it was back in Hawaii. She sent packages every so often, and I remember my brother, Taylor, writing once to ask if he could have my baseball card collection after I died. Other than that, no one wrote me. I didn't have a girlfriend back home and my high school and college buddies had moved on with their lives. Some guys, like Pineapple, got "care packages" from home on a regular basis—boxes of home-baked cookies and cakes and other delicacies. Whenever packages of food arrived, it was party time, with everyone sharing the contents.

I was beginning to think my time in the 'Nam would pass very uneventfully, which was just what I wanted. After several weeks in the field, I still hadn't heard a gun fired in anger. Then, as we were bedding down one night, Smyth came to my hole in the ground and said the CO had called for me to attend an urgent meeting. I trekked across to Prion's place in the small camp, worried that it must be an important meeting for him to have called it so late at night. As it turned out, there was good reason for my concern. Forty-eight hours later, I lay wounded in a hospital bed at Chu Lai, while Prion was headed home for the last time.

CHAPTER FIVE

Speaking from experience, I can honestly say that being a patient in a military hospital isn't so bad, unless, of course, you're seriously hurt or dying from wounds. Fortunately, that wasn't my case in June of '69. The bullet that Prion shot into my leg had passed clean through without hitting blood vessels or vital muscles. I didn't know that at the time, only that my leg hurt like hell and blood was oozing out from one side. It wasn't until Doc, our field medic, shot me with some kind of painkiller and bandaged the wound tightly to stop the loss of blood that I began to feel better. After that, my leg just felt numb, except when I made awkward movements, such as what happened with the girl on the chopper.

Once on the ground at Chu Lai, I got the best of care. After watching my young airborne companion walk away with the MPs, I was turned over to a medical team at the runway, rushed to the 27th Surgical Hospital, placed on an operating table, and poked with a needle that caused my eyes to go heavy very fast. When I next opened them, I found myself in a soft bed, the smell of scrambled eggs and bacon in the air, and a gentle breeze coming through a nearby window. After a few seconds adjusting to my surroundings, I looked down and saw that my leg was still there, along with fresh bandages on the area where I'd been injured. I reached down to touch it and realized to my relief that there was no pain. I could even move the leg slightly, although it felt heavier than usual.

"You'll be all right," said a voice to my left and I turned to find a nurse serving breakfast to another soldier propped up in another bed. There were just the three of us in a small room that also contained a medical cart filled with equipment and one window through which the wind was blowing. "They said it was just a flesh wound," she said, smiling down at me. "You'll be up and walking about in a few weeks. In the meantime, just relax and enjoy this place."

That was great news and good advice.

For the next five weeks or so, I did enjoy myself at the 27th Surgical. True, there wasn't much to do except sleep, eat, read, and talk to the fellow who shared my room and the few visitors we had, but I didn't complain. The hospital was infinitely better than being in the field with B Company, and every day spent there was one day closer to home. Besides, I was something of a celebrity.

Somehow, word got around that I was the sole survivor of a firefight. After that, the hospital staff treated me like royalty, with someone always there fussing over me with homemade snacks or the newest PX magazines. Once, a big orderly came in the room and gripped my hand in a fierce handshake. He didn't say a word, just stood there looking down with clenched lips and pumping my hand, until I ask if he was all right. "Yes, Sir," he said, with obvious emotion. "I just wanted to shake your hand." Then he smiled and left the room. It was dumbfounding. I couldn't understand how anyone could get so emotional just shaking hands with a complete stranger. I still don't get it, but I've met a number of people like him over the years, and while I still don't fathom how their minds work, their kind do come in useful from time to time.

During my second week at the 27th Surgical, a bird colonel came around and pinned a Purple Heart and a Bronze Star on my nightgown, while a bunch of docs and medics all stood at attention and posed for a picture with me. Afterwards, they congratulated me and even wheeled in a big cake shaped like a Purple Heart. I played the role of a modest soldier and told them they shouldn't have done it because I hadn't really done anything special. I was telling the truth, of course, but they didn't know that. To them, I was a hero. Looking back, I think most of them probably didn't really care. They just came for the colonel and the cake.

All that attention taught me a lesson I've not forgotten—its image that counts, not reality. People need heroes, someone they can look up to and admire, and they'll invent them, if necessary. No one at the hospital ever asked me about the fight in the sand dunes. They didn't really want to know any details. They just assumed I was a hero because they'd heard I'd survived when the others had been killed.

But there were some people I couldn't fool. Later the same day, after the awards ceremony, they took me down the hall to a small office and somehow hooked me up by telephone with my family back in Hawaii. It had apparently been arranged several days prior, because my parents and one brother, who were waiting when the call went through, already knew that I was wounded and at a hospital. My mother was first on the phone and overjoyed to be talking to me, but quite concerned about my injury. I had to repeat at least three times that I wasn't seriously hurt before I felt she believed me and the subject changed to whether or not I was eating right and getting enough sleep. Next came all the news about my brothers, and then my cousins and aunts and uncles, and so on. She must have yabbered on for half an hour before finally running out of hometown gossip. Then my father got on the phone.

He didn't waste words with pleasantries. "How'd it happen?" he asked right off.

"You mean my wound?" I replied.

"Of course! What else are we talking about?" he said. So I described the fight in the sand dunes, changing the story somewhat to make it appear I'd fought fiercely and, of course, been shot by the enemy, rather than my own commanding officer. When I had finished, there was a pause on the line and then my Dad said, "Frank, did you tell this story to the army?"

"Yes, Sir."

"And they believed you?"

"Yes, Sir, it's the truth," I said, trying my best to sound convincing.

"Uh huh, here, tell it to Alan," he replied, and then my brother was on the phone. I repeated my story, and at first, I could tell Alan didn't believe it either. But I stuck to it, and I noticed there was less doubt in his voice when he finally turned the phone back over to my mother. Truthfully, I wasn't too surprised by the reaction of my father and brother. They knew me far too well and simply could not imagine me acting courageous. But then, I wasn't really concerned with their opinion. All that mattered was how the army saw me, and in that regard, I was viewed favorably. After all, I had just received two military decorations and they didn't give those away to just anyone.

Unfortunately, the Purple Heart and Bronze Star were not my ticket out of the infantry. I stayed at the Chu Lai hospital a little more than a month, dragging it out as long as possible by grimacing in pain, or limping, whenever a doctor was around. But eventually, the docs decided my leg was fine, since it had only been a minor wound in the first place, and released me to go back to my unit. I was in no rush though and was able to convince the 196th's Rear Detachment that I was supposed to stay there for a bit, just to make certain the leg was truly okay. It bought me three more days of vacation at Chu Lai, mostly relaxing at the beach during the day and the officer's clubs at night. Then, figuring I'd better not press my luck too far, I caught a chopper back to Battalion headquarters at LZ Baldy, where I found my unit doing a turn as bunker guards.

It was the same old bunch of grunts, rude mannered and simple minded. But they welcomed me back as a long-lost brother and afforded me a respect I hadn't had before and certainly didn't expect, considering how I'd been treated previously. Bryson made it logical when he explained that combat soldiers can be among the most superstitious people on earth. It wasn't that the troops suddenly liked me so much, as they saw meaning in the fact that I was the sole survivor of the fight in the sand dunes. To them, I was more than courageous—I was lucky—and that went for a lot out in the field. Naturally, I did nothing to dissuade them of that idea, such as tell them I'd cowered at the edge of the fight and gotten involved only at the end when I had no choice.

Another reason I was so welcomed back was the assignment of a Captain Lawrence Grovich as Prion's replacement. Grovich had joined the unit during my hospitalization, and while he was certainly dedicated to the cause, it only took a few minutes to realize he was no Captain Prion. While Prion had inspired respect and fear, the men viewed Grovich as an incompetent and went so far as to crack jokes about him.

A medium-sized man who grew up in the northwest, Grovich partly brought it on himself, dressing like he was on parade with shiny boots and brass and always lecturing the troops about military protocol, as though that meant anything to a bunch of cannon fodder. Veteran platoon sergeants, like Mann, pretended to give him respect while often ignoring Grovich's orders, or changing them to their own liking.

I got the same kind of dismal impression when Grovich and I first met. We sat in a small office at Baldy and, after nearly an hour of talk, I was sure the army had made a mistake sending him to the field. Grovich said straight to my face that he would have been much more comfortable working at some office back at headquarters. "I've had all the required training," he said, "but I'm just not comfortable leading a unit in combat. This is real, not some classroom assignment back in the States. People's lives are at stake and I can't afford to screw up. I'm going to need the support of veterans like you who I can turn to for advice."

That statement, I realized, was made based upon the only thing he knew about me, which was my survival of the firefight in the dunes. Like everyone else, he was giving me credit for something I hadn't done. I wasn't about to dissuade him. Instead, I purposely spent a lot of time the next few weeks getting to know Grovich, talking about the unit, our lives back home, and playing the card game, 500 Rummy, which he loved. I almost always won but threw a game now and then to make him feel good. It wasn't that I was a nice guy, far from it. I wanted to know him better and get his trust, figuring the time might come when I would need his goodwill and support. Like most smart investments, it paid off.

In time another unit replaced us at Baldy and we were flown west to take part in a sweep along the Laotian border where there were reports of Vietcong activity. As soon as I stepped off the chopper and breathed in the open air, old fears rose up in my throat. I'd been out of the field for nearly two months, but it was like I'd never left. The heat, the bugs, and the strange smells were all still there, waiting for my return. Except this time, unlike my earlier weeks in the field, I got the full experience of living in Vietnam.

It started that first day, as we climbed up a thick jungle trail that rose gradually along the side and then up to the peak of a tall hill. The heat, as usual, was in the high 90s. My rucksack, filled with canned food, ammo and water, not to mention my ammo belt and rifle, crushed down on me like a ton of bricks. We hadn't gone more than a hundred yards up the mountain before sweat was pouring down my face, my chest was heaving, and I was stopping every few feet just to catch my breath. I could tell the other guys were hurting, too, but no one wanted to be the first to complain. Besides, we all knew stopping on that trail was dangerous because the enemy could sneak up within a few feet before being heard or seen. So on we went, climbing higher and higher up that infernal mound. Finally, after ascending for some six hours, we reached the crest, where we set up a defensive perimeter and dug in for the night. Completely worn out, I collapsed on the ground and lay there for sometime before spreading out my air mattress and blowing it up. I was desperate for a good night's sleep.

It wasn't to be.

Sometime after midnight, I woke to the sound of voices coming from the jungle far below. I wasn't the only one. Almost to a man, I saw the company poised along the edge of the hilltop, peering down at the thick trees hundreds of feet below us. The voices we heard were high pitched and definitely Vietnamese. Since there weren't supposed to be any ARVN units in our sector, and since civilians would never have been out in the jungle at night, we assumed the voices belonged to Charlie.

It was creepy. Anyone who's ever spent the night in a forest knows that sounds travel loud and clear through the dark. We certainly knew it. Once the sun went down, no one spoke above a whisper or turned on any kind of light. It was too easy for snipers to take a bead in the dark, burst off a few rounds, and then just fade safely away. That's what made the sounds we heard from below so surreal. The gooks weren't making any attempt at all to hold down the noise. In fact, as we lay there, staring down in the dark, straining to make out their words, the dinks started to sing. Right there, in the dead of night, in the middle of a war, Charlie had a party going on.

I would have just let them be—why bother someone who's probably well armed, having fun, and most likely not even aware of our presence? Grovich had other ideas. He locked in the approximate position of the singers and had his RTO call in an artillery strike. A few minutes passed and then we heard a whistling sound fly over our heads, followed by a bright-white explosion in the air above the forest. The artillery boys had shot an airburst to mark the position of their target, which Grovich quickly verified.

Almost immediately, the singing stopped and a hush fell over the woods. That lasted all of fifteen seconds. Then the most uproarious laughter broke out down below. It was beyond belief. If that artillery round had detonated over my head, I would have knocked down trees trying to get away, but those guys thought it was funny. So did some of us up top. No sooner had the dinks started laughing than I heard muted chuckles from our ranks, along with such things as "What the F...?" and "Those guys are crazy!" But it was no joke to Grovich. He ordered "fire for effect," and soon after, three 155-rounds came knifing through the dark and exploded directly on what appeared to be the location of the partygoers.

When the noise of the explosions dimmed out, a hush fell over the forest and I turned back to my bed, sure that it was over. But incredibly, after a short time, laughter again broke out down below. This time it gave me the creeps. "They're out of their minds," I said to myself, and edged over closer to Bryson, who was peering down into the dark with his mouth open. Ghost stories I'd heard as a Boy Scout ran through my mind and I imagined phantoms floating up through the dark to slit our throats.

Grovich had never heard such stories. He ordered in a second, more massive artillery barrage on the laughing boys that lit up the forest below and caused the earth to shake. This time, the laughing stopped for good and the forest again became quiet. Whoever they were, whatever they were doing, I was sure they were dead after being hit like that. Grovich gave the order to resume resting, but few of us slept the rest of that night; we were too spooked by what had happened.

The next morning, being unable to see much from above, Grovich had the unit ascend back down the hill and move through the area that had been bombarded. We spent more than hour digging through smashed foliage and battered trees. We located several pits where the bombs had hit, plus pieces of clothing and chunks of flesh scattered about, but nothing close to an actual body. Whoever had been there was no more. It was possible some of them had di-di mowed away from that death zone hit, but given the laughter we heard, much more likely they'd all been blown to bits by the heavy barrage.

The best explanation anyone could come up with was that a bunch of gooks had been high on some kind of dope and just didn't realize the danger when the artillery started. It was easy to believe. We'd been told that the VC often took drugs to get up their courage before a battle and they had certainly acted like a bunch of drunks or druggies, singing loudly and then laughing when the artillery first started. Nothing else we imagined could explain their actions the night before. Whatever the reason, I was glad we didn't find anyone waiting for us when we climbed down there.

While searching the area though, I chanced upon a shiny object at the base of a tree, still attached to a shredded remnant of clothing. It was a medallion, circular in shape with an image of a star in the center and Chinese letters engraved on the back. Figuring it was a good souvenir, I stuck it in my rucksack and then forgot about it.

Besides, there were other things to think about that morning. Our assignment for the day was to search a couple of local villages, which G-2 suspected of harboring Vietcong. Since we were only thirty miles or so from the Cambodian border and the infamous Ho Chi Minh Trail, it was probably true. It was common knowledge that small isolated villages in the countryside were at the mercy of any armed band, and with government soldiers rarely getting out that way, such little towns often served as rest and resupply places for Charlie. Our orders were to locate and destroy any illegal stockpiles of food or munitions we found and to capture, or terminate with extreme prejudice, anyone suspected of being a Vietcong, which could have been interpreted as any man between fifteen and fifty years of age.

I didn't think about it at the time, being preoccupied with keeping myself alive, but I now realize the people who lived in the Vietnamese country provinces probably suffered more than anyone in that war. Both sides—the communists and the Saigon government—threatened them, took their sons away to fight, and gave nothing back in return. I would have moved to a metropolitan area as fast as my legs could carry me, but those poor bastards hung in there, eating scraps, sleeping on dirt floors, and being abused daily by both man and nature. I suppose they were just too ignorant and too settled to go anywhere else.

It took us about an hour tramping through the underbrush before we emerged near the first small village. It was a typical country hamlet of ten to twenty small thatched-roof dwellings, surrounded by a stream on one side and rice fields on the others. From our vantage point, I could see a few farmers out in the fields doing something, as well as five or six water buffalo lounging about, munching away at whatever water buffalos eat. From that short distance, it all looked very serene.

Grovich had me position the Third Platoon as a "blocking force," while he took the other two platoons through the woods and around to the far side of the village. The idea was for them to enter the village from one side while making a lot of noise. Experience told us that if there were any VC in the village, they would be frightened and run out the back door in our direction, trying to escape rather than fight.

Mann spaced out the members of our platoon in a wide semicircle, and then we sat low and out of sight and waited nearly half an hour for Grovich to come in from the other side of the village. When he finally did, there was some yelling and a few loud voices, but no gunfire and no one running out our direction. If the Vietcong had been in that place, they weren't there that morning.

Still, we stayed in place and waited a bit longer before word came over the radio that the village was indeed secure. Only then did we move out and slowly advanced along the edge of several rice fields to join the rest of Company B. When we entered the small town we found that the First and Second Platoons had already rounded up the villagers and placed them under guard in a central courtyard. There couldn't have been more than forty of 'em, all cowering in fear and seemingly all under twelve or over fifty years in age. That wasn't unusual in the Vietnamese countryside back in '69. Men, when they reached a certain age, either went off to the bigger towns and cities to escape the war or else they were off fighting, probably for the NVA. And for some reason, I hardly ever saw any young women in those country hamlets either, which didn't really make sense because there were always some children around. Almost all the women in those little villages were craggily faced old hags, hunched over with blackened teeth from eating too many betel nuts.

As we came on the scene, one old man was talking to Tran, our Kit Carson Scout, who was translating for Grovich. "The chief say no VC in village," said Tran. "Say not see VC long time. Say GIs Number One. VC Number Ten." Good ole Tran. He had a way of explaining things so well. I figured he was a Texas A&M grad, but he played dumb the one time I jokingly asked him about it (which made me suspect it all the more).

"Okay," remarked Grovich to Tran. "Tell the chief we won't hurt anyone." Turning to the company first sergeant, he said, "Tell the men to stop searching and take a break for lunch. We'll rest here a short while and then head for the next place."

I thought the first sergeant might say something, but he didn't, so I stepped forward and said, "Sir, don't you think we should at least finish checking out this village? What if the chief's lying or there's stuff stashed about out of sight?"

"I don't think he's lying, Lieutenant," answered Grovich. "Look at him! He's scared to death! He wouldn't dare lie with us right here in his village. Besides, we've looked. There's no sign of any Vietcong here."

"But what if they're about, Sir?" I replied. "They're always down in some hole or tunnel. They wouldn't be part of a welcoming committee, you know?"

"Yeah, I know that, Lieutenant," said Grovich, who I could tell was becoming a bit annoyed with me questioning his orders, "but I still don't think he's lying. Would you lie to ninety armed men?"

Well, I would, if it'd save my hide, but telling that to Grovich just then would have been a waste of time, so I dropped it, shrugged, and walked off. I still had an uncomfortable feeling, but my apprehension pretty much disappeared as the villagers began to ignore us and go about their business, which meant doing pretty much nothing except standing knee-deep in rice fields.

As we sat there eating our lunch, one old lady brought out some *nuoc mam* and offered it to our guys to go with their Cs. The Vietnamese loved the stuff and ate it like catsup. Mann took some from her and spread it on whatever he was eating, but the smell of *nuoc mam* always made me sick, so I looked the other way when she approached. The old lady couldn't take a hint though and pushed the *nuoc mam* at me. I tried to shove it away politely, and when I did, our eyes met. For just a second, I sensed an intense hatred from that tired old face, then she turned away and the feeling was gone. But the look in her eyes stayed with me. Several times in the following weeks while asleep, I dreamed of her staring hard at me and woke to find myself wet with sweat. Even now, years later, if I lie in the dark and think back, I could feel the malevolence in those eyes. Needless to say, I was glad I didn't eat the *nuoc mam*.

But I did take a bath. One of the Third Platoon guys found a well at the edge of the village and decided to cool off. Before anyone could stop him, he stripped down to his shorts and straddled the top of the well, while one of his buddies hauled up water and poured it over him. It looked refreshing and the commander didn't say anything, so a bunch of us, including me, ended up doing the same thing. The dirt from our bodies washed back into the water at the bottom, which was probably the village's drinking water source, but we didn't care, it wasn't our well. And besides, we were used to living with dirt. In fact, as we left that place, a number of troops filled their canteens with water from the well. They stuck in iodine tablets to disinfect it, but I doubt that helped much. The truth was most infantry in the 'Nam really didn't care if they got sick, because if they did, it usually meant a trip to a rear base camp where they could recover. That was a damn sight better than being out in the bush.

After resting for about an hour, we headed west, with the intention of searching a second hamlet several clicks away. Having found no VC in the first village and filled our bellies with food, we must have relaxed our guard as we moved inland. That was a mistake. We hadn't gone more than a quarter mile, strung out in a long line, when a burst of gunfire from the front drove us to the ground. My platoon was last in line, so we couldn't see what was happening, but the cry "Man down, man down" came through the prick-25 loud and clear. The lead platoon had walked smack into an ambush and taken casualties.

Like many firefights, this one didn't last long as our superior weapons and numbers came into play and quickly decided the outcome. Before long, only a few scattered shots came back in our direction and then none at all. As he would do a thousand times that year, all across the country, Charlie had hit and run.

This time their ambush had been a success. Three of our guys had been shot in the initial volley, including the company point man, who had been killed outright. While the wounded were tended to, Grovich sent the Second Platoon off in pursuit of the fleeing dinks. They soon came back, with Platoon Leader Kitchen saying the VC were nowhere to be found. It seemed to me they hadn't looked too hard because they'd returned to our position in what seemed like a very short time. But no one questioned their actions. We all remembered what had happened to Captain Prion when he had aggressively pursued the enemy just a few weeks earlier. Kitchen wasn't about to repeat that mistake.

The medics were still tending to our wounded though, so Grovich held a brief war council to decide what to do next. "The worst thing," he said, conveniently forgetting about our dead, "is that we've lost valuable time. Our orders are to search both villages today. Either we disobey orders or we have to move really fast to reach the second village before nightfall. Both alternatives are bad. We can't ignore orders. Yet, we'll just tire out if we rush to get there."

I thought he'd been out in the sun too long. We'd come under fire and taken casualties, so it was obvious our original orders were no longer valid. But the other platoon leaders, Kitchen and Williams, just stood there like mutes, so I spoke up. "Sir, we all want to carry out battalion orders, but given what's happened here, those orders don't make sense any more."

"Why not?" he asked.

"There's no chance now of sneaking up on the second village unawares," I replied. "Whoever hit us could easily run ahead and warn them before we could arrive. To make it worse, now there's a chance of walking into more ambushes. They'll assume we would go that direction."

Hearing that, even the mutes nodded their accent.

"So what do you suggest, Love?" asked Grovich.

"Our first concern should be for the dead and wounded, Sir," I said. "Let's take them back to that first village where they can be safely medevaced. Then we should return to where we dug in last night. We've lost the element of surprise, and that hilltop is safe and easy to defend."

"But how do I explain this to higher-ups?" asked the idiot, still not understanding our situation.

"They'll understand, Sir," I answered, becoming somewhat exasperated. "Just think for a minute. If this looks bad, how will it look if we have more KIAs? You can bet that will happen if we head for that second village now. There's no way for us to sneak in unseen like we did this morning." It was obvious stuff, but Grovich, like many young career officers, was afraid to buck the system. He didn't want to take responsibility for changing the orders he'd received from a higher headquarters. The truth was (and I'd made a career of this), officers who displayed common sense and initiative were often the ones who usually got the attention and respect of the big brass. Not to mention awards and promotions.

Grovich didn't know that though and just stood there with his chin in his left hand staring down at the ground, obviously thinking about what to do. Fortunately, Williams finally spoke up and said, "Sir, I agree with Loveless. Best thing now is to medevac out our wounded and repair for the night. We, at least, did one place today. We can always ask battalion about doing the second village tomorrow."

"I agree, too, Sir," said Kitchen, who had also somehow found his voice.

That did it. With all three of his platoon leaders in agreement, the light somehow finally dawned on Grovich. So we turned about and headed back towards our campsite from the night before. On the way, we stopped at the first village, where we'd had our lunch, to have our wounded picked up by a chopper and flown back to Chu Lai. We'd only been gone a short time, but when we arrived back at the small country town, there was nary a soul at home. That made sense as the residents had probably heard the shooting and fled as fast as they could. Only the old chief was still there, found hiding inside a grass hooch.

Why he remained, when the others had gone, I never understood. My guess was, as the village elder, he had a responsibility to remain behind, whether he liked it or not. Whatever the reason, he soon regretted it. I was on the far side of the village and didn't see it, but heard afterwards that two guys from the First Platoon dragged the old man out from his hiding place, carried him across the compound, and dropped him head first down the well where we'd washed ourselves earlier that day. He must have died when he hit bottom because when I looked down the well a short time later, there was no movement or sound from below.

When Grovich learned what had happened, he called the platoon leaders and sergeants together and demanded we turn over the people who had killed the old man, threatening to court-martial them on murder charges. But it was a hollow threat. The whole company was certain the villagers could have warned us about the ambush. Even though many of them knew the names of the culprits, no one was about to turn in their fellow soldier. It was war, and horrible things happened in war.

Eventually, Grovich realized he was wasting his time and we moved on, leaving the village for our mountaintop retreat of the night before. It took us more hours of hard labor to climb back up the hill, but we willingly did so because it was a relatively safe location to bed down. Or so we thought. That evening, just as the sun was going down, I heard several zinging sounds going overhead, followed fast by the cracking sound of an AK-47, the weapon of choice for the Vietcong.

I hit the ground, along with nearly everyone else, alert to hear and respond to any follow up gunfire. But there wasn't any. For several long seconds, I lay motionless on the ground, and then crawled into a shallow crevice nearby, dragging my rifle on the way. I crouched there, listening to the sounds of people scurrying about and talking, but heard no more gunfire. Before long the sun was gone, bringing on the darkness of night and bringing the camp back to a level of normalcy. We all assumed that a sniper had snapped off several shots from somewhere down below and then slunk away to safety. He didn't hit anyone, but it spooked the whole company and kept me on edge most of the night. The next morning, I waited until most of the others were up and walking about before I rose from my air mattress, just in case the sniper was still in the area.

Not long after rising, we received new orders from brigade headquarters, instructing us to abandon the crest of hills bordering Laos and to now move east towards the coast. We did so for three days, staggering our pace and alternating our route at times in case we were being watched, while checking out any villages that we came across with along the way. We never found any VC or contraband, but Charlie was always nearby. Each day, just before nightfall, the local neighborhood sniper shot off several rounds in our direction. It was always the same, the sound of rounds zinging through the air, followed by the crack of an AK-47. He never hit anyone, but always sent us scattering about like a flock of panicked sheep. After the second time, we expected it would happen and took more precautions on where and how we set up camp. It was obviously the same guy, and even though the sniper had been more nuisance than threat, it was only a matter of time before he hurt someone, so we tried various tactics to finish him off. We returned fire, set up snipers of our own, and even tried a night ambush—all to no avail. It might have gone on for weeks, if we hadn't linked up with another unit on the fifth day of our sniper encounters.

Orders had arrived sending us to one of the bigger towns in the region, so it was arranged that we could ride back there with an armored platoon that was operating close in our vicinity. When Grovich heard that, he called ahead and informed the armored platoon's leader about the sniper in the hopes that we could use their firepower if the sniper made another appearance.

Late that afternoon, we arrived at the rendezvous point to find our armored escort—about a dozen APCs and two tanks, well camouflaged behind sand dikes and shrubbery, with their engines turned off. They were so quiet and well hidden, we didn't see them ourselves until we were within a few yards of their position. The tracks were a welcome sight for me. Not only did they look fearsome with their big cannons and .50-caliber machine guns, but for the first time in days, I could stop traveling by foot.

The officer commanding the tanks and APCs had listened to Grovich and positioned his vehicles well. Not only were they well hidden, their guns were all aimed towards a solitary wood line about a hundred feet away. If there was a sniper following us, that was the most likely place for him to hide and shoot. The soldiers from the armored convoy had set up their bivouac area off to the side, so we settled in with them, trying to make it appear that everything was going on as normal. We didn't want the sniper to think there was anything unusual, hoping that he would make an appearance.

Sure enough, as dark descended, we heard the familiar *crack, crack* of an AK-47 and the whine of bullets flying over our heads from the direction of the trees. Almost immediately, we opened up with everything we had, close to a hundred men and more than a dozen armored vehicles blasting away at the woods. We lit up the dark and the sound was earsplitting, especially when the tanks boomed away with their cannons. Even I rose up on my knees and emptied my M16 towards the woods, sure that the sniper wouldn't dare try to return fire during that murderous barrage.

When it was over some minutes later, we lowered our guns and looked out at a forest in shambles—grown trees lay on their side, split in half, smaller shrubbery chopped to ribbons from our fusillade and virtually nothing standing that was taller than two to three feet in height. The scrubland that had stood there just minutes before was virtually gone, obliterated by our massive barrage. Our entire line of troops looked out in silence, amazed at what we'd done in such a short time. "Holy shit," said someone to my right and I turned to find Bryson standing there. "If we didn't kill him with that, then he probably died from a heart attack."

I nodded my head in agreement and said, "Yeah, that's the end of that," and turned to sit on the ground just as a familiar *oweee, oweee* sound whizzed over to our left, followed by the sound of an AK-47.

It was unbelievable! Not only had the man survived, he had the temerity to shoot back! I flopped onto my back and looked left and right to see fellow soldiers all leaning down behind the embankment with the most incredulous look on their faces, not believing what they'd just heard. Then, from somewhere down the line, a cheer went up and increased in crescendo as others added in their voices and even firing their weapons into the open air. I joined in, more laughing than cheering. It was unreal! We were applauding someone who had been shooting at us every day for the past week.

Maybe it was because no one had actually been hit by the sniper, who was obviously a bad shot, or maybe it was our way of paying our respects to a fellow soldier, even if he was the enemy. Whatever it was, our cheerfulness was a natural response. I think we all felt good because we sensed that this particular gook was somehow a comrade in arms with his "never give up" attitude. It was our way of saluting his persistence and also our farewell. After a few minutes, we all relaxed and bedded down for the night, sure that we'd heard the last from our friend.

The next day, we packed up and left the field, but only after a quick inspection of the torn-up wood line where we found nothing. Whoever he was, he had departed the scene and was out of our lives. Still, I don't think anyone who was there that night has ever forgotten the sniper who refused to quit.

I sat on the back of one of the tanks as we rode in from the field. It was not the most comfortable ride, bumping across open fields or down dirt roads, but it sure beat humping on the ground with a heavy load of gear on your back. Over the years, I've heard tankers complain about how they have it worse than the infantry, since track vehicles make bigger targets for the enemy. But, for my money, there's nothing worse than being an infantryman, except maybe being an infantryman for the other side. Grunts might be smaller targets, but in wartime they're full-time targets, who rarely get to enjoy a hot meal or a roof over their head. Besides, while they may complain, I don't recall ever meeting a tanker who voluntarily joined the infantry.

We were supposed to go to an LZ named Hawk Hill for a few days of rest and resupply, but on the way there, we got diverted to the provincial capital of Tam Ky, which lay midway between Chu Lai and LZ Baldy. Nixon's Vietnamization program was just kicking off at that time and someone up top had decided American and South Vietnamese troops should spend more time getting to know each other. Since we were already in the neighborhood, it was decided Company B should stop by Tam Ky and link up with a local ARVN unit stationed in the town.

So we headed east and spent another hour bouncing over land before we came to what must have been a main thoroughfare by Vietnamese standards, a straight, two-lane paved highway. It looked somewhat familiar to me. When one of the other tank riders said it was the road that connected Chu Lai to Baldy, I knew I'd been on it before. The driver of our tank later said that road stretched the length of the country. I'm sure it did, but I don't remember seeing anything but military vehicles that entire morning, although there were a number of water buffalos trudging down the sides of the road, pulling carts of people and goods behind them.

After traveling another thirty minutes or so, we arrived at Tam Ky, riding the tanks and APCs straight through the middle of the town to an ARVN camp on the far side. The highway through Tam Ky wasn't much more than a hard-packed dirt road, lined on both sides by two-storey buildings and lots of open-air markets or small business stalls. Almost all the structures had open air windows and colorful designs, with some hanging large advertising banners across the front of their upper levels. Many looked rundown, with broken doors, boards hanging loose and paint peeling off, pretty much like the small town in Michigan where my dad's relatives lived. Occasionally, we caught glimpses of larger structures off to the side, most of which looked like churches or temples. One had a statue of Mary on the front lawn, which meant it was probably a Catholic church left over from the French occupation years earlier.

Fortunately, there were no other vehicles in Tam Ky that morning, at least not out on the road, although we had to dodge plenty of bikes and motor scooters, scurrying back and forth, with their drivers often struggling to balance baskets of goods. I say "fortunately" because there was no sidewalk and the road was packed with activity. Vendors of both sexes and all ages squatted next to carts or large wicker baskets of goods, shouting as we passed by in the hopes of making a sale.

But it was the children that I recall most when I think about that drive through Tam Ky. There were dozens of them, running alongside, waving and calling out "GI Number One" as we drove through town. Some of the guys threw money at them and laughed as the kids scrambled for it, while others tossed cans of C-rations at the little urchins. I thought that was a bit dangerous, given that the cans were nothing more than heavy, flying projectiles. But the little munchkins went after the canned food like hungry tigers attacking their last meal. Of course, grown-ups were there with the children, but they mostly stood back and observed, just waiting, I thought, until we were out of sight before retrieving the goodies from the youngsters. I must admit it was a power trip, sitting on that tank and watching the townsfolk cling to the sides of the street, watching in awe as we roared though. All in all, it's one of my more pleasant memories of Vietnam.

The ARVN compound on the far side of town, like most of the other ones I came in contact with in the 'Nam, wasn't anything to brag about. There were about a dozen one-storey buildings circling an assembly area, and several three-storey guard towers facing away from Tam Ky. The camp was surrounded by concertina wire but security didn't impress me as being too tight. I felt certain the VC would have had no trouble getting inside the fortification if they really tried. We were met by an ARVN lieutenant who, after being introduced to Grovich, escorted us to a pair of one-storey buildings set apart from the rest of the structures. Inside, we found cots for sleeping, with one shower to share in each building. Toilets were outdoors in their own sheds but that was no different from many of the American encampments. Besides, after living outdoors for weeks, no one complained.

That evening, Grovich and the three of us platoon leaders were dinner guests with the local ARVN commander, a Major Ngo Dinh, and his senior officers. We sat around a large rectangular table in a room that looked as though it was from some fancy restaurant back home. There were paintings on the wall, several ceiling fans above, and plush chairs which sat on an actual carpet. In order to become better acquainted with each other, the Americans sat separated from each other by a Vietnamese counterpart. We were served food and drinks by lower-ranking Viet soldiers as though we were in some fancy restaurant, which I found it to be interesting.

While I'd previously had casual interactions with a few Vietnamese military types during my short time in-country, Major Ngo, whom I sat next to, was the first ARVN soldier with whom I really struck up a conversation. We spent most of the dinner time exchanging our histories and thoughts and, I believe, took an instant liking to each other. Like many in the South Vietnamese leadership, he came from a family with influence and money. It must have been big money, because he spoke excellent English and claimed to have attended school in Europe as a boy. There was no doubt he was in charge of the ARVN base. Whenever he spoke to the group, the other Vietnamese stopped talking instantly. Once, when he rose to his feet, the other dinks jumped to their feet like he was royalty, which he may have been for all I knew. Despite appearances though, my gut instinct told me Ngo was cut from the same cloth as I, serving in the military only because he had no other choice. I felt at the dinner, and in later interactions, that despite our different upbringings and cultures, he and I were quite similar. Of course, he had more money and power.

Grovich and the others didn't seem to share my sentiments. They appeared to be uncomfortable throughout the dinner, hardly touching their food, and barely engaging Ngo and his officers in conversation, even though the Vietnamese all spoke some English. Perhaps my fellow Americans were bored by Ngo's stories, which admittedly were mostly about himself and went on endlessly. Or it may have been the first real Asian meal for most of them and they didn't quite know what to think of the strange vegetables and meat products on their plates. Coming from Hawaii, and having lived in Korea for two years with my parents, I had no such problem, having eaten Asian-style food most of my life. Besides, for me, anything was better than the stupid C-rations we'd eaten for weeks.

As dinner drew to a close, Ngo extended his courtesies in a new direction. "Captain Groveech," he said in his thick Vietnamese accent, "your men are tired from the field. May I invite you to join me at the camp carwash before you sleep?"

"Thank you, Major Ngo," said Grovich, "but we've had a long day and I think its best we get back to our men now. We should make sure they are okay this first night. Perhaps we can see the carwash tomorrow morning."

"In the morning?" chuckled Ngo. "If you wish, Captain, but such a place is much better at night and I would be pleased if you were my guests."

I knew what Grovich's answer would be, so I piped up, "Sir, since Major Ngo has been so gracious to invite us, perhaps at least one of us should go. I don't mind visiting this place with him this evening."

"All right, Love," said Grovich, somewhat surprised at my suggestion. "Maybe you're right. You can represent us tonight."

"Excellent," said Ngo, delighted to have at least one companion.

Soon after, with dinner completed, as we left the building, Grovich grabbed me by the shoulder and whispered, "Thanks, Love. I don't think I can take too much of this guy. Just watch yourself."

"Don't worry, Sir, I'll be fine," I replied, knowing Grovich would surely have stopped me from going if he'd understood the term "carwash." But he didn't know until the following day, and by that time, I had an explanation all cooked up to maintain my all-American image.

In Vietnam, lots of military camps had "carwashes" just off post. It's possible vehicles got cleaned at some of them, I don't really know. But for sure, lots of GI's got their insides cleaned out for as little as five bucks a shot at "carwashes," while being able to select their own cleaning woman. While at the hospital the month prior, I'd learned from one of the nurses' aides that the carwashes outside the gate at Chu Lai were strictly off-limits to post personnel because of the high rates of VD in-country (although they somehow still managed to stay in business). But since we weren't at Chu Lai, and I was a guest of the local Vietnamese commander, I reasoned it was only proper for me to attend the local carwash with Ngo.

Sure enough, the place he took me to was but a few minutes' walk from the camp. Although right off a main road, the building wasn't very inviting. It was a typically dilapidated three-storey place that from the outside appeared to have only one light, hanging overhead at the front door. It was made less inviting by the fact that two mean-looking thugs were standing guard at the entrance. One of them was the biggest Vietnamese I ever saw, well over two hundred fifty pounds and thick like a sumo wrestler. I felt their hackles rise when I walked up, but at the sight of Ngo who'd been slightly behind me, their demeanor changed. They ushered us into the interior where we were introduced to a middle-aged man, whom I took to be the proprietor. A short, rather plump man, he ignored me and led us down a hallway to a small lobby where five or six women reclined on sofas and easy chairs, smoking cigarettes and drinking. Like the building, they weren't much to look at, too skinny and too homely for my taste. I would have ignored all of them back home. But I wasn't at home, and it *had* been weeks since I'd been with a woman, and it *was* Ngo's treat—so I decided to do my best given the situation.

While I'd been inspecting the merchandise, Ngo had been introducing me to our escort. "Reeutenant Roveless," said Ngo, tugging on my sleeve and attracting my attention back to him and the other man. "Please to meet Mr. Nguyen. He is owner."

"Happy to meet you, Sir," I said, extending my hand to Nguyen. While he did offer a somewhat limp handshake, I felt somehow he didn't share the sentiment as he grunted something and turned quickly back to Ngo. While the two of them talked, I gave another glance at the girls and noticed someone I'd missed before. She had entered the room from another door and was addressing one of the reclining harlots. She was no Waikiki beauty queen, but her face looked decent even without makeup and the slacks she wore amplified a round and firm body underneath. She was definitely the best of the lot.

As I stared, Ngo turned to me and said, "All settle now. Please, Reeutenant, you pick girl."

"That's easy, the young lady in the white blouse," I said, pointing towards the pretty one, who must have overheard because she cut off her conversation with the other whore and looked in our direction. As I pointed, the proprietor turned to Ngo and said something in Vietnamese. By his tone, I could tell he wasn't pleased with my choice. Ngo listened and then said something back, which seemed to agitate the merchant, who raised his voice a level and stepped closer to Ngo. As they talked, the object of my affections walked slowly in our direction and looked straight into my face, before passing behind me and giving a tug on my shirt. That clinched it! A woman who wanted it was much more fun than one who didn't. I'd made the right pick.

All this was missed by the proprietor, who continued to argue with Ngo, even raising his hands in the air and yelling something that obviously wasn't polite. The end result was Ngo slapping the whore-master hard across the face with the back of his hand. The man stumbled backwards against the wall, nearly falling down. For a second, it looked like he was going to strike back at Ngo, as a fierce look came across his face. But then he obviously thought better of it and settled back into a crouching position, staring down at the floor.

Ngo walked forward and stood over the crouching merchant, yelling obscenities down at him. At least I assumed they were obscenities, not understanding a word he said. The owner never said a word, just kept looking down at the floor. I could see his one hand was clenched and it seemed to me he was shaking, but I couldn't tell if it was from fear or anger. Whatever the case, he had the good sense to stay down on the floor. Ngo must have yelled for a full minute and then, his anger vented, he turned away from the cowering man and back to the women, who were all standing wide-eyed, watching the scene unfold. Ngo called to two of the little strumpets, who jumped up at his command and then beckoned to my girl, who was standing in the near doorway, a fearful look on her face.

"Come," he commanded, grabbing my arm and leading me down a side hallway with the three women in tow. As we left the lobby, I looked back to see the owner, who had returned to his feet and was glowering at me.

"What was that all about?" I asked Ngo on the way down the hall.

"You pick owner daughter," he said, as casually as if I'd selected the best grapefruit in the marketplace.

"You mean this is his daughter?" I asked, looking back at the one I'd chosen, worried that my selection could lead to more trouble. "I didn't know that. I can pick someone else."

"No! You Ngo guest! You pick girl! No worry! Owner not important," answered my newfound friend.

That was enough for me. I didn't want to argue with him, and if Ngo wasn't worried, why should I be? Of course, if I'd been more experienced, I would have insisted on another woman since it's never good to make enemies when you can avoid it. But I was young and hot-blooded at the time and didn't figure on ever seeing Mr. Nguyen again. Besides, the woman, who was holding on to my shirt as we walked, *wanted* me.

Houses of prostitution in Asia are viewed quite differently from those in the States. For one thing, they're not always hidden in out-of-the-way locations, away from the so-called decent folks. Whorehouses can be found in some Asian cities right around the corner from schools or places of worship. It's a cultural thing. Men who frequent Cat Houses in Asia aren't looked down on as sinful or evil, they're just guys out having a good time, who are expected to go home to their families afterwards. That's true even in Asian countries with lots of Christians, like Vietnam and Korea. Some places, like the Miari District in Seoul, are virtual communities with thousands of customers each night, many of whom are respectable businessmen or community folk.

Another difference has been that Asian women have tolerated such places better than their Western counterparts. Perhaps that's because they lacked much power outside of the home, or maybe they've just been indoctrinated by centuries of tradition to let their men run wild. Whatever the reason, it's been a paradise for men for hundreds of years. But it's a paradise that could soon fade from memory. The advent of Western culture, to include women's lib and the influx of women in the workplace, has begun to slowly change some attitudes. While they rarely run things, Asian women in recent years have become much more involved in community affairs and decision making than in the past. It's probably only a matter of time before such exotic places as Bangkok and Seoul are as exciting as Louisville and Bangor.

Even the way they get down to business is different in Asia. Ngo and I spent more than an hour with the three girls; drinking whisky, eating, and singing songs before going separate ways to our private rooms. It seemed to me to be a very civilized way to run a bordello, and I've since experienced the same way of doing business in other Asian countries, with even groups as large as ten or twenty partying together before pairing off alone. The hookers certainly seem to appreciate it. After all, they could always justify their work by claiming to have sex only with men who are their friends, not just some stranger off the street.

Anyway, sometime near midnight, I finally settled in a tiny one-window room with my Vietnamese honey, whose name I'd learned was Mai. We had hardly shut the door when she jumped on my back, dragged me to the floor, and began tearing off my uniform, stopping just long enough to laugh at my green underwear. I took the smile off her face though when she popped her flimsy garb off and jumped aboard for the ride.

It was a wild one. We thrashed about from wall to wall, knocking down furniture, what little there was of it, and finally getting stuck in some kind of a wooden depression in the corner, where I released weeks of pent-up demand, and she apparently did, too. We'd been in the room less than ten minutes, said nary a word, and not even touched the single low-lying bed in one corner.

I propped myself up in the corner of the tub, for I could see now that it was one, and leaned back exhausted, full of myself. She lay on her back, fully nude, with one leg cocked up on the edge of the tub, and jabbered away in words that meant nothing to me, pausing every now and then to laugh at some unknown joke. Being young and confident, I was sure she was saying I was the best thing she'd ever experienced, or words to that effect. Looking back now, from a distance, I'm not so certain she was talking about me at all.

When I finally dragged myself up to the bed, she followed, and soon we were both fast asleep on one of the hardest sleeping mats built by man. But then, it wasn't built for sleeping. I woke sometime later to feel a woman's hand between my legs, urging me back into action. It succeeded, and did again once more later that night. I have to give Mai credit. She wasn't any great beauty, but she had as much desire as any woman I've ever known; no man could ask for more.

The next morning, she surprised me by asking for money. I knew Ngo had already paid for the night's entertainment, but I gave her some of my MPC anyway. It didn't really matter to me. MPC wasn't like real money, and I rarely had a chance to spend it. As Mai escorted me out of the building a short time later, we passed Papa in the lobby. I tried to ignore him, but could feel his eyes boring a hole in my back. An hour later, after changing into my other set of fatigues, I reported to Grovich and informed him as to the exact nature of a Vietnamese carwash. I figured it was better for me to tell him about "carwashes," than have him learn about them from someone else.

Knowing his character, and high opinion of me, I left out the details of my encounter with Mai, telling him instead that I had reluctantly agreed to stay the night in the same room with a woman so Ngo wouldn't lose face.

"You didn't do...?" started Grovich.

"Oh no, Sir, I didn't do anything," I said. "The girl took the bed and I slept in the corner on the floor. She was just a kid. Kind of reminded me of my own sister. I wouldn't have felt right taking advantage of her. Even now she's probably talking about the strange American who stayed the night without even touching her."

I half expected him to laugh in my face. I would have at such an obvious lie, but he just put his hand on my shoulder and said, "Sorry to put you through such a thing, Loveless. We won't worry about Major Ngo's losing face anymore. We've done our duty, thanks to you. But don't tell anyone else about that place. If the men hear about it, they'll all be down there."

"Yes, Sir, I see your point," I answered. "But you know, this is a small compound. We can't keep the men cooped up here day and night. They'll be looking for ways to go into town and they do deserve some time off, Sir. It's just a matter of time...."

"You're right, Love," he said, looking serious. "We all deserve a break. But I don't want anyone going to a place like that and getting sick. We've lost more men in this war to VD than combat, you know. How will it look if a bunch of our guys come down with that kind of infectious disease?"

"Yes, Sir, I understand. Still, there must be something we could do..." I said, leaving it open for him to ponder.

"I'll give orders that the men can take turns going into town—but only during the day in groups of four, and always with a senior NCO or officer. That way, there's less chance of anyone getting in trouble. But I'm not comfortable with it. These guys are no dummies," said the dummy. "It's just a matter of time before they find out about this place and start sneaking down there at night."

It was just what I wanted Grovich to think. "Hmmm," I said with a grave look on my face. "You know, Sir, maybe there's one way we can make sure no one goes to that place."

"What's that?" he asked.

"Well, I met the owner last night. We seemed to get along pretty well. Perhaps, if I went to him and told him his place was off-limits to our troops, he'd make sure none of our guys got in."

"Are you sure you can trust him?" replied Grovich."

"Pretty much. Ngo and I exchanged words with him and he seemed to take a special interest in me last night. He probably would work with me. On the other hand," I said, putting my chin in my hand, trying to look serious, "it is his business and he's not going to like losing money. Of course, we could just pay him a something to work with us. Then we'd only have to worry about the women. And that's another problem. That place is in a dark alley and has several entrances. It would be easy for them to slip our guys in, if they really wanted. The only way we can really make sure no one goes there is by stationing a guard at the place each night."

"No, that'll never work," he replied quickly. "After one night, everyone in the company will know about the place. They'll be fighting to be on guard duty there."

"Not if we personally select people we can trust, Sir," I stated. "We just need a few men. Have them take turns guarding the place and tell them how important it is that no one else finds out about it."

"It couldn't be senior people," he answered, showing some interest. "That would be too obvious."

"Yes, Sir," I said, turning to one side, trying to look thoughtful, and then turning back to Grovich. "You know, there are a few soldiers I know who we can trust. I'm very close with the two who came in-country with me. If I ask them to take on this job and keep quiet about it, they'll do it! And I'm sure they'll tell me if any of our other guys try to frequent the carwash."

"Who are they?" he asked.

"My RTO, Corporal Bryson, and Sergeant Baker in First Platoon, Sir," I responded. "I'd trust them with my life. We can have them take turns down there at night and I can even drop in on them now and then to make sure everything's okay. Of course, you'd have to get Baker assigned to me for the time we're here."

"All right, let's try it. You set it up with that whore-master. See if he'll agree to work with us and," Grovich paused for a second in thought, "let's pay him a little something just to make sure. I can chip in a hundred bucks. And I'll tell Kitchen to release Baker to your care for the next week while we're here. I guess that's the best we can do given the circumstances."

"Yes, Sir! But don't worry. Nothing will happen that I won't know about," I stated, fully confident that would be true.

"By the way, Love, I didn't know you had a sister," said Grovich.

"Ohh," I stammered, caught off guard for a second. "Oh yes, Sir, I...I don't. What I meant was...*if* I had a sister I'm sure she'd be like that nice girl last night."

"I see," he said, turning away, as I reminded myself to be more careful in the future. I'd forgotten that unit commanders could access any soldier's personnel files and learn about their family history.

That night, accompanied by one of our Kit Carson scouts, who was paid to keep his mouth shut about where we were going, I introduced Baker and Bryson to their new duties. At first, I didn't let them know what was up, only telling them they'd been chosen by the commander and me to protect a warehouse of fresh meat. Baker was the first to speak up. "But, Sir," he said, "why us? You know we'd do anything for you. How come we get this duty? Why didn't you take care of Johnny and me?" Bryson was quieter, just muttering a few swear words and staring at me like I'd just sold him out like a slave.

They complained all the way to Nguyen's place, asking over and over why they had been singled out for such a dumb job and why our unit had to protect raw meat. But once at the carwash their attitude changed. When I escorted them into the main parlor, where about ten women sat waiting, Baker turned to me, grabbing my arm, and said, "That's the meat?" Bryson's only comment was "holy shit," as he walked up to the nearest whore and introduced himself.

For the next week, the three of us spent every night at the carwash, enjoying ourselves, but also taking turns stationed at the front door to make sure the girls weren't bothered by any nasty GIs from back at the camp. I would venture to say we were probably the only American soldiers in the history of the Vietnam War to be assigned the job of guarding a whorehouse.

My two comrades may have sampled every woman in the place before we left; Bryson was especially popular, I think because he was younger and probably stronger than we other two. Baker played the field, too, but I stuck with Mai, the shopkeeper's daughter. She was enough, a ferocious lover with boundless energy who never seemed to tire. Besides, I felt certain her energy would have turned destructive if I slept around with any of the other women.

The amazing thing was, no one in the unit ever caught on. Oh sure, we were careful to alter our route to the carwash each day, and kept up a pretence by dragging ourselves back to the barracks every morning—exhausted from lack of sleep—which we were, by the way—but you'd think someone would have figured out we were up to no good. I could only credit it to the simplicity of Grovich and the stupidity of the others.

All in all, it was probably the best week I had in Vietnam. I was pleased. Baker and Bryson were pleased. The girls were pleased. Even Grovich was pleased, once actually congratulating me for managing to keep the carwash a secret from the troops. I assured him it was nothing, just doing my duty.

The only one not pleased was Papa Nguyen. Each time I entered his place, I got looks that could kill, but he never said a word. Frankly, I didn't give a damn. I figured he was just a pimp who couldn't stand up to Major Ngo when his daughter was taken away by a foreign soldier. Just to be safe though, and to reinforce my relationship with the local warlord, I went there one more time with Ngo later that week.

Mai, on the other hand, turned out to be tougher than her Dad. I've only met a few women in my life that enjoyed sex as much as Mai. She always did ask for money in the morning, but I didn't care. It was just MPCs anyway. I figured she needed the cash more than me and didn't ask why. You could imagine my shock when Major Ngo came to me the day before our scheduled departure from Tam Ky. "Reeutenant," he said, all serious, "it good idea you don't go carwash today."

"Don't go? Why not, Sir?" I asked.

"Mr. Nguyen daughter. She run away," he said, looking me in the eye.

"Run away! You mean she's gone?"

"Yes, she get money someone and run away. Maybe DaNang," said Ngo. "Nguyen not know, but he angry."

Well, Ngo was right. I didn't dare go back. If Mai had run away, it was with my money for sure and she had timed it well. She knew I would be departing Tam Ky soon and the free money would end, so off she went. I was certain that Papa would blame me, even though she was probably running away from him. So, that last night the boys and I stayed in camp, when we packed up and left Tam Ky the next morning, I went with no regrets. Mai had been fun, but that was about all. There was no real attachment between us, just sex and money. By the time we arrived at Chu Lai, I'd already forgotten her. But I hadn't been forgotten.

CHAPTER SIX

After Tam Ky, we went back to Chu Lai for something called "Stand down," which was basically three days of rest and relaxation, or R&R as the army calls it, for infantry units. We didn't have to do any kind of labor, not even guard duty. As I'd done the last time I'd been at Chu Lai, I spent my days hanging around the beach reading magazines and my nights partying at the Officer's Club. There weren't any women to spend time with—the hooch maids who cleaned our barracks all looked old enough to be my mother and the few nurses and such on post were already taken—but other than that, I had no complaints since no one was shooting at us.

They put us up in Quonset huts with metal roofs, high on a cliff overlooking the ocean; prior occupants had filled the walls of my room with photos of women in various stages of undress, mostly from *Playboy* magazine, which made interesting décor. We even slept on real beds with mosquito nets draped over them—well, actually, army cots, but they seemed like real beds to us infantry types. Lying there in the dark, surrounded by *Playboy* bunnies, with the wind coming off the ocean, and the rain pinging off the roof made for some of the best sleep I've ever had.

While I'd been at Chu Lai twice before, once during my in-processing and then at the hospital, Stand down was the first I really checked out the big army post. Our first morning there, I hiked up to the top of a hill in the middle of the post and looked down on row upon row of metal-roofed buildings stretching into the distance. In between were motor pools, ammunition storage bunkers, warehouses, and other administrative buildings. There were also several outdoor movie theaters—white-painted walls faced by rows of folding chairs—and one large outdoor arena, where I assume they had stage shows for the permanent party troops. Far off on the west side of the base, I could see the Chu Lai runway, from where the medevac and resupply choppers were based, while in the other direction, the South China Sea beckoned with its blue waters. I'd seen it all when flying in several months earlier, but being there on the ground, it all made a much bigger impression. The development of a military post like Chu Lai was no small undertaking and must have took years to get to that stage.

I spent most of that first day at the main PX, buying souvenirs for myself and my family—things like stationary and envelopes with maps of Vietnam, plus some Americal patches and shirts with the division logo. I also bought a boonie cap—a lightweight, camouflaged hat with a broad rim to keep the sun from my eyes. Everyone carried their combat helmets in the field, but we usually hung them from our rucksack and wore them only during firefights. The rest of the time they were too heavy and uncomfortable in the 'Nam heat. Boonie caps, on the other hand, were light and practical and, while discouraged back at the big base camps, were worn by many soldiers in the field.

Our Chu Lai Stand down began at a historic time. The day before, President Nixon had announced the first large-scale withdrawal of American soldiers from Vietnam since the war began. The *Stars & Stripes* newspaper said American strength in Vietnam would be reduced by 25,000 troops before year's end. Of course, they didn't name which soldiers or units would be affected, and in reality, as the plan was implemented, no one really went home early. Sure, some unit colors were retired and sent back to the States. So officially, we withdrew some units from Vietnam, starting with the 9th Infantry down in the Delta. But that didn't mean individual soldiers in those units went home early. Those who hadn't completed their one-year assignment in-country were just reassigned to other military commands in Vietnam. "Withdrawals" in Washington, D.C. talk really meant that fewer people would be sent from the States to replace the guys who were already there, so that over time, our involvement would decrease. You couldn't tell that to infantry grunts though. Two of the guys in our First Platoon took the army at its word and walked into division headquarters, volunteering to be among the initial 25,000 soldiers withdrawn. They were politely told to rejoin their unit.

For me, the highlight of that Stand down came on our last night at Chu Lai. I had gone to the Officer's Club early that night and was enjoying the sight of a young Asian girl up on stage swaying to the sound of a Vietnamese rock and roll group doing a poor rendition of the Animal's "We Gotta Get Outta This Place," when I spotted Alan Baker coming in the front door. Figuring he'd been sent by Grovich, I bent down behind the bar and pretended to be looking for something on the floor, hoping Baker would not notice me. But he was persistent and soon found me out.

"Sir," he said sounding short of breath and tapping me on the shoulder, "I've been looking all over for you. We need you down at the beach."

"What for?" I questioned, looking back up at him and rising back to my seat.

"Some of the guys have something to show you that I think you'll be very happy to see," he replied.

"Well, why don't you just show it to me tomorrow? I like the view from here just fine," I answered, motioning up at the dancing girl. The last thing I wanted to do just then was join a bunch of drunks down at the beach, especially that bunch of drunks that I would be stuck with in the weeks ahead.

"You don't understand, Sir. We have a surprise that you don't wanna miss. I know you're gonna love it!" he said. I looked at him hard and felt that he was sincere and what he was saying didn't sound too bad. Given his tone, I figured they had a woman for me, so I nodded ascent and followed him out the door.

Baker had a jeep. God knows where he'd got it; I didn't ask. But it only took us a few minutes' drive to get across the post and park on a road running along above a beach, which I immediately recognized. It was the same shoreline where I'd had a pleasant evening some months earlier with the Vietnamese girl from the in-processing office. Just down the street I could see the Reception Station and Combat Center, both of which brought back bad memories and made me wish I'd stayed at the O' Club rather than follow Baker.

The sight of my men made me wish it even more. There were about a dozen of them, just as I'd imagined, sprawled around on the sand down below, all in various stages of inebriation. They had a couple of women all right, women who were so old and worn out that even my brother Bob would have tossed them back. I was horny, but not desperate.

"So where's the surprise?" I said to Baker with a hint of irritation.

"It's coming soon," he said. "Just wait, Sir."

"It's not something like that, is it?" I asked, pointing to the women.

"Oh no, Sir! It's better, much better! You're gonna love it! Just wait here," and he jogged down to talk to one of the other troops, leaving me with the jeep, alone on the roadside. I grabbed a Carling Black Label from a cooler in his backseat, sat down on the road, and leaned back against the jeep to wait. I'd already made up my mind to head back to the club if nothing happened in the next few minutes, but I didn't have to wait that long. Halfway through my beer, Baker came running back, grabbed my arm, and yelled, "Come on Sir, they're here." He dragged me up alongside the road, with the rest of the guys and their whores following close behind.

Across the street from us, some fifty or sixty feet away, there was a two-storey building that looked like a typical housing barracks. Most of the lights in the building were out, and I saw a military police jeep with two soldiers, most likely military policemen, parked at one end of the building. Inside the barracks there were shadows moving behind some of the windows. Other than that, I saw nothing unusual.

"So, what up?" I asked.

"Just watch, Sir," said Baker, his eyes riveted on the building across the street.

I did, and before long a second jeep with military police markings drove up next to the first vehicle and stopped. It looked like there was some kind of conversation between the occupants of the two jeeps, and then the second one drove to the opposite end of the building and also parked. A short time later, a pair of MPs got out of each jeep and entered the building from both ends.

"What the hell is going on, Baker?" I asked, becoming ever more curious.

"Well, Sir. You know how you're always telling us that you should never have been in the field and all? How some sergeant changed your orders and sent you out with us because you'd messed with his woman?"

"Yeah, so?"

"I'm not sure, Sir, but it looks like the MPs are about to find dope in that Sergeant's room," said Baker matter-of-factly with a slight smile on his face.

"Dope? Are you sure? The same guy? What's his name, um, Sergeant Bowers?"

"Yeah. That's the guy," he answered.

"What the…? But how do you…? Who says he uses dope?" I asked.

"Didn't say he used it," replied Baker, "just that the cops are going to find it in his room."

"What? Yeah, but still, how do you…?"

"Well, let's just say nobody fucks with B Company and gets away with it," said Baker, "especially some idiot REMF."

I asked no more. Whatever Baker and the others had done, it was better I didn't know about it. So I stood there with the rest of them, watching the barracks and waiting to see what would transpire. For nearly half an hour nothing did, so about half the group, with entertainment at hand, took the trollops back down to the beach, leaving just Baker and me on the street with four or five of the others. The wait was worth it. Not long after, three of the MPs came out one end of the building, pulling someone behind them. I couldn't tell who it was, being so far away, but he was definitely resisting and making enough noise to wake up anyone asleep in the building.

"You guys wait here," said Baker, motioning to the other troops, "the LT and I are going to see who they got," and he started across the road. I tagged along, still curious about what Baker and the others had done and wondering if, indeed, Bowers was the man with the MPs.

So, pretending to be two soldiers just out for a midnight stroll, we crossed the road, strolled along the side of the barracks, and drew close just as one of the MPs was pushing their prisoner into the backseat of a jeep. At that close range, I had my answer. It was Bowers, the sergeant who had screwed me out of a safe assignment, in the rear, handcuffed and arguing at the top of his voice with the MP who shoved him. I gave a silent chuckle and walked up to the side of the jeep.

"What's the problem here, Sergeant?" I asked, walking up to the military policeman who looked in charge. He was filling out some kind of notebook, but glanced up and stopped when he noticed my rank.

"Nothing much, Sir," said the MP. "We're taking this man in. Caught him with drugs in his room."

"That so?" I said, looking over at Bowers, who at that point broke off yelling at the other cop and turned in my direction. I looked him straight in the face and said to the MP with the notebook, "Well, I guess you have to do your duty then, Sergeant. If our senior NCOs break the rules, they should pay the penalty. We need to set an example for the younger soldiers."

"Wait a minute, I know you," hollered Bowers, who tried to rise from his seat but was pushed back down by the MP next to him. "I do know you…." but I could tell from the look on his face that he wasn't certain about who I was.

"I don't think so, Sergeant. I'm not into drugs," I replied. "Now, for your own good, I suggest you just sit back and don't give these officers any trouble."

That did it. Somewhere in the deep recesses of his mind the lights turned on. "Hey! I do know you! You're that guy," he yelled! "What are you doing here? You're supposed—"

"What will happen to him?" I said, turning back to the MP and pretending to ignore Bowers.

"Don't know, Sir, that's up to the provost marshal. We got a tip he was selling it and found this stuff in his footlocker," replied the MP and held up a small white bag.

"That's a lie!" Bowers shouted, still trying to rise from his seat while being held down by one of the MPs. "I didn't put that fuckin' stuff…Wait a minute! You did it," he yelled, pointing at me! "You put that shit in my room! You're trying to frame me 'cause you got sent to the field!" And then he turned to the MP holding him and said, "Call Captain—"

I wasn't about to let it go any further, as the MP with the notebook was starting to give me a strange look, so I interrupted Bowers's ranting and said, "Don't make it worse on yourself, Soldier. You've got enough trouble already." And then I turned back to the cop and said, "Carry on, Sergeant, you've got your hands full. As for me, I've got a big date back here tomorrow, so I better get some rest." And I started back across the road, followed by Baker.

"You fucking shit!" screamed Bowers from behind as we walked away. I was sure he thought I was referring to the girl, which, of course, I was. It was all a bluff, but Bowers didn't know that.

From across the street we could still hear him shouting as they drove away. I figured he'd take one last look back at me, since he thought I was the person who set him up. I would have. Sure enough when he turned and looked, I was ready, having pulled one of the whores over and put my arm around her shoulders. I gave Bowers my best Aloha Smile and nodded at the fast-receding jeep. I was sure he appreciated the irony. I held on to her until they were out of sight and then pushed her away, before wiping off my arm.

If that seemed petty and vindictive, it was. But that was the reality of Vietnam, especially for infantry soldiers, who hung together in the worst of times. Everyone in my platoon had heard me complain about how I'd been assigned to the field by Bowers. None of them felt sorry for me, yet they helped to set him up. To them, it was simple. Someone had messed with a member of their unit and they were evening the score. Most likely, when interviewed, Bowers tried to make the MPs think I had planted the drugs in his room. But I had a great alibi, since a number of people had been around me all-day long. Anyway, I never heard anything more about the case, so I guess the higher-ups didn't believe what he said.

Bowers didn't have to worry about his girlfriend. I didn't have time for her. The next morning, our unit Stand down ended and we were sent north, to the small farming town of Qui Xuan, a few kilometers west of LZ Hawk Hill. I headed for the field that morning more relaxed than at any time since coming to Vietnam. Our assignment sounded simple enough, and after several weeks of the carwash and Chu Lai, I was well rested. I was certain my luck had turned for the better.

In some ways it had. We spent nearly a month in a small camp the army had built near a rock quarry, less than a mile from Qui Xuan. The surrounding area was wide open, with very little vegetation and small chance of anyone sneaking up on us. As a result, it wasn't nearly as stressful as regular field duty. There were five or six small buildings where we bunked and a multi-use place where we got served hot meals twice a day and saw movies on a small screen several times a week. It wasn't Chu Lai, but it wasn't bad duty for the 'Nam.

Each morning, I met with Mann and went over our platoon assignments for the day, and then spent my time lounging about, reading, playing cards, or talking philosophy with Grovich. I learned that Grovich had a good grasp of history and politics, as we often discussed the antiwar movement, civil rights, and the other causes that had impassioned our generation. They hadn't impassioned me, of course, as my passions have always been turned on by more traditional methods. But my time spent with him did help to make the days go by faster.

It was during our talks at Qui Xuan that I realized Grovich didn't really believe in the war. I had thought from our first meeting that he was not the combat type, and he confirmed it at Qui Xuan. Grovich believed strongly that his country was a positive force in the world and had voluntarily gone to Officer's Candidate School while in college, receiving his commission as an army officer upon graduation. But after nearly four years of active duty, and just two months in Vietnam, Grovich had clearly lost the passion for military duty. He often spoke of returning to Kansas to settle down and teach elementary school. As a scholar, he definitely felt out of place in the infantry, but what could he say? The stupid ass had volunteered for combat. He was in a hell of his own making and he knew it.

Our assignment at Qui Xuan was to guard two bridges on the country's main north-south highway and also the rock quarry, which was used for military construction. Protecting the bridges made sense. If they were blown up or damaged, traffic along the critical route would have curtailed. But the rock quarry was another story. It seemed like we were just guarding a bunch of rocks. It wasn't like Charlie was going to steal them. Or blow them up, for that matter. But no one complained. It was easy duty and each day that passed brought us one day closer to going home.

Grovich rotated the platoons so that they took turns guarding the three different sites. One of the bridges was within shouting distance of the quarry, so in case of trouble, we could reposition support fast. But the second bridge was more than a mile farther down the highway. The platoon watching over that site could only count on a nearby ARVN unit for help in case of an attack, which meant they were pretty much on their own.

As an officer, I didn't have to pull guard duty. Late in the afternoon just before sunset, I toured the five or six bunkers assigned to our platoon to make sure everyone was in place, and then retired to my bed in a small shed. Bryson, as my RTO, and Mann, as our First Sergeant, also had cots there, but Mann rarely slept in his. He preferred spending the night out in the bunkers, looking after the troops and trying to be one of the guys. I thought he was stupid, but said nothing since it justified my ability to sleep comfortably at night.

The village of Qui Xuan would have been a truck stop in one of our big western states—a main street with an open-air market and a half-dozen stores, maybe fifty thatched huts and rice fields in all directions. The people were the same as in every other Vietnamese town—mostly old folks who ignored us or children who ran after us. There was a carwash, too. I stopped by for a look-see several days after we arrived but held on to my money. The women were so bad I left them for the other guys.

I had better luck in the marketplace, when I stopped to check out a vegetable's girl's melons. She couldn't have been more than seventeen years old, but then I was only five years her senior. We flirted with each other for about ten minutes. I got her to laughing by making strange sounds and fondling her tomatoes and bananas, while she made gestures with her eyes and spoke softly as I touched the fruit. Neither of us understood what the other was saying, but we managed to communicate. When I brought out two oranges from my rucksack that had been delivered earlier that day as part of a rations shipment from the rear, her eyes widened. Oranges didn't grow in Vietnam's heat and were considered a delicacy. She took the oranges from me and held them up to her chest, smiling and making it plain she was willing to trade. We ended up in the back of a nearby shack while some little boy, possibly her brother, watched the vegetable cart. I would have gone back for more, we had plenty of oranges, but it was soon after that when I met Suzie.

Suzie was a so-called Coke girl, someone who rode around selling cold sodas and beer from the back of a bicycle. Amazingly, they sometimes balanced upwards of four cases of drinks, encased in dried ice, on their bikes. And the more enterprising ones were mini-lunch wagons, with rice cakes and *banh da* cookies on the side. Coke girls, and sometimes Coke men, had regular routes planned so they could maximize sales from American soldiers working in their neighborhoods. When they showed up on their routes, we always stopped what we were doing to have a cold drink in the shade.

The beer and sodas were all black market, probably sold to the Vietnamese by our own people up the line somewhere. We paid an outrageous price to buy it back—as much as five bucks for a soda—but we didn't care. The bottom line was: the Coke girls regularly got cold drinks out to the field where it was often above ninety degrees hot, something our own supply guys had a hard time doing. We could have saved money by refusing to pay their high rates, or just took the drinks from the girls by force. But that would have meant cutting off the supply, which would have been stupid. Besides, we didn't have anything else to spend the MPC money on anyway, so we just paid the high price. At least, we almost always paid it.

My association with Suzie began one evening on my way back to the compound when I chanced upon a commotion involving her and three GIs. As I approached the rear gate to our camp, my attention was drawn off to one side by the sound of someone yelling. I looked over and saw a soldier, about thirty feet away, holding a young woman from behind by her arms and laughing at a small mongrel dog, which was darting in and out and yapping its head off. Nearby, a bike lay on the ground with what looked like some kind of food and drink cans scattered about. Two other soldiers, also laughing, were having fun pouring cans of some kind, soda or beer, onto the ground. The woman, who I figured was a Coke girl, was kicking and screaming, but could only watch in frustration as her inventory flowed away in the dirt. I muttered something to myself and kept on walking as I had no intention of getting involved, but then the girl yelled out, "GI help! GI help!"

Instinctively, I looked in her direction and saw that she was short, with a round face, and somewhat more plump than most of her countrywomen; nothing special by my standards. But the look on her face got to me. She was desperate and pleading for help. Call it your "damsel in distress complex," but it was one of the rare times in my life I made someone else's problems my own. Besides, I didn't recognize the three soldiers, which meant they were not from my platoon and undoubtedly lower in rank.

So I strode over and, between dog yelps, asked one of the soldiers holding the girl, "Aren't you boys going a little too far?"

"Butt out, Lieutenant," said the soldier in an insolence manner. "This bitch is ripping us off, so we're teaching her a little lesson." The girl also tried to say something, but I held my hand up and motioned for her to keep quiet, which she did, although she continued to stare hard at my face.

"Kind of hard to butt out when you're pouring my drinks on the ground," I replied. At that, the two others, who were emptying cans on the ground, stopped their labor and looked at me.

"Your drinks?" asked one.

"Yeah. Actually, they're the Third Platoon's drinks. We're having a party today and this girl was supposed to supply the beer and soda," I said matter-of-factly. "'Course, now I don't...."

"Well...." said the big talker, loosening his grip on the girl, "we didn't know about no party. We just got tired of paying for our own beer. You know, this stuff's supposed to be ours and this bitch is—"

"Yeah, I know," I interrupted. "It's a raw deal, having to pay for beer that we should get for free. But it's better than nothing. You know where else we can get cold beer all the time?"

"Well.... the other girls—" he started.

"Won't bring anything after they find out what happened to her," I interrupted, "unless we stop this girl from talking somehow."

"Christ, Lieutenant. We can't shoot her," cried one of the others, looking at the girl, who obviously understood what we were saying and was suddenly more frightened than angry.

"Yeah," I thought out loud. "Well.... then we better pay her for the stuff you poured out and hope she keeps her mouth shut. I'll tell Sergeant Mann the party's off."

"Sergeant Mann! Shit! Don't do that, Lieutenant," said the talker. "We'll take care of it. We'll get ya some beer and soda. No need to tell Mann." Like everyone else in the company, he knew Mann's reputation and had no desire to anger him.

"Well, okay, if you're sure," I said, and at that the big talker let go of the girl, giving her a small shove in the process, and the three of them walked off. Sure enough, a short time later, they stopped by our platoon with several cases of beer and soda. Mann wasn't there to greet them, but when he returned I told him we were having a party courtesy of the First Platoon, which he thought was great, especially as we hadn't been planning a party.

The girl, who went by the name of Suzie, got her money, too, and from that day on was my close buddy. Early each morning she came by on her bike to share breakfast, and every afternoon ended her route back at my position. We had only several weeks together, but in that time, Suzie became the best, if not the only, Vietnamese friend I made. In broken English, she introduced me to the food and customs of her people and kept me informed about things happening in the town. Before that, I'd paid little attention to the Vietnamese things around me, except certain women, of course. Thanks to Suzie, I learned enough about their culture that I could actually understand why they acted certain ways and could blend in with the Vietnamese much better than previously.

More than that, Suzie made me realize I had a gift for foreign tongues. I'd learned pretty good Korean in school years earlier when my Dad was stationed in Seoul with the air force, and I knew a bit of Spanish from college classes. But I never really thought of myself as any kind of linguist, until Suzie came along. She carried an English-Vietnamese dictionary around with her, and so, with nothing better to do, I started writing down frequently used words or phrases I learned from Suzie and then practiced them on the other Vietnamese working with the unit. I think it made quite an impression on her, as Suzie said I was the first American she knew who tried to learn her language.

By the time I left the rock quarry, I could understand lots of useful Vietnamese phrases and several hundred words, many of which I still recall. I don't say that I became fluent in the language, but after less than a month with Suzie, I knew more of the local lingo than anyone else in our unit. My advice to any young man (and old ones, too) wanting to learn a foreign language is to have an attractive female instructor. It's a great motivator that's helped me learn Japanese, Chinese, and even a bit of Arabic over the years.

In those late afternoons, Suzie and I spent most of our time together in a bunker on the far side of the compound nearest the quarry. The guys knew it was our hideout and left us alone. It was well they did because Suzie was a screamer. She was so loud the first time, I thought she'd rouse the whole camp. I had to stick a sock in her mouth to quiet her down. When I pulled it out, she gave a big smile and pretended to zip her mouth shut. Unlike Mai, who'd been a little too rough for my taste, Suzie was a pleasant lover. She cuddled and cooed and used her hands like a pro. Afterwards, she always took the time to wash me down with a wet rag and bring me a cold drink from her bike.

I suppose Suzie fell in love with me. She certainly acted like she did, always making sure I had food and drinks and told me repeatedly that I was the nicest man she'd ever known. There were times I noticed her just staring at me with a faint smile on her face, as though in a trance. Once, she handed me a small package that contained a photo of her, dressed nicely and standing in front of some kind of shrine. I felt sure she had arranged to have it taken just to show her feelings for me. Later that week I returned the favor, presenting her with a photo of myself standing in front of our bunker. Given our situation, I tried to treat her with respect and kindness. I think she was hoping I'd take her with me back to America, but as much as I liked her, there was no chance of anything permanent. We could relate well enough in Vietnam where we were both prisoners of the war in our own ways, but she would have been out of place in the states. Besides, at that age, marriage was the last thing on my mind.

I still have an old photo of the two of us, standing with men working in the rock quarry to our rear. She's clinging to me tightly with a mischievous grin on her face, while I've got her in one arm and my M16 in the other. On my head is the boonie cap, with a necklace of red and white love beads dangling around the rim. Suzie gave me the necklace and said it would protect me from danger as long as I kept it. Perhaps it has. I'm still here after twenty plus years, having had more narrow escapes from death than I care to think about. Somebody, or something, has been looking out for me. I wore the boonie cap, beads attached, at a parade of Vietnam Veterans just last year. I'm sure Suzie would have been proud.

During the first three weeks we were stationed at the rock quarry, it seemed like the war was far away. We never saw fighting and rarely had even a hint of enemy activity in our area. That may have been because there were several South Vietnamese military units stationed around Qui Xuan that helped guard the town and sent daily patrols into the countryside. I spent some time visiting the ARVN units with Grovich the first week we were there and I wasn't especially impressed. Although we'd shared guard duty with Major Ngo's troops tat Tam Ky, Qui Xuan was the first time we actually worked with the Vietnamese in the field.

The South Vietnamese had some excellent military forces, like the marines and rangers, who had distinguished themselves in numerous engagements. But those units were almost always down south near Saigon or on the Cambodian border, not up in our area. Up north, we had the regular ARVN divisions and local militias, which, while better than nothing, weren't always the most reliable partners.

The commanders in many of those units, like Major Ngo, were akin to the Chinese warlords of a half century earlier. Most of them were graduates of the Vietnamese military academy, but it was well known that appointment to the academy was often based on family or favors. As a result, some of the people who graduated from the academy were not really that knowledgeable or dedicated to their jobs.

Officers were usually assigned to the provinces where they grew up and were often given political responsibilities in addition to their military ones. As a result, division commanders, while having military clout, also could control government jobs, access to critical supplies like food and equipment, and even the ability for someone to travel in the provinces. It was immense power and, because of it, corruption was a way of life in many ARVN units. Promotions and assignments were frequently the result of political and family connections or bribes, with money and equipment going to those in favor, not necessarily those in need.

Like is often the case in Third World countries, the people at the very top were the most corrupt. There was an unspoken feeling that many of the top government and military people in South Vietnam had little faith in the future of their country and were just trying to grab as much money as fast as possible so that when the end came, they could flee the country. I only came in contact with the elite once during a trip to Saigon, so I can't really affirm that it was true, but everyone, from lowlife farmers to government bureaucrats, said the ARVN top generals bought and sold positions on a daily basis, often using wives and mistresses as "go-betweens," delivering promotion lists for bags of cash. At the end of the war, these same people could, and probably did, fly out with their families to the bank accounts they'd stashed away in Switzerland or Hong Kong. The guys down below weren't so fortunate.

Most of the troops controlled by these warlords were conscripted from villages within their own province. That was good because it meant local commanders had loyal soldiers, but it also meant they didn't like to risk them in big battles, because support in the villages could go away if casualties were too high. As a result, whenever one of the regular ARVN divisions got into heavy combat, they often pulled back and left the brunt of the fighting to the few national army divisions—or to us Americans.

There was even some suspicion that the ARVN worked closely with the VC when it fit their purposes. There were just too many times that American units walked into firefights while ARVN units, only a few clicks away, were untouched. Tran, our Kit Carson scout, told me once that the ARVN commanders always made two sets of orders whenever they were going to assault a location—one for themselves and one for the VC so no one would be there when the ARVN troops arrived. I still find that hard to believe, but Vietnam was a true civil war between fellow Vietnamese, so anything was possible.

Not surprisingly, morale was not that great in many South Vietnamese units. I never thought ARVN soldiers were cowards, but their training was poor, their equipment old, and their leaders inept. And, unlike us Americans who would return home after a year, they were in the war for the duration.

At the very bottom of the Vietnamese military pecking order were the Regional and Popular Forces, better known as "Ruff-Puffs" by us Americans. They were akin to our National Guard in that they were normally assigned to defend a particular village or province where they lived. But half of them didn't even have uniforms and the other half couldn't have shot their way out of a 7-eleven store. The only thing I ever saw them do exceptionally well was steal chickens and pigs from farmers in the small villages. That may be a biased opinion, as I read somewhere that more than eighty thousand Ruff-Puffs died during the war. Perhaps they did perform well in some parts of the country. But from my experience, a well armed L.A. gang could have wiped out every Ruff-Puff unit in our area of operations in less than a month.

I speak with some knowledge of the "Ruff-Puffs" because I got to witness their caliber up close. It happened during the fourth week at Qui Xuan, when my platoon's turn came to guard the bridge down the road. I had visited the site early in our assignment and wasn't comfortable with it. The bridge itself wasn't a problem. It was short, maybe fifty feet across, spanning a dry gulch that supposedly became a river during the monsoon season. But it was important because of its location on a main thoroughfare.

The problem defending the bridge was its isolation. Qui Xuan and the rest of our company was more than a mile away. If the bridge ever came under attack, it would take critical minutes for relief to come, even in the best of conditions. At night, along a dark road, it would take even longer because reinforcements, wary of an ambush, would travel much slower. And Charlie always attacked at night

We Americans guarded one side of the bridge from a fortified position that was about fifty feet across by thirty feet wide, surrounded on all four sides by five-foot high sandbag walls. The north-south highway ran along one side of the little fort, with a line of trees some fifty or sixty yards behind the road, while the creek, which was all it was during our time, ran along the opposite side. There were two reinforced bunkers in the camp, one at the corner closest to the bridge and one on the far opposite side. Inside this miniature stronghold, we had a few lean-tos for shelter from the sun and rain but not much else. Across the gulch, a Ruff-Puff unit stood watch on the other end of the bridge from a similar-sized camp.

All but a few of our platoon were assigned to guard the bridge at night, while during the day we rotated small shifts so that about half a dozen could stay back and relax near Qui Xuan. The platoon members guarding the bridge, in addition to their own personal weapons, were also armed with an M60s and a full complement of claymore mines. The "Pigs" were positioned in the two bunkers, so we could cover all four sides of the compound. Claymores were planted along the two ends of the camp, but not along the sides facing the highway and the stream. Of course, we also had our commo equipment to keep us in touch with Grovich and the rest of the unit back at the quarry just in case of trouble.

The Vietnamese on the other side of the creek were similarly armed; I made a protocol visit to their camp the first day and met some officer whose name I couldn't pronounce. They appeared to have about twice as many people as we did, but most of them seemed to be doing nothing but sitting in the shade while I was there, which didn't give me much confidence. I did notice the Ruff-Puffs had a mortar tube, which was some consolation, as that could mean additional firepower in case of an attack.

The first several days we guarded the bridge, I left Sergeant Mann in charge at night, while I stayed back at the main compound, safe in my bunk. Each afternoon I went out with the relief column to make sure things were okay, and then returned to Qui Xuan with the people coming off duty. I would have stuck with that routine, except about a week into it, Mann's R&R came through and he flew off to enjoy himself in Hong Kong. I had it in my mind to send another sergeant in his place, but Grovich made it clear that without Mann, my presence was needed at the bridge. So I gave up the comfort of my bed and spent the next few nights sleeping under the stars.

I mention the stars because, except for those few occasions when I didn't sleep alone, the nighttime sky was perhaps the most pleasant thing I remember about Vietnam. As a child, I'd gotten the astronomy bug when my father brought home a toy planetarium. My brothers and I spent many a night lying on our bedroom floor locating the Big Dipper, Orion, and other constellations. In the Vietnamese countryside, where city lights were scarce and the sky was clear, the stars spread like a blanket close above our heads.

It was fascinating for me because the pattern of stars in the Southern Hemisphere are different than what we see back home in the states. I'd seen the southern sky during my trip to Nigeria two years earlier, but that was only for a few weeks and the nights had often been overcast. But in Vietnam, I had plenty of time to lie on my back and look up at the dark sky above. It was like having the planetarium all over again.

My third night at the bridge started out like any other—quiet and clear with thousands of stars blinking down. The men were on four-hour shifts, six on duty at a time, with me and an RTO named Benson as reserve. Benson was filling in for Bryson, who had been called back to Chu Lai for some medical thing. I could hear laughter coming from the Vietnamese military camp across the river, where they were obviously having a good time. It was a sharp contrast to the stillness on our side, where the loudest sound was Benson slurping on some kind of fruit. It was all very tranquil as I lie on my back, looking up at the Southern Cross.

I may have dozed off, I'm not sure. I just remember being very much at peace when suddenly I felt a tremor in the ground, followed by a muffled explosion and someone yelling "Incoming." Instinctively, I grabbed my rifle and staggered to my feet, but hadn't gone three steps before I stumbled and fell to all fours, my head still groggy from lying on my back. I was down for only a few seconds, but in that time, the sound of someone painfully screaming came from the far side of the camp and I heard the unmistakable cracking of AK-47s mixed in with our own weapons.

I wiped the sleep from my face and rose back on my feet just seconds before another explosion went off. This time, chunks of dirt, mixed with pieces of what felt like fiber, perhaps clothing or parts of sandbags, fell around me like raindrops. "Shit, they've got mortars," I said loudly to myself. I knew only artillery rounds could make such loud impacts and cause dirt to fly up like that, and since the dinks didn't have any big guns, I reasoned they had targeted us with a mortar tube. That meant trouble. Our sandbag walls gave us some shelter from bullets towards the camp, but they were no protection from mortar rounds dropping in out of the sky.

I started running for the nearest sandbag embankment, with just one thing in mind—to get the hell out of that place. The rest could stay there and die if they wanted, but I'd take my chances on the outside, hiding in the dark until reinforcements came. In a few bounds, I reached the facade nearest the road and was headed over the top when I felt strong hands grab me about the waist and drag me backwards. I kicked back in an attempt to break free of the person gripping me, but lost my footing instead and crashed to the ground, pulling my assailant with me. I hit the ground with a hard thump, but fortunately kept a clear head. I came up fast to find myself facing one of my own men, who was himself getting up off the ground. "You stupid shit," I screamed. "We're all gonna get killed here."

My ferocity backed him up for a second, but then he pointed at the wall I'd just tried to mount and started to shout back. "But LT, they're over—" He never finished the sentence. One second he was standing directly in front of me, and the next, he was lurching violently up and to the side, twisting like a rag doll in midair before collapsing face down in the dirt. I cried out and fell back against the sandbags, my eyes locked on his body, which lay motionless on the ground. For long seconds, I crouched there, afraid to move and afraid not to. Then I turned and peered over the embankment into the dark where it sounded like the shot had come from. Seeing no sign of movement, I scurried over to the soldier's side and tried to prop him up, but dropped him right away. Then I threw up. The entire back of his head was gone, just brains and gore oozing out on the ground. He must have been killed instantly from a bullet round, and it happened while he was trying to keep me from going over the wall. He'd saved my life and died in the process.

A shudder ran through my body, causing me to slump forward on my knees, my breath coming loud and hard and my eyes fixed on his dead body. I'm not sure how long I slouched there, probably not more than a few minutes, but long enough for another explosion in our perimeter that blew me back to my senses. I grabbed around for my rifle, which was lying a few feet away, and then crawled back against the sandbags to take stock of the situation. What I saw wasn't reassuring.

The bunker on the far side of the camp must have taken a direct hit from the mortar and was a shambles. I couldn't see clearly all of the damage, but it was obviously torn to pieces, and the three men manning the bunker, along with their M60 machine gun, were gone. Across the way, close to the wall facing the creek, I could see two bodies on the ground and to my left another lay sprawled out, in addition to the soldier near me. The machine gun in the fortification nearer the bridge was active, cracking away at something in the dark, and I could see other soldiers in my platoon crouching and shooting over the wall from several locations. But that was it. Counting the soldier at my feet, it looked like we'd lost at least a half of our group.

It was a desperate situation. Under bombardment and possibly surrounded, we could die from the mortars if we stayed put and be shot by the dinks if we tried to leave. Our only hope was reinforcements coming from the company area. They were at least a mile away but would have surely heard the explosions and gunfire. *If we can hold out long enough, they'll come to our aid*, I thought, and then I remembered Benson and the radio. He would certainly have reported our position and called for help the moment the shooting started, which meant Grovich probably already had the unit on its way. We just had to stay alive until they got to us, and the best chance of that, I reasoned, was for the remainder of our platoon to stay together in a group so we could best defend ourselves.

With that thought in mind, I crouched low and sprinted to the remaining machine gun position, diving in head first and bowling over one of the occupants with the force of my arrival. He screamed profanity as he fell over me and I felt the other defenders jump back in alarm. "Don't shoot!" I roared. "It's me, Loveless!"

"Shit, Lieutenant, you wanna get killed?" came a familiar pissed-off voice. It was Tex, the cold-blooded killer who I'd crossed months earlier on the day of Prion's death. We didn't have much love for each other, but I was glad to have him around just then because he was a real fighter.

"Yeah, that's why I volunteered for this place," I said, getting up off the ground. Once up, I took a look around my new surroundings and decided it wasn't all that bad. The bunker was in the corner of the camp closest to the bridge. It comprised a space about five feet by eight feet, with high sandbag walls all around, except for the entrance facing back towards the center of the camp that I'd just tumbled through. It offered pretty good protection from small arms and we had a working M60 that would keep help the gooks off our backs for a while. The other two soldiers in the small bunker—Frankowsky, a Detroit boy, and a Corporal Brown—weren't killers like Tex, but they were grunts. And they were armed.

"What're we gonna do, Lieutenant?" asked Brown, looking more nervous than I felt.

"First thing, let's get the others in here with us," I answered, suddenly feeling more confident of staying alive. "Frankowsky, you go and tell the rest of them to get back here. And have 'em bring all the ammo they got. And be sure to find Benson. We need that radio."

He hesitated for a moment. Then Frankowsky slipped out of the bunker and vanished in the dark. I turned back to Tex, who was staring out towards the bridge. Visibility was limited to no more than twenty or thirty feet, but between us and the bridge was open ground, which made it hard for the enemy to sneak up, and the walls of the bunker were solid. "We'll be fine in here, so long as we don't take a hit from that mortar," I stated to no one in particular.

"The mortar is over there," said Tex, pointing to some flatland east of our position. "I don't think they got a spotter. They hit us first a couple times, and then tried the bridge, but missed. The last couple rounds have been closer to the ARVN's camp. They're all over the place."

I looked in the direction he pointed to, and sure enough, after a few seconds, I saw a flash of light in the distance, followed shortly by an explosion near the Ruff-Puff camp across the way. Tex had it right. The dinks had lined up the mortar during the day and were just spacing their rounds in a pattern. Their gunner was shooting in the dark and most likely didn't even know what damage he'd caused. Even so, he'd hit our place hard, taking out one of our two bunkers, and their last round had fallen directly on the other camp.

"Well, better them than us," I answered, referring to the camp across the river. "When we get the radio we'll call in some artillery and shut that thing down," I added, hoping that Benson would soon join us. But it wasn't to be that easy. Soon after, Frankowsky returned with four others in tow, but no Benson.

"Where's the RTO?" I queried.

"Dead, Sir," said one of them, pointing across the camp. "He took one in the back over there."

"And the radio?"

"No good, Sir. We tried. The round went through it. Couldn't even get static," he said.

"Damn! We needed that radio to call in fire support! We've got to stop that mortar," I said in a tone of sheer frustration!

"The Puffs have one," said Tex. "Maybe they already called for redleg?"

"I wouldn't bet on it," I answered. "The closest artillery base is Hawk Hill and that's American. They probably figure we're calling for support. So we just have to hope that mortar keeps shooting at their side of the bridge—that is, unless one of you wanna go ask if we can use their radio."

"I don't mind," said Tex, looking me straight in the eye, "it's better than just sitting here doing nothing."

You meet them every once in a while—men who're willing to die just for the chance to be a hero. I've known more than a few in my years in the army, and each time, I've wondered how such neurotics could stay unnoticed for so long. Don't get me wrong. I have the utmost admiration for bravery. No one respects heroism more than a coward like me. But it's one thing to be courageous in battle and another to get your ass blown off just trying to show how tough you were.

"Right," I said to Tex. "You'd be dead before you got halfway to the bridge! Maybe you haven't noticed, but we're surrounded!"

"Well, maybe we are and maybe we aren't," he answered arrogantly. "Yeah, we've been taking fire from all sides! But I think it's only three or four dinks moving around out there! It's all single fire, like one guy! No sustained shots, nothing heavy! Besides, if there's so many of them, why don't they just come in and overrun us? It's easy to see we don't have much left here! Let me try! I can make it over there!"

He was insane, of course. I wouldn't have tried to go over to that ARVN camp just then for all the money in the world. But he did have a point. Why hadn't they charged us? Anyone could see we didn't have that much firepower. And, if he were right—that there weren't many of them—then, unless the mortar hit us, we had a good chance of holding out until daylight or until Grovich and the others came to our rescue. I still believed in my heart that the rest of the company must have heard the gunfire and were headed our way.

But the more I thought about it, the more comfortable I got in letting Tex make a run for the ARVN camp. If he made it, then we'd get our hands on a radio and have a shot at shutting up the mortar. Even if he didn't make it, we would only lose one man and the rest of us still had a good chance of holding out against a small group until help arrived. That meant Tex was expendable. *Why not let him try for the radio?* I thought. "Well, I don't want to order anyone to go, but if you think you can get to the other side and—" I began.

"I'm outta here," he cried, and he began stripping off his helmet and M60 ammo bands. Then he rolled down his sleeves, blackened his face with dirt, picked up his rifle, and said, "Cover me. I'll be back as soon as I can," just before sliding over the wall and fading away in the night.

I expected to hear a burst of gunfire any second, signaling the end of good ole' Tex, but the seconds went by and then the minutes, and I began to think the psycho had actually made it to the other side. I stared into the night anxiously, hoping to see the area around the mortar tube explode from artillery fire, but when nothing happened after more long minutes, I started to have second thoughts. I was sure something had gone wrong and the others felt it, too.

"Maybe he got caught," said one of the troops.

"No, we'd have heard shots if he was caught," said another. "He's over there trying to get the Ruff-Puffs off their butts."

Or maybe he got smart and he's run off and left us on our own, I thought to myself, just as a volley of gunfire illuminated the area to our front, causing me to instinctively duck down below the wall. Outside I heard shouting in the distance, followed by the zinging of bullets over our heads and the sound of more shots.

"Those are AKs," said one of our group, which meant Charlie was doing the shooting.

Then someone yelled "It's Tex," and I looked out to see a figure running out of the dark towards us! It *was* Tex! Bobbing and weaving like a fullback, he came sprinting across the open space between us and the bridge. Behind him we could see shadows moving and the flashes of guns as they tried to bring him down. I was amazed at how fast a big man like him could run (although I've set a few land speed records myself with death on my heels), when someone yelled, "Cover him," and we began blasting away at the flashes. I doubt we hit anything, but it gave them pause, and that was enough to let Tex come scrambling over the wall back to our little group. He dropped exhausted at our feet, trying to catch his breath while two of the guys groped at him to see if he was hit.

"I'm okay. I'm okay," he said, waving them off. "Lieutenant?"

"Here," I answered. "What about the radio? Did you get across? Did you talk to the Vietnamese?"

"They're gone," he replied, still panting.

"Gone! What d'ya mean gone?"

"Just that," he said, starting to catch his breath. "I got across. Right up to their camp. But no one's there. I could smell tea still cooking and there was a dog sniffing around, but the place was empty. Nobody home."

"A whole company of soldiers doesn't just disappear," I said, incredulous.

"Well they did, Lieutenant. I think them fucks just di-di-maued as soon as the fighting started."

"Shit! And took their radio with them, I suppose," I griped.

"Who knows? I didn't bother with an inspection," said Tex. "I headed straight back here. When I passed close to the bridge, I saw six or seven gooks standing around. So I stayed down and watched. After a few minutes, most of 'em headed off for the ARVN side. But two of 'em stayed. I crept up real slow and saw 'em trying to tie these under the bridge." He held up two battered bags. They were satchel charges, the closest thing the dinks had to plastic explosives. "Figuring to blow it up, I guess. So I zapped 'em and took these and lit out for here. Just a few steps ahead of the posse!"

Well that took it! The Ruff-Puffs had run off and left us alone to guard their stupid bridge! We had no radio to call for help, and now the VC, having just seen our gunfire, knew the rest of us were in one location. It wouldn't take much for them to concentrate their attack on our position.

"We're outta here! Grab your stuff," I said, starting for the back door to the bunker.

"Where're we going, Lieutenant?" asked Frankowsky.

"Don't know. But if we stay here, we're dead. Charlie knows where we're at and that there's not too many of us. It's just a matter of time before he zeroes in with that mortar or gets close enough to lob in a grenade. I don't plan to wait around for that. We're better off trying to escape in the dark up the road to the quarry."

"It seems to me we should stay here, Lieutenant," piped up Tex, apparently recovered from his run, and quick to be a voice of dissent again. "I only saw four or five other dinks out there. No way they're gonna take us if we stay put. And the mortar's for shit. It's just luck if it hits us. This is the safest place in the camp. If we go out in the open, even one guy can take us down."

"You stay here if you want," I answered. "I don't like the feel of this place. Anyone else feel lucky like Tex?"

Well they didn't, of course, and since I was the officer, they took up their gear and followed me out the door towards the far side of the little camp. Not wanting to be left alone, Tex trailed behind. It would be easy, I figured, to go over the back wall and escape in the dark. The dinks would think we were still in the bunker and would concentrate their efforts there. By the time they figured out we were gone, I hoped, we'd be far up the road.

To this day, I still think we'd have made it safely out of that place, if there hadn't been so many of us. I've snuck out of plenty of tight spots, but almost always by myself or with one other. Eight fully armed men was another story. None of us carried our packs, only weapons and ammo, but we clanked and scrapped along the ground with every step across that camp. I kept trying to shush them up, but a brass band couldn't have announced its presence much better than we did that quiet night.

Still, we got to the other side of the compound and even climbed over the sandbag wall and dropped down into open ground beyond before Charlie opened fire. I was one of the first over the wall, and had gone no more than a few steps, when I heard the guns cracking and the sound of bullets zinging by and thunking into the sandbags behind me. I flattened myself to the earth, bawling with fear and frantically searching for someplace to hide. But there was nothing, just open ground to both side and the flash of Charlie's guns from our front.

Caught in the open, the men from my platoon who had already come over the bunker wall were desperately trying to fight back. To my left, I saw two of them shooting from the prone position, while behind me several others huddled with their back against the sandbags. At least one was already dead, a few feet away, and as I watched, another slammed back into the sandbags and slumped to the ground.

I was terrified, but had enough sense to know it was death to stay put. Staying low to the ground, I crawled backwards towards the wall, yelling at the others to follow. Once close, I jumped to my feet and scampered up the outside of the sandbags like a monkey. I hit the top in a flash and was almost over when something smashed into me from the rear, throwing me in the air. I crashed to the ground with a thud and came up screaming, my left shoulder in agonizing pain and blood oozing down my arm. I ripped open the bandage pouch on my pistol belt and started fumbling with the contents, sobbing out loud, "Oh God, oh God, oh God!" My left arm seemed to dangle helplessly and, with only the right, I couldn't get the damned bandage out of its wrapping.

I was trying to tear the package open with my teeth, when suddenly, someone was there was, taking it from my hands. "I've got it, I've got it, just hold still," he yelled, and in seconds he was wrapping the bandage around my shoulder in quick, strong, circular movements. "You'll be fine. It just scraped your shoulder." I recognized him as Brown, who I'd previously thought of as a weak soldier. Perhaps he was, but he knew his business with a dressing. In a flash he was tightening it with a final tug, and then, with a "Come on," he ran back to the fight.

I shifted my position on the ground to look back at where he'd gone. What I saw was Tex standing inside the wall, firing an M60 machine gun out into the dark, with Brown beside him, feeding rounds. One other soldier lay between them and me, facedown on the ground. The rest were still outside the camp, I guessed, fighting for their lives.

I looked anxiously for my rifle, but it wasn't there as I'd dropped it when I got hit climbing over the wall. With an effort, I got to my feet and headed for the security of the other two, my left shoulder throbbing with every step. As I passed the dead soldier, I stopped long enough to pick up his rifle and then joined Tex and Brown at the wall.

I leaned up against the bunker wall, rested my gun on top, and surveyed the scene. It was just as I'd left it just a few minutes past—a killing ground. Several motionless bodies were visible in the dim starlight just outside the wall—the men left behind when I'd bolted back into the camp. But that was all. There was no one shooting from the other side of the wall where our guys should have been, and I couldn't see any flashes from Charlie's guns, which meant they weren't shooting at us anymore either.

Tex and Brown were only a few feet away though, still laying down a stream of bullets into the night. I grabbed Tex by the arm and yelled, "Stop! Stop for a minute!"

He threw off my grip and kept on firing, so I grabbed him again and pulled him towards me. "Stop! What are you shooting at? There's nothing there!" I yelled.

He turned on me with the look of a man gone berserk and hollered, "What the fuck are you doing?"

"Listen, just listen for a second," I screamed back and pointed outside, "they're all gone!" This time, I got through. The glare went from Tex's eyes and he turned and looked out at the dark. It was eerily quiet.

"Where'd they go?" asked Brown in a frightened voice.

"I don't know," I answered. "Maybe they're just staying down. Or maybe they're trying to get around behind us." I turned to look at the empty camp to our rear, but saw nothing there. "I only know they're not shooting from over there anymore."

"Frankie, Frankie," Tex shouted out into the night, but no reply came. Then Brown yelled some other name that I don't remember, and again there was no response. Just silence.

"They're all dead," I said solemnly. "We're the only ones left."

"Jesus, sweet Jesus," cried Brown, suddenly finding religion.

"We've gotta get back to the bunker. It's the safest place now," I said, turning to move back across the camp, while trying to ignore the pain in my shoulder. Brown and Tex held back for a few seconds, still looking over the wall. Then they followed, lagging behind.

This time we went across the camp faster than before, but not fast enough. Halfway to the other side, gunfire exploded from the wall to our left. Bullets streaked past, one coming so close to my face I could smell it. I saw Tex stagger and fall to his knees, just before I dove in a slit trench and buried my head, face-down. While the sounds of guns reverberated above, I lay there in the muck, quivering from head to foot, sure that my death was seconds away. Yet somehow, I was able to poke my head above the rim of the ditch, and that probably saved my life.

Brown was still fighting, some ten feet away with his back towards me, kneeling over Tex and firing the M60 towards the wall. For the time being, he seemed to have the upper hand, because no one was shooting back in our direction; the heavy fire from the machine gun probably kept the dinks down. It was too good a chance to pass up. *You'll be rewarded in heaven, my son*, I thought, and away I went for the back of the camp as fast as my legs would move. Brown could be a hero if he wanted; Frankie Loveless was getting out of that hellhole.

But nothing went right for me that night. I hadn't gone twenty steps when my feet got tangled up in something, causing me to stumble and fall to my knees with a clank. I reached down to get free and found I'd snared myself on one of the leather pouches full of explosives that Tex had brought back from the bridge. He must have dropped it on our first trip across the compound. I pulled it off and started to throw it away, but a voice from somewhere deep inside made me pause. I looked down at the pouch, then back in Brown's direction, then in the direction of the bridge.

At that moment, I knew what had to be done—the bridge had to go! If it was blown, I reasoned, those killers would go away and leave me alone. After all, I reasoned in desperation, they'd come to blow up the bridge, not get in a big fight with us. Perhaps I was mad with terror. Certainly, I would be called a coward and a traitor if anyone ever learned what I'd done. But that didn't matter. Only one thing was clear in my mind just then—it was a choice between the bridge and me—which meant the bridge would soon be history.

I threw the satchel charge across my shoulder and stole along the shadows at the back of the camp. I wanted to get as close as possible to the bridge before going into the open to reach that cursed span. Behind me, I could hear Brown still engaging the VC. If he could keep their attention long enough, I thought, the night's horror would soon be over.

Indeed, my plan might have worked, but I never got the chance to find out. I was almost back to the bunker that eight of us had left only a short time before, when a deafening explosion blasted me off my feet and sent me skittering across the ground. Debris fell around me like rain and I choked on a thick dust swirling in the air. How I kept consciousness, I'll never know. My eyes went black, my head was ringing, and now in addition to my shoulder, my right leg hurt like hell.

For a few seconds, I thought I'd been blinded, but that fear faded as my sight slowly returned. I wasn't so lucky with my leg. Through teary eyes, I saw at least three small shrapnel wounds. I tried to pull my knee up to get a closer look, but the pain was so great I cried out and fell back. Tears welled up in my eyes and I began to sob again, partly from the burning in my leg, but also from the knowledge that I couldn't even run away anymore.

I groped along the ground on all four, coughing at the dust, trying desperately to find a place to hide. But it was hopeless. The bunker was a mess, literally demolished by the explosion, and the outer wall around it was blown away in all directions, leaving scattered sandbag remains and nary a shadow of shelter. I put my forehead to the ground and sobbed in despair, when I heard a scrapping sound from my rear. I held my breath and twisted around to see an armed man standing there just a few feet away, looking down at me.

He wore black pajamas and held an AK-47 in one hand and was waving some kind of paper in my face with the other. Certain I was a dead man, I slowly raised my hands above my head and forced out the words, "Don't shoot! Please! I give up! Please!"

He seemed to pay no attention and instead walked forward, grabbing my left wrist and pushing the paper in my hand. "*Chieu Hoi*," he said, and repeated it several times while looking back over his shoulder as if looking for someone else. "*Chieu Hoi. Chieu Hoi.*" I guessed he was looking to see if there were any more of his kind coming up, and only then, when he looked to the center of the camp, did I realize the M60 had gone quiet. Brown was no longer fighting, which meant he was most likely dead. That meant I was the only American left alive.

With survival in mind, I answered, "Yes! Yes! *Chieu Hoi*! I give up!" I pushed myself up on my haunches. As I did, I took a close look at the paper.

It was yellow, the size of a dollar bill, and it had the flag of South Vietnam printed on one side with the words "Safe-conduct pass to be honored by all Vietnamese government agencies and allied forces." I flipped it over and saw on the back a photo of President Thieu of South Vietnam and similar wording. Then it came to me what he was saying and trying to do! "*Chieu Hoi*!" I said out loud. "*Chieu Hoi*! That means you want to surrender to me!"

"GI Number One," he said, kneeling down in front of me and flashing the "V" sign, and then said again, "*Chieu Hoi.*"

I'd learned about the *Chieu Hoi* program during my in-processing and hadn't given it a thought since. I knew that it was an amnesty program we Americans dreamed up a few years earlier to get the Vietcong to defect to our side. I'd been told that Tran, our Kit Carson scout, was a former *Chieu Hoi* person, but other than that, I'd never given it a thought. All any VC had to do was come forward with a *Chieu Hoi* leaflet and agree to stop fighting the South Vietnamese government and they would receive a cash bonus and get resettled in some distant province where they could start life anew.

We dumped thousands, maybe millions, of the *Chieu Hoi* leaflets by air over enemy controlled areas, urging the Vietcong to surrender. We poured so many of them over the jungle, it was said, that Charlie started using them as toilet paper. To stop that activity, I had heard, our side began dipping them in acid before dropping them over the woods.

Supposedly, some 150,000 Vietcong came forward during the war to switch sides under the *Chieu Hoi* program. At least those were the official numbers. The word was, Charlie would turn himself in, take the government's money, have R&R for six months, and then go right back to fighting for the Cong. I remember Tran saying he knew one guy who'd changed sides four times.

Needless to say, I was somewhat skeptical about the character standing over me as I was obviously helpless at his feet. A bullet had gone through my shoulder, my leg was riddled with shrapnel, I'd lost my weapon, and here was this gook who was trying to surrender by waving a piece of paper in my face. But he was the real thing. He leaned down, put his arm around my back, and helped me to my feet. It must have been a strain on him as I was definitely heavier than he.

He practically carried me over to the demolished wall, propped me up against some sandbags, and started talking like crazy, all the while gesturing out towards the bridge. I knew a few words from my time with Suzie, but he was going way too fast for me to understand much that he was saying. I just nodded agreement, figuring he was trying to tell me something about how he was going to blow up the bridge. Of course, he didn't know I'd been trying to blow it up myself just a little earlier.

We couldn't have been there very long, with him blabbing away and me pretending to be interested, while struggling against exhaustion and pain. Then some kind of commotion from across the camp caught our attention. He turned and peered into the dark for a long moment, then faced back and said, "VC," as he took hold of my shoulders and helped me to lie down on my back. Then he rose to his feet, looked down, and repeated, "GI Number One," and motioned for me to stay put, before heading off across the camp. I watched him go, until he disappeared in the dark. Then I started crawling again. He might have been a real *Chieu Hoi*, but there was no guarantee he would return and I still needed someplace to hide.

I quickly realized that getting anywhere else was not that easy, as the wounds in my leg, while not serious, had gotten even more painful. Every time I dragged that leg forward, I let out a sharp gasp of anguish and struggled to keep conscious. Then, from somewhere on the other side of the camp, there was another explosion, followed by heavy gunfire and men yelling. It struck me that some poor sucker, most likely Brown, had been found alive and was making a last stand. Crippled and unarmed, I was sure they would find me next. "I can't die like this, not for some stupid bridge," I mumbled to myself just as another explosion went off somewhere. "No more, no more," I cried, finally giving up and laying down on my back to get one last glimpse of the stars above.

CHAPTER SEVEN

I don't think there's ever been a morning when I've woke up and been so surprised to find myself still part of the world. As consciousness slowly returned that next day, my first thoughts were of the night before. I had vague memories of being picked up off the ground and carried by someone, and later feeling a strong, pleasant breeze flow over my body and thinking, *So this is what it's like to die*. Well, I didn't die, but I must have been out of my mind and half-gone with pain when they found me. Who wouldn't have been after the night I'd gone through?

It was bright lights and the sound of voices that brought me to my senses. When I fully opened my eyes, I found myself in bed with a circular fan rotating slowly above and two faces, both American, staring down at mine. "How do you feel?" one of them asked, and I noticed then he was dressed in all white, like a doctor.

"Okay," I answered, somewhat hoarsely. "Where...?"

"Chu Lai. You're at the Chu Lai hospital, Lieutenant," he said.

"Am I, am I...." I started to ask. My leg felt strange, like not there at all, and I tried to rise up and look down at my body, but the effort caused a sharp pain in my shoulder, making me cry out.

"You're fine," said the medical-looking one, pushing me gently back down to the bed. "When they brought you in last night, you were pretty badly shot up. We pulled some iron out of your leg in a few places and patched up a hole in your shoulder, but there was no permanent damage. You'll carry some scars around, but other than that, you should be like new in a few weeks."

"My leg feels...."

"It's raw," he said. "You lost some flesh and some nerves were scraped, but no bones were broken. We tied it down so you won't roll over on it. Don't worry. You'll be up and walking in no time."

"Thank God," I murmured, truly relieved. If he was telling the truth, and I had no reason to doubt him, I had somehow lived through the bloody fight at the bridge. I felt a wave of relief wash over me and closed my eyes in silent prayer. I had survived! I was back at Chu Lai safe and sound, while so many others were dead, lying in the dirt of that awful place. But then it struck me! What about the others? Had any of them made it out alive? What about Tex and Brown? They were alive the last I'd seen of them, although Tex looked mortally wounded! For sure, I'd run off and left Brown—left him alone to fight the dinks. If he had survived and were to talk, it could be bad for me. The penalty for desertion in combat was…"The others," I pleaded, looking up again at the two strangers, "what about…?"

"You were the only one, Lieutenant," said the other man, who was dressed in regular army fatigues and somewhat younger than the one who had pronounced me okay. "Your unit was in a bad fight. Only you were found alive and brought here. I'm sorry, but the others didn't make it."

I shuddered with that thought and again shut my eyes in silent prayer. *Is it true?* I thought. *Are they all dead? Could I really be the only survivor?* It didn't seem possible, but it was confirmed the next day when the company sergeant major came to visit. He'd been at Baldy and missed the action, as usual, but he got the story of the firefight from the unit and relayed what he heard back to me.

Grovich and the rest of the unit back at the Qui Xuan camp had heard the mortar rounds exploding by the bridge and tried to raise us on the radio. Grovich didn't know, of course, that Benson had been killed and the radio damaged. But he couldn't get an answer on the radio, so Grovich roused the troops and got them on the march towards our position. Fearful of walking into an ambush in the dark, they moved slowly along the road—much too slowly, as it turned out.

By the time they arrived at our camp, the shooting had stopped. Nonetheless, still cautious of walking into a trap, Grovich split the company in two parts and entered the little compound from opposite sides. That's when they found four dinks, huddled in the middle of the camp, busy stripping gear off dead GIs, so busy they didn't notice the approach of our guys from two sides until it was too late. Rather than risk a crossfire that might have injured or killed some of our own men, Grovich ordered grenades thrown at the dink scavengers. The last explosions I'd heard were from those grenades, which killed the four VC.

With the enemy all dead, the unit looked around for survivors and found only me, badly hurt and, I was told later, going in and out of consciousness. The sergeant major said our firefight was big news in the division and described the memorial services that had been held that morning for the others. "It's very hard to lose so many good guys,' he said, "but we're all very glad you're still with us, Sir."

I could only nod in agreement.

Two days later, while propped up in bed reading a magazine, I got another visit. This time, a Brigadier General, who I guessed was one of the Division's deputy commanders, entered the room with a group in tow, including a full bird Colonel and several of the hospital staff.

"Well, young man," he said, briskly grabbing my hand, "how do you feel? You gave us quite a scare, you know?"

"I'm fine, Sir," I answered meekly, "just a little banged up." It was true. I was feeling much better than the first morning, but I stayed down on my back, thinking it was better just then to play a sympathetic role.

"I'll bet," he said, gripping my hand tighter. "You're the talk of the whole Division right now. You must have gone through hell the other night. You know, some of my staff are telling me we should name that bridge you saved in your honor."

That was something I never expected to hear, especially since at one point, I'd been actually trying to blow up the bridge. But only I knew that. Instead, I wisely answered back, "There's no need for that, Sir. The other guys gave their lives. They deserve the credit, not me. I was just lucky."

"You don't know how proud I am to hear you say that. And you're right. We'll call it the B Company Bridge," replied the General, turning to face the others. They shuffled their feet and nodded their heads in approval and I swear the Colonel looked like he was going to cry.

To this day, I can't understand how people can get so sentimental over a few words. The fact was I didn't want that stupid bridge named in my honor. It would have meant going out there again for some kind of ceremony and I didn't want to ever see that place again. The only thing I did want at that time was to extend my stay in the hospital. So I asked, "How long will I be here in recovery, Sir?"

"How about it, Doc?" asked the one-star general, looking back at one of the hospital staff, who'd been around to see me several times, always asking questions.

"You'll be up and around in a few days," he answered, looking down at me. "Your leg should be completely healed by then. You'll have pain in your shoulder for some time. That was a nasty wound. But just don't try to strain it too much and that too should be fine in time."

"Then I guess I'll be back with my unit soon," I said to no one in particular, with a solemn look on my face.

"Not unless you want to, Son," said the Colonel, speaking up for the first time. "You're twice wounded so there'll be no more field duty for you, unless you really want to go back out there?"

"That's right," echoed the General. "We've got a desk job lined up when you get back on your feet, so you'll finish your tour right here at Chu Lai. But that's not the biggest news! You've been approved for the Silver Star and you're going to receive it from the President himself!"

Those words nearly brought me upright in the bed and, dumbfounded, I asked the General, "I'm going to the States, Sir?"

He chuckled, looking at the others. "No, not quite. The President's coming here, to Vietnam. You're going down to Saigon in a few days to be part of a special awards ceremony. That is, if you're up and able to travel by then," he said, looking over at the medic.

The medic nodded and replied, "Should be no problem, Sir."

Well, that was big news all right, except the General got it backwards. For me, getting out of the field was the best possible thing anyone could have said. Having the President present an award was just a bonus. I wanted to shout with joy, but had the sense to keep my mouth shut. They were all thinking I was some kind of hero. If they'd known the full truth about my actions at the bridge, I might have been court-martialed. But they didn't, and I wasn't.

Three days later, I left the hospital with a slight limp and a still aching shoulder, but with spirits so high I hardly noticed the pain. I was escorted from the hospital by a soldier who introduced me to my new place of assignment, some kind of special correspondence office that handled congressional letters and other sensitive writings. I had lunch with the office boss, a captain who hailed from Pennsylvania, and was shown the Quonset hut nearby where I would have my own small room for my time off and sleeping. I did spend one night there, but I didn't start to work. That would have to wait for my return from meeting the President.

The following day, I flew to Saigon on a cargo plane, sitting once again on nylon strap seats and hanging on for dear life every time we hit air bumps. It was an uncomfortable but mercifully short ride. We landed at Bien Hoa, where I was met by a major who escorted me to the Caravelle Hotel. It was a big colonial-looking building in the center of town, made of faded white stone with large columns at the entrance and an elegant lobby that reminded me of the Royal Hawaiian Hotel back home. I had expected to stay in a barracks at one of the army bases, but since I was meeting President Nixon in a few days, the major said I got VIP treatment. And I wasn't the only one.

I'd thought it strange that the President of the United States would come all the way to Vietnam just to present me with an award. At the hotel, I learned that wasn't the case. Three other soldiers, who were already at the Caravelle, were also getting pinned by the President and several more were still on their way to Saigon from other locations in-country. All of us were being placed under the guidance of several army protocol people at the hotel. They were to instruct us on all the details involved with the awards ceremony and how we should act. During a short briefing, they explained that Nixon's trip to Vietnam had come about because the President had gone to the west coast a few days earlier to welcome back the Apollo 11 astronauts (Suzie and I had been making it in the bunker when they landed on the moon). Afterwards, he just kept going west to meet and discus world affairs with the leaders of several Asian counties, which undoubtedly included talking about the war in Vietnam.

Since Nixon was going to be in the area anyway, it was arranged that he would make a quick stop in the 'Nam to meet with the troops. The highlight of his short visit, all set up for the media, was to be a ceremony where he would recognize a bunch of us so-called heroes and, at the same time, of course, get some favorable news coverage.

The President wasn't due in Saigon for a couple more days, so the following morning, with nothing else to do, I took a stroll around town. Since I'd lived in a large Asian metropolis for three years as a teenager, when my father was assigned to Seoul, Korea, I expected to find a similar place. In some ways it was, with lots of street vendors and, of course, an Asian population. But Saigon was also quite different. While the feel of Seoul can be similar to big American cities like Houston or Chicago, Saigon seemed to me to be as much European as Asian. Built and named by the French, who occupied Vietnam for many years, it was more like a small town than Seoul.

I didn't see that many tall office towers, blocks of solid construction, or streets packed with automobiles like I did in Korea. Instead, the main streets were broad, tree-lined boulevards complete with street-side cafes, boutique stores, and bakeries. Side streets were considerably narrower, but likewise crammed with open markets and vendors hawking their wares, often fruits, vegetables, or flowers, from small tables or large wicker baskets.

There were plenty of automobiles and trucks in Saigon, but the main modes of transportation appeared to be motorcycles, bikes, and rickshaws. On several corners, I came across bike racks with upwards of a thousand parked bicycles. That shouldn't have surprised me, as the streets were packed with people walking about, mostly shopping or selling something. They had to get about somehow, and there were few on-street parking places. The population of Saigon was supposed to be about one and a half million at the time, and I believe it given the numbers I saw that day.

Despite the ongoing conflict, the people of Saigon struck me as open, colorful, and friendly. Instead of the drab grey or dark blues I had experienced up north near Chu Lai, the Saigon Vietnamese dressed in a variety of colors, often bright ones, especially the young women in their long, flowing *Ao-dais*. Moreover, everyone seemed overly gracious and good humored.

Even though I was a foreigner, I felt relaxed and accepted as I walked the streets. That may have been because the people of Saigon were used to having outsiders in their town. In fact, throughout that day, I must have come across several hundred non-Vietnamese shopping, eating in restaurants, or just walking the streets. About half were US soldiers. That was to be expected, but many other non-Asian-looking people were in suits or civilian clothes and not carrying weapons.

There were plenty of signs that a war was ongoing, what with policemen on all the main street corners and armed men in uniforms everywhere. But it was the one-legged men who caught my eye. I saw more of them that one day than I've seen over the rest of my life. They were pitiful, hobbling from place to place or sitting on street corners, hands out, begging for money. Seeing them reminded me of just how close I'd come to losing my leg not long before and, watching what they were going through, I decided then I'd rather go home in a box than as a cripple.

Given the history of Saigon, I expected French influence to be everywhere, and there were a great number of stores, restaurants, and even street signs written in French. But I was surprised to find Japanese trade names, like Sanyo and Honda, on billboards and buildings all over the city. In the early to mid-60s, "Made in Japan" was still sort of a joke back home in the States. We just assumed any product that came from Japan was cheaply made. That may have been an impression pushed on us by our own corporations, worried about the competition. Little did we know that in a few years the whole world would become familiar with the names of Japanese companies.

I walked about ten blocks that day, from the center of town all the way down to the docks that separated Saigon from its sister city of Cholon. The whole time, I had my eye out for young women. Given what I'd heard about the city, I hoped to be approached by prostitutes, but the only women who stopped me were elderly, trying to trade in their MPCs for Vietnamese money called Dongs.

From time to time MACV, our national military headquarters, would try to shut down the black market economy by issuing new MPC currency. The new stuff always had different design and colors, which made any prior-issued MPC worthless. It was no problem for us Americans. We stood in line and just traded in our old MPCs for the new stuff. But the Vietnamese weren't supposed to have MPCs. So they often ended up being stuck with the worthless paper unless they could sell it to an American. Somehow, the word was on the street that day that a currency change was in the air. I don't know how the dinks found out about something like that, since we weren't even told about currency exchanges until the last minute. But I figured what the heck and ended up trading less than a hundred dollars of Vietnamese Dong for more than a thousand dollars of MPC that day. I'd have bought more if I'd had more of the Dong.

About midday, I stopped for lunch at a restaurant that appeared to cater to foreigners, as their signs were in French and English and several soldiers were already eating inside. While there, I sat beneath an outdoor overhead canopy, only a few feet from the road, and witnessed a scene that has stayed with me for many years. Across the street from the restaurant, an old man sat on a small bench next to several large wooden cages that held colorful, noisy birds. A number of people walked past the old fellow and he ignored them, except for the foreigners, who he would engage in conversation, pointing at and obviously discussing his birds. The first few people he stopped appeared to listen politely, looked at the birds, and then moved on. But he persisted and seemed to hit pay dirt when two young GIs, probably not more than twenty years of age, ambled up. As with the others, he enticed them to his position and began to talk and point at the birdcage. The two soldiers listened to the old man for some time, and then one of them reached into his pocket and handed the vendor something, which I assumed was money.

I figured the soldier would walk off with a bird in hand, having bought one, but instead the old man reached in the cage, pulled out a bright red-feathered fowl and threw it up into the air. The bird fluttered for just a second, and then made a low circling motion before flying straight up in the air and disappearing out of sight above a nearby building. I watched until it was gone from sight and then glanced back at the old man and soldiers. The one who appeared to have paid for the bird gave the old man a pat on the back and walked off down the street with his companion. Only then did I understand what had happened. The soldier hadn't bought the bird—he'd bought its freedom. I chuckled to myself and went back to my meal, thinking how ironic it was that an American could buy a bird's freedom while he himself was trapped in Vietnam.

It was just by chance that I glanced up a few minutes later to see a bright red bird come swooping down from above, to land gently on the old man's outstretched arm. He reached up, stroked it, seemed to speak to the bird, and then placed it back in the cage, ready for the next customer. I watched for a few moments more and then headed back for my hotel, more determined than ever to get out of the 'Nam.

The next morning, they woke me and the other heroes early, had us put on new, starched uniforms, and flew us out to a base camp called Di An, about ten miles north of the city. It was the headquarters for the 1st Infantry Division and looked like a typical large army base, but with one big difference: there wasn't a Vietnamese in sight, not even a hooch maid. When I asked about it, our escort said it was just a precaution. The army was taking no chances with the President coming to visit.

They drove us to a small airfield where we were joined by several other soldiers, who were also to receive awards. There was also a small elite group of infantry troops standing by, who were to be the honor guard for the ceremony. Each of us awardees was interviewed by an army captain, who was apparently the person in charge of making sure the ceremony was conducted properly. When my turn came, I was surprised to learn that while he knew my name, he had no other information about my history in the 'Nam, including specifics as to why I was receiving an award that day.

"We were told the Americal was sending someone down," he said, "but not much more. I just got your name yesterday after you arrived in Saigon. We'd already planned the ceremony and had to add you at the last minute. So, your name's not in the official program, but don't worry, we'll have the citation all ready to go for the President." It was typical army planning as far as I was concerned, but I really didn't care whether I was a last-minute add-on or not. Main thing, I was out of combat and getting a prestigious decoration from the President himself.

The next several hours were spent standing around looking at each other, getting briefed repeatedly on the ceremony protocol, practicing getting pinned with fake decorations, and being told how to address the President, just in case he spoke to us. It was over-preparation, but not a surprise. I've been in hundreds of army ceremonies in my career, and for every minute spent on the actual event, triple that time was spent practicing for it. We all felt it was a little too much, but no one complained since the President himself was coming to take part. Still, when we finally heard that the President would soon be there, we were much relieved.

Even then it took another twenty minutes before a big helicopter, escorted by Hueys and Cobras, came in from the southeast and landed on Di An's runway off to our left. During that time, were we joined by several hundred more soldiers, all of whom lined up in formation facing an elevated platform, with us honorees standing in the front rank. We didn't wait long. A few minutes after the big chopper landed, out popped the President wearing a blue suit and striding forth in a fast pace. He was surrounded by the news media and so much military brass that I wondered who was at work running the war.

They put him up on the platform, which made him a good target for snipers, had there been any around. After we were brought to attention and gave the perfunctory salute, the President started into a speech about how we were fighting the most difficult war in America's history—as though we didn't already know that. I distinctly remember he said something about the American people not understanding why we were in Vietnam, at which the guy in formation next to me muttered something like "Neither do we." He probably spoke less than ten minutes, but in that sun it seemed much longer.

When he finally ran out of stuff to say, Nixon was escorted down from the stage to the formation and, while some adjutant read the orders and the media took pictures, he walked down the line with several of the military brass and presented the awards to the eight or nine of us. When my turn came, I stared straight ahead and tried my best to look serious, like a real hero, as they recounted my participation in the Battle of the Bridge. The President was handed a medal, which he clipped to my shirt pocket, and then, after taking my salute, he stepped back, shook my hand, and said, "Congratulations, Lieutenant. I'm sure your family is proud of you." I was barely able to utter a "Thank you, Sir," before he moved on to the next person in line.

As he did so, I glanced down and saw that the medal was indeed red, white, and blue in color, which meant it was a Silver Star, as I'd been told. I brought my eyes back to the front just as the adjutant began to read the citation for the next awardee and at that very moment felt the Silver Star slip off my shirt and heard it hit the tarmac with a loud clang. Instinctively, I stooped to pick the medal up, but one of the army coat hangers following the President beat me to it, pushing me back up and securely fastening it back to my uniform, while I went back to standing at attention. I'd been at ease long enough to see that Nixon had turned at the sound of the medal hitting the ground, and given me a strong, curious look before going on with the next award. I kept my eyes forward, but in my mind, I thought, *God knows I don't deserve it.*

I ran across that Silver Star a few weeks ago while rummaging through some old boxes. Even though some twenty years have now passed, it seems like yesterday when I stood across from Nixon. I've since received many military decorations, including one more in person from a President. But, coming so early in my career as it did, I suppose I value that one Silver Star more than the others. Still, I'd let it go for the right price. I mean, what can you do with military awards except impress other military types, and I'm beyond that now. Trouble is, no one seems to want Nixon souvenirs nowadays, so I guess I'm stuck with it.

After he'd pinned on the last award, the troops in formation were allowed to relax and gather around as the President, accompanied by about half a dozen cameramen, plunged into the ranks of soldiers wearing steel pots to shake hands and talk story. I wasn't more than a few feet away and heard much of what transpired, mostly lame conversation between a President and soldiers who had little in common with each other. For example:

President: "Where are you from, Son?"

Soldier: "Texas, Sir."

President: "Think the Cowboys can beat the Packers this year?"

Soldier: "I hope so, Sir."

President (to another soldier): "Where's your home, Son?"

Soldier: "Chicago, Sir."

President: "Have you seen the Cubs this year? Are you a Cub or White Sox fan?"

I hoped the guy would ask him how the hell he was supposed to see the Cubs play when he was stuck in Vietnam. But he did almost as well.

Soldier: "I'm a Yankee fan, Sir."

Then the President, seemingly buoyed by his success as a conversationalist, turned to a Black soldier and asked, "How about you, Soldier, where are you from?"

Soldier: "North Carolina, Sir."

President: "Do they ever get any black-eyed peas and collard greens out here?"

The Black, who was probably expecting another sports question, just stared back at him with a puzzled look on his face. Nixon may have realized he'd said something dumb and turned away without waiting for an answer, practically walking into me. For some reason, he bent down close, so no one else could hear, and said:

President: "How about you, Soldier? Where do you call home?"

Loveless: "Used to be Honolulu, Sir, now I'm from Chu Lai."

President: "That's nice. I'm from California myself. Keep up the good work."

And off he goes, probably thinking Chu Lai was somewhere in the southwest. He spoke to just one more fellow, a guy from San Clemente, before he boarded a jeep with the generals and Secret Service, who took him back to the helicopter.

Later on, Nixon was criticized for his conduct of the war, but at that point in 1969, it seemed to me he was on the right track. He'd started the Vietnamization Program and announced the first withdrawals of American troops after only six months in office. I was never his biggest fan, but I give him credit. At least Nixon tried to end the conflict honorably, and he actually went to the field and met face-to-face with the troops. When LBJ had visited the 'Nam three years earlier, he'd told the boys to "come back with that coonskin on the wall," but he didn't get out of Cam Rahn Bay, one of the largest and safest military bases in the country. At Di An, Nixon came as close as he could to the field without donning a rucksack.

Soon after the President left, we boarded our own chopper and headed back to the Caravelle Hotel. We were joined on the flight by a reporter from the army paper, *The Stars & Stripes*, who took our pictures and questioned us about our awards. It was my first time being interviewed by the media and, being young and cocksure, I spun a pretty good story about "just doing my duty," and how I could "hardly wait to get back to the field to rejoin my boys and finish the fight…" the kind of stuff I figured would be appreciated by the army higher-ups. At best, I thought if they even printed anything, it would rate a line or two in the next day's paper, nothing more.

The newspaper interview was already forgotten when later that night, one of the other awardees, a guy named Gil, and I hit the streets, ready to celebrate. I was in particularly good spirits, and why not? By the Grace of God I'd survived three months in combat, been awarded a Silver Star by the President, and now, for the rest of my time in Vietnam, I'd be on easy street at some desk job, servicing the hooch maids on a regular basis. I was looking forward to the rest of my tour. If I'd known that the worst was yet to come, I would have crawled under my bed in the Caravelle and never came out. But I didn't know, so off I went dumb and happy to enjoy the Saigon nightlife.

Gil and I hit a number of bars that evening, drinking and checking out the local stock, and were pretty snookered by the time we reached The Princess Nightclub. Two steps in the door, I knew we'd made our last stop. I remember a long bar at the back of the place, a small dance floor with a few women circling each other, and a dark room thick with smoke, loud music and more "hostesses" than I could count. They were all busy earning their keep by flirting with customers and getting them to buy shots of beer or tea for a few bucks.

With so many young men away at war, or dead, Vietnamese women were often the breadwinners for their families. Most of them stayed at home or worked in the family business, usually something small. But some of them chose the easy life, making a few dollars night after night while serving drinks to strange foreign men assigned to duty or doing business in Saigon. The girls all spoke broken English and were very friendly if they thought you had money. "Hey GI," they'd say, "You buy me drink? I no butterfly. I give you good time." But if you begged off, they showed a different side. "Hey what! You *Ba Muoi Lam*! You number ten!" Gil, who was an old hand at the Nam club scene, advised me to be patient until I saw someone I liked and then concentrate on that one. With luck, and some cash, he said, I might get laid. He was half right. It didn't take luck.

I'd heard about hostess clubs in my teen years when my family lived in Korea. In the years since Vietnam, I've learned that nearly every major Asian city has similar hostess clubs. Businessmen with customers to impress and large expense accounts frequent these clubs on a regular basis, sometimes spending thousands of dollars in an evening for food, drinks, and a little music. If that sounds like a colossal waste of money, you have to realize some of the biggest business deals of the last half century have been made in such places. Asian businessmen value personal relationships. Getting drunk together has often cemented some of the best friendships and business deals.

Over the past two decades, I've been in hundreds of these clubs all over the Orient and found that they are different in different countries. For example, the working women places like in Japan and Hong Kong are mostly hostesses, serving drinks and being friendly, but they are not hookers. The only way to get one of them to bed is with a lot of patience or an extreme amount of money. The same can't be said for poorer countries like Thailand and the Philippines where, with a little side cash to the club's mama-san, you can take a woman out for the night. That was the case in Vietnam during the war, where twenty bucks bought an all-nighter.

If I'd been smart, I would have avoided bar women that night. VD was rampant in Saigon, which reportedly had more than 50,000 prostitutes. Besides, with the possible exceptions of Suzie and Mai, I was never that attracted to Vietnamese women. With their small breasts and thin bodies, most of them were too delicate for my taste. But I was in exceptional high spirits that night and being smart when it comes to women has never been one of my strong points.

As it was, Gil and I found a wobbly wood table in a back corner of the Princess.

We were drinking our *ba muoi ba* and checking out the offerings when a fairly attractive young lady came up to the table and stood there looking me straight in the eye. The booze must have been having some effect because she looked exactly like a high school girl I once had a crush on, a beauty who once told me she'd rather date a slug than spend an hour with me. It's hard to deny fantasies when they're available three feet away, so I stared back and gave her my broadest smile. At that, she reached down, grabbed the front hem of her dress, and lifted it up to her neck. A supple, naked body stood before me, leaving nothing to the imagination except the shape of her shoulders.

"You like?" said a muffled voice from beneath the pulled-up dress. Well, I did, so I asked her to join us for a drink. Ten minutes later, introductions done, we were off to her place. I left Gil to pay the tab, which was near fifty bucks at that point, telling him I was just going outside for a minute. I figured to be long gone by the time he noticed he was stuck with the bill.

The girl and I didn't linger on the streets. We both knew curfew was approaching. While it probably wasn't the case most of the time, by law, anyone caught outside after 10 o'clock could be shot on sight, no questions asked.

She led me on a short but hectic march through several back alleys and past the front of a big holy looking building before we entered a plain three-storey apartment building with just minutes to spare. Once inside, I followed her up a narrow stairwell to the second floor, where we found her room in the middle of a long, dimly lit hallway lined with multiple doors. I was relieved to be there, as I'd begun to wonder if it had been the right thing to have followed her home.

On the way there, we hadn't seen more than fifteen to twenty people on the street, possibly because of the late hour. But several of the folks we'd passed had given me strange looks, as if surprised to see an American in that part of town. One had actually stopped in his tracks and watched until we went around a corner and out of sight. It made me nervous for sure. Although I had a knife tucked inside my boot, as was my custom when off post, I knew that wouldn't be much protection in case of real trouble.

Fortunately, we'd encountered no one inside her building, so the thoughts of danger went away once we entered her room. It was no more than eight by ten feet in size, with a bed, a small table, and a lamp near a window on the opposite side. A wooden chair leaned against the wall near the door and, in the corner, there was one of those portable closets that used to be popular in Asia, the kind that zipped up and had wheels on the bottom. The place wasn't much to look at, plus it smelled like a storage bin for dead fish. I wouldn't have lived there on a bet, but then she was a whore after all, in a city full of whores.

"Nice place," I said, trying to get her to relax.

"Tank you. I give beaucoup good time, GI, you see," she replied.

Figuring that was enough small talk, I lifted her up, plopped her down on the bed, pulled up her dress, and had one of those young boobies in my mouth before she had time to ask me if I wanted something to drink. I think it took her by surprise, because she gasped and gave out a squeal before settling back to enjoy the action. But she didn't relax for long. I was just starting to contemplate Miss Left when I felt a tapping on my shoulder and heard her saying "Wait, GI, wait!"

"Wait? Wait for what?" I cried. "I'm ready now?" And I was, too. After nearly two weeks without a woman, I was fit to explode.

"Take off laundry," she said, trying to rise from the bed.

"Laundry! What laundry?" I asked dumbfounded, at which she pointed to my uniform. "Oh, you mean take off our clothes? Well, yes. Yes. By all means." I sat up in the bed and began unlacing my boots.

She rolled off and knelt on the floor nearby, like mother's little helper, placing my boots in the corner and then neatly stacking my uniform on the chair. I made sure the knife was in one of the boots and was down to my green underwear when she rose to her feet and said, "GI, now I go bathroom."

"Bathroom?" I exclaimed. "You want to go to the bathroom now woman!"

"Please, *Tieu-uy*. No can help. Soon come back."

"Where is the bathroom?" I asked, somewhat annoyed and noticing for the first time there wasn't one in the room.

"In hall. I back soon. Please wait," and off she went, closing the door behind her.

I sat back down on the bed, facing the door and the chair, which held my clothes, and leaned back to wait. Suddenly, the door opened; she popped her head in and said, "You want something drink?"

"Drink? No! Fuck no, I don't want a drink! Just hurry up," I stressed, becoming more irritated! So out she went again, slamming the door behind her. I stretched out on the bed, propping my head up on a pillow and stared at the ceiling, wondering how women could be so simple minded at such a passionate time.

It was the slightest sound that made me glance over at the chair. When I did, I saw a sight I'll never forget—a panel had opened in the wall just above the chair, and a hand had just snatched my uniform and pulled it through the opening.

I bolted upright and, for just a second, sat there with my mouth agape, not believing what I'd just seen. Then I jumped forward, grabbed the door handle, and yanked hard. My clothes had just gone out a hole in the wall and into the hallway! But the door held fast! Something, I didn't know what, was stopping it from opening!

I yelled loud and jerked on it again, as hard as I could, and nearly pulled my arm out of its socket. I pounded on the door and kicked it, causing yet another shriek as pain shot up my still-injured leg. But it still wouldn't budge. Somehow the bitch had locked the door tight! So I drew my knife out from the boot, plunged it into the door, and started cutting away at the wood near the door's jam. It took a few frantic minutes, but I was finally able to cut through enough to loosen the hardware and pushed the door open. I rushed into the hall and found five or six Vietnamese watching me from other doorways down both sides of the hall. They had all undoubtedly been roused from their sleep by my pounding and shouting.

I gave a wave of my hand, smiled broadly, said, "Hi," and stepped back into the room, softly pushing the door shut behind me. The girl and my uniform were forgotten as the danger of my situation dawned on me. I was in a building, God knew where, that was full of Vietnamese, who were now alerted to my presence. I had no clothes except my boots and underwear, no way to contact any Americans, and no weapons, except the knife. I paced back and forth, cursing my luck and thinking furiously on what to do.

One thing was for certain, I couldn't stay in that room. There was little chance the witch would come back, but if she did, it would certainly be with people not to my liking. Even if she didn't return, any of the new friends I'd just made in the hallway could turn out to be on the wrong side. I had to get out of that building.

But I knew going outside was nearly as dangerous. It was already past curfew, which meant I'd be a target for friend and foe alike, especially any Vietnamese who supported the other side. We'd all heard about groups of the VC who roamed the streets at night. Still, as I thought on it, at least outside I might find a place to hole up until daylight. For sure I couldn't hide in that room. So, with no further hesitation, I put on my socks and boots, picked up the knife, and pissed on her bed. Then, after making sure the coast was clear, I crawled out the window above the bed and dropped onto the ground below. I banged my knee into my face when I hit, but managed to not make too much noise before slipping away into the night.

I immediately set a course that I was certain was the direction of the Princess Nightclub. If I could locate the club, then the odds of my getting back to a US military compound or the Caravelle Hotel increased considerably. Fortunately, I was aided in my passage by the darkness of the streets. If Saigon had streetlights, they weren't in my part of town. Only the stars above and an occasional beam of light shining through the cracks of buildings helped illuminate that gloomy night.

I must have looked the sight that night—a tall white man sneaking from shadow to shadow in the empty streets of Saigon, wearing only green underwear and a pair of combat boots. I can laugh about it now, but it wasn't funny then. I was absolutely terrified someone would find me, so I moved slowly and cautiously, sticking to the shadows as much as possible and searching out every street corner and intersection before darting across.

But while there was little light, there was plenty of noise—dogs barking in the distance, voices from inside houses I passed, and every once in a while the sounds of trucks on nearby streets, most likely military patrols. I froze at every sound, then resuming movement only when I was sure it was safe. The dogs scared me the most. I'd been afraid of dogs since childhood, when a big German shepherd I'd been teasing took a bite out of me. In my mind, I could just see some stupid dog alerting the Vietnamese to my presence, causing me to be captured and tortured to death in a basement, forever listed as "missing in action" on some official report back in Washington. It was a crazy thought and I should have known better. There were no basements in Vietnam.

After about an hour of wandering through the dark, I realized that I was lost, though my path had been back in the direction of the Princess Nightclub, but only God knows how far I'd gone, or where I was at that point. The only things I knew for certain were constant fear and a feeling of total exhaustion from a night that had already been far too long. I sat down against a building, pulled my knees up to my chest, and buried my face in my arms. I intended to rest for just a minute, but must have dozed off slightly because on my next conscious moment, I felt the presence of someone nearby. My first instinct was to bolt straight up and run like hell. Instead, I kept stock still and peeked over my arm towards the ground, to my front. What I saw made the hairs stand on the back of my neck—two bare-sandaled feet, only a few yards away, facing my direction.

It was clearly a Vietnamese and, given the late hour, most likely someone up to no good. If he'd been armed, I would probably have been dead on the spot. I could only assume he didn't have a weapon and was surprised to have stumbled across someone sitting there in the middle of the night. While he didn't see my face, the light color of my legs and arms, not to mention my combat boots and green underwear, must have given away the fact that I was a foreign soldier. As it was, after several long seconds when neither I nor the sandaled feet moved, they began to slowly, and quietly, back away. As the feet went from view, I waited just a bit and then tilted my head ever so slightly higher to get a better look at the owner of the sandals. What I saw was the back of a man, probably young by the way he moved, and obviously trying not to make noise. He got across the street about forty feet away, took one last look in my direction, and then started running up the block.

A second later I was off in the opposite direction as fast as I could go. Unfortunately, that wasn't very fast. My leg, still not fully recovered from the shrapnel wound at the bridge, was all right for walking, but running was another matter. I couldn't go that fast and every time my leg struck the ground, I felt a shock run through me. Still, fear made up for the pain and I tore down the road, no longer concerned with concealment.

I must have gone for about three blocks before stopping to catch my breath. As I did so, I heard the faint sound of motorbikes coming from the direction I'd just fled. As I listened, they seemed to be getting louder, moving towards me. That was bad news. Americans didn't ride in bike packs, at least not in Saigon, and certainly not late at night after curfew. Whoever they were, I assumed they had been alerted to my presence.

I searched desperately on the street for somewhere to hide, where I could get down and out of sight, but every building was boarded up and locked for the night. There were a few small tables and such, but nothing large enough to provide cover for a human being; not even a tree to climb or a car to crawl under. The only thing that appeared to provide shelter was a large mound of garbage piled at the side of the road half a block away. I limped down to it and found the pile to be at least five feet high and more than a dozen feet across. It wasn't much, but with no other choice, and with the sounds of their engines coming closer, I piled in and buried myself in the midst of the rubbish. In doing so, I was nearly overcome by the stench of the junk, as it smelled like something had died there. I held my nose with one hand, closed my eyes, and prayed that the bikers wouldn't think to look for me in a trash pile.

I didn't have to wait long to find out. Within minutes they drew near, gunning their engines and yelling to each other as they came down the road. From the sound of it, there were probably half a dozen of them, spread out and going slowly but steadily down the street. As they approached, I bit my lip to stop my body from shaking and tried to sit absolutely still.

As they drew abreast of my position, it sounded like one of the bikes had stopped nearby, as its engine was idling. Then I heard something hit near the top of the garbage pile and soon after felt a cold liquid flowing down onto my back. A less-experienced man might have leaped up and run, figuring they were spotted, but I stayed perfectly still. My father had frightened me out of a hiding place years before by throwing something in my direction, and I wasn't about to fall for the same trick twice. Take it from someone who's been in hiding all over the globe—you're not found till you're found.

Staying under the garbage proved to be the right decision. The gang of gooks, including the idler, continued to move slowly past and, before long, the sound of their engines began to fade in the distance. I'm not sure why they didn't search the garbage pile as there certainly wasn't anyplace else to hide on that road that night. Perhaps they figured no American would ever bury himself in such a filthy place. Whatever the reason, I'd chosen my hiding place well.

I waited until there was only a faint echo from their engines and then carefully slid from beneath the rubbish heap. As I emerged, something in the pile must have become unstable, because there was a terrific crash as glass bottles and some kind of metal cage went banging into the street. In an instant I was on my feet, listening intently for any sounds from down the road where the bikes had gone. As I'd feared, the report of the crashing junk had carried in the still night air. Within seconds, the sound of the motorbike engines was no longer diminishing but becoming louder. I turned and ran back in the direction I'd originally come from, hoping that I'd heard wrong. But those hopes were dashed seconds later when I looked over my shoulder and saw first one and then a bunch of lights pop into view on the street. They *were* coming back, and this time they knew I was there.

I ran as fast as my legs could carry me, frantically searching for another hiding place and was so focused on the bikes to my rear that I failed to notice some other lights until I raced around a corner and found myself face-to-face with them. Only these lights were bigger, brighter, and headed straight for me. I screamed out in shock, threw my arms in the air, fell to my knees, and then went facedown on the street. A blinding light filled the air around me and I expected to feel bullets tearing through me any second as a number of vehicles screeched to a stop in front of me and to my right.

There were voices, and then a vehicle on my right tore past, headed in the direction of the motorbike gang. I looked to the side and got just a glimpse of a jeep with someone sitting high in the back as it passed by, heading in the direction I'd just fled. A few seconds later, the sounds of gunfire came from around the bend, and I guessed the bikers had found more than they'd bargained for.

The bright-light people were obviously military. But I had a new worry if they were ARVN, as I didn't trust any Vietnamese just then. Unfortunately, there was no way to discern who confronted me. The glare in my face was so bright I could only tell by the sound of their engines that there were two vehicles remaining at my front. So I stayed still, not moving, facedown to the ground, praying they were friendly. Then, from the front, a voice boomed out, "Stand up!"

I let out a sign of relief. It was an American voice! For the first time since I'd left the girl's apartment, I felt safe. I took a deep breath and yelled, "Don't shoot!" I gradually rose to my feet. "I'm an American! I'm an American!"

"Come forward! Slowly!" said the voice.

"Don't shoot. I'm an American officer," I hollered back, walking towards the shining lights with my head still facing downwards and my hand shielding my face from the light.

"Stop," came back the voice just as quickly, "and put your hands back in the air."

I raised my arms and stood still, while turning my head to the side to avoid looking directly at the lights. "Look, I'm Lieutenant Loveless of the Americal Division," I said! "I'm lost. I need to get back to base!" But there was no reply, just the loud humming of the vehicles for what seemed like a long time. "Hello?" I asked, hoping for a reply. But again there was no answer and I started to get a bad feeling. It was crazy, but I thought, *What if they are Americans who are out on their own doing something illegal?*

For a brief second I thought about flight, and then the light suddenly went out and a voice close to my front said, "Turn around and put your arms behind your back."

I looked up to see the shapes of two men only a few feet away, clearly Americans by their size. "What for? What're you gonna do?" I asked, turning around to face the other direction. "I've told you who I am."

"Just a little precaution. No one is supposed to be out after curfew, and if you're who you say you are, these will be off soon enough," one replied as I felt handcuffs lock around my right wrist and then my left.

"There's no need for that," I protested, twisting around to face two enlisted soldiers, the younger of whom had a pistol aimed directly at my stomach. "I'm really an army officer."

"Oh, we believe you, Sir," said the older one who was wearing sergeant's stripes, as he pushed the other's pistol down and away. "We find lots of officers wandering the streets late night in just their shorts and boots. That's why we're doing so well in this war." Both of them chuckled.

I wanted to damn them on the spot and order them to unlock me, but considering my situation, I knew it would be much better to wait until we got to an army base. There were too many stories in the 'Nam of officers being killed by their own troops and I'd just met these two worthies. They could have shot me and dumped me in a ditch and no one would ever have known, except the soldiers in a second jeep, who were casually watching the scene and were undoubtedly their friends.

So I kept my mouth shut as they escorted me to their vehicle and had me sit up front next to the driver's seat. "I'll be right back here, Lieutenant," said the older fellow in a demeaning manner as he crawled in and sat directly behind me. Then off we went, following the path of the third jeep that sounded like it had engaged the bikers. We found it parked on the side of the street about a block down the road, along with several overturned motorcycles and a couple of bodies lying on the pavement. One American was taking pictures of the motorcycles and bodies, while a second continued to man the machine gun on the back of the jeep just in case, I guessed, that the Vietnamese came back. We parked alongside and then the older guy behind me got out and engaged in a discussion with the picture taker. Before long, he came back and then, leaving the dead gook's bodies on the street, we all took off, headed for a military base several miles away, I was told.

Once there, the handcuffs were removed as I was turned over to the military police and taken to a small wooden building where a sergeant interrogated me for nearly an hour, while other MPs scurried about doing whatever it is they do to look busy. I told my story to the interviewer, explaining how I'd left the Princess Club to find something to eat, gotten lost, and was trying to find my way back to the Caravelle Hotel when I slipped and fell into a small stream and soaked my clothes. I'd taken them off for just a few minutes with the intention of drying them off, I said. But then the motorbike gang came along and I had to run like hell to get away, leaving my uniform behind.

It was weak, but the best I could come up with on short notice, and while it made logical sense, the sergeant was very skeptical. Twice I had to repeat myself, practically word for word as, I thought, he tried to catch me contradicting myself. When that didn't work, he started using sarcasm. "Let's see," said he, "you claim to have gone out for a nighttime stroll, by yourself, in a city you only arrived at two days before in the middle of a war. Is that right?"

"That's right, Sergeant," I said, pretending to lose my patience. "And I got wet and I took off my uniform and I got chased by a gang of cutthroat bikers and now I'm being questioned over and over like some common criminal! Now I've told you who I am! I am an officer in the United States Army! Just today I was in a ceremony with the president of the United States! I suggest you call the Caravelle Hotel right now, Sergeant, or I'll—"

"Or you'll what Frank?" asked a voice to my rear.

I spun around quickly because I knew that voice. It belonged to… "Deeds! You're here," I exclaimed, staring at him in disbelief. It was my old OCS roommate all right, leaning against the far wall with a smirk on his face. He was wearing an "OD" armband, which meant he was an officer in charge of something that night, most likely the MPs in that building, including the very person who was questioning me. I'd not given Deeds a thought since leaving Fort Benning, but at that moment, he was a most welcome sight.

"Thank God, it's you," I said, rushing forward to grab him by the arm. "Tell them who I am," I pleaded, turning to face the MP sergeant. But Deeds shook me loose and walked over to a table to pick up a newspaper.

"No need for that, Frank," said he, folding open the paper. "Everyone in the 'Nam knows who you are by now." And he handed me the paper. I glanced down and there, on the front page, was a photo of the president pinning a medal on one of the guys at Di An, with me standing just to the rear. A bold headline read "NIXON HONORS VIETNAM HEROES."

"You're a hero, Frank. Says so in the paper," said my old roommate, with a touch of envy, I thought.

"Well, it wasn't anything really," I said, starting to regain my composure.

"I'm sure of that," Deeds replied sarcastically.

I ignored him and shot back, "Well this does prove who I am." I turned back to him and took the paper to the sergeant who had been interviewing me. "So how about helping me get a new uniform and taking me back to my hotel now?"

"Afraid that's not possible, Frank. You'll have to stay here for the night," said Deeds, calm as can be.

"What?" I asked, turning back to Deeds. "Why? You know who I am. There's no reason to keep me here now."

"Regulations," he replied. "Anyone caught outside after curfew has to be locked up over night. We have no choice. Tomorrow you'll have to meet the Provost Marshal and explain to him why you were out on the street that late."

"I've already explained all that to this sergeant here," I spat out, pointing to the desk sergeant who was obviously being amused by our conversation.

"I know, Frank. I know. And I'm sure your story is all true. You're an honest guy," he said, which told me I was being screwed with since he knew I was anything but. This was his chance to take revenge for Fort Benning and the little toad wasn't about to let me slip away so easily. "The Provost Marshal will read your report and you'll probably be back in your comfortable hotel by noon. But tonight, you have to stay here. If we make an exception, even with a famous hero," he continued sarcastically, "then we could all get in trouble. You wouldn't want us to break regulations, would you?"

Well, I did, but I couldn't say so with so many witnesses around and it wouldn't have made any difference. So I muttered something about wanting to do things right, and then Deeds puts his arm around my shoulder and said, "Don't worry. You'll only be here a few hours. Tomorrow, we'll get this whole thing straightened out."

"We better," I replied, keeping up a bluff front.

"Hey! You're a hero. You don't have a thing to worry about," said Deeds, which made me worry all that much more.

The upshot was I spent the night in an army cell, sleeping on a cot instead of next to a sensual woman as I'd planned. Still, considering how close I'd come to cashing in my chips earlier that night, I couldn't complain.

The following morning, three MPs took me back to the Caravelle Hotel and waited while I changed into a clean uniform. Then they drove me across town to yet another small military compound, surrounded by a high concrete wall, and ushered me into a big, impressive building. It was made of some kind of white stone and had marble steps leading up the front, making me think it must have once been the residence of some kind of royalty. That impression was reinforced by armed guards everywhere, which told me there must be high ranking officers in the area. When I asked the MPs who we were going to see, they just said their orders were to take me to that location. They had no idea who I was to meet. I assumed it was the area Provost Marshal, as Deeds had said, and I was prepared for him. Although my stomach was in knots, I'd rehearsed my story that morning and was confident the Provost Marshal would hear me out and send me on my way.

After waiting for a short time in a large outer room, a major came and escorted me up several flights of stairs and down a long hallway to an office. Stepping inside, I found myself face-to-face with a Lieutenant General, sitting behind a big desk. I'd seen him the day before at Di An, so he must have been someone high at MACV. I was so shocked at seeing three stars that I never noticed the name on his uniform. But I kept my composure and snapped off a brisk salute. "Sir, Lieutenant Loveless reporting, Sir!"

"Thank you, Lieutenant," he said, returning the salute and gesturing to my rear. "Can you please join us?"

I turned and saw two officers seated on a sofa. One of them was Deeds, doing his best to look serious. The other was a Lieutenant Colonel whom I'd not seen before. "You know Lieutenant Deeds, I believe. This is Colonel Sandowski, our Public Affairs Officer," said the general, who had come from behind his desk and led me to a seat directly across from Deeds.

"We've heard about your adventures last night from Lieutenant Deeds," said the three star."

"I didn't do anything wrong, Sir," I protested quickly, concerned that Deeds had given a variation of my story. "It was just a freak chain of events."

"Oh, I'm sure it was, Son," he said, putting his hand on my shoulder for reassurance. "We're aware of your excellent record and don't doubt your story. Lieutenant Deeds here has vouched for you personally. I understand you're friends from OCS?"

Well, that didn't sound good. Deeds was anything but a friend. But I couldn't say otherwise until I knew more of what he'd told them. "Yes, Sir," I replied, glancing over at Deeds who sat with his hands clenched in his lap, looking down at the floor. "We were roommates for a while."

"He's told us of your unselfishness at OCS and how you always took the time to help the other cadets," said the general. That sounded even worse. Why would Deeds say that after what I'd done to him? But he just sat there quietly, not daring to look me in the eye.

"Your division commander says you're one of the bravest soldiers in his unit," continued the general, "and I myself was with the President yesterday when you received your award. There's no question that you're a soldier we're very proud to have in this command. But you see, because of last night, we have a little problem."

"A problem, Sir?" I said, becoming more concerned, if that was possible.

"It seems the press got hold of what happened," he replied, "and now they're talking about running a story that could be embarrassing to us all, including the President."

"The press," I blurted out. "How did they find out?" But I knew the answer even as I asked—Deeds! He'd blabbed, or had someone in his office leak the story to the press. No one else knew about the night before.

"We don't know, Son, but they did," answered the general. "And you know these goddamned media types. They're happier reporting a scandal than they are helping with the war effort. If they print that one of our most decorated young soldiers, a soldier who just got the Silver Star, from the President, no less, was found drunk and stripped of his uniform... Well, that will be very embarrassing."

"But I wasn't drunk, Sir," I protested. "I was just lost. I'll tell them the truth. I'll tell them I lost my uniform when that gang chased me and that the MPs came and rescued me. There's nothing wrong with that."

"I'd like to believe you, Lieutenant," he answered. "But the media have already talked to the MPs who found you, and they said you were brought in drunk. Unfortunately, the fellow you went to the bar with has corroborated their story."

"He says you left the bar with a prostitute, barely able to stand up," broke in Sandowski.

"Well it's a damned lie," I answered in anger. "I had a few drinks, but I was nowhere near drunk." But I knew Gil was paying me back for walking out and sticking him with the bar bill.

"That may be true, but he's pretty credible. After all, he got an award from the President, too. Besides, like I said, the press is always ready to believe the worst about our people. When they approached him this morning, Colonel Sandowski here tried to reason with the media to kill the story. But they're like wild dogs. They smell blood and they're out for the kill, demanding that we let them talk to you. Freedom of the press and all that shit," said the general, practically shouting, before regaining his composure and then going on to say calmly, "Anyway, we've got to protect the army. This war is unpopular enough already. We can't afford any more scandals like that Green Beret thing last month. I've talked about your case with the Old Man and he agrees. We've got to get you away, where the press can't talk to you. The PAO here thinks," and he pointed at Sandowski, "if the media can't get an interview, they will just drop it. After all, it's just a rumor right now. In fact, Sandowski," he said, turning to the lieutenant colonel, "see if there is a way to just tell the media, if they ask, that Loveless should not even have received the award yesterday, that it was just a mistake he was up on the reviewing stand. That might kill the story altogether. But don't you worry, Son," he said, turning back to me, "you can keep your medal, and it will still appear on your official records. With luck, the PAO here can make it look to the outside world that we made a mistake when your name was included as an award recipient. Anyway, we'll do what we can and Lt. Deeds here will make sure his men don't talk to the media. We've just got to make sure they don't get to you. So," and then he put his hand back on my shoulder, "we've decided to send you back to your unit."

"My unit, Sir?" I said meekly. "You mean the Americal?"

"No. Yes. Yes, the Americal," he said. "But I mean your unit. That infantry company you were assigned to. If we get you back out in the field, there's no way the press will be able to talk to you. The press can get on Chu Lai and then find you, but not if you're out in the field. Besides, the PAO here has already tried to cover for us and told the press you flew out this morning, eager to get back to your soldiers. If we don't get you back there, it'll look all the worse—like we lied."

Well, they had lied, and because of it, I was about to get screwed. Nothing could have been worse news. "But, Sir, I've been wounded twice," I pleaded. The regulations say—"

"I know the regulations, Lieutenant," he said sternly. "But we don't have much of a choice. The army made the regulations and can adjust them if necessary. The alternative would be embarrassment for the army and the President. You wouldn't want that, would you?"

Well, the army could go to hell for all I cared, but I daren't say that, certainly not to a lifer. So I bowed my head and muttered something like, "No, Sir, I wouldn't want to make the army look bad."

"I knew you'd see it our way, Son," said the brass, "and believe me, this will work out best for your career. I'll make sure this is reflected in your record, and as soon as this thing has died down some, maybe in a few months, we'll get you back to a rear job. Don't worry!"

I thanked him and we talked some more, but I was in such a funk that I don't remember what else was said. All I could think about was going back to the field and the horror that meant.

An hour later, as I left the building with Deeds and Sandowski, I was still in a state of shock. The absolute worst had happened. Instead of going back to Chu Lai to live in a Quonset hut complete with hooch maids and work at an office job for the rest of my 'Nam tour, I was headed back to Bravo Company and the horror of combat. I could only walk silently towards the post exit, completely disheartened. My old roommate, however, wasn't so depressed. At the front entrance to the compound, as Sandowski and I got into a jeep, Deeds turned to me and said piously, "Sorry it turned out this way, Frank. I did my best to help you."

Go fuck yourself, I thought, but with the PAO present, I replied, "I appreciate what you did, Charlie. I'm sure we'll meet again someday so I can return the favor."

"I'll count on it," he said, turning his back and sauntering off, whistling. I watched him walk off, never expecting to see him again, but hoping that somehow, someday, our paths would cross.

That afternoon, they put me on a plane and two days later I rejoined B Company in the field. I've never been back to Saigon, but that's fine with me. After the war, the North Vietnamese renamed the place Ho Chi Minh City and cleaned up the hookers and street gangs. By the early 90s it was such a respectable place, the Vietnamese tried to make it into a tourist destination, even welcoming back ex-GIs. I read somewhere that a lot of 'Nam vets have made the trip, but I'll never go back. For me, it'll always be Saigon, where a hand through the wall stole my clothes and nearly got me killed.

CHAPTER EIGHT

The moment I arrived at the Chu Lai airport, I was met by several military policemen and a captain. They hustled me aboard a Huey and had me flown directly back out to LZ Baldy. I had been hoping to delay my return to the field by hanging out at division headquarters for a few days, but obviously, the higher-ups had talked and they were making sure the media, who rarely went to the field, couldn't get to me. When I landed, Bryson, Baker, and several of the other Bravo Company guys were there to welcome me with open arms, but that was little consolation. I'd hoped to never see their faces again, except perhaps at some post-'Nam reunion years down the road. Even so, I put on a good face and pretended to be happy that I was back with my old comrades in arms.

Not much had changed in my absence. Grovich, naturally, was eager to have me back since he had an inflated opinion of my value and, as always, needed fellow officers in which to bounce off his decisions. He definitely was the same as before and still prone to worry and overreact about nearly everything. There was also a new officer just assigned to the company. A Lieutenant Jeremy Burns had replaced Lieutenant Kitchen as boss of the Third Platoon and was more than eager to be my friend. Only Sergeant Mann didn't seem all that pleased by my return. He glanced up when I entered our command office, said, "Welcome back, LT," and then continued to answer only to himself.

A few new troops had joined the unit while I was gone, primarily replacing those we had lost at the Battle of the Bridge, but mostly they were the same bunch of miscreants I'd left weeks earlier, each soldier just treading water and counting the days until they rotated back home. Don't get me wrong. Having observed American soldiers, and those of numerous foreign nations, over many years, I have the utmost respect for the people serving in our military. The young men and women I have known are mostly dedicated, honorable people who proudly serve their country. On the whole, I'd more likely trust the people I've met in the army than most of the civilians I've encountered. But when you eat, sleep, and live with soldiers day in and day out, especially in an unhealthy environment like the 'Nam, anyone can become stale meat.

The good news was that the company had been assigned guard duty at Baldy just days before my return, so for the next three weeks, I mostly sat around during the day reading or playing cards and spent a few minutes each night checking on the guys who were on the bunker line. If we'd stayed there for the rest of my tour, it wouldn't have been so bad; boring perhaps, but not bad. Unfortunately, in those days, the army had a thing about putting combat units in combat situations. Our reverie was broken early one morning in late August when we woke to learn that we had orders to reinforce some other Americal infantry units that were heavily engaged in a place called Que Son Valley. The sun was still climbing up over the South China Sea as we boarded a bevy of choppers and headed south.

I sensed even before we landed that it wouldn't be just another small-time enemy engagement. The valley we flew into was long and narrow, surrounded by steep-slopped mountains with triple-canopied jungles. It ran east-west, with its far end pointing straight at Cambodia and the Ho Chi Minh Trail. Down the center of the valley, I saw a slim, meandering river flowing silently between green hills and the morning sun reflecting off multiple rice paddies. It all made for a very tranquil scene, but brought me no comfort. My gut instinct said we were headed into something very bad.

Our Intel reports said that that Que Son was an agricultural grain house, with small farm communities overseeing acres of rice, corn, and vegetables. But it was also a conduit for the North Vietnamese, as their units could traverse the valley straight from Cambodia into the center of our operations. The place had been a hotbed of activity for years, with both sides doing their best to establish control. To hear our G-2 talk, the enemy had done the better job. They'd infiltrated Que Son in '65 and either killed or chased off all the local government officials. Most of the valley hamlets became deserted at that time, as the inhabitants fled to refugee centers in Tam Ky. To take back control, our side ringed the valley with mountaintop LZs (with poetic names like West, Center, Ross, and Siberia) and sent in both American and Vietnamese infantry units to conduct ground patrols.

It took a while, but in early '69, the Vietnamese government announced that Que Son was under their control again. To prove it, they resettled hundreds of farmers and their families in the village of Hiep Duc. Apparently, that caused a big loss of face to the ever-sensitive Vietcong, who vowed to retake the valley. According to the Intel guys, the enemy had been sneaking agents into Hiep Duc for months, warning the locals that their village would be wiped out by September. Now it appeared they were trying to make good on their word.

The week prior, Charlie had launched a predawn attack on LZ West, one of our more prominent firebases overlooking the valley. Before they were driven away, fifty-nine enemy fighters were killed in a bloody battle along the perimeter wires. While our side won that fight, it was a wake-up call in that it showed the dinks were serious. They would never have gone after a firebase that size and risked losing so many men unless they had a considerable force in the valley below.

Five days later, two of our infantry companies walked into separate ambushes at the bottom of a well-known precipice, which the locals affectionately called the "Mountain of the Black Leeches." We didn't know it at the time, but they'd stumbled on a network of bunkers and tunnels where an entrenched NVA regiment that had little interest in conserving ammunition had been hiding.

Encircled and vastly outnumbered, the two Americal units were badly mauled, suffering up to forty percent casualties in a day and a half of fighting. They were being slowly destroyed by the time brigade headquarters was able to rush five other infantry units in to join the fight. The influx of hundreds of American soldiers stabilized the situation for a bit, but the next morning, the dinks fiercely counterattacked, inflicting dozens of more casualties and, in the process, shooting a battalion commander's helicopter out of the sky. He and seven others were killed when the chopper hit the ground, but no one knew that at the time. Our side just knew the helicopter had gone down behind enemy lines and it was our duty to reach the site and rescue any possible survivors. That was when brigade HQ called in more reinforcements, including our unit and some U.S. Marine infantry types from up north at Danang.

We landed several miles from the site of the chopper crash, on a hilltop well away from the fighting and beyond range of any weapon the dinks might fire. I no sooner got off the helicopter than I noticed that the valley was unfathomably hot. After more than four months in-country, I thought I'd already experienced the heat of Vietnam, but Que Son set a new standard. Surrounded on all sides by mountains that cut off any hope of a breeze, and it being the middle of summer, the heat in that valley was unbearable. Doc, who carried around some kind of portable thermostat, said it was one hundred ten degrees Fahrenheit the day we landed and one hundred thirteen degrees the following day. Even if he was off a bit, it was still the hottest weather I'd ever experienced.

But hot or not, we had a job to do. Once we'd unloaded ourselves and our gear from the helicopters, Grovich brought the platoon leaders together and filled us in on what to expect. "We're going in with some other units," he said, "to find that chopper that went down yesterday. Battalion's pretty sure everyone was killed since it was seen bursting into flames in midair and an explosion was heard when it went down. But we've gotta make sure. Our job will be to recover any bodies and, just in case someone is still alive, bring them back out."

The others were just nodding their heads, but it sounded like a crazy assignment to me, so I spoke up and said, "Sir, if they are all dead, and the gooks are down there in packs, aren't we just gonna get more people killed trying to get those bodies? That doesn't make any sense."

"Maybe, Love," he answered, using the nickname he'd given me. "But you know we never leave our dead for the VC. And we're not going in alone. Two companies of the 3rd of the 21st, plus one from the 4th of the 31st will be with us. We'll be supported from the east, too—a battalion of marines is pushing west from LZ Ross. With luck, we'll catch Charlie between us."

With luck, I thought to myself, *the dinks will just give up the fight and go back across the border, and we can all go back to Baldy.* But I kept my mouth shut and nodded along with the others. Even though my opinion was by this time well respected by Grovich, I figured it best to not push my luck. Besides, the orders were from battalion headquarters, not from him.

At least Grovich was right about the help. We spent most of that morning hacking our way through some pretty thick foliage as we humped about a mile down into the valley and then back up another ridge, sweating all the way, before linking up with the other army units. They were at the top of a place called "Million Dollar Hill," so named because several of our helicopters that had been hit by ground fire had crashed on its slopes the year before. There were, indeed, three other American companies strung out along the top of the ridge, mostly staying out of the sun, sleeping in the shade, waiting for us to arrive.

At first, it was reassuring to see so many friendly faces, even if they did seem to mock us as we passed through their ranks to find our own spot to set up at along the mountaintop trail. Combined, our four infantry companies added up to about 400 men, which made me feel a lot more comfortable about the task at hand. I knew that many troops, plus the division's air power and artillery that we could draw on, should be more than enough to fight the communist force in the valley.

While Grovich made the rounds to meet with the other commanders, I reclined beneath a small bush to relax and catch my breath. Within minutes though, Sergeant Mann came up and broke my reverie with new information he's learned about the ongoing battle. The other three companies had all arrived on scene two days earlier, he said, and had since undergone nearly sixty hours of constant combat, resulting in high casualties. One unit in the 3rd of the 21st had gone from ninety able-bodied men to about sixty, and another had supposedly lost forty percent of its strength the day before. The remaining soldiers were both physically exhausted and mentally spent, Mann said, which explained why reinforcements, including our unit, had been called into the fight. It also meant, I realized, that we would probably be expected to carry the brunt of the battle the next day.

Mann then walked me out to a high point overlooking the valley and tried to explain the terrain and what we were up against. The site of where the chopper crashed was less than a quarter mile away, on a prominence called Hill 102, but it might as well have been on the moon. In two days of heavy fighting, our side had made no progress against the dug-in NVA forces. Even aerial bombing hadn't been able to dislodge them, as the night before, naval jets had carpet bombed the area surrounding Hill 102 with napalm. Normally, that should have been enough to drive out even the cockroaches, but no one thought the gooks were on the run. I got that loud and clear from one of the platoon leaders in the 3rd of the 21st a little later that morning.

"We'll never get 'em outta there," he lamented. "They've got the whole area dug out with tunnels and bunkers and they ain't hurting for ammo. Them's regular NVA, not VC," he said. "Yesterday, we walked right into a crossfire and had fifteen of our guys pinned down all day. They were only thirty feet away, but we couldn't move up to get 'em, and they couldn't move back to join us, and it was too close to call in arty. It was dark before we got 'em outta there, and by that time, we'd lost three more KIAs. Fuckin' dinks are all gonna die before they leave that place."

Unfortunately, the headquarters staff back in the rear didn't share that attitude. Shortly before noon, word came in from Baldy that it was time to make another attempt to reach the downed chopper. So off we went, four infantry companies side by side, headed down into a ravine that separated us from Hill 102, leaving behind only a small field hospital and security detail. As I'd suspected, our company took the lead, followed by the others. My platoon was second in line, in the middle of our formation, generally the safest position in case of hostile fire.

We hadn't gone fifty feet when a shot rang out, chasing us all to the ground. It had to have been only a single bullet, which meant it was either a sniper or a stray round going off. Even so, we were all in a nervous funk and stayed down until a report came over the radio that someone in the 3rd of the 21st had shot himself in the leg and was being taken back up the hill for medical evacuation. Without knowing any details, word spread quickly through the ranks that he'd shot himself on purpose, as he probably figured it was better to be injured with a flesh wound than to go back into that ravine again.

Considering where we were headed just then, I actually thought about that option, but decided it wasn't for me; deep down I'm as afraid of ridicule as I am of getting hurt. Besides, it's not easy to shoot yourself without inflicting permanent injury, although some years later, I did pull off a similar gambit in the Mideast. As it was, I dismissed the idea and started back down into the Valley of Death behind Bryson, who had gotten instructions over the radio for us to resume the decent.

At first it was easy. Strung out behind each other, the four companies proceeded slowly down Million Dollar Hill. No one was in a rush and we couldn't go fast anyway, thanks to the thick foliage that grew ever denser as we neared the bottom of the hill. Our intent was to move as quietly as possible, as we hoped to get up close to the dinks before they realized we were coming. Plus, the weather seemed to slow us down. I don't know if it was fear or the heat, but sweat was pouring down my face. While I'd often worn a towel around my neck to absorb moisture in Vietnam, that day was the first time my towel ever got soaking wet from just wiping my face. My breath was coming hard and I was drinking like a fish, going through two canteens of water by the time we crossed the ravine and reached the base of Hill 102.

Once in the ravine, we repositioned so that the four units were in a wide line, with our company situation on the far left. Only then did we begin to move up Hill 102. There was definitely a tense feeling in the air, but we were able to move steadily forward without incident until we were nearly halfway up the hill. I was beginning to hope that the NVA might have actually wised up and gone away, when a barrage of gunfire rang out on our right.

Being on the far side of the formation, it was obvious our company wasn't the one under fire, but with bullets zinging overhead, we quickly fell into a defensive posture, our weapons aimed away at the quiet jungle on our left. Charlie was well known to feint attacks from one direction and then hit from the opposite side with their real offensive, so we reacted to make sure that wouldn't happen. After a few minutes though, it appeared that a fake attack wasn't the case. The terrain in front of us remained silent, while behind us, on the opposite side of our large formation, the sound of small-arms fire grew louder and louder. I recognized the rat-a-tat of M60 machine guns and the popping and cracking of M16s and AK-47s, but there was also a loud snapping sound that I'd not heard before. "That's a .51-cal," said Pineapple, one of our M60 gunners, who was just to my rear. Like me, he heralded from Hawaii, only he was of Japanese ancestry. The two of us had hit it off right away when he joined the unit some weeks before as we were both from the 50th State and could relate as only islanders can. "Only the regular NVA has those," he said. "They usually use 'em to shoot at helicopters. Now they're using 'em on us." His hearing was soon confirmed when Grovich came down the line and gave us the skinny on the situation.

"Companies A and D are pinned down by machine-gun fire from bunkers on the hill," he said. "They're under heavy fire from two, maybe three, machine guns, and can't move forward. The 4th of the 31st is gonna stay in position, to keep Charlie from coming in on this side. We're supposed to go around to the left and flank the bunkers." He drew a diagram in the dirt, trying to show the location of the bunkers relevant to our position.

"And what happens if *we* get pinned down, sir?" I asked, concerned that we could easily become isolated from the other companies, with no other units in reserve.

"Brigade thinks that won't happen," he replied. "They think the NVA won't figure on a force as big as ours, so we have a good chance to get on top of 'em unseen. If we can knock out that first bunker line, we should be able to take this hill and get to the chopper."

I wasn't so sure it would be that simple, given how well dug in the NVA appeared, but there was no sense arguing with orders coming down from the top. Grovich would have marched on Moscow if brigade gave the command, so I just nodded my assent and watched as he went forward to inform the lead platoon of the plan. A few minutes later we were off, circling around the left side of Hill 102, fortunately still hidden somewhat by thick shrubbery, and every man alert to any unusual sound or movement. We hadn't gone more than a hundred feet before we came to a stop. "Williams must have spotted them," I said to no one in particular, referring to the Second Platoon leader, who was in front of us.

"Not exactly LT," said Bryson, who was nearby, monitoring the prick-25. "Lieutenant Williams found gooks all right. But it sounds like they're all dead!"

"All dead?"

"Yes, Sir! And it sounds like there are lots of 'em."

Sure enough, Williams had found dead NVA all right. He'd stumbled on a mass grave containing hundreds of them. Our platoon came on it a few minutes later when we resumed our advance. I smelled the gravesite long before I saw it as the midday sun was causing the bodies to rot where they lay, making a horrible stench. There were rows of dead bodies in a big hole in the ground, apparently placed there with some care because the bodies were all facing the same direction, the ones on top with their hands folded on their chests. It looked as though someone had started to cover the grave with dirt, but left before the job was done. It was a gruesome sight that temporarily left me spellbound, just staring down into the hole.

An explosion of bullets from the hillside brought reality back fast as lead whizzed through the air around us, ricocheting off trees and clipping the branches and leaves of nearby bushes, sending everyone to the ground yet again. Private Lopez, a Puerto Rican kid standing just feet away, made a little sound like he'd been punched and then fell over backwards, dead with a bullet through his chest. The sight of him falling down stunned me, and if not for Bryson who dragged me to the ground, I might have been hit by the second volley, which followed a few seconds later. I crawled behind a small tree and lay flat on my stomach, shaking and praying for the gunfire to stop. The lead whizzing around us was heavy and steady and included that snapping sound I'd heard earlier. The Second Platoon, at the head of the formation and hidden from view by the thick vegetation, had obviously found the NVA in strength.

Within seconds, Grovich, who was in the rear of the formation with the First Platoon, tried to raise Williams on the radio. "Dragon Two, Dragon Two, what is your situation? Give us your situation!" he yelled.

"We need fire support, Sir," came back a voice on the radio, "and a medic! We've got men down up here! Lieutenant Williams is shot and some others, too! We need help!"

"Can you pull back, Dragon Two?" yelled Grovich.

"Negative! We're on the ground with little cover! There's bunkers to our front about fifty meters away! We're engaged with them and we need help! Get us out of here!" yelled the voice.

"Roger that! We're coming your way, Dragon Two," replied Grovich. "Just hold on! Hold on!" And then he said, "Dragon Three, Dragon Three, do you copy?"

That was our call sign, so I grabbed the received from Bryson and replied, "Yes, Sir! We're pinned down up here, too!"

"Well, get ready. I'm coming up," was the reply, and sure enough, in a few minutes, Grovich and the First Platoon leader, Lieutenant Jeremy Burns, came running up the line, doing their best to keep low to the ground. They plopped down next to me for a quick powwow on what to do.

"Sir," I said before Grovich had a chance to open his mouth, "I hate to say it, but it looks like brigade was wrong! The NVA know we're here! There's no sense going on with this flanking business! We're just gonna get more people killed! Let's pull back, rejoin the other units, and combine our strength!"

"Roger that, Love, but first, we've got to get the Second Platoon out of there," Grovich answered. "Burns and I will move forward from here with the First and try to see what's up with their position! You take your people and go around more to the left! And keep it quiet! They won't expect us in that direction! Once we're all in position, you open up and keep their heads down until we get our guys out of there! You're the key, Love! You have to give us cover! If anyone can do it, you can!"

To me it was just one more stupid idea—I was supposed to take my platoon on yet another sweep around to the left, just minutes after walking into a firefight while trying the same kind of operation. And how could Grovich know we wouldn't just run into more dinks as we continued to move to the left? It just didn't make sense to me, but I couldn't think of anything better and there was no sense haggling about it. Grovich would never leave the Second Platoon stranded and alone, and who better than me to go to the rescue, what with my reputation as a fearless, gung-ho soldier with a lucky star over his head? Hadn't I already escaped sure death at least twice? Further talk was useless, so I conferred with Sergeant Mann, who got the platoon together and we crawled out of the kill zone.

We kept low to the ground and moved as stealthily as possible, praying we could get close enough to take the dinks by surprise. My insides were quaking with dread, but we stayed undetected, and after what seemed like an eternity of creeping along, we were in the right position relative to the enemy machine guns. I couldn't see any NVA, but the sound of gunfire and some light smoke was coming from a low position directly to our front, maybe twenty or so feet lower than our location and twice as far away. It was most likely a dugout bunker, with the dinks inside concentrating their fire towards where the Second Platoon was located.

I passed the word back and at my signal, all thirty-plus of us opened up on the enemy site. It worked. In fact, it worked too well. The machine gun went silent all right, but only for a few seconds; then, instead of firing towards the Second Platoon, it turned on us, along with an accompanying salvo of AK-47 gunfire from multiple weapons. We'd flanked the enemy and stopped their broadside against the main force of our company, but now they were madder than a nest of disturbed hornets and we were their target.

No one can imagine how terrifying a machine gun is until they've been in front of one with bullets splattering all about. It shook me, I'll tell you that. Unlike the two previous times that day, when we were incidental targets in the rear, this time our platoon was clearly the object of the VC barrage. I felt my pants get wet in the first few seconds as I fell flat to the ground behind a small lump of ground. We had to get the hell out of there or we'd soon endure casualties, but I knew our platoon couldn't pull away until Grovich had time to relieve the Second Platoon, which I hoped was ongoing since the gooks were now focused on us.

So I kept down to the ground and waited three or four minutes as both sides engaged in an intense barrage. Then, figuring that was enough time for the First Platoon to pull back, I started crawling on my hands and knees away from that damned machine gun nest as fast as possible, telling the others, most of whom were actually engaging the enemy, to follow along. But I move faster than almost anyone alive when death is knockin' on the door. Before I knew it, I'd crawled out behind the troops in my platoon, gone around a small bush, and came face-to-face with two NVA soldiers crawling fast towards me on *their* hands and knees.

I screamed at the sight of them, causing the lead fellow to also yelp and stop fast in his tracks. The second dink who was still coming forward stumbled into the first, causing both to fall forward on their chests. In a flash, I rolled on my side to fire the M16 but couldn't control it because the sling had tangled on my arm. Instead, I desperately grasped for my pistol. As I pulled it from the holster, I looked up to see a rifle point rising up towards my face. I hollered in despair just as a burst of gunfire exploded so near to my head that my eyes went black. When I opened them a moment later, the two Vietnamese lay dead, their bodies still twitching just feet away, and Pineapple stood behind me laughing. "What's the matter, *Haole*, you never heard a Pig before?"

I grumbled, my ears ringing from being so close to his M60. "Yeah, I heard one. Next time, get here a little faster, *Brah*," I said, using a Hawaiian word for friend and staring hard in his face as the rest of our platoon began coming into view, crawling or hunching over as they left the battle site.

As our guys came into view, the forest suddenly went quiet. With us no longer firing at them, the VC must have realized we'd moved away and they, too, ceased fire. With the woods serving as a protective screen, I figured it was safe to get up, so I rose to my feet, shoved the pistol back in its holster, went over and kicked the two dinks to make sure they were dead, and walked away from the scene like nothing had happened.

It was a game piece of acting if I say so myself. By a miracle, I'd just missed being killed and my heart was pumping like crazy. But in front of the troops, even a comrade like Pineapple, I had to act like it was no big deal. If you think that's easy when your insides are mush and you feel like throwin' up, just try it sometime. Vietnam showed me that it's not who a man is, but who he appears to be that counts. And I've always been good at appearances.

Once Mann confirmed that our entire platoon had pulled back, and that we had no losses, we retreated back to the big gravesite, where I found Grovich and Burns in a heated discussion. "We got 'em all out but two guys, Love," said Grovich. "Williams and three other KIAs, plus two wounded. But we couldn't get to the Point man and one more. They're still up there lying out on the ground. We're thinking how to go back for 'em.'"

The imbecile was crazy, but instead of just arguing with him, I tried to convince him with some reverse logic. "You can count on the Third Platoon, Sir. My boys are pissed off now and ready to fight. But we shouldn't rush back in there too fast. Those dinks are really dug in. We were lucky that time because they didn't expect us coming in the back door, but it won't be the same the next time. Sure, maybe we can get our two KIAs back, but we could lose more good men in the process. You have to ask yourself if it's worth it. And there's a second point to think about, Sir. As you said earlier, our mission was to pull a surprise flank attack so the main thrust could succeed. Well, we did that. We came around here and engaged the enemy. But let's face it, we didn't succeed 'cause the dinks are still in their bunkers and now the element of surprise is gone. It seems to me the best thing we could do now is go back and talk with the others about this strategy. Since we don't hear anymore gunfire from the other units, they've probably pulled back anyway to rethink the attack."

"But we can't leave our dead behind, Loveless," interjected Burns, the stupid ass. "The gooks will strip them and leave 'em lying in the dirt."

"I know how you feel, Jeremy. I really do," I said, as calmly as possible. "But you see," and I put my hand on his shoulder like an older brother, "we can't always do what we want in wartime. You're right. We all want to go back for them, but we also have an obligation to the rest of our men here." I waved my hand around, indicating the other soldiers, some of whom were eyeing us as we talked. "If that was me lying dead up there, I'd understand if the company didn't come back just now. The VC may take their weapons and clothes, but like you said, they'll just leave the bodies on the ground. We can always go back later when it's safe."

"What you say makes sense, Love, but I still don't know…" said Grovich, wavering in his typical indecisive way.

"Well, there's one more thing, Sir," I said. "I know it's not right, our men and the mission come first, but I was worried about you, too."

"Me? Why are you worried about me?" he queried.

"Think how it looks, Sir," I replied. "We failed in our flanking attack and we lost men. If we hang around here now and just keep doing the same thing and losing more men, when we might be needed back there, it'll just look worse for you as the company commander. It's commendable to try and retrieve our KIAs, but it's more important to win the fight. We need to talk to the other units to coordinate our efforts. Still," and here I paused for effect, looking very solemn and looking him straight in the face, "I understand how you feel, Sir, so if you'd like, I can stay here with maybe half my platoon and we'll try to get those men back after it gets dark. The VC are dug in, expecting us to keep coming back. I doubt very much that they will come out on the attack. They'll stay in their bunkers and, hopefully, after dark, they'll relax a bit. That's when we'll try to sneak in there and get out our KIAs." It may seem as though I'd lost my senses by making such a suggestion, but I knew my man.

There was no way Grovich could go back and tell brigade that he'd left behind part of a platoon to carry out a recovery operation on their own, especially since all four companies were supposedly already on a mission to recover dead bodies from the downed chopper. Even my volunteering wouldn't justify him leaving us behind.

"No. No, we can't do that, Love," he came back quickly, as I'd hoped. "We have to stay together."

"Are you sure, Sir? I really don't mind and there are some others—"

"No, I appreciate your offer, but we must stay together, and you're right, we must go back. We'll take this hill, and when we do, we'll get our men back," he said with determination.

So, exhausted and minus a half dozen men for our effort, we returned to rejoin the other three companies still engaged in the main battle. It didn't take too long to go back, since we were just retracing our steps through where we'd already gone earlier that morning. When we arrived at the main AO, things were just as bad as when we'd left, probably worse. The NVA was still entrenched in their bunkers, there was still plenty of lead flying in both directions, and another dozen on our side had been killed or wounded. It was just as dangerous in the air. A medevac chopper had been hit trying to fly out the injured and had gone down, fortunately without any injuries, while a second chopper had landed back on Million Dollar Hill, but wouldn't take off because of the .51-cal machine guns. Can't say I blamed the pilot, considering how things had been going.

While Grovich again went off to confer with the other chiefs, I got yet another look at how bad things were going. We'd set up to the rear of the other three units, so I was able to sit back and watch as dead and wounded were carried past our location to be placed on medevac choppers for transportation to Chu Lai. In the short time I sat there, probably five wounded soldiers were brought back. Once, a soldier with his eyes bandaged shut was led past my location by a friend who held his hand. I don't think the soldier was blinded, just wounded near his eyes, but the thought gave me shivers as I'd rather be dead than blind.

However, the most unusual sight I saw while sitting there was a soldier being helped to the rear by two buddies. For a second, I thought he was drunk. Although able to walk on his own, he was very wobbly in his steps and was mumbling wildly, but it looked like he didn't have a scratch on him.

"What the matter with him?" I asked as the three of them went by.

"Heat casualty," answered the one nearest to me. "We've had four or five guys collapse today from this heat."

"Heat casualty?" I intoned, thinking it strange since we were all hot as hell. "What do you mean? What's a heat casualty?"

"Our medic says it's not unusual in the 'Nam," he answered, pulling to a halt, most likely because I was an officer. "Sometimes people get so drained of water they can't sweat, he says. After a while, they get dizzy and confused and just lie down on the ground. If we don't get them out of the sun, they can get sun stroke and maybe even die. But if we can get them in the shade or some-place where their temperature can get down to normal, then they're okay. This is our second guy this morning. Our medic has us take them back to the rear where they pack 'em in ice on a Huey and then take them back to Chu Lai. He said heat casualties usually return to the field in two or three days, unless they really get it real bad, but that's rare."

That was news to me. Even though I'd been sweating profusely, I hadn't thought until then about the possibility of someone actually getting killed by the heat. But it did make sense. It was hot as hell in that valley, with all of us working in a constant sweat. I'd gone through three canteens of water in the last few hours and was still thirsty just sitting there in the shade. "Okay, thanks," I said as they continued on their way. But I thought to myself, *Just one more way the 'Nam can kill you.* Then I put it out of mind.

Before long, Grovich returned, looking serious but bringing with him the best news I'd heard all day. "The NVA's dug in too deep," he said. "We're not making any headway and now another Huey's gone down, so brigade's or-dered everyone to back off the attack. We're all to go back up the hill and then they're gonna send in jets and try to blast 'em out of there."

That made a lot of sense to me, and within minutes, all four of the com-panies hit the trail out of there. We were hot and beaten, but full of new energy now that we were moving away from that damned bunker line. In fact, we were so energized it took us only half as much time to hike back to the top of Million Dollar Hill as it had to go down it earlier that day.

Just as we reached our morning jump-off point, I heard a screeching sound overhead, followed by a thunderous explosion back at Hill 102. I turned around to see a jet fighter pulling up into the sky after having dropped his load on the bunker site. A few seconds later, a second jet swooped down and hit the hill again, this time causing a ripple of explosions. That was normal attack mode for jet fighters in the 'Nam; they always came in pairs, so one could watch the backside of the other. Everyone knew that pattern, including the NVA, because as the second jet rose away, the dinks opened up with a ma-chine-gun barrage. They failed to hit the second jet, but it must have been a scare for that pilot. I stood there watching the second jet roar away as a grunt standing nearby said, "They've been doing that for three days."

"Doing what?" I asked.

"The gooks," he said. "They stay down when our fighters come, then they come out and blast away at the second jet. They know they're safe 'cause the first plane don't have time to turn around and target 'em. But sooner or later, we're gonna lose one of those fighters. It's just a matter of time."

I could see his point and mentally agreed that it was probably just a matter of time before we lost a jet, but at that moment I really didn't care. I'd nearly been killed myself that day and was for letting the NVA keep Hill 102 and the rest of that accursed valley, if they wanted it so badly. All I wanted just then was some water to drink as my canteens were bone-dry empty. A few minutes later I got what I wished for, and a lot more.

All that morning, clouds had been rolling in from the central highlands, slowly covering the valley, and bringing some much-needed shade. The screeching of the jets must have loosened something upstairs, because no sooner had the last of three separate pairs of jets flown off in the distance than it started raining, and raining, and raining. At first it was a welcome relief from the heat as the water was cool and refreshing. Along with dozens of others, I sat on the side of the hill overlooking the valley, looked straight up into the sky, and let the rain wash over my face. After a bit, I turned my helmet over, let it fill with water, and drank it down, and then filled and drained it again. It was the finest rain I'd ever known, for about half an hour. After that, it was just one more miserable Vietnam experience. Outdoors, with only a few trees for shelter, we all soon became soaked to the bone. I wore my boonie cap and ended up pulling out my air mattress and stretching it over my body as much as possible, but to little avail. There was a constant torrent of water pouring from the heavens and all we could do was get wet!

By the time the rain finally stopped, night had fallen, and so had the temperature. Even though it was still about eighty degrees Fahrenheit, for us that was a thirty-degree drop from earlier in the day. In wet clothes, it was just one more hit as we passed the night huddled against each other, shivering with the cold. That, plus an on-and-off bombardment of Hill 102 from our artillery back in the rear, kept me awake the most of the night.

The next morning's heat chased away the chill in my bones but did nothing to stiffen my spine. I woke up hopeful the brass had finally seen the light and would take us out of that accursed place. It just didn't make any sense to have infantrymen banging away at an enemy that was so well entrenched. "They should pull us back and just send in the B-52s," I told Bryson. "When they're dug in that deep, the only logic is to just blast the fuckin' dinks out. We're just gonna lose a lot more men if we go back in there like yesterday. Only an idiot would order that again."

Sure enough, around eight o'clock, the idiot sent down word for us to again try and take Hill 102. So we dragged on our rucksacks, slung our weapons over our shoulders, and got ready to move back down into the ravine. Then something unusual happened that kept us in place and delayed the attack.

I was standing with Bryson, waiting for our orders to head down into the valley, when a lieutenant from one of the 4th of the 31st companies came up and asked if he could use our radio for a conversation with his battalion commander. That was strange since he should have had his own radio and RTO. But there was no reason to object, so I nodded approval and Bryson pulled it off his back and handed it to the officer, who walked a short distance away before starting to talk. Curious, I edged over just close enough to overhear; his conversation went something like this:

"I'm sorry, Sir, but my men have refused to move out." There was a pause and then he said, "I think they understand, but some of them have simply had enough. They are broken." Then another pause, followed by the lieutenant again, saying, "That's the problem, Sir. Most of our squad and platoon leaders have been killed or wounded. The men won't go." Another short pause, and then he said, "Yes, Sir. I understand, Sir." At that he walked past me, returned the radio to Bryson, and headed, I assumed, back to his own unit.

It was one of the strangest conversations I'd heard in more than a year of army duty. It sounded like the officer's unit was refusing to go back into the fight, but I knew that couldn't be true. No soldier would dare refuse a direct order; they could be court-martialed and imprisoned for deserting under fire. Even though I'd heard what he said, I couldn't believe it until word came back up the line that soldiers in one of the units had refused to move forward. Their action, or inaction as it was, brought the whole advance to a halt. That was okay since no one wanted to move forward anyway, so we all reclined to the ground and held in place while the situation was resolved. That didn't take long.

Within half an hour a chopper came in and dropped off a major and a ser-geant major; the latter looking very much like my father, which meant he was someone not to mess with. I watched as the two lifers, both looking very grim, walked past our platoon on their way to talk to the reluctant group of soldiers. Not long after that, we got word that the soldiers who had refused to join in the advance had apparently changed their minds and would now go along, so it was time to get off our butts and resume moving towards the enemy posi-tions.

We didn't know it at the time, but the next week, that little episode ended up being front-page news across America. I found out just how big a story it was some months later when I saw a *New York Times* article titled "TOLD TO MOVE AGAIN ON 6TH DEADLY DAY, COMPANY A REFUSES." Newspapers and broadcast networks all across the country had somehow picked up the story, making it sound like five of Company A's troops had led a mini-mutiny, telling their lieutenant, who was fairly new to the field, that they had had enough and weren't going to fight anymore. It might not have been such big news, except, in addition to the battle of Hiep Duc Valley being the biggest con-frontation in Vietnam at the time, the Secretary of the Army just happened to be visiting in our area right then. Lots of media trailed in his wake and, true to their nature, were looking for something controversial to report. So it wasn't surprising that it became a big story.

Still, when I read the *Times* article, it seemed to me they blew it way out of proportion.

The story that we got later that same day was somewhat different than what the media reported. We were told that five soldiers, who spoke for the entire unit, hadn't actually refused to go into battle. They just wanted to talk to the IG or someone higher in the command—to complain about the lack of rest and food and stupid orders that seemed to have no purpose, except get-ting more men killed trying to recover dead bodies. I saw their point, of course, having had the same thoughts myself. Once the sergeant major and senior officer talked to them, they must have realized the futility of their complaints, or at least felt they had been heard, because they went right back to work as combat soldiers.

Unfortunately, with the so-called "mutiny" over, the war started again. Down the hill in a line we went, four companies strong, although somewhat less strong than a day before. I had an ominous feeling going back down that trail into the Valley of Death, as it was called years later in a book. I knew it was only by the grace of God, and Pineapple's Pig, that I hadn't been killed the day before and now we were headed back into the same hellhole.

At least we weren't alone. Just before we reached level ground, a jet shot across the sky and unloaded on the bunker site up ahead, setting off a loud explosion. We stopped our march, waiting for the following jet, and sure enough, it came thirty seconds later, dropping straight out of the sun and touching off a second fireball on the hill ahead. It set off the dinks, too. Just like the day before, they opened up with a heavy machine gun as the second jet pulled up and away. They might have got him too except this time the combat airmen, knowing what to expect, had planned ahead. As we watched fascinated, a third jet came screeching in low over our heads, causing me and many others to nearly jump out of our skins. It roared in just above treetop level and then pulled straight up in the air, as the pilot plastered the bunker line with napalm bombs. It was the first time any of us had seen a trio of jets on the attack and I'm sure it caught the dinks by surprise. Flames roared across Hill 102, followed seconds later by a loud, reverberating boom. Thrilled that the fighters might have hit pay dirt, we let out a cheer that was nearly as loud as the explosion. It was stupid, of course, because it just alerted the dinks that we were on our way, but it was a spontaneous reaction that we couldn't hold in.

We had no sooner finished cheering than orders came over the radio, telling us to proceed to the base of Hill 102 and prep ourselves for an assault on the bunker line at the top. Only this time, the order of attack was changed. "Us and D Company are taking the lead today," said Grovich over the radio to me, Burns, and some sergeant who, with Lieutenant Williams gone, had assumed command over the Second Platoon. "We'll be on the right, D on the left," Grovich said, "with the others trailing behind in reserve. I know it's tough being up front," he added, "but arty's been hitting this place all night and that last bomb drop must have hurt the gooks. With luck, they're ready to throw it in, or maybe they've already moved out. This could be our chance to shine, so pass the word that we don't let up until we take the top," said the simpleton. "Love, put your platoon on the left, next to D Company. That'll be the center of attack. We're gonna need your experience there. Then the Second Platoon in the middle, and Burns, you take your guys to the right."

I wanted to tell him that my experience was really nothing more than keeping my head down and hightailing it away from trouble as fast as my legs would go, but Grovich would never have believed that. After all, hadn't the President just cited me? So, with no chance the attack would be called off, there was nothing left for me to do but to carry out his orders and hope to God Grovich was right about the NVA.

Up the cursed hill we went, slowly picking our way through the brush and keeping an eye out for booby traps, while keeping as quiet as possible. We stopped frequently to observe what lay ahead, and drink down water, as the heat from the prior day was back in full force. There was some shade going up that hill, but almost all of it from short, scrubby bushes that offered little relief. Even trying to conserve my water, I quickly drained two of my three canteens and would have gone through more if the dinks hadn't opened up on us.

Like most firefights in the 'Nam, the enemy got off the first shots. Not yet halfway to the top of the hill, we hadn't expected to make contact so soon. Luckily, I had just stooped over to catch my breath for a second when they hit us with small-arms fire from what seemed like a very close distance. I saw one man go down on my right as I fell forward to the ground and rolled behind a small bush. Instinctively, I began crawling backwards as fast as possible to get away from that deadly fusillade, with Bryson close by dragging the radio along.

We ended up behind a mound of dirt, which protected us somewhat from direct gunfire and gave me a chance to look around at what was happening. What I saw was my men all low to the ground, returning fire fast and furious towards the top of the hill. But it was probably for naught. The dinks had planned their attack well and were virtually invisible, except for a few flashes of gunfire now and then. All we could do was blast away at the brush and trees up ahead and hope to hit somebody.

I grabbed the handset from Bryson to call for support, but Grovich beat me to it. His voice came crackling through the receiver "Dragon Two, Dragon Two, move over and link up with D Company. They're under heavy fire and need support!"

His words caused me to turn to my left and look in the direction of Company D's position. While I couldn't see them, since we were about a hundred feet apart, I could hear several loud explosions and the sound of gunfire from that direction was definitely louder than where we were. They appeared to be getting it worse than us and probably did need help, but it was near impossible for us to move from our own position because of the gunfire.

"Dragon Six," I shouted back, "we're under fire, too! We have people down and are fully engaged! We can't possibly move from here now! Out!"

There was a pause at the other end, and then, "Roger that, we're moving in your direction," came the answer. So for the next minute or so, I kept down behind the dirt pile, doing my best to stay calm and watching the action take place around me. Then Grovich was back on the radio. "Dragon Two," he said, "you must move over and link up with D! That's a direct order from brigade! You must go and support their attack!"

"But we have several wounded, Sir. They can't be moved," I argued back.

"Then leave someone behind to watch your wounded and take the rest! We're on our way and should be there in a few minutes! We must support D. It's not an option!" he yelled.

I didn't dare refuse a direct order, so I replied in the affirmative and then Bryson passed the word along to the men that we should evacuate any wounded and move back down the hill to get below sight of the enemy. As we did so, I linked up with Sergeant Mann and informed him of the company orders. He volunteered to stay behind with six or seven others to look over the wounded, which ended up being just two individuals, and to keep the dinks occupied until relief arrived. He said if his few troops could just maintain a semblance of firepower, the enemy might not even realize we'd pulled out until Grovich showed up with the reinforcements. I thanked him and then he turned away to start gathering up the soldiers who would stay behind with him. Shortly thereafter, the rest of us departed.

It took a little time to move back down the hill, and once we'd got to where it felt safe, we stood upright and started humping in the direction of D Company. They couldn't have been that far away given the loud volume of sounds we heard, but we never got there. Midway through a small clearing, we suddenly came under fire again, although this time it only sounded like just a few enemy combatants. Nonetheless, caught in the open, we took off running as fast as possible for the nearest shelter. I sprinted for a big tree and dove under it, landing on my stomach and banging my face into my rifle, which I'd carried in front of me. I rolled on my back to catch my breath and wiped off sweat that was flowing down my neck and forehead. That was when an idea flashed through my mind that I realized might get me out of that cursed place. It may seem strange that someone could even conceive of what came next, but I've noticed over the years that my best inspirations often came when danger beckons most. Perhaps that's why I've survived so many dangerous encounters.

I glanced around and saw that no one was looking my way. Bryson and several others were close by, but were focused on the direction of the enemy fire, which was already easing, and not watching me. So, I let go of my rifle, looked up at the trees above and began taking in rapid, heavy breaths while tossing my head from side to side. I continued that routine for a short bit until Bryson crawled to my side and looked down at me laying there, my head rolling, my mouth open, and my eyes blinking rapidly.

"Jesus! Medic!" he yelled loudly, as he came to his knees beside me. "Are you hit, sir?" He was in a near panic as he grabbed hold and turned me on my side to look for any wounds. I responded by babbling some nonsense and continuing to roll my head from side to side.

"Medic!" he yelled again. "Medic, man down!"

Seconds later, with the VC gunfire now sporadic, our doc and several others came running up from somewhere. Doc also gave me a quick look-see for any wounds, then put his hand on my forehead and said, "Heat prostration. We've got to cool him off."

I could have given him a hug, but that would have blown my cover. So I continued my act of breathing, blinking, and rolling as they lifted my head up, took my backpack off, and loosened the front of my shirt. It was then that one of them poured water down on my face and chest and I almost blew it. The shock of that wet liquid hitting my hot body brought me instantly upright on my butt. Fortunately, after a split second, I had the sense to maintain a blurred look in my eyes right, jabber some nonsense, and fall back to the ground.

"We've got to get him to the rear," said Doc. "He can't go on, and if he stays here, he could die. Help me get him to his feet." Strong hands began to lift me off the ground.

""Hold it," said a voice, and back down on the ground I went. There was a short discussion above me between Doc and another and then, between blinks, I saw Mann's face looking hard into mine.. I had no idea how he'd caught up to us when we'd just left him up on the hill, but I wasn't about to ask. I was more worried that he would see through my game and call me out. To my surprise, he said, "Yeah, get him to the rear. I'll take over the platoon. Shadley, you and Yancy take the lieutenant back. Bryson, you come with me." And then he was gone. Mann might have thought I was faking it, I'll never know. But with me out of the way, he would be in charge. That certainly would have appealed to him as he liked giving orders and probably figured the platoon was better off with me out of the way. He would have been right, of course, but I didn't give a damn. I just wanted out of there.

The two soldiers lifted me up and carried me back down the hill, with one leading the way holding my legs while the other grabbed under my arms and across my chest. They must have stopped to rest a half dozen times and were constantly complaining about my weight, which I thought was petty, since by doing that job they were getting farther and farther away from the firefight. It took a while, but we made it down the hill and eventually came to a place where other Americans were gathered. The whole time I continued to act incoherent, mumbling and keeping my eyes closed or unfocused, but I could tell we'd reached a safe rear location because of the surrounding sounds.

My two stalwarts lay me down beneath a small canopy of some sort and then the leg-holder went away, returning a short while later with a several other grunts. One of the new guys must have been a medic because, like Doc, he felt my forehead and asked questions of the two who had brought me down the hill. I overheard him say something about "a chopper," and then soon after, he and my two escorts were gone. I was left lying on the ground with one soldier, who placed a wet rag on my brow, as a guard. As I'd hoped, my deception had worked and no one questioned my condition. The heat stroke casualties from earlier in the battle had set the stage, and everyone just assumed I was one more.

I don't know how long I lay there, having my forehead cooled, my eyes closed and pretending to be semiconscious, but it had to have been more than an hour. During that time, the sound of gunfire in the distance went away, which probably meant the battle was drawing to a close. Not long afterwards, I heard the sound of a chopper approaching and landing nearby. Then I felt myself being lifted again, placed on a stretcher, and then carried towards the sound of the helicopter, where I was gently lifted aboard and loosely tied to some kind of hooks on the chopper floor. During all this, I did not open my eyes,, except for occasional blinks and mumbled nonsense. I lay there tied to the floor no more than a few minutes, during which I heard the crew talking and helping several other wounded come on board. Then we were off, the tail of the chopper rising first and then a forward thrust that lifted me up and away from Hiep Duc Valley.

As we rose in the air, a cool wind blew through the chopper, and I felt a surge of exhilaration flow through my body. I was out! Away from the heat and slaughter of that damned place. I'd cheated death again and, hopefully, kept my reputation intact. All I had to do was fake a slow recovery back in the rear. For the first time in days I relaxed.

And then someone, a medic I suppose, put an ice pack to my forehead. I gave a shout and bolted upright to find myself face-to-face with a soldier who was holding a wet cloth and, of all people, Sergeant Mann. I rolled my eyes and fell back to the floor, moaning. But it was too late. Mann had seen through me.

"Feeling better, Sirrr?" he slurred down at me from what felt like just a few inches above my face. I didn't respond, except to turn my head away from him and breathe deeply. "You'll be happy to know, Sirrr," he went on, "that we took the bunker line. And that I'll be your bunk-mate for a while. I got a little wound here in my arm, so I'm going back, too. But you just relax. We'll be at division soon. In the meantime, I'm sure this ice pack feels good for a hot head," and he placed that freezing rag back on my forehead, holding it tightly. I was ready for it this time and didn't jump. But it sent a chill down to my toes and would have soon given me a giant-sized headache if something more pressing hadn't intervened.

One second we were gliding gracefully through the air. The next I heard a loud "Bang!" and felt the chopper rock sharply to the left. "Shit, we're hit!" yelled one of the door gunners, and the ice pack fell away from my head. I shot up to a sitting position and saw with horror that smoke was pouring from the rear of the ship. The pilot pulled it level, but the Huey shuddered violently, as though hitting bumps in the air. We were clearly in trouble.

I struggled to free myself from my bindings. I didn't want to be tied down if we hit the ground. There were several other soldiers nearby, all grabbing whatever they could to keep from falling out of the rolling, whirly bird, and I saw Mann on his knees, up behind the pilots, watching the scene unfold. He'd forgotten all about me as the pilots struggled to keep us airborne.

Several times the chopper tried rolling over to its left side, and each time the pilot managed to right it. But he was definitely losing the fight and we were definitely losing altitude as the helicopter slowly wobbled downwards towards the ground and the cabin filled with smoke. I freed myself from the final binding just as the pilot turned on his headlights, probably to get a better view as he landed. I glanced outside to see a large rice paddy coming up fast and braced myself hard against the rear of the cabin, grabbing hold of a metal bar and lifting myself up off the floor. There was a tremendous jolt as the chopper hit the ground, bounced up, and then came down hard again before sliding along the ground to finally tilt over and rest on one side.

The final impact of hitting the ground loosened my grip and threw me down and across the cabin. I smacked the back of my head hard against something, but remained alert. As we came to a halt, I scrambled to pull myself up and out of the smashed wreck. In doing so, I stepped over an unmoving body that looked to be partly crushed by the crash. He may or may not have been dead, but I had no time to worry about anyone else as I reached up, grabbed the side of the cabin, and pulled myself out of the Huey. With nothing to grab on to on the side of the downed bird, I slipped and fell face forward into rice paddy slop, landing next to someone else. He helped me to my feet and then the two of us stood there for just a second, looking around to catch our bearings. We were in the midst of an open field stretching away on all sides, with a tree line off to one side in the distance. I heard some sounds coming from inside the downed chopper, but when my companion shouted, "Let's go," I took off following him as we ran low across the rice field towards the forest. We were in enemy territory and didn't want to be there when the Cong showed up.

CHAPTER NINE

The sun was just going down in the west as my companion and I fled the spot of the crash. Contrary to the day before, when we had a heavy downpour of rain, it looked like the skies would be clear that night. That was good because it meant the two of us would be able to move easily through the countryside. But it also meant that pursuers, if there were any, would have an easier time searching for any crash survivors, so we needed to put as much distance as possible between us and the crash site.

For five or six minutes we ran along rice paddy banks, headed for a group of small trees in the distance. Then there was a loud banging noise from behind us, and we both hit the ground and buried ourselves in rice paddy goop. Cautiously, the two of us then raised our heads slightly and peered back towards the downed chopper in the distance. The sound had come from there and, sure enough, I saw about half a dozen figures, silhouetted against the fading sun, headed for the Huey. At least one of them held a weapon with a banana-shaped clip, which meant they were either VC or NVA.

They spread out in a semicircle as they approached the chopper but then disappeared from my sight as they got up close and the sun glared directly behind them. Seconds later, several shots rang out from the direction of the wreck and then it was quiet again. We assumed they'd found someone alive and finished them off; I shuddered, realizing that could have been me.

"Oh sweet Jesus, we're gonna get killed," said my partner, who was in the muck beside me, in a low voice.

"Come on," I whispered back, pulling on his arm. "Just be quiet. I don't think they know we're out here." I began moving away, this time staying hunched over as much as possible to avoid being seen. He lingered for just a second and then came after me. Behind us I could hear faint shouting, which told me the dinks were probably ransacking what was left of the helicopter. The two of us stayed low to the ground, moving steadily towards the trees, and I kept glancing back every few seconds to see if there was any movement in our direction, but saw nothing. Then suddenly, a second burst of gunfire split the silence of the night.

I dropped to my knees and froze in place, but my partner, probably thinking the shots were aimed at us, went erect and ran full speed ahead, making himself an easy target in the moonlight. As he pulled away from me, I, too, thought it would be better to run than remain in place and I went to my feet. But in doing so, I looked back towards the sounds of gunfire and realized that the dinks were not shooting at us. The flashes of their guns, which clearly lit up the evening sky, appeared to be going in the opposite direction and increasing in frequency as they went. That could only mean, I told myself, that someone else had survived the crash, and the dinks were in hot pursuit. It also meant the bad guys would be distracted for a while, which gave my companion and I a good chance of getting away from there. I turned back to the front and saw him disappearing into the trees about fifty feet ahead and then took off sprinting towards where he'd gone.

He was waiting for me when I arrived, calling out in a low voice as I got close. I hit the ground near him and then turned to watch the firefight that was still going on back across the rice paddy. It sounded like the gooks had their hands full because there was definitely an M16 steadily popping away amongst the AK-47 fire. But it was only one against many, which meant the end was inevitable. Sure enough, after a few minutes, the sounds of gunfire and the flashes melted away. I wondered at the time if that lone fighter had been Sergeant Mann. I hadn't seen him when we fled the chopper, and no one else would have tried to hold off so many VC by themselves. As much as he'd disliked me and gotten in my way a number of times, I had to give him credit, Mann was one tough soldier. "That's life," I muttered to myself, and then turned back to my new partner in flight.

The rest of that night the two of us moved steadily away from the location of the crash, heading in what we thought was an easterly direction, where we figured there were more American bases. At first, the woods were jungle thick, almost impenetrable, which made for very slow progress. I cut myself numerous times on thorns and bushes as we fought our way forward and was elated when, after several hours, we stumbled across a trail through the forest. Already exhausted from fighting through vegetation, we decided to follow the trail, even though we both knew it could be dangerous. A pathway in the middle of that kind of jungle in Vietnam could only have been worn down by the sandals of many people over a long period of time, which probably meant VC bringing weapons and supplies from up north. But we weren't thinking too clearly that night. We just wanted to get far away from the spot of the helicopter wreckage.

It must have been well after midnight before we felt it was safe enough to stop and rest. Drained of energy, we moved away from the trail, spread out some very large leaves, and lay down on the ground to rest. I must have slept soundly, because the next thing I knew the sun was up and soft raindrops were splashing on my face. I rose slowly from the hard ground, my body stiff in a half dozen places. As I moved, my partner jerked up quickly, looking around desperately in all directions. I calmed him with a wave of my hand and then for a few seconds, we listened to see if there were any sounds of movement near us. It was all quiet like a forest should be, with only the rustling of trees and birds flittering above.

"Frank," I said, breaking the silence and holding out my hand. He came back with "Clay," and for the next few minutes, we exchanged stories about ourselves. I told him about my time in the 'Nam and learned that he was copilot of the chopper and a true short-timer, having been in-country for nearly a year. Other than that, and the fact that his home was in California, I didn't learn much about Clay, which was just as well considering how things turned out. From somewhere he came up with a Butterfinger candy bar that we shared for breakfast and then we were off again, moving towards what we hoped was the ocean and safety.

We walked all morning, following the trail as it meandered up and down the hills and ridgelines of the forest. By midday, we were near numb with fatigue, having gone for miles with just the candy bar for food and no water. We were lucky, having a canopy of trees for shade, but we'd both been without water for nearly a day, and with the sun as hot as it'd been the day before at Hiep Duc, we were shriveling up from the heat. My eyes actually began to blur from the loss of moisture and I wondered how it would feel to die from thirst. Inwardly, I laughed at the irony of it and imagined how the newspaper headline would read: "Hero Frank Loveless dies in the jungle from thirst after faking heat stoke the previous day."

Clay, who was in the lead on the trail, was the first to hear what sounded like water gurgling nearby. I thought he was having delusions but then I heard it, too, coming from slightly below us on the right. So we turned off the trail and stumbled along for just a short distance before finding a small mountain stream that was flowing through the forest. We didn't hesitate a second, jumping in face first and nearly drowning ourselves as we frantically gulped in the water. I sank to my knees and then lay down on the stream bottom, with just my head above the water. It was clear and refreshingly cool, considering the overhead sun poking through the trees above. I could feel my body starting to come back to life as my pores drank in the life-giving liquid.

After a while, we pulled ourselves onto the stream's bank and lay there discussing what to do next. We decided to follow the water flow, since it seemed to be headed in the right direction and we didn't know when we'd be able to find water again. We also thought there would be a better chance of finding food along the stream, although we really had no idea of what kind of food there would be in the woods.

For the next several hours we walked in the stream's bed as it meandered through the forest. It was more difficult than walking down the trail, but it felt safer and it was certainly a whole lot cooler. I don't think we had gone very far, certainly no more than a few miles, when the stream emerged from the woods into more open ground. Initially, we hesitated to leave the shelter of the forest, but we certainly couldn't turn back, and to the front we could see several small pockets of foliage along the stream bed where, in an emergency, a person could hide to avoid detection. So we pressed forward.

It was late afternoon, with the forest far behind us, when the stream finally merged into a larger river, which appeared to go in a more north-south direction. Because the flow of water was wider and deeper than the smaller stream, we hesitated before deciding how to proceed, finally choosing to walk along the shallow edge of the water as it went in a southerly direction. We didn't know where that would take us, but given the direction, we were confident of not ending up in North Vietnam. Our bigger concern was that the land had begun to look cultivated and we were worried about running into any Vietnamese.

Our fears proved well founded a short time later when we came around a bend in the river and found two men a bit farther downstream, standing knee-deep in the water with what looked like fishing poles. They saw us at about the same time and one of them yelled something and waved, probably assuming we were fellow fishermen. They couldn't have been soldiers, standing there fishing, so I waved back, and turned around slowly to reverse course and walk away as though nothing was wrong. But Clay wasn't as calm. He bolted like a startled deer and started sloshing through the water back in the direction we'd just come. "Wait! Stop!" I screamed, but to no avail, as Clay was too panicked. I watched for a second and then looked back to see that the two fishermen had dropped their poles and were climbing out of the water! They'd seen Clay run and must have realized we weren't your ordinary Vietnamese.

With no more thought of deception, I plowed after Clay, yelling at him to head for the shore. He heard me and soon we were climbing out of the river on the opposite bank from the Vietnamese. We paused for direction and then took off running as fast as we could to get away from the stream, going through several open fields, clambering up a small hill, and then going around a couple of fields with tall crops before stopping to rest in a small gully. As we did so, we heard the sounds of people, seemingly far away but coming from different directions. "They're trying to encircle us," I said, and off we went again.

This time, we went until my legs literally gave out from under me. I stepped on something and my left leg, which was still not fully healed, buckled and I fell to the ground. Clay, who was close behind, stumbled over me in his haste. We dragged ourselves up in a flash, and then paused in disbelief. The voices were still audible, but sounded like they were getting closer, not farther away, even though we'd run several miles.

I fell back against a tree, panting hard as Clay, standing no more than six feet away, asked "Which way?" At that very moment, a shot rang out and he lurched sideways to the ground, hollering in agony and holding his side. I went down nearly as fast, looking desperately in the direction where I thought the shot had come from, but saw no one. I went to Clay's side and saw that, indeed, he was hurt bad. A bullet had torn through his left side, coming out his back.

"Get up!" I yelled, grabbing him by the shoulders and trying to pull him to his feet. But he just sagged to the ground and lay there looking up at me.

"Frank," he gasped, in obvious agony. "I'm done for. Please tell my family—"

"You'll be all right!" I cried, trying again to pull him from the ground. "You've got to get up!"

"No, I'm finished. Please. Give this…give this to my wife," he said in pain and pulled a small wallet from his back pocket and pushed it in my direction. "Promise. Promise…that you'll take it to her."

Well, I don't need to be told when a discussion's finished. He'd made up his mind to die and I honestly thought he was done for anyway as his breaths came fast and heavy. So I said, "I promise, Clay." I stuffed his wallet down the side of my boot, laid him gently on the ground, had one more fast look around, and took off running.

I didn't go far. I ran over a small hill, somehow tripped on something with my bad leg, and proceeded to tumble face down into more water. I came up gasping for air and found myself in a small stream that looked very much like the one we had been in hours earlier. *Christ*, I thought, *we've been going in a circle*.

But there was no turning back, so I began forging across to reach the other side. As I neared midstream, I heard the sound of a rifle locking a round and a voice from behind say, "No. No." I stopped and raised my hands above my head and then turned slowly around to see a man, armed with a rifle aimed straight at me.

"Oh God," I said to myself, and then out loud, I said, "Okay, okay," hoping he understood I was surrendering. He yelled something loudly and was soon joined on the bank by two others. None of them wore a uniform.

As they gathered together, one of them motioned for me to come out of the water, which I did, keeping my hands above my head. Then he walked behind and, putting his hands on both of my shoulders, pushed me down to my knees. It hurt when I hit the ground, but I was so frightened, it was a minor inconvenience. One of the three stood in front of me, his weapon aimed straight at my face, while the fellow from behind searched through my pockets. He found nothing, which made sense since I rarely carried anything on my person. All my letters from home and family photos were in my rucksack. That, along with my M16 and .45 and even my knife, had been taken from me when I was put on the medevac chopper the day prior and were, by that time, probably resting comfortably back at Baldy. However, he failed to check my boots, where I'd just put Clay's wallet and somehow he missed in one pocket the small medallion I'd found weeks earlier in the jungle. Satisfied I was hiding nothing, the dinks tied my hands behind my back with some kind of cloth and motioned for me to get up and start walking back up the little hill. I did so, and they followed.

They took me back up to where Clay lay silently, having passed on. One of them searched through Clay's clothes, but again found nothing, and then the four of us headed back down towards the stream. We soon came across a fairly wide trail that we followed for a short distance before entering a small clearing surrounded by eight or nine small hooch's. As we came into the center of the little village, about twenty Vietnamese of all ages gathered about us. A few of them pointed in my direction and made threatening gestures, but most just stayed away, not wanting to get too close to the foreign devil, I guess. We stayed there only a short time, sitting in the dirt near a fire pit of some sort, until a somewhat older man showed up.

He was probably a village chief of sorts because as he entered the clearing, one of my three captors approached the fellow and began talking to him in a deferential manner. As he listened, the elder kept his eyes focused on me and nodded repeatedly. Before long, he silenced the talker with a wave of his hand and then turned and pointed in a westerly direction while telling something to my captor. He must have given instructions of some kind because not long after, we were headed westward, only this time I had two more escorts in addition to my original three. I tried to ask where we were headed, but it was plain none of them understood English. So I tried a few Vietnamese words I'd learned from Suzie, including the word for town, which I've now forgotten. I'm sure it surprised them that I could speak anything in their language, but I was like a two-year old trying to make himself understood. They just chuckled and made jokes with each other whenever I spoke. So I soon gave up and stuck to sign language the few times I needed to communicate.

We spent the rest of that day moving steadily west with the sun going before us. Mostly we kept to jungle trails, but once in a while, we would enter a small village and a similar scene would be repeated—the guards would have me sit in the village square while the residents would circle around, make menacing gestures and occasionally throw small rocks in my direction. They might have been expressing their true feelings for Americans, but at times, I felt they were just putting on a show for the VC because a lot of it was just noise. Whatever the case, the guards always made sure I wasn't harmed, which told me they were taking me someplace special and would protect me until we got there.

Soon after darkness arrived, we entered a much larger village with dozens of huts spreading out in a small valley. It was different in another way, too, because when we entered the village square, instead of gathering around to see the strange foreigner, the townsfolk kept their distance. In fact, the few who saw me acted as though it was no big deal to see an American, which I thought was strange since we were far from any American camps. Shortly after arrival, we were met by a man, who appeared to be in his thirties or forties and apparently had some authority. He talked to my escorts a few minutes, after which they placed me on the ground near a hut and untied my hands. Most of them then went away with the town guy, leaving just two of the guards watching over me. That was enough though. I had no intention of trying to escape from even one armed man, much less two, so I just leaned back against the hut and waited for whatever was going to happen.

As I sat there, I began to think that maybe I'd reached the end of the line. We were obviously waiting for something, and in my mind, that meant someone was deciding my ultimate fate. I had pretty much resigned myself to whatever was to come when an old woman approached our trio and handed out rice soup to me and the guards. It was pretty bland stuff, but having not eaten all day, I eagerly scooped it down. More than that, it was very reassuring because, if they were feeding me, it meant I wasn't going to be killed; at least not that day.

About the time we finished eating, the headman returned with one of my original escorts and indicated I should get back on my feet and follow along behind him. I did, and this time I was led to a solid mud-packed structure at the edge of the village that looked similar to constructs I'd seen in other Vietnamese villages. Somewhat larger than regular family dwellings, it had much thicker walls, no openings for windows, and a short entryway that forced adults to stoop over when entering or exiting the thing. Built because of the war, the place was like a bomb shelter. A direct hit by an artillery round or aerial bomb would have blown the building to smithereens, but it did offer protection from bullets or flying hand grenade and artillery fragments. As we came to the front of the reinforced hut, the leader of the guards grunted something and indicated I should enter. So I bent down to the small entry and crawled inside. It was cramped and dark in the interior, with the only light coming from the entryway.

As I entered, a familiar voice spoke up. "Well, look who's here. It's the hero lieutenant!" It was Mann! In the dim light I could see him sitting on the ground and leaning forward, with someone else next to him leaning against the wall.

"Sergeant Mann," I said, ignoring his insult, "so they got you, too?"

"Not without a fight," he replied cockily. "I shot three of 'em before they took me down. I'm sure you gave them hell, too, *didn't* you, Lieutenant?"

"I didn't have a weapon," I said, paying no attention to his insolent tone and crawling forward into the space, "but I managed to elude them for a day at least." There was another man in there. "Who're you?" I asked the other fellow.

"Sergeant Fitzgerald, Sir. From the 121st Evac," he replied, and I realized he was the medic from the chopper.

"He's been my savior," said Mann. "I took one in the arm. The Doc here patched me up good." And I saw that Mann's right arm was in a sling of sorts.

"We're lucky to have him," I said, but truth be told, I was kind of concerned to see them together. They were the only people who could make a claim that I'd faked being a heat casualty, as they were both there when I reacted to the ice pack in the chopper. If we all made it back alive and they ever went public, it could be the end for me. The army would be more apt to believe my word against either one of them, since I was an officer, and a decorated one at that. But if they both testified against me, it might be another matter. On the other hand, it was somewhat comforting to have them around.

Since being captured, my only thoughts had been about wondering if I would ever see home and family again. With two fellow Americans, I began to have some hope. After all, since they'd not already killed Mann or Fitzgerald, it probably meant they were going to keep us alive for some reason. Plus, I recalled reading about an American who had escaped from the Vietcong and made it back to the world sometime earlier in the war, so there was some hope. That night, before going to sleep on the dirt floor, I made up my mind that, no matter what I had to do, I would survive.

The next morning, the three of us prisoners and at least ten Vietnamese armed guards resumed our journey west. Most of the time, we Americans were unable to talk to one another because they separated us from each other. The only times we could communicate was when the group stopped to rest or eat, which wasn't that often. The scenery was similar to the day before, lots of hills and trees and unbearable heat, as we kept to well-worn trails. But the terrain was definitely becoming more remote. The day before, we'd met a number of people on the trail, almost all of them farmers carrying loads on their backs. Now, as we moved steadily farther inland, there were fewer dwellings and we rarely passed anyone going in the opposite direction. Three times that day we stopped—once to eat, once to avoid detection from a pair of American jets high above, and once to rest at a barber shop along the way. At least, I think it was a barber shop. Three of our guards took turns having their hair cut by an old man, while an equally old woman fed us some rice and bananas.

That night we slept in the open along the trail, then rose at dawn the following morning and walked for another half a day before arriving at what we quickly realized was our final destination. We'd traveled so far by that time that we might have passed into Laos. I'll never know for sure where we ended up, but I was certain that we'd reached our objective as soon as it came in sight between thick trees. Not only were our guards suddenly more animated, the place ahead just didn't have the feel of a typical Vietnamese village. There were grass-thatch hooches, but they weren't spaced out like in other hamlets and several of them were very big, much too large for even an extended family. Also, unlike other villages I'd seen in the 'Nam, the woods grew in very close about that place. Some tall trees had even been pulled over and tied down atop some of the buildings, probably for concealment from planes flying overhead. I had expected to end up in some kind of prisoner-of-war camp, and I was surprised to find that there were no watchtowers or barbed wire around the place we entered. There was only a bamboo fence that stretched around most of it, and not a very good one at that. At the rear of the camp, there appeared to be no fence at all, only a stream or small river flowing along.

They marched us down to a large open space in the middle of the camp and had us stand in line, at attention, until a bow-legged man, who was less than five feet tall, came out of one of the buildings. He stood in front of our formation and addressed us, and unlike our escort guards, he was dressed in a military uniform and could actually speak some English.

"You now prisoner of war," he said in a loud voice, as though we didn't know it. "This is prisoner camp. You live here. You not escape, you be okay. If you try escape, you die." He then pointed at the surrounding forest. Then he walked along the line of us, stopping close in front of me first and shouted, "You name please!"

I shuffled my feet and looked down at him and said, "Loveless, Sir."

"Love less?" he replied. "What you mean love less? No talk love. I want you name!"

"My name *is* Loveless, Sir," I answered, trying to seem sincere and subservient, as the last thing I wanted was to anger him. The little man looked at me strangely, probably wondering whether I was lying or crazy. After a few seconds of scrutiny, he turned to Sergeant Mann, who was next in line.

"You name please," he demanded.

Mann gave me a glance and then looked down at the gook and said, "Mann."

"I know you man," barked the little Viet. "I want you name!"

"My name *is* Mann," said Mann in his own serious tone, and I worried that he might strike out at the little guy. Fitzgerald didn't share my alarm as I felt him force back a chuckle. The gook certainly didn't think it was funny. He got red in the face, glaring at Mann, and then at me, and then back to Mann.

"You think this joke!" he cried. "This not joke! You prisoners! You not soldier now! You disgrace soldiers! You follow rules, maybe you go home! You not follow rules, maybe you die!" He was clearly getting excited and might have lost it completely but for an abrupt interruption.

Suddenly, there was an ear-piercing scream from behind us. I automatically turned to see who had made the noise, but saw just a blur of someone running towards us and then felt a sharp crack across the side of my head. The blow sent me sprawling on the ground, my head exploding in a succession of colored lights. Several other vicious whacks to my back and legs followed, sending shock waves pulsing through my body and causing me to howl out in pain. I curled up to protect myself, and then, as the blows thankfully stopped, tried to crawl away. Someone shouted, causing a guard to block my path and hold me down; then a second one grabbed my arms and the two of them pulled me up to my knees. I hung there between them, trying to clear my head as blood trickled down my cheek. I muttered, "Please, please don't hit me." Then my head was yanked violently back and I found myself looking straight at a face I'd hoped to never to see again—Nguyen, the owner of the carwash in Tam Ky.

I shrieked in recognition and tried to pull away, but the guards held me fast and forced my face back up into Nguyen's, who was delighted that I had recognized him. He stood there, staring down at me and smiling, savoring the moment. In his left hand was a stick that looked nearly as thick as a ball bat. I was sure he meant to kill me on the spot. But instead, he pushed his face about an inch from mine and screeched something as loud as possible. I shut my eyes from the sound and wished I could shut out the smell as well because his breathe was horrible. Then the smell went away and I opened my eyes to see Nguyen, a few feet away, talking to the short English speaker.

The little man looked down at me and then said, "Captain Nguyen very happy see you. He say you hurt daughter. He say you no die, but never leave prisoner of war camp."

"No. No, it's not true," I wailed. "I respected his daughter. I loved her. Tell him I loved her!"

The little man said something in Vietnamese, but it just infuriated Nguyen, who snatched a rifle from one of the guards and chambered a round.

"No!" I bawled, struggling in vain with my captors. "No. I did love her. I'm your friend. Remember?"

But Nguyen remembered me only too well. I was the man who'd defiled his daughter and caused her to run away from home. And now I was helpless at his feet. He grinned at me and raised the gun to my face. I pulled and yanked to get free, knowing death was but a second away.

Then the little man who spoke English stepped forward and said something to Nguyen in a quiet but commanding tone. Nguyen lowered the gun and responded angrily, but the little man calmly replied, holding out his hand, palm upwards. Nguyen shouted at him and gestured towards me, but the little man stood his ground, thank God! Whoever he was, he had fortitude to stand between me and that murderer. He had power, too, because after one last shout in my direction, Nguyen thrust the rifle to the ground, turned on his heels, and walked away, obviously not pleased.

The two guards released my arms and I dropped to the ground, shaking from the near death experience. The little man walked forward, looked down at me, and said, "Commander come back soon. He decide you. Tonight you sleep here so Captain Nguyen happy." He pointed at the ground. Then he spat out something to the guards, most of whom then led Mann and Fitzgerald away, towards some hooches on the far side of the camp. I was left behind, slumped in the dirt, attended by two of the dinks who looked nearly as frightened as I, even though they had guns.

The rest of that day, I stayed on the ground in the middle of the camp. My two guards gave me a rag that I applied to the side of my head to stop the bleeding, and late in the day, they brought me some bananas, nuts, and tea. But mostly they just talked to themselves and smoked something in bamboo sticks that didn't smell like tobacco. Just before sunset, the little linguist came back and had them drive stakes into the ground and tie me to them, spread-eagled, with my back flat against the dirt. I was sure they'd learned that trick from watching old cowboy and Indian movies, which proves there's a limit to how much of our culture we want to share with foreigners.

I spent the night like that, going in and out of consciousness, my wrists and ankles hurting from the tight knots around them, and constantly trying to shift my weight away from small rocks that poked me in the back. It was damned uncomfortable, I'll say that, but it was worse the next morning. I woke to find myself covered with ants and other bugs. Unable to knock them off with my hands, which were tied down on both sides, I yelled and shook myself as best I could, but most of the bugs hung on, little bothered by my movements. One of the guards came over to see what the fuss was about and found it amusing enough to call over two of his friends, who were no more sympathetic to my problem.

All three of them stood there munching on food and talking like I was some kind of new plant they'd just discovered, while the bugs slowly ate me alive. The only time my guards showed any expression was when I shook myself trying to get rid of the tiny tormentors. Then the gooks would point at different places on the ground and jabber like a bunch of gamblers betting on a game. They were enjoying the scene so much it could have gone on all day. Fortunately, my cries must have had some effect, because after a while, another Viet came up and ordered me untied, which they proceeded to do. Even when the ropes came off, it still took time for circulation to return to my arms and legs, before I could rise to my feet and knock off the remaining bugs. When I was finally able to walk, the guards took me over to one of the large buildings in the middle of the camp.

As I entered, several people rose from the floor to greet me, one of them being Fitzgerald. The other was an American, too, but his appearance wasn't very reassuring. He was tall, perhaps six-four, and very thin. I guessed that he weighed less than one hundred twenty pounds, his hair was matted and grown down beyond his shoulders, and he moved very slowly. His clothes, which were black Vietnamese pajamas, looked like he'd lived in them for months.

"Sorry for the rough appearance," said the apparition, sticking out his hand. "You'll look the same after you've been here as long as me. Name's Franklin. Ted Franklin. Major Franklin if you prefer, but we don't use rank around here much."

I took his hand, which felt like sandpaper, and introduced myself. As I did so, I couldn't help but ask, "How long have you been here?"

"I've been a prisoner a little over three years," he answered. "Been in this camp about half that time."

"You've been here all that time?" I stammered.

"Don't worry," he said, grabbing me by the arm and leading me over to sit on a straw mat. "It's not that bad. If I can make it, so can you."

It was then that I looked around at my new surroundings. The hooch was about fifteen wide by thirty feet long in size and dimly lit, with just a few holes in the corners of the roof and along the sides to let in light. The only sign of furnishings were seven or eight straw mats laid out on the floor. I couldn't image living there for a few weeks, much less for years.

We sat down and, while Fitzgerald, who was a Medic after all, removed my boots and rubbed my ankles, which were swollen from being tied up all night, I told Franklin how I'd been captured, leaving out only those details that would have done me no credit, such as being a fake heat casualty. When I was finished, he still had one question, "What did you do out there to make 'Happy' so angry?"

"Happy?" I asked, not understanding the question.

"The fellow who knocked you down. We named him after one of the seven dwarfs because he's always smiling. I couldn't see everything from here, but he sure didn't look happy with you," he said.

"Oh! Him. His name's Nguyen. I met him in Tam Ky. He thinks I took his daughter away from him. Truth is, she just ran away from home. Can't say I blame her, having him for a father."

"You're lucky to be alive," said Franklin.

"The lieutenant's always lucky," said a voice brazenly from the back of the hooch, and Mann came walking out from the shadows. "He has a knack for getting out of tight spots while everyone around him is getting killed. Isn't that so, Lieutenant?"

If we'd been alone, I would have suffered his insolence, but with the others present, I thought it best to play a more forceful hand. "We may be in a prison camp, Sergeant Mann," I said, "but I am still your superior. You'd best not forget that."

"I never forget it, Lieutenant. I know exactly who I am and what you are. And I know how fortunate we are to have you here, because in this kind of place only the strong survive," he added menacingly, with emphasis on his final words.

I started to rise to my feet to confront him, but it was hard to get up, especially since Franklin put his hand to my chest and Fitzgerald kept hold of my ankles to keep me on the ground. "If there's some sort of trouble between you two, you'd best get over it quick," said Franklin. "We all have to stick together in this place."

"Yes, Sir," said Mann, responding. "You can count on me." And he stared hard in my direction and then walked back into the shadows.

For the next several hours, Franklin told me about the camp and I filled him in with news about the outside world. I learned that in addition to him, there were two other prisoners at the camp who happened to be somewhere else just then. He said their names were Eddy, who'd been a door gunner and survived when his chopper was shot down, and Rodrigues, a Puerto Rican infantryman. We were the first Americans they had seen since Rodrigues had been captured more than six months earlier.

There were less than twenty Vietnamese soldiers patrolling the place, he said, mostly NVA from up north, plus a few women who did the cooking and cleaning. As Franklin had mentioned, the American prisoners had named the most prominent Vietnamese after the seven dwarfs. Nguyen, who they called "Happy," came to the camp only once or twice a month on short visits. The rest of the time, I assumed, he was in Tam Ky spying on us and the ARVNs.

The camp commander was called "Bashful" because he was rarely seen. Franklin thought him to be a literate, cultured man because he treated the prisoners well. From time to time, Bashful and Franklin would even play chess because, said Franklin, no one else at the camp understood the game. The short English speaker was called "Doc." He was the camp politician and held classes for the prisoners, educating them on the history of Vietnam and about how the evil country of America would lose the war. Franklin said there were times he felt that Doc, who was most likely a member of the North's Communist Party because of his speeches, had more power than even the commander. Given the way he had stood up to Nguyen the day before, I didn't doubt it.

Two of the other guards were named "Grumpy" and "Sleepy" for their demeanor, although I found Grumpy to be mostly show. While there were times he seemed to snap at us Americans for no reason at all, I noticed that when he wasn't being watched by the other guards, he was much more calm and easygoing.

"No Snow White and the Old Witch?" I asked Franklin, half joking.

"Oh, we've got them, too," he said. "You'll meet Snow White soon enough—at dinner tonight. She's okay, the only thing good to look at around here, but strictly off-limits. As for the Witch, you better hope you never meet her. She's part of their military, or at least some military. Her uniform is different from any we've seen before. And sometimes, I think she speaks a different language from the other gooks."

"What does she do?" I inquired.

"Asks us questions mostly," he said. "She and her sidekick—a guy we call "Dopey"—show up here several times a year and stay for a while. They take turns with each of us, asking about our family, our friends, where we're from, stuff like that. Not military questions like you'd expect. They always end up telling us how our family is suffering or how our wives and girlfriends are out running around while we're sitting here in this place."

"Do they speak English?" I asked.

"Yeah. At least she does. And she knows a lot about the war and what's going on in the world. I lied to her about my family once and, somehow, she found out. The next time she came here, I paid for it. They staked me out like they did to you, only I stayed there until she left more than a week later."

"But what do they want if they're not asking military stuff? Maybe she just wants to brainwash us or make us feel bad about this stupid war," I said.

"That's the point, isn't it?" replied Franklin. "I don't think they expect to get anything from us. Most of us have been prisoners too long. We don't know what's happening out there. They just enjoy playing a game torturing us."

"But they don't actually torture us, do they?" I asked, worried. "Except for staking us to the ground?" It was a question that meant a lot to me. From the moment I'd been captured, I'd thought frequently about how I'd react if tortured. Deep down, I knew I'd say or do anything to keep matches out from under my fingernails.

"Not usually," he said solemnly, looking off into the distance, as if recalling a terrifying experience. "But once last year, the Witch took a guy from here at night. A young black guy. An hour after he left, we heard a loud scream. Then another.... Then another.... It went on for a long time, maybe several hours. And then silence. The next day, they said he'd escaped and run away in the jungle. They even punished us for it. Made us sit in the sun all day without water. But we knew better. We knew she'd killed him. Even the guards couldn't look us in the face after that. She's the devil! The devil in female form!

"But other than that," he said, turning back in my direction and deliberately changing the subject, "living here is very routine. On days when it rains, everyone just stays in their wood buildings or attends indoctrination classes taught by the Doc. When it isn't raining, which is most of the time, the Vietnamese guards usually take us prisoners out to work in a banana patch or do menial tasks around the camp. Other than that, we just sat around and wait for time to pass."

The other two Americans, Eddy and Rodrigues, were out working the fields when I arrived at the hooch. Franklin had been left behind because he had come down with a sickness called beriberi, and he proved it by pulling up his pants to show me his swollen legs. "My balls are as big as golf balls," he said, "from eating too much rice."

"When do you eat?" I asked, trying to change the subject and realizing that I hadn't had any food since the night before.

"They give us a daily ration of manioc and rice," he answered. "Sometimes, we get some fruit, and once in a while, pork or chicken. But don't plan on putting on too much weight." He chuckled, rubbing his very thin stomach. "We're fed twice a day, but lucky if we get one good meal out of it." I found out later that they had made their own stove in one corner of the hooch. It wasn't much, just some mud-packed rocks holding up a piece of metal, but it worked on the few occasions they had something to cook.

We were still talking when the other two prisoners came back to the hooch late that afternoon. Rodrigues was physically thin like Franklin but quite different in personality. He kept to himself in one dark corner of the room and seemed to be sullen and depressed at all times, someone who had just given up on life. During my time at the camp, I don't think we exchanged more than ten words, and those were just simple greetings. But Eddy was something else. Even though he'd been at the camp for nearly a year, he seemed healthy, almost robust, and his spirits were high. He talked a lot about his life back in the States and pumped me with questions about what had happened back home since he'd been captured. He clearly had not resigned himself to being a prisoner of war forever. That evening, as he and I sat staring out the small entrance to the shack, I asked him a question that had been on my mind since arriving at the camp. "Have you thought about escaping?"

"Of course, I've thought about it," he said. "But it's near impossible. Out back the river's lined with *punji* sticks. They're below the water level so you can't see them, but they're there all right. If you step on one, you won't go very far with a hole in your foot. The only other way out of here would mean going through the gook's living area to the front gate, and there's always someone on guard there, day and night. You'd have to have one of the guards help you to get through there. And even if you made it out of this place, where would you go? We don't know how far we are from civilization, much less a friendly

American base. Sure, we know enough to head east towards the ocean, but traveling through that jungle without food or weapons, with every gook in the neighborhood looking for ya—you'd be just asking to die. Nah, I've thought about it, but I'll take my chances here."

"We're safer here," piped in Franklin, who was listening nearby. "As long as we keep our mouths shut and do what they say, we're treated all right. Sooner or later, this thing will end and then we'll all go home."

That sounded good to me. I didn't mind sitting out the war, even as a POW, so long as we were safe like Franklin said. But Franklin didn't have to worry about Nguyen. I was sure the carwash owner would kill me if he had the chance, and that could come sooner or later. In the back of my mind, I knew I had to escape if the opportunity presented itself.

That evening, I met Snow White. She and an older woman came around and gave us several baskets of food for the following day's ration. The other woman, who could have been anywhere from age forty to sixty, was obviously the boss and didn't seem too friendly. When Franklin pointed at me and said my name, she gave a blank look in my direction and turned away halfway through my "How do you do?" I noticed she was coughing every few seconds and thought she might have pneumonia. "Sneezy," Franklin said as she left the hooch.

Snow White was different. She was about eighteen years old and fairly attractive. Both Eddy and Rodrigues said hello when she entered and she nodded back in return. I'm sure they both fantasized about her, and that she knew it. When she drew near, I gave her my best smile and looked long and steady into her face. She diverted her eyes to the ground at first, but then returned my look with a knowing smile that told me I'd scored. I wasn't surprised. Women of all ages and all nationalities like to be admired. This one had just come of age and was stuck in the middle of the jungle with few men to choose from. I was probably the best thing she'd seen in a long time, and I'd made plain my attraction to her.

From then on, whenever I had the chance, I greeted Snow White in my rudimentary Vietnamese and made a point of expressing my interest. Once, when we passed close to each other, I brushed her side with the palm of my hand. Her mouth dropped open in surprise and then, I swear to God, she started to blush. If we'd been anywhere else, I think we would have consummated the union right then and there. Under the circumstances, of course, that was impossible. Still, I felt certain she was soft on me, and it gave me something nice to think about in that hellhole.

Two days after our arrival, we three new guys joined the others in their daily routine. We rose with the sun, did stretching exercises for about ten minutes, then ate breakfast and went to work. As Franklin had said, it was make-do jobs like digging trenches or gathering manioc. I'm sure it was mostly for show, just to keep us busy, especially since we spent most of the day sitting around waiting for instructions from the guards.

We did have some entertainment at the camp. Late each afternoon, they marched us down to an outdoor area near Doc's quarters and made us sit on the ground while listening to Hanoi Hannah on the camp radio. She spoke English and had a half-hour program that was mostly bullshit propaganda. But Hannah always played a couple of American songs, which we welcomed, and once in a while, by listening to her, we could catch a hint about what was happening back in the world.

About a week after my arrival, they changed our schedule. Instead of making us listen to the radio broadcast, we were taken to a separate building and made to sit through a political lecture. The so-called classroom had several rows of wooden benches and signs in English on the walls that read "VIET-NAMESE WILL WIN JUST WAR. FREEDOM FOR VIETNAMESE. AMERICA WILL LOSE." The six of us sat in the front row and had to stand up at attention when the Doc came in. He welcomed us and then spent the next four hours talking about the Vietnamese people's historic struggle against the Chinese, the Japanese, the French, and the Americans. During my time there, we learned all about Vietnamese heroes from the past, including a couple of sisters, whose names I forgot almost immediately. It was boring stuff really. It's no wonder people were always fleeing Communist countries, if that was what they had to endure in school.

This routine went on for about a month with little variation. With little else to keep me occupied, I got to know a lot about each of the other prisoner's, except for Rodrigues, who hardly ever talked to any of us. I tried to practice my Vietnamese with the guards or Snow White whenever the chance arose, hoping to establish some kind of rapport with them. But of the guards, only Grumpy seemed to respond, and even then not in a very friendly manner. The rest of them acted like I had leprosy.

At night, I had a hard time sleeping on the dirt floor, and there was never enough to eat, but other than that, I had adjusted to being a prisoner of war quite easily. Even my early fears about Nguyen gradually diminished. He'd not made an appearance since that first morning, and I was beginning to think I could just sit back and wait out the war. Then the Witch came.

We knew something was up when the Doc showed up at our morning exercise period. We rarely saw him before noon and never that early in the morning. As soon as we were done with breakfast, he had us line up in formation in the middle of the compound. We stood there, at semi-attention, for nearly an hour before we heard a hubbub at the far end of the camp. Soon after, a group of eight or nine people came around the corner headed in our direction. "It's the commander, Bashful," whispered Franklin to me, and then, "Oh God! And the Witch!"

I saw her as soon as he spoke, and I knew what he'd meant by different uniforms and different language. Her clothes were different—sharper and more professional—and I could guess what language she spoke. She may have looked like just another Oriental to the others, but I knew right away, having lived in Seoul as a youth, that she was Korean and, based on her uniform,

North Korean at that. And she wasn't alone. There was another Korean trailing along behind her, a big brutish-looking man also in a uniform similar to hers, undoubtedly the one Franklin called "Dopey."

As they drew near, Doc ordered us to stand at attention, which we did of a fashion. The commander, a medium-sized person, wearing a NVA uniform, greeted Doc and then proceeded to give a short speech, translated by Doc, which basically welcomed us newbies and informed us of how lucky we were to be prisoners of the humane National Liberation Front. He ended by reminding us that we would be treated well so long as we did not try to escape, but that we would be killed if we tried to get away, as though we didn't already know that.

While he was talking, I paid attention to the Koreans standing directly behind him. It was well known that there were several South Korean army units helping us in Vietnam, mostly in the central part of the country. But I'd heard nothing about North Koreans being involved in the war. Yet they were right in front of me, big as life. I felt sure their presence at the camp would be big news if any of us ever got back to the world and reported what we'd seen.

The man was your typical Korean soldier. His immaculate uniform was tight to his body and the look on his face, as he watched us, was harsh and menacing. I marked him down as someone to stay away from. The woman was far more interesting. She looked to be in her late twenties or early thirties and was slightly over five feet tall, with one of the best figures that ever graced a pair of fatigues. An attractive face peered out from beneath her cap with a smug look on it. Surprisingly, it was she who stood next to the commander during his monologue, which meant the woman was senior to the man. I say surprisingly because women rarely rise to a position of influence in North Korea.

When the commander finished his speech, Doc led him forward to meet each of us new prisoners, starting with me. He chuckled when Doc explained my name and said, "Welcome to POW camp," and held out his hand, which caught me by surprise. But I grabbed hold and shook hands, thinking Franklin was right. Bashful was probably a nonviolent man, who would have been a teacher or bureaucrat in another time.

As he moved down the line to greet the others, the rest of the entourage followed along and I soon found myself confronted by the female, standing directly to my front and staring hard at my face. I averted my eyes down to avoid her look, concentrating on the uniform name tag, which translated out as "Kim." As I did so, I couldn't help but notice her breasts. They were magnificent—slowly heaving up and down in the most sensual manner, like they were straining to burst free of that tight... I realized my peril and shut my eyes quickly, but it was too late. Against my will, I felt a lump rise in my pants. Keeping my face forward, I tried to glance to my left to concentrate on what the commander was saying to Sergeant Mann, standing on my left. I was hoping she would follow my glance, but she didn't.

"This one is very interesting," she said in Korean to her countryman standing to her left rear, and then she placed her hand flush against my chest, which made my discomfort all that more pressing.

"He is a criminal! The enemy of our people, and not worthy to live!" angrily replied the man, who was clearly not one of my biggest fans.

"Yes. But his name is strange," she said. "I have heard it somewhere." And then she spoke directly to me in Korean, saying, "Are you famous my Loveless?"

Her question was so unexpected that I almost answered her in Korean. I already had part of the first word out of my mouth, "An...." when I caught myself and started to cough. But she, too, had been caught off guard, not expecting a response in her own language, and especially from an American. A puzzled look came across her face, and she came closer, only inches away, and spoke to me in her native tongue again, this time quieter. "Do you understand Korean, Loveless man?"

This time I was prepared. I smiled weakly and, as though I was apologizing for the cough, said, "Sorry, Ma'am, I chocked on something." It gave her pause, but that's all. Her dark eyes searched my face and peered deep into my eyes to see if I was lying. I gave a blank look back, but felt the sweat on my forehead and knew somehow that she wasn't fooled. Fortunately, I didn't have to keep the bluff up for long. I heard the Doc call out to her and, after a quick nod in his direction, she said, this time in good English, "We'll talk again." Then she moved on down the line, followed by Dopey, who cursed as he went past. As she moved away, I took a deep breath and whispered, "Thank God" to no one in particular. Something told me it would be very unhealthy if she knew I understood Korean.

But the Witch wasn't through with me just yet. A few seconds later, there was a commotion to my left. I turned to look and saw her standing in front of Fitzgerald, who was third in line. She was slowly unbuttoning her uniform blouse and looking back in my direction with a smug look on her face. She had already opened up halfway and had both the commander and the Korean soldier shouting at her. The Korean was particularly agitated, waving his hands and yelling something about her family and the Fatherland. But she silenced him with a sharp rebuke and ordered him to back away, which he did, although reluctantly, I thought. Then she pulled the commander off to one side and spoke quietly to him, while the rest of us looked on in fascination. After a short exchange of words, it was clear that she was going to have her way. She returned to confront Fitzgerald and continued unbuttoning her blouse. Bashful might have been the commander, but she was the one in charge.

Fitzgerald was beside himself. He was young, I think maybe a bit more than twenty, and terrified by what was happening. He was pumping his feet up and down, blubbering, "Please. Please don't," and turning his head left and right for help. But there was nothing any of us could do, except look on in astonishment. In short order, she had the last button undone and then, with a final look in my direction, pulled open her blouse.

The Good Lord can strike me down if I ever see a better chest than that one, because everything will be downhill from then on. These days, women pay thousands of dollars to get tits like that, but hers were as superb and real as nature intended. As she had probably intended, since she was again looking at my direction, I felt a stirring rise up once more.

But her attention quickly went back to Fitzgerald. Visibly shaken, he had closed his eyes, refusing to look down at the bounty below him. It was a useless gesture, as she meant to have her way. She reached down, took hold of his hands, and placed them on each of her breasts. Fitzgerald reacted as though he'd been burnt, yelling, "Ahhh," and yanking his hands behind his back. She just smiled, moved closer, and spoke to him so softly that I couldn't hear from just six feet away. Then she reached down, took his hands gently into hers, and once more placed them on her breasts.

This time he left them there, his eyes now wide open. She took hold of his arms at the elbow, smiled satisfyingly, and leaned back slightly, so that everyone could get a good view. For a few moments, Fitzgerald remained stiff, and then, you could tell, he began to relax and enjoy the work within his grasp. He was gawking straight down at her boobs with a smile on his face as his rough hands squeezed and massaged her bosom. He did such a good job that before long, her eyes had closed and small gasps of pleasure were coming from her mouth. I thought my pants would burst from just watching and I nearly yelled, "I'm next!" when her eyes flashed open. She then pulled back her right arm and smashed her fist into Fitzgerald's face.

The blow staggered Fitzgerald and he stumbled backwards off his feet. He lay on the ground, propped up on his elbows, while she stood with clenched fists above him, screaming curses and threats. It reminded me very much of the famous scene when Muhammad Ali stood over a fallen Sonny Liston at the end of their second fight. I thought to myself that he was done. She had played with him as a cat does a mouse and would surely kill him now. But that was not her plan.

She barked out some orders and two of the Vietnamese guards snapped to and dragged Fitzgerald, who was pleading, "Please! Please! I did what you said!" back to his feet. She slapped him hard across the face and shouted in clear English, "Shut up. Do not talk." He stopped with the words, but stood there whimpering, his arms held tight by the guards, while she calmly re-buttoned her blouse and tucked it back into her fatigue pants. When she was done, she spoke to one of the guards, who came forward and began to strip away Fitzgerald's clothes. He protested for just a second, but stopped just as fast when one of the guards slapped him and it was plain no one could help him. When they were finished, Fitzgerald stood there as naked as the day he was born, and probably just as confused.

The Witch gave him a look-over, smirked at his nudity, and said something to Doc. Then she walked away from the formation, followed by Bashful and Dopey, who had stood by during the whole episode. As she departed, she went directly past my front and I heard the words "*Dasi Manapsida*," which is how a Korean would say "see you again" to an inferior. I pretended not to hear, but it struck me then that the whole thing with Fitzgerald may have been just a demonstration to impress me with her power. If so, it had worked. From that moment on, she had my attention.

Sadly, Fitzgerald's ordeal wasn't over yet. "Punishment is for to enjoy too much touching Colonel Kim," said the Doc, addressing our group. "Sergeant must stand here with no clothing." Apparently, it was one thing to have touched her, and yet another to have enjoyed it.

So, while the rest of us were soon released and allowed to return to our hooch, Fitzgerald was made to stand out there in the steaming hot sun the entire day, a spectacle for everyone in camp. He stood there until his legs gave out, and then went down on his knees for more hours until the sun finally disappeared from sight. Only then did he get any relief as two of the guards came out and carried him back to our living place. When they dropped him and his clothes at our entryway, his body was burnt and dehydrated, something terrible. Franklin and Eddy carried Fitzgerald inside and gently placed him on the ground, and then pulled his clothes on him. For the next hour or so, we took turns dousing Fitzgerald with cool water from the river while he just lay there with tears on his face.

That night, Fitzgerald killed himself. We found him the next morning, his wrists slit lengthwise up the arm, probably by a sharp stone that we found near his body. Mann said Fitzgerald was a very religious person, so we just assumed the poor fool couldn't live with his shame and had slowly bled to death while we slept just feet away. We buried him out back of the camp, next to the graves of two former POWs, who Franklin said had died a year earlier while trying to escape through the jungle.

Very little out of the ordinary happened during the next week or so as we went about our daily routine. I saw the Witch up close only once in that time, when she was our "guest teacher" in class, telling us about the paradise of North Korea and how much better it was living there than in South Korea, with its corrupt puppet government. She also let us know, by the by, that the United States was going to hell for its crimes against the workers of the world. I swear it looked as though she was getting through to simpleminded Rodrigues, who seemed to eat up her every word and who even asked her several dumb questions. But I don't think she really cared if any of us bought her baloney. More to the point, she just enjoyed having us stand at attention and answer up whenever she wanted. She would ask each of us in turn such things as "Who had started the war in Vietnam?" or "What is the most evil country in the world?" and so on. The correct answer was always the United States, and we always told her what she wanted to hear. Only a fool would disagree with her after what had happened to Fitzgerald. I was still worried that she might question me again about my Korean language ability, but as the days went by and she never brought it up, I began to think she'd forgotten me. I should have known better. Women rarely forget Frankie Loveless.

CHAPTER TEN

The reunion I'd worried about came several days after our class on Korean history. I had just pulled myself beneath the burlap sack that served as my blanket and was ready for some shut-eye when Grumpy and another guard came in the door calling out my name. I rose from the floor and hesitatingly walked towards them. "Don't worry. It's probably nothing," said Franklin as I passed him on the floor. But I could see in his face that he didn't believe his own words. This was the first time since my arrival that any of us had been called outside after the sun had gone down and horrible ideas were running through my head. I walked slowly, trying to think of something, anything that could keep me in the room. But it was futile, as nothing came to mind. As I neared the entryway, Grumpy gestured towards the door with his rifle and said, "*Ongoai*," which meant for me to go outside.

"*De lam gi?*" I answered riskily ("What for?").

"*Kim dai ta*," he said, meaning Colonel Kim.

"Christ," I said out loud, with both Fitzgerald's ordeal and Franklin's story about the Black flashing through my mind.

"Oh God," said Franklin from behind. I stopped in my tracks and turned to see him rising from his mat, as were others in the room. "Do whatever she asks," he said, running up and grabbing me by the shoulder. "Whatever you do, don't make her angry. Just submit to her will."

It seemed to me he knew more about her than he had let on earlier, but there was no time to discuss such things just then, what with a rifle prodding me to get moving. I exited with the two guards, accompanied to the door by everyone except Mann, who had stayed on his mat with a smirk on his face. He probably thought he was seeing the last of me.

I'd expected to be taken directly to her hooch, but instead, the guards walked me up the hill to a building that I knew to be the dink's latrine. At the door, Grumpy handed me a bar of soap and a razor and said something in Vietnamese. I didn't understand his words, but his meaning was clear enough—he wanted me to clean up. To that, I had no objection as the only bath I'd had in weeks happened days earlier when I slipped and fell into the river behind the camp on our way to work. Shaving was rare, too. They made the five of us share just one razor, so we just took turns trimming our beards. Not that it mattered much; with our poor diet, the hair on my face grew slowly anyway. But the most important thing about being able to wash and shave was that it gave me some mental relief. I knew if they planned on killing me, it made no sense to have me get cleaned up.

I spent half an hour making myself as presentable as possible, given the ragged clothes I wore, and then the two guards took me across the compound to the big hooch that served as Colonel Kim's living quarters. Grumpy knocked on the door, and when a female voice answered, he pushed it open and gestured for me to enter. As I did, he took hold of my arm with a firm grip and, much to my surprise, winked at me and said, "Be Okay." I stood there gawking for a second, but only for that, because a clear voice from inside had said, "Come in."

When I did, I found myself in a room about twenty feet square in size. There were two small screened windows on opposite ends of the place, and a second door directly across from the one I'd just entered. Off to my left was a military cot, covered by a mosquito net, while nearby were a footlocker, a small desk, and some shelves. I noticed uniforms stacked neatly on the footlocker, as well as some personal items and a mirror on the desk, but not much else. The owner of the room sat to my right at a small wooden table, wearing pants and a sweatshirt that read "California" on the front. Unlike the several previous times when I'd seen her in uniform, this time, Colonel Kim looked very relaxed, sitting there with her hair hanging down, munching away at a bowl of noodles. A second bowl, with chopsticks at the ready, was on the near side of the table, steam rising from it.

Even though it was a peaceful scene, I thought it best to play everything straight until I knew exactly why she had called me there. I didn't want to end up like the last soldier who had been called to her quarters. So I walked up to the table, went to attention, and rendered a salute with a "Lieutenant Loveless reporting, Ma'am."

"*Anehaseyo*, Lieutenant," she said, mixing her English and Korean and, I noticed, chuckling to herself, and then added "sit down" in Korean. I didn't take to the bait, but remained standing at attention, as though not understanding what she'd said.

"You may stand if you want, Lieutenant," she said, returning to English, "but it is foolish. I am sure you know my language. I know many things about you. I know that your father was a member of the American military clique. You have three brothers and you went to Michigan University and you lived in Korea as a youth." Then she paused for a second, as I digested her words. "It was that time you learned to speak Korean, was it not?" she asked, reverting to her native tongue.

It seemed foolish to continue the ruse, since she obviously had learned that much about me, so I answered in her native tongue, "Yes, Ma'am. I know a little of your language." And I sat down at the table.

"Please eat," she said, gesturing towards the bowl of noodles. "I think you must be hungry."

Starving was more like it, since they fed us like mongrel dogs. I took hold of the chopsticks and dug in, wolfing down the hot noodles and soup.

She watched me carefully, no doubt entertained by the gusto with which I ate. As I neared the bottom of the bowl, she spoke again. "It is good that we can continue our talk. I have many things to ask you. It was difficult to do when the commander was here. He is gone now. But first, please do not think I am alone. Captain Soh waits behind that door," she said, pointing towards the door at the back of the hooch. "He will come if I call."

"Yes, Ma'am," I answered. I had no intention of trying anything anyway. Even if I overpowered her, what could I do then, with no weapon and no plan of escape?

"I say this because I know that you are a brave man," she continued. "And you are big. You may be tempted to take advantage of a small girl like me."

"I am not so stupid, Ma'am," I replied. "I know my situation. Thank you for the food."

She smiled at my reply and then went on. "You are the first American hero I have met."

"I'm no hero," I said, "just another prisoner."

"But you are a hero, Loveless-man," she replied, as she pulled out from underneath a pile of papers on the corner of the table a copy of the *Stars & Stripes* with my photo on the cover. "Even the criminal Nixon says so."

Well, the Witch had done her homework and had me again. Still, I thought it best to continue denial. I knew from experience that Asians are not impressed with people who blow their own horns. "I was very lucky," I said. "It was nothing."

"Perhaps," she answered, smugly I thought. "But to your countrymen, you are a hero. And now, you are my hero." At that, she rose from her chair and slowly walked past me and sat on the cot. "Please join me, my hero," she spoke invitingly, her hand patting the cot beside her. "I don't meet many brave men, and I think in your home country, you are not really loveless."

Only then did it finally dawn on me why I'd been brought to her cabin. Call me dumb if you will, but when you're a prisoner of war, your mind is on survival, not getting laid, and especially not by someone with a reputation as fierce as hers. But now that she'd made the opening, I was ready to do my part. Sure, I knew the military Code of Conduct forbids giving aid and comfort to the enemy, but I couldn't remember reading a thing about not having sex with them. Besides, what choice did I have? She was, after all, a higher-ranking officer.

My conscience thus clear, I went over and sat next to her on the cot. But even then I wasn't quite sure where to begin. It's not every day that a fanatical female communist asks you to bed; I didn't want to do anything to upset her. Fortunately, she was used to taking charge. "I hope you are as strong as you look, my Loveless," she purred, "slipping her hand down between my legs in a most distracting manner."

"I will do my best, my love," I answered, warming to the occasion and pulling her forward to kiss her full on the mouth. She took to it with gusto, thrusting her tongue in my mouth and clasping her hand behind my neck. *Right move*, thought I, pushing one hand underneath California to grab a handful of pleasure. But I had barely started to work when she backed away and sat there looking at me with those ebony eyes, her mouth open, and her tits rising up and down with each breath. For a second, I thought about Fitzgerald when he had enjoyed himself too much and thought, *Oh shit!* But the fear went away immediately as she reached down and pulled California over her head, revealing those perfectly shaped boobies. Then she followed up by standing up and sliding out of her pantaloons, leaving only a pair of white lace panties to cover her modesty. I'd thought she was well built, but only then did I realize how much I'd underestimated her. She wasn't that tall, to be sure, but I never saw a more perfect female body, and even at that age, I'd known plenty.

"Show me your strength," she whispered, reclining back onto the cot. That was enough for me. In a thrice, I stripped off my rag of a uniform and mounted up. Almost at once, I wished I hadn't. She was a tiger, clawing and scratching and screaming as we bounced first on the bed and then off onto the floor. She was easily the most vicious woman at lovemaking I've ever known. When we were finally through, my backside felt as though it had been whipped. I had aches and pains in places I'd never experienced before. But I was content and so was she, purring like a pussycat. "*Nola-umnida*," she said, which meant "that was wonderful."

I carried her back to the bed and held her in my arms, falling asleep soon afterwards, only to be awakened some hours later by a soft hand on my face and a voice whispering my name. I groggily came to and we went at it again, even more fiercely than the first time. By the time morning came, I was exhausted. I wasn't at my peak strength anyway, not after weeks of being a prisoner with barely enough to eat, but Miss Kim might have proven too much even at my best.

I stayed with her for more than one week, eating well, resting often, and getting all the sex I could handle. The only times I left her place were to go to the bathroom and once when I attended her weekly lecture on the evils of capitalism. Even then she had me sit apart from my comrades, all of whom looked at me with questions on their faces, except Mann, who tried to ignore me. It's possible, if there'd been air conditioning and a color TV, that I might still be hard at work in that little hooch.

She had boundless energy and an insatiable appetite for coupling. There were times I wanted to yell, "Enough already!" But I didn't dare refuse her. I'd seen what she did to Fitzgerald, and I remembered the story about the Black soldier. In fact, after several days there, as I began to feel more secure, I brought up the subject of the Black. She just looked me in the face and said simply, "He didn't please me," and left it at that. I didn't pursue the subject. I was just thankful that I seemed to please her.

She told me a lot about herself during that week. I learned that her full name was Myung-Mi Kim; that she'd traveled widely around the world, although not to the States; that she enjoyed Western films; and that, indeed, her father was some sort of high official with the North Korean government. She'd learned her English from an American tutor, she said, which I found strange since few Americans were known to have ever gone to North Korea.

At first, she was all formal, very much the communist, except when making love. As the days passed though, and we got to know each other better, she became more and more a woman. When the time came for me to return to my own hooch, I think she'd actually gone a bit soft on me, asking if I had enough to eat and if I were cold at night, the kind of things women do for their partners. I didn't take to her quite as much, liking my women to be softer and more pliable, but I never let on; I pretended to be overwhelmed by her beauty and my good fortune, which, in a way, I was.

There are some, I suppose, who might consider me a traitor if they learn what I did in that camp. But unless they've been a prisoner of war, as I have been several times, they haven't earned the right to criticize my actions. I've learned there's only one thing that counts when you're a POW, and that's coming home alive. Besides, I didn't give away any military secrets or rat on my fellow prisoners. And believe me, there were some who did, who really did collaborate with the enemy in the 'Nam. I was just doing what I had to do, even if I did enjoy it in the process.

Several times during my stay in Myung-Mi's hooch, the other Korean was present. The first time he saw me, he made a comment that sent her off. She pounced on him, slapping him across the cheek, yelling profanities and driving him into a corner of the room. He took it meekly like a whipped dog, apologizing for his impertinence, and left with his tail between his legs. From then on, whenever he saw me, he kept silent, but the look on his face whenever she wasn't watching showed that he didn't bare me much goodwill.

The day before the commander returned to the camp, I was sent back to live with the other prisoners. They were thrilled to see me and bombarded me with questions the moment I entered the big hut. I felt it best not to tell them the truth and reported, instead, that I'd been treated like a slave, cleaning and cooking and doing manual labor for her pleasure.

"Did she torture you?" asked Eddy, anxious to know every detail.

"Not really," I said, "except once in a while she took a switch to my back." I pulled up my shirt to show the nail scratches on my back.

"Fuckin' bitch," said Eddy, "taking advantage of a man like that."

Mann, as usual, sat off to one side just taking it all in. He was no doubt disappointed that I'd returned, but kept it to himself. Franklin was the surprise. Late that night, just before we turned in, he slid over to my mat and engaged me in small talk. We spent time talking about what had happened during my absence, and how Eddy's health seemed to have deteriorated. Then, towards the end, he let out with a question that caught me by surprise. "When you were with Colonel Kim," he said with a searching look on his face, "did she force you to do anything sexual?"

"Sexual? Good Lord, no," I answered quickly, "unless you call washing her feet each night sexual, or massaging her shoulders! She thinks she's some sort of queen, that one, and I was her man-servant! I slept on the floor without even a blanket to cover me."

"That's good, I mean that's good that she didn't treat you badly," he replied and away he went to his bed on the floor. After he left, I thought about it and remembered his comments the night I'd been called to her hooch and something that Myung-Mi had told me one evening—that she'd tried several white men before me but hadn't enjoyed them. It didn't take much to figure out that Franklin must have been her lover at some time and still had feelings, maybe even felt jealousy regarding her. He always called her "The Witch," and, while that was true to a point, he may also have been expressing his own anger over her rejection of him. I decided to be careful from then on whenever discussing Myung-Mi with him.

The next morning, we were fed a larger-than-normal breakfast and allowed to stay in our hooch instead of going to work. We speculated that the good treatment was in celebration of the commander's return, but Franklin said that hadn't happened before when the commander had gone away and returned, which meant something different was up. We stayed curious until near midday, when the guards came and ordered us out into formation.

When we fell out, the commander was already waiting, as well as Myung-mi and the other familiar faces. But there were several new Vietnamese soldiers, too, and someone else I'd hoped not to see again—Nguyen. The bunch of them were lined up in formation behind the commander, while the guards stood at attention along both ends of our line. It was the only time I'd seen them so formal since coming to the camp. I glanced over at Myung-Mi, who returned my look, but gave no hint as to what was up.

Once we took our place across from them, Doc came forward and started to speak. "Commander Hoang say good morning to esteemed prisoners of war. Today is special day. It is day to finish this prison camp. From today, you will go to north to live in very fine camp with other prisoners. Soon, I think, you will return to your home."

I felt the excitement flow through the five of us. Eddy grabbed my arm, tears in his eyes. To the side, I saw Mann grinning from ear to ear. It was the only time I'd ever seen him smile, and why not? It was the best possible news! We'd all known that peace talks were going on in Paris, but none of us had been so optimistic to think the end of the war would be reached so soon. In truth, of course, it would be another three years before any kind of terms were reached that would allow American prisoners to return home, but we didn't know that then. We just had the Doc's word that we might soon go home and that was enough. Then he continued.

"To make journey north," he said, "we have new uniform for you," and he waved to some guards standing alongside, who brought out a stack of clothes and placed them at our feet. "Please wear new uniform."

We looked at each other, still not believing what was happening, and then fell to our knees, rummaging through the clothing. Sure enough, there was a new pair of pants, a shirt, and even socks for each of us. We separated them and, with Doc's encouragement, began changing on the spot. I took off my shirt and trousers, after first emptying the contents of my pockets on the ground. There wasn't much—a P-38 can opener on a string of beads, the NVA medallion I'd found near the Laotian border on my first mission with Grovich, and Clay's small wallet.

I pulled on the new pants over my boots and stuck Clay's wallet in the pocket and had just picked up the P-38 when there was a shout from one of the Vietnamese, who ran forward and grabbed the medallion that was still on the ground. He examined it closely, turning it over in his hands. I heard him mutter something in a low voice and then he flew at me, shoving the medallion in my face, pushing me backwards and screaming a stream of invectiveness. I fell back, bewildered, and holding my hands in front of my face to fend him off. I heard the commander shout something, but the dink had lost his composure and just kept coming at me as I backed away. Finally, several of the guards grabbed his arms and kept him at bay so the commander could intervene.

For once Bashful wasn't calm. He shouted at the soldier and tried to force him to back down, but the dink just shoved the medallion in the commander's face and yelled something back. Bashful took the medallion from the soldier, and then he, too, observed it carefully, while the dink kept up his tirade, pointing at the medallion and then at me and talking so fast I couldn't pick up a word of what he was saying. By this time, the other Vietnamese had broken their ranks and gathered around the two antagonists. I looked over at Myung-Mi, hoping to get some idea of what was happening. But her face was a mask, so I could only stand back from the group, wondering what I'd done to cause such a commotion and fearing the worst. It didn't take long to find out. The commander finally got the crazy soldier to settle down somewhat and talk, although he was still plainly agitated. Then he handed the medallion to Doc, who walked up to me and asked, "Where you get this?"

I thought it best not to say I'd found it after an artillery strike on some dead gooks, so I said, "A friend gave it to me back in Chu Lai."

"When get?" he continued.

"Oh, about three months ago," I said, thinking fast on my feet and pretending to think hard on his question. "He owed me some money and gave me this for a souvenir instead."

"Where friend get medal?" asked Doc.

"I don't know," said I. "Why? Is it important?"

But Doc didn't answer. He gave a long blank look at my face and then went back into discussion with the commander. This time Myung-Mi joined in, but so did Nguyen, which wasn't reassuring. They talked for about five minutes and when they finished, Bashful pointed my way and voiced another order. Then Doc turned to me and said, "You not go to north now. We decide you later." Then he spoke to the guards, causing two of them to grab my arms and began leading me away.

I couldn't believe it; on the very day of my deliverance from that accursed place I was being separated from the others because of some stupid medallion that meant nothing to me! It was crazy, horrible! I had to stop it! I dragged my feet and struggled with the guards, yelling back at Doc or Bashful or anyone who would listen. "No! Wait! Wait! Where are you taking me? I didn't do anything! You can keep the damn medal! You can keep it! I don't want it! Franklin, tell them!" I protested, but to no avail. Behind me, the dinks had already turned back to the other Americans, who were back putting on their new clothes like nothing had happened.

They pulled me over to a small outdoor cage close to the hooches where the Vietnamese guards lived and pushed me in. I no quicker hit the dirt than I bounded back up and grasp the bars of the cell, imploring the guards to bring Doc or the commander or Colonel Kim. If someone would just listen to me, I was sure the whole mess could be straightened out. But the two guards just laughed at me and sat down under a nearby tree to keep out of the sun.

Seeing it was futile to talk to them, I sat down in the dirt and surveyed my new surroundings. I'd noticed the little cage my first day in camp; Franklin had said it was where they put prisoners who were being punished, but no one had been in it since my arrival. Now I was there, all because of some stupid medallion I'd picked up in the field. It was a simple enough cell, about ten feet square, surrounded by a fence about six feet high. It was made entirely of bamboo, but secured tightly. I probably could have broken out by ramming my body repeatedly against the bamboo poles, but that wouldn't do, what with two armed guards sitting twenty feet away and another dozen or more right around the corner.

Several hours later, I watched as the other Americans, escorted by most of the Vietnamese guards, were marched out from the POW camp, presumably headed for their new home up north. I watched them with tears streaming down my face, yelling at them as they left. "Wait! Wait! Don't leave me behind." I don't even know if they heard me, although I think they must have. Only Mann looked back, and then just for a second, before the group disappeared from sight into the forest. I was left clinging to my prison bars in the most dreadful state of mind, imagining they would all soon be free, back home in America, while I would be dead, just another statistic in a senseless, stupid war.

Here's some advice for anyone who may become a prisoner. Try to keep your mind focused on something positive. If you don't, you're sure to go crazy in short order. For me, sex is usually best. I close my eyes and imagine myself in an exotic setting, slowly seducing different women I've known in my life.

True, my situation doesn't change, but my mind stays clear and my body relaxes as best it can. Besides, thinking about women gives me something to live for.

Unfortunately, back in '69, I was little experienced at being a prisoner, so I spent that day conjuring up the most horrible fate for myself. I'd heard stories in my childhood about Americans being held by the North Koreans, and I envisioned myself growing old, digging ditches in Hanoi, my family long resigned to the fact that I'd died in a jungle prison camp. I had only one hope—Myung-Mi.

That hope flowered briefly in the early afternoon, when her lackey came up to the cage and passed a note through to me. As he did so, he smiled smugly and passed his finger slowly across his throat, a sign that didn't need translation. It was clear where his sympathies lay. Unfortunately, the paper reinforced his act. It read: *"Your crime is too great. There is no help. Confess and you may live. —Kim, Myung-Mi."*

I was dumbfounded. Just the day before, she'd been in my arms purring like a pussycat and now she'd thrown me to the dogs without so much as a "by your leave." Yet I felt sure about her feelings. What the note said didn't make sense. *I didn't even know what crime to confess to. If I can just get her to talk to me in person*, I thought.

I waved the paper at Dopey and said in Korean, "Please tell Colonel Kim I must talk to her. I want to confess." I realized he had no love for me, but also knew that he dare not deliver my message. After all, she'd asked for my confession.

"I will tell her," replied the big Korean, "in the morning. If you are still alive." He walked off like he'd just scored the winning touchdown.

Shortly thereafter, I had another visit, this time by Doc and Nguyen. The carwash owner said nothing, and didn't have to. He'd come along to gloat and watch me beg for my life. I didn't disappoint him. As soon as they drew near, I grasp the bars of the cage and pleaded with Doc, offering to do anything if they would just let me go away with the other Americans. Doc listened, but basically ignored my pleadings, as he had his own script to cite. "I must tell you," he said solemnly. "The medal you have very special. Give by President Ho Chi Minh to only few soldiers. That one belong to soldier from village close here. He great hero. He missing long time."

"But I didn't kill him damn it! I got the medal from someone else!" I cried, near hysterical.

"Maybe you not kill. But big crime. Someone must be punish. You the only one."

"Wait, I remember now!" I squealed. "Your hero isn't dead! My friend said he got the medal from a captured Vietnamese! Your hero must be alive in a prison camp, just like me! You could trade me for him! I can help do that!"

Doc gave me a hard look, repeated what I'd said to Nguyen, and for a minute, they discussed it among themselves. Then Doc turned back to me. "That cannot be," said he. "Hero of the revolution die before to lose medal."

"No! It's the truth!" I lied. "Take me back to Chu Lai! I promise to find your hero! You have my word! I'm an officer! We're not allowed to lie!" But my words were wasted. Nguyen was grinning widely, visibly enjoying my squawking, while Doc watched me with a look of disgust on his face. I didn't care. It didn't matter what they thought. I had to get out of there. "Please," I begged, dropping to my knees, "please, in God's name...."

But this only brought a retort from Doc. "Colonel Kim say you hero. But I think you no hero. You not proud officer." He turned and walked away, followed by Nguyen.

After they left, I sagged to the ground, weeping and shaking uncontrollably. I believe my mind finally gave way about then because I remember dreaming about Nguyen slowly roasting me to death over a flame while I kept repeating over and over that I loved his daughter, and that I wanted to marry her and take her home to Hawaii. In my delusions, I could see the two of us surfing on the North Shore, telling Vietnamese jokes while my family cheered us on and my mother...my mother! I could see her clearly. She was praying for me... she'd said so in her letters. Perhaps if I prayed, too, our combined prayers would save me, and I fell into all the hallelujahs and holy names I could think of, praising Mary and Jesus and Moses and Allah and Buddha and even Martin Luther King.

I'd been a poor Christian up to then, not believing in God, attending church only when forced to by my parents, and, once there, concentrating on girls instead of religion. Prayer, I had thought, was a waste of time. But even the basest of sinners finds religion when facing certain death. So I prayed that day, telling God that if He would get me out of that mess, I would devote the rest of my life to spreading his Word and living a life of modesty and virtue.

The pious will think me a hypocrite, crying to God like that after ignoring him for so many years. Perhaps I was, but how many men turn to God on their final day? Most, I'll wager. And who knows? Perhaps calling on the Lord did help because suddenly, I felt myself back in the cage and was aware of the presence of someone else. I spun around to find Snow White peering through the bars at me.

She'd come to bring my supper, but in my state of mind I imagined her as salvation itself, an angel sent by God. I had to let her know that I was a changed man, that I was no longer selfish and greedy, but was instead ready to do God's work. But how? She didn't speak English. *If only I could send a sign*, I thought. And then it came to me: Clay's wallet! I would show her Clay's wallet and explain how I had to go back to America to see his family! I'd promised to do that! It was my sacred duty! God couldn't let me die until I'd fulfilled my promise!

I reached in my pants and yanked out the wallet. I had to show it to her, to let her know my story was true, but I was so nervous, so shaken with fear and the Lord, that the wallet fell from my hands, spilling paper and photos on the ground. I tried to scoop up the contents, to show her, but fumbled that, too, mixing dirt in with everything else, all the while crying, "No! No! It's

Okay! It's Okay!" I must have looked the sight, sitting there on the ground, tears running down my face, jabbering on in a language she didn't even understand. She might well have thought I was crazy, which of course, I was, if only for a little while. But even if I wasn't a truly repentant sinner, she certainly was an angel. Snow White reached through the bars of the cage and calmed me by placing a soft hand on mine, causing me to look up and see her tender face staring back at me, with tears rolling down her cheek. In her other hand, she held one of the photos from the wallet—a black and white picture of a young woman and two small children. It must have been Clay's family. "Yes!" I cried. "Yes, I must go back to that family! I must tell them...."

She started to say something, but one of the guards shouted at us and started over, so she dropped the photo on the tray of food she'd brought and passed it into the cage. Then she was up and gone, holding her face as she ran.

I stayed alone the rest of the day, except for my ever-present guards. As night came with its cool weather, I slowly regained my senses and realized again the futility of my predicament. I found some kind of cloth bag lying in the dirt and pulled it over me and lay against the bars, trying my best to calm my mind. I must have fallen asleep because sometime later, I felt a tap on my shoulder and heard someone whisper my name. I jerked up with a start, pulling away. But the other person hovered over me, holding my shoulders down and calming me by softly speaking in English, "Lieutenant! Quiet! Quiet!" I caught my breath and leaned back to see who it was, and then I grabbed his arms and pulled closer to get a better look at his face and saw that it was Grumpy.

"You speak English?" I asked, bewildered.

"ARVN," he said, pointing at himself. "No talk now. Come. We go."

I couldn't have been more astonished if Nixon himself had shown up at the camp. It was hard to believe that Grumpy was a member of the South Vietnamese Army. He was one of the most feared of the guards, always threatening and taunting us prisoners. Besides, it didn't make sense that an ARVN soldier would, or could, stay under cover for that long. Surely, the dinks would have seen through him after a while. It was just too improbable. I shook off the bag and rose to my feet, and then it came to me—what if it was a trick? What if Grumpy was working with Nguyen and leading me to my death? He had moved to the cage door, but I held back, thinking how I might make a break for it and run away, and then, I saw a body on the ground, not five feet away. I approached and recognized that it was one of the guards, lying face up, mouth open.

"He dead," said Grumpy. "Come." And he passed out of the cage.

This time I followed, satisfied that he was telling the truth.

My relief at getting out of the little prison was short lived when I realized Grumpy was leading me straight towards the dink's living area. Again, the thought of a double cross went through my mind—if he was trying to help me, why were we walking into the lion's den? Most of the Vietnamese might be asleep, but there were always several guards on patrol. It would only take one of them to rouse the entire camp. Grumpy had a rifle, but that wouldn't be much good if they were on to us. I grabbed at his back, causing him to stop, and then gestured towards the far side of the camp. "That way," I whispered.

"*Punji*," he said, pointing in the direction I'd indicated, and then, "this okay," pointing back towards our front. He was a man of few words, but I understood his meaning. The back side of the camp was bordered by the river, which had the *punji* sticks along the bottom that Franklin had told me about. I'd seen some of their tips sticking up from the riverbed in the daylight, but at night, they would be hidden from view—at least until one of us stepped on one. If that happened, the escape would be over before it began. I knew Grumpy was right. The only way out of the camp was straight through the dink's living area and right out the front gate, which was never guarded. We just had to avoid being seen by any of the other Vietnamese. So we padded along softly in the dark, moving slow and staying close to the buildings, Grumpy in front and I close behind.

We were nearly to the main camp entrance when the sound of voices drew us up short. I knelt behind as Grumpy dropped to his knees and peered around the edge of a hooch to get a look at who was talking. I couldn't see them, but there were two different voices and they were getting louder, which meant they were coming our way. There was no sense waiting for an introduction. I took off back in the direction we'd just come, looking desperately for a place to hide, with Grumpy hard on my heels a second later. We hadn't gone far when a door opened in a building to our front and out stepped one of the dinks, causing us to stop and back into the shadow of the closest hut. Then we watched anxiously as he sat down on the steps of his hooch and lit up a cigarette, oblivious to us hiding less than twenty feet away.

It was a desperate situation. We couldn't go forward without being seen by the smoker and from behind two guards would be coming around the corner of the building next door in mere seconds. Grumpy realized our predicament and dropped to his knees, facing back towards the two approaching guards and quietly pulling the AK-47 off his shoulder. I looked up to heaven, made a silent prayer, and then crouched down behind him, ready to run as soon as the shooting started. And then I looked up again and was inspired by one of the best ideas of my life. That's saying a lot, when you consider that I've talked or tricked myself out of a number of ticklish situations over the years. But that night, I was brilliant.

By looking skyward, I'd realized we were hiding in the shadow of Myung-Mi's hut, which had a North Korean star on the door. It was a long shot, but rather than risk a gunfight with the guards, who clearly outnumbered us, I decided to try and pull off a sham. I tapped Grumpy on the shoulder and stood up behind him. "Come," I said, stepping out of the shadows with my hands held high. At first he gasped and didn't budge, probably thinking I was trying to surrender, which would have meant the end for him. Then I quietly said, "Colonel Kim," and started towards the stairs of her hut. At that, he saw what I was up to and fell in behind, his rifle pointed at my back.

Seconds later, two guards did, indeed, round the corner and reacted to my appearance by raising their weapons up to fire, but lowered them when they saw Grumpy. They came forward and said something to him, to which he replied, and then they continued on their way. Even the smoker in the next hooch, who had stood up and watched when the guards came, sat back down to finish his cigarette. As I'd hoped, they all thought Grumpy was taking me to see Myung-Mi. Everyone in camp knew she'd kept me in her room the week before, so they figured I'd been called back by her and didn't suspect we were trying to escape.

We walked straight up the steps of Myung-Mi's hut and knocked on the door. At first there was no response, but a second knock brought faint sounds from inside. Then the door suddenly opened and Myung-Mi was standing there, still buttoning the top of her uniform and looking at me as though she'd seen a ghost.

"*Mian hamnida*," I said, apologizing for disturbing her. For a long second, she just stared at me with a stern look on her face, like one might greet a salesman at the door. I began to fear she would turn us away, so I gave her a smile and said in Korean, "May I speak to you, my love?"

At that, she looked back at Grumpy with his rifle, said, "*Dro-osipsiyo*," and led us into the hut. Behind us, I could see the two guards strolling past the next building and continuing on.

As soon as Grumpy had closed the door behind us, Myung-Mi whirled to face me. "Why do you come here, Lieutenant? I can do no more to help you! Captain Soh told you this!" she lectured.

"I came to say good-bye, my dear," I replied calmly. "It would have been rude to leave the camp without saying farewell."

"Leave the camp!" she laughed. "What do you mean? You are not leaving this camp."

"Sorry to disappoint you, Colonel, but I have other plans," I replied and I stepped aside as Grumpy leveled his rifle at her stomach.

I should have anticipated her reaction, but didn't, probably because I surrender whenever someone aims a gun at me. Not Myung-Mi. She walked straight into the barrel of the rifle and screamed something at Grumpy in Vietnamese. It scared the bejesus out of me, but only for a second, then I grabbed the back of her head with one hand and covered her mouth with the other. She tried to turn on me, but I twisted her head away hard and threatened, "Shut up! I'll kill you myself if you do that again!" It was a bluff, but by then Grumpy had raised the point of his rifle up to her head. She saw that he was serious and I felt her relax in my hands. "This is not a game, Colonel," I said in a still-serious tone. "If you want to live, keep your mouth shut. Do you understand?" Her eyes glared at me above my hand, and then at Grumpy, and then back to me again, and she slowly nodded her head. I gave her a long, hard look and took my hand away from her mouth, ready to grab again at the slightest sound. But she didn't say a word. She just stood there, her chest heaving, one hundred ten pounds of fury ready to rip my eyes out. "We just want to get away. You won't be killed if you keep quiet."

"You will not kill me," she spit back, her confidence returning.

"Perhaps," I replied, pointing at Grumpy, "but he will. Now wait here." I walked to the back of the room where a clothesline was strung across one side. I ripped it off the walls and used it to tie Myung-Mi's hands behind her back while she muttered some not-for-public Korean phrases. Then I forced her down on the floor and ran the clothesline beneath her butt and secured it around her ankles. She was trussed up tighter than a pig at a luau.

"Must keep quiet," said Grumpy, who came up with a cloth that we jammed in her mouth and tied behind her head so she couldn't scream for help.

Before I did though, she managed to blurt out one final threat. "I will find you, Loveless. You cannot hide, Coward."

"I understand your anger, my dear," I answered, tightening the rag. "It must be difficult for you to be around men who aren't helpless prisoners. But there are far better women waiting for me back home, so if you don't mind…" and I gave her teat a squeeze, "I'll be going now." She cursed me from beneath the gag and tried to lash out with her feet, but only succeeded in falling over. Truth be told, she was an attractive woman and a damn good lover. But I didn't feel like giving her any credit just then, and after all, she was a communist. That done, I started for the door, anxious to be on my way again. But Grumpy held back.

"Wait," he said, grabbing my arm. "I go see gate. Come back soon."

"We go together," I replied, somewhat anxiously.

"No, Lieutenant. I go. See no guards. Then come get you."

Well, I didn't like the idea of sitting in that room alone with Myung-Mi, even tied up like she was. But what Grumpy said made sense. By himself, he wouldn't arouse suspicion. He could make sure the coast was clear before we made another try for the front gate. So I agreed and he slipped out the door alone.

For the next few minutes I waited for his return, doing my best not to look in Myung-Mi's direction. It's damned unnerving knowing someone was just a few feet away, giving you a death stare. I didn't like it one bit and was starting to wonder if Grumpy was ever coming back when there was a quiet knock on the front door. I opened it easily, but instead of Grumpy, I found myself looking up at the big Korean. His eyes bulged out at the sight of me, and he grunted out an "Ahhh," as he lost his composure. I started to slap the door in his face, but was too slow. I noticed his glance go behind me, to where Myung-Mi was securely tied on the floor, and he let out a bellow, charging headlong into the room and knocking me off my feet.

We bowled over together in the middle of the floor, but as we did, I twisted just enough to the side so that I regained my feet first. As he tried to rise, I kicked him in the side of the head and sent him back down with a cry, and then I scrambled to find a weapon—something—anything to hit him with, because there was no doubt he was the stronger of us two. I took hold of a table chair and smashed it downwards at him, but the Korean moved fast so that it bounced off his side with little impact and splintered on the floor. I threw a piece of the chair that was left in my hand at him and turned to flee for the door, but he was faster, grabbing one of my feet out from under me and bringing me down with a crash. I tried to rise, but he pulled me back and in a flash was atop me, pushing me down on my back, his hands round my throat, and his body weighing me to the floor. I struggled and pounded with my fists at his face, leering above just inches away, but he held on tight. I twisted furiously to escape his grasp, but it was hopeless. My eyesight began to fade and I could feel the life leaving my body as I gasped for breath. Then suddenly, my face was sprayed with something wet and I felt the Korean loosen his grip and fall away.

I rolled to one side, gulping in air and looked up to see Grumpy kneeling down next to me. Behind him, the Korean lay a few feet away, a knife protruding from the back of his neck and out through the front, with a steady stream of blood dripping on the floor.

"You okay, Lieutenant?" asked Grumpy, pulling me up to a sitting position.

"Yes. Yes, I'll be fine in a minute. What took you so long?" I answered, still gasping for air, just as I noticed that Myung-Mi had rolled herself across the floor and was nearly over to the front door that was wide open. Grumpy saw her in the same instance and jumped over to slam the door and then drag her back to the middle of the room, while she struggled like a demon against his efforts. He was clearly the stronger though, and once he got her against the back wall, he tied her to one of the corner stakes that held the hooch together.

As he finished tying her down and my breathing returned to normal, I asked, "How's the gate?"

"Gate okay. We go now," said Grumpy matter-of-factly as he started for the door.

I rose to my feet and followed, but turned to Myung-Mi one last time. "By the way," I said, looking down at her, "I went to Michigan State, not Michigan." And then I passed from the hooch, closing the door behind. Given who she was, I was confident the guards would not suspect anything or check her hooch for many hours. By the time they found her tied to the floor, we would have been long gone. And Grumpy was right. This time, as I followed him towards the front gate, the coast was clear and we walked straight out the camp without so much as seeing anyone else.

It didn't take long after we left the compound before we entered the jungle and veered off on an easterly direction on one of several trails. It was all too easy, but certainly understandable, what with the only prisoner in camp supposedly tucked away with his Korean lover, the dinks just let their guard down, so to speak. I'm sure someone had to answer for it later on, but that wasn't my problem. At that moment, I was jubilant and wanted to cover as much ground as possible before we were discovered missing from the camp.

We hadn't gone more than a minute in the woods when a shadowy figure, carrying a rifle, stepped out in front of us on the trail. I gave a yelp and turned to flee back up the path, but Grumpy grabbed me by the shirt and held on, saying, "It okay! It okay! My friend! She my friend!"

I stopped and glanced over his shoulder and saw that the strange apparition, now walking towards us, was a woman, and not just any woman. It was Snow White, dressed in black and armed with an AK-47 and another rifle of some kind. Grumpy greeted her warmly and they spoke for bit, while I looked around nervously for others. It was difficult for me to think of her in that context as she'd always been such a sweet, young, innocent thing. I couldn't imagine her carrying a weapon, much less taking a risk by helping me to escape. As they finished exchanging words, she came over to me and, looking up into my face, placed her hand on my cheek and said something soft in Vietnamese.

"She say she help Lieutenant get you family," said Grumpy, and for a second I thought he meant that she wanted to make a family, which goes to show how my mind works.

Then I remembered the photos in Clay's wallet and knew what she meant. She was going to help me get back to the family in the photos, which she took to be mine. I smiled back at her and said, "*Cam on ong*," which was the basic "thank you" in Vietnamese. I really meant it. I could see then that I had her to thank for my freedom as much as Grumpy. She must have gone to him after having seen the photos of "my family," and together, they had plotted the escape.

We didn't linger long to renew old friendships. Snow White kept the one weapon but handed me the AK-47 and a light bag, which I found to be full of food, and then we were off, following a narrow trail that cut through the forest. We went single file, Grumpy in the lead, with me in the rear and Snow White between us. It was hard walking through the bush in pitch dark, but we traveled as fast as possible before stopping to rest some hours later. Not surprisingly, I was exhausted and very much welcomed the break. I'd just gone through one of the most hair-raising days of anyone's life and wasn't exactly in the best of shape after living weeks as a POW.

We sat down in a small grove of trees and I leaned back against a big, broad-leafed plant and soon fell asleep, waking sometime later to find a light rain splashing on my face and Snow White warmly snuggled up against me and Grumpy snoring away across a small clearing. It was all very pleasant, and danger seemed far away, so I pulled her closer and shut my eyes again.

When I finally did wake up, the sun was already high above the trees and my companions were snacking on the food Snow White had packed. I joined them for a bite and then we were off again, headed eastward, trudging up and down and around small hills thick with vegetation. But unlike the night before, we were now pestered by millions of bugs whirring about, doing their best to feast on the slow-moving humans. They probably were there during the darkness, too, but either the rain drove them off or they'd been sleeping themselves. In the daylight, they certainly were a major annoyance.

The other thing I noticed in the morning light was that my forearms were red with dozens of small cuts from the elephant grass and thorns that crowded the trail. During the night, I'd felt myself getting nicked as we walked, but wasn't aware of how badly until I saw my arms in the daylight. Fortunately, the cuts weren't painful, and since the Vietnamese shirt I wore was small, with sleeves that only went down to my elbow, I just did my best to keep my arms clear of the sharp plants while we walked. At least in the daylight, I could see and avoid the nasty things.

We covered a lot of territory that morning, probably more than five miles through the jungle, which wasn't bad considering the primitive trail we followed. We rarely spoke as we moved, stopping only a few minutes every once in a while to rest and listen for anyone who might be pursuing us. In what must have been early afternoon, we came upon a stream running through a small valley and decided it was time for a longer break. Confident that it was fresh water coming down from the mountains to our rear, all three of us drank lustily from the stream and then we waded in, clothes on, and immersed ourselves in the cool water.

I sat there with water up to my chest for what seemed like a long time, washing blood from the nicks in my arms and rejoicing in the fact that the bugs didn't seem to like sitting down on wet skin. Grumpy and Snow White were enjoying it even more, splashing water on each other and laughing out loud like two little kids.

We might have stayed there longer, but a rifle shot suddenly broke the stillness of the day and brought us to our feet. It came from our rear, the direction we'd just been a short time before. I looked over at Grumpy with a question on my face, and as I did so, a second shot rang out, this time from the opposite direction where we were headed. In unison, the three of us clambered out of the stream, grabbed our weapons, and started making tracks parallel to where we were and away from both gunshots. We all recognized the sound of an AK-47 and knew someone was close by.

We scrambled through a thick forest of vines for about ten minutes before emerging in an area of less dense vegetation. We could get more solid footing in that open area, but our path was blocked by a hill directly in front that rose up several hundred feet. Proceeding up the hill meant we would be in open country and exposed to enemy eyes. But with no other real choice, we started up and around the corner of the hill, staying as low to the ground as possible. We went perhaps another hundred yards, with me falling slightly behind the other two—partly from fatigue and partly from the fact that I still had one leg that had never quite healed.

Snow White and Grumpy were racing past several very large boulders on the side of the hill when they suddenly stopped dead in their tracks and sunk to their knees, causing me to nearly fall over them as I arrived seconds later. I caught myself with one hand on the ground and bounced up ready to continue my flight, but Grumpy grabbed at me and pulled me back to the ground, going, "Shuu, shuu." My eyes darted to and fro, searching for what had made them stop, but I saw and heard nothing. When I looked to Snow White, she pointed up the hill to our front, but I still saw nothing other than a line of trees, perhaps fifty to sixty yards away. Then the faint sound of voices floated down from above, and soon after, I made out shadows moving through those same trees. It was people all right, and from the sound of it, there were a number of them—coming straight at us.

"Go back," I urgently whispered to Grumpy, grabbing him by the arm and turning to look back down the hill. But no sooner had the words escaped my lips than a familiar sound came up from down below that I'd heard many times on patrol in thick woods. People were coming up the hill, hacking away at the thick vines we'd struggled through just minutes before.

We were trapped, with dinks before and behind, herding us, like hunters on a wild animal safari. We couldn't go forward and we couldn't go back. I frantically looked around and saw that the only way out seemed to be sideways, down the hill to our left, where the jungle again grew thick with trees. Once there, we might be able to avoid detection and get away. But getting there wouldn't be easy because it meant running over open ground for several minutes and exposing ourselves to the soldiers coming down the hill, who would definitely have a clear field of fire. Still, I thought, at least it was a chance. If we sat still, we'd either be dead or prisoners in minutes, and I didn't relish the thought of either of those options.

Grumpy must have had the same thoughts, and why not? Sure, I was an American, a foreign invader who had been scheduled to die and then had escaped from their own prison camp. But in the eyes of the VC, Grumpy would be viewed even worse—he was one of their own, a traitor who had gone over to the enemy. They would most certainly make a meal of him if we were caught. I turned my head to tell him we should run down to the trees and found him sitting back on his haunches with his eyes closed, his arms crossed in front of his chest, humming a tune. It was downright weird! I was wetting my pants with fear, and he sat there calmly, droning away on some stupid song!

I was sure he'd lost it and was about to run for it by myself when he abruptly stopped humming and opened his eyes. He looked at Snow White and then pulled her close and whispered something in her ear. Then he turned to me and said, "Two minutes. You wait. You go trees. You okay." And he pointed at the thicket down the hill that I'd been eyeing.

"What do you mean?" I asked. "What are you going to do?"

"Two minutes," was all he answered, and he raised his hand with two fingers extended. Snow White touched the palm of his hand with hers, and for just a second, they searched each other's face. Then he began crawling away from our position to the right, moving across the ground like a snake. I watched him, wondering what the devil he was up to, until only his boots and legs were visible, and then they, too, disappeared from sight. That was when it struck me that he might have played the two of us for fools. *What if he'd de-*

serted, I thought, *leaving us to be caught by the Vietnamese while he slunk away to safety?*

I wasn't about to take any chances. I got down on the ground to crawl after Grumpy, waving at Snow White and urging her to come on. But she took hold of my ankle and held on, chattering away fast in Vietnamese. I didn't get a word of what she was saying, and didn't care to. "You don't understand," I wailed, "we'll be killed if we…!" I didn't finish the sentence because an AK-47 off to our right began blasting away.

Instinctively, I looked for the shooter and realized that someone was firing an AK-47 all right, but he wasn't shooting at us. In fact, the shots seemed to be coming from the direction Grumpy had just gone, and from above, I could hear people shouting. It didn't seem possible, but it looked like the fool was single-handedly firing up the hill at the advancing dinks. For a moment I just watched the scene, not believing he would do something so stupid! Then I became aware of Snow White tugging at my leg and going on like crazy, trying to get my attention. I glanced back and she pointed down at the groove of trees and only then did I realize what was happening. Grumpy was attracting the attention of the dinks, taking their fire and giving us a chance to escape.

It was all the encouragement I needed. In an instant, I was up and running, my feet flying over the ground, the pain in my leg gone, or, more likely, not noticed. I hit the tree line with a fury and plunged right on into the forest until I fell to the ground out of breath. I crouched there on all fours, my rifle slung out on the ground beneath me, gasping for breath, when suddenly, there were footsteps breaking through the woods behind me. I fell to one side and was grappling for the gun, as Snow White burst into view and collapsed on the ground a few feet away.

We both lay there, panting hard, for what seemed like a long time. Behind us, back on the hill, we could still hear the guns firing, which meant Grumpy was yet engaged, holding off the bad guys. Snow White's full attention was in that direction, and I thought then, and still do, that she was considering going back to help him. I was more certain of it when I caught my breath after a bit and rose to my feet to go farther into the forest. She stayed on the ground, still facing the hill behind and listening intently to the gunfight. I could feel her reluctance to move on, so I took hold of her hand and spoke to her gently, saying that we had to leave there, that going back would just mean our deaths, too. She didn't understand my words, but I'm sure she understood my meaning. She wasn't happy, but after a bit came to her feet and fell in behind, following me into the woods. It was five, maybe ten minutes later that the sound of gunfire ceased. I glanced at Snow White and saw tears in her eyes. She knew that Grumpy had undoubtedly met his Maker.

The two of us walked steadily the rest of that day, always keeping the sun to our backs, and keeping to the densest parts of the forests. That night, we slept under another large tree, huddled together against the coolness of the night. Snow White was warm and soft, but I didn't make a move on her. We were both tired beyond belief, but more importantly, she was clearly shook up at losing Grumpy and I wasn't about to do anything that would alienate the one person I needed just then.

The following day was more of the same, a sparsely populated countryside that was hot and bug infested, but this time it was a bit tougher because we were hungry, having run out of food nearly a day earlier. We had already gone three to four hours on foot that morning when we stumbled across a large tree that Snow White clambered up and threw down some kind of fruit. It was dried up, something awful and tasted like rubber, but at least it was filling. Afterwards, we made better time.

Several times that day, airplanes had flown over our position as we moved steadily eastward. They were mostly jets, but once, a C-130 lumbered across the sky and then came back several times in a lazy circle as if looking for something. I thought hard about how we could signal them, like starting a fire to get their attention, but was concerned about drawing attention to ourselves in case the VC were nearby, so I let it go. Then, in early afternoon, as we neared the top of yet another steep hill, I heard the faint but distinctive sound of a helicopter.

I couldn't tell which direction it was coming from, but the chopper was definitely headed our way, because the sound of its blades snapping through the air was growing louder and louder. I stopped in place and searched the sky, but the trees were tall and thick, blocking most of my view, which also meant there was almost no chance they could spot us down below. I looked frantically around for a way to signal the chopper and saw what looked like a clearing further up the hill.

A surge of energy went through me and I sprinted towards the open area, desperate to reach it so I could try and signal the helicopter crew. I ran up and up, with the noise of the chopper steadily growing louder, and just as I emerged from the trees, a Huey shot by directly overhead, only a few hundred feet above. "Wait! Wait!" I hollered, firing my rifle into the air, hoping against hope that the crew might hear the gunshot. But no such luck. The chopper kept on its course, going over the top of the next ridgeline, the sound of its engine growing fainter and fainter until it disappeared from sight.

I was still there, standing in the middle of the clearing, watching the distant ridge top, when Snow White caught up to me. She put her hand on my shoulder, and when I turned to face her, I felt wetness on my cheek. I wiped it away with my hand and realized it was from my own tears. My distress at having come so close to being rescued was obviously very emotional. I pulled Snow White to me for a hug and might have stood there feeling sorry for myself a long time, but my grief was interrupted by the whine of bullets zipping past us, followed seconds later by the sound of gunfire. The crew of the Huey hadn't spotted us, but someone else had. The two of us went to the ground just as another round of bullets whizzed past, and then crawled behind a small mound of dirt to hide.

From the sound of it—the shots were too random—there were probably not more than two or three people shooting at us. I looked towards the top of the small clearing, as it went up the hill, and saw first one and then another person in tan clothing jump up and run forward a short distance. That confirmed their number was small and told me they were probably VC. A large group, or even a small regular NVA unit, would have just come down and blasted us out. These guys were working their way down to us slowly so as to avoid casualties.

But even if there were only two of them, and I felt sure there were more, it was just a matter of time before they cornered us and we were either captured or killed. We had to do something, and do it quick, if we were going to get out of there. I fired off a few rounds to let the dinks know we were armed and then frantically looked about for someplace to run. I didn't see much choice. The only way out was back down the hill, to the trees we'd just left. They were thick enough that we might slip away yet again. But just like the day before, if we got up and ran for the woods below, we would be out in the open and easy targets for our friends up the hill. We could try and crawl there, but that would only work if someone provided cover for us while we went slowly along the ground. "Here's where we need Grumpy," I said to myself, and then I was struck by another brilliant idea.

I took Snow White by the arm. "Wait! Two minutes! You wait," I said, pointing at myself and the trees below and then holding up two fingers, just as Grumpy had the day before. I then took the hand that was holding her weapon and raised it to imply that she should shoot at the guys on the hill, which would, of course, give me some cover to reach the trees. She nodded in agreement, sure that I had a plan like Grumpy's that would get us out of there. I gave her a brave smile and then was off on my belly, crawling to the thick growth below.

It took me several minutes to get inside the woods and up on my feet, out of view from above. Then I was off as fast as I could, running parallel to the clearing, while keeping inside the tree line. I was sure that once they caught Snow White, the dinks would assume I'd fled straight down the hill, which was the easiest and most logical escape route. By going sideways, I figured on flanking around behind them and buying myself some time. How much time would depend on how long Snow White could hold them off and how long they searched for me in the forest below the hill.

I suppose there are some who will think the worst of me when they read this account. They'll say that I had no honor, that I ran off and deserted someone who had risked her life to save mine. But I've never lost sleep worrying about do-gooder bleeding-heart types. Few of them have ever been in such a desperate spot, or I'll wager they might have done the same thing. For me, it wasn't a question of honor. It was survival, plain and simple. Besides, I was sure then, and still am, that Snow White was not in any danger of being killed by the VC. She was Vietnamese and could always say that I'd forced her to help me. Why wouldn't they believe her? She was young and a woman. I, on the other hand, was an American and would surely have been killed if caught. I'm sure she was quite upset when I didn't reappear to help her escape, but that afternoon, with death in pursuit, her feelings were the least of my worries.

I went a good mile or so inside the trees, steadily circling around below the top of the hill, in an attempt to put space between me and the VC. Only when it felt safe did I ventured out into open ground and again start climbing up towards the ridge. That took a while, but in time, I went over the top without trouble and quickly descended down the far side.

For the next several hours I plodded on, following a narrow canyon filled with trees and surrounded by high cliffs on both sides. Certain the dinks would come in my direction once they realized I'd given them the slip, I kept constantly moving. It was late afternoon before I saw another human being, and again, it was a most unexpected sight.

After leaving the canyon, I crossed a shallow mountain stream and stopped for a few moments to cool off before heading off into more open country that lay beyond. As I did so, I again heard the sound of an engine. This time, it sounded like it was on the ground and not that far off. Curious at what kind of a vehicle it might be, I got out of the water and went back into the woods, cautiously moving towards the sound. After a short time, I came upon an opening in the trees and crawled forward to get a view at what was making the noise. What I saw sent my heart pounding! There in the middle of a small field, several hundred feet away, sat a Huey with several of the crew walking around outside. It was the most beautiful sight of my life!

I ran from the woods towards the chopper as fast as my tired legs would move, shouting at them to wait for me! But my mouth was dry and my voice practically gone from the last two days on the run. What the helicopter crew saw was a poorly dressed man, armed with a rifle, running towards them and yelling! That was apparently enough to frighten them because I watched in horror as the crew scrambled back aboard and the pilot revved up the engine. The blades on top began to rotate faster and I realized that in a few moments they'd be off the ground, leaving me behind. I threw the rifle to the ground and ran with both hands above my head, so they could see I meant no harm. But it did no good; before I was halfway across the clearing, the chopper rose into the air, rotated in a circle, and took off above the trees.

I screamed at them, imploring them to stop, but there was no chance they could hear me. I fell to the ground and pounded the dirt, yelling after the chopper, "Why? Why did you go?" It just didn't make sense that they would they flee once I'd thrown down my weapon.

My question was answered a few seconds later as the thumping of the Huey's blades began to grow louder instead of more distant. I looked up and saw that the chopper had reversed course and was coming back in my direction, but with its guns blazing. I was sure they were shooting at me and went to the ground behind some tall weeds, just as a rocket from the chopper screeched overhead and exploded well behind me. I turned to see what it had hit and saw several pajama-clad men had entered the clearing and were firing back at the chopper. They were the target, not me!

I thought about my rifle, but realized it would have meant going back towards the pajama men, even if I could find it. That would have been suicide, so I forgot the rifle, jumped to my feet, and began running across the clearing. I wanted to get as far away as possible while the dinks were engaged with the helicopter. From somewhere, I found a reserve of energy that helped me fairly fly across the ground towards the woods on the opposite side. They were coming up fast when suddenly the earth exploded nearby and a torrent of dirt splashed in my face and I felt myself flying through the air.

When I came to some time later, it was to a blur of sounds and feelings. I was cold and the ground was vibrating with a loud constant thumping. But worst of all, someone was hitting the side of my head with something hard. When I tried to raise my hands to ward off the blows, I found that I not only couldn't move them, they hurt something awful. I blinked my eyes open only to find myself lying on the floor of a helicopter, my head banging the metal grating every time we hit a bump in the air; my hands were bound tightly with some kind of tape and tied by rope to my feet, which were also taped together. I rolled to my side and felt another sharp pain as I propped myself up against the chopper wall. My head was spinning with lights and sounds and I couldn't understand why I was tied up.

Then I became aware of men talking just a few feet away. I looked around and saw three men in an open doorway. Two of them were Americans, laughing and gesturing and enjoying themselves. The third was Vietnamese and, like me, bound hand and foot. He was chattering on as fast as he could, most likely pleading for his life, since he sat perched on the edge of the open door. The two GIs didn't understand what he was saying, much less care. They were having too much fun tormenting the poor fellow.

"What's that you say?" said the smaller of the two Americans. "You don't like my friend here? Whatd'ya think about that, Bob? He doesn't like you!"

"He doesn't?" replied the bigger one. "And here I am trying to give him flying lessons. How's that for gratitude, Al?"

"I don't think he appreciates your help," replied Al sarcastically.

"Well then, he can just learn to fly on his own," said the tall one, and to my horror, he put his boot on the Viet's side and pushed him out the door. I could hear the dink scream for several seconds before he faded out.

I was stunned. I'd heard stories about VC prisoners being pushed from helicopters but never believed them. Yet it had just happened right in front of me. I looked down at the chopper's floorboards, shaking my head to erase the picture of it from my mind, when an even greater horror struck me—they thought I was Vietnamese! That's why I was tied up! And why not? I'd lost weight and gained a considerable tan from being outdoors so much and my clothes were definitely Vietnamese. To them, I was just another captured dink.

I recoiled at the thought, pulling back against the chopper wall, and looked up at the two Americans just as the small one said, "Hey, the other one is awake."

"Are you ready to meet your maker, gook?" said the big guy, sliding over and leering down at me.

"You stupid jerk! Can't you see I'm an American?" I shouted. "I'm an American officer! You just rescued me! Get me back in one piece. You'll be heroes to the whole world!"

He pulled back, with his mouth wide open and his eyes popping out. Then the short one bent over, looked in my face, and said, "Jesus, Bob, this gook speaks English."

Thus ends the Vietnam memoirs of Colonel Loveless...

Glossary

AO, Area of Operation

APC, Armored Personnel Carrier – an armored vehicle that could carry up to a platoon of infantry soldiers, often equipped with a .50-caliber machine gun

ARVN, Army of the Republic of Vietnam

Ba-Moui-ba, Vietnamese beer

Ba-moui-lam, Vietnamese for lover or playboy

Carwash, a house of prostitution near American military bases in Vietnam

Charlie, a slang term for the Vietcong

Chieu Hoi, the Vietnamese "open arms" program to encourage the enemy to surrender

CO, commanding officer

CQ, Charge of Quarters – the officer assigned to oversee and barracks when soldiers lived

Di-Di, Vietnamese for "scram"; also, di-di mau

Dinks, a slang term for the Vietcong

DMZ, Demilitarized Zone that separated North and South Vietnam

Dust off, the US Army's medical helicopter evacuation system

FNG, fucking new guy, a slang term

Gooks, a slang term for the Vietcong

Grunt, an infantryman

Haole, the Hawaiian word for "foreigner," usually used to note a Caucasian

IG, Inspector General – Army judicial investigator

KIA, killed in action

KP, Kitchen Patrol – persons assigned to clean army kitchens

LZ, Landing Zone – a large, cleared-off area, often on a mountaintop, that allows helicopters to land safely; frequently, LZs in Vietnam were headquarters for infantry and artillery companies, batteries and battalions

MACV, Military Advisory Command Vietnam – the highest American military headquarters in the war

MEDEVAC, acronym for "medically evacuated"

MIA, Missing in Action

Nuoc Mam, a Vietnamese sauce made from fermented fish

NVA, North Vietnamese Army – the NVA were the "regular" full-time soldiers from North Vietnam, as opposed to the VC or Vietcong

OCS, Officer's Candidate School – the army has several of these to train new officers in various specialty areas such as infantry, armor, engineer, and artillery

OD, officer of the day

PAO, an army Public Affairs Officer – a PR person who handles the media for the military (later in his career, Loveless served as a PAO)

Point Man, the lead soldier cutting a path through dense vegetation in a line of soldiers

Punji, stake; razor sharp bamboo stakes sometimes coated with poison and usually hidden under the ground or water

PX, post exchange

REMF, slang for rear echelon motherfucker

ROTC, Reserve Officer's Training Corps

R&R, rest and recuperation – soldiers in Vietnam were allowed one week of R&R during their year-long tour, often to such places as Hong Kong, Hawaii, Thailand, and Australia

RTO, a radio telephone operator in an infantry unit – this person was key to supplying artillery and airpower support during battles with the enemy

Silver Star, one of America's highest military awards for valor in combat

Stars & Stripes, the military newspaper, published in Tokyo and delivered to American soldiers in Vietnam (later in his career, Loveless was assigned as deputy publisher of the newspaper)

TAC, tactical officer – someone, usually in the grade of captain, who trains candidates at the various US Army officer schools

Tieu-uy, Vietnamese for 2nd lieutenant

WIA, wounded in action

XO, executive officer

Notes

Americal Division	Formed in New Caledonia during World War II, the Americal saw action in a number of Pacific battles during that war. It was reactivated in 1967 in Vietnam and deactivated again in 1972. The Americal had three light infantry brigades under its wing, the 196th, the 198th and the 11th. Its area of operations stretched from the South China Sea to the Laotian border and south from Danang for about 100 miles.
Bien Hoa	The large US military airfield in Vietnam; located close to Saigon. Bien Hoa was perhaps the world's busiest airport in the late 1960s in terms of daily takeoffs by fixed and rotary wing aircrafts.
Chu Lai	A coastal city about 40 miles south of Danang that served as headquarters for the Americal Division.
Division	A large Army unit, comprising about 20,000 soldiers in the American army. Divisions have smaller units broken down into brigades, battalions, companies, and platoons. Battalions are the basic fighting unit of the army, with four companies each. Most companies have about 100 soldiers assigned, divided into three platoons.
Fort Benning, Georgia	The US Army's Infantry School headquarters. Ft. Benning is home for the army's officer and non-commissioned officer infantry training and also for the army's airborne training.

Fort Dix, New Jersey	The army's largest East Coast training facility for new recruits.
Helicopters	The most common helicopters found in Vietnam were the Huey, used to transport small numbers of men and supplies; the Chinook, used to ferry large numbers of men and materiel; the Cobra, a two-passenger gunship strictly used for combat; and the Loach, a small, fast observation helicopter. All of these had official designations but were known by their nicknames.
Kit Carson Scout	Kit Carsons were former Vietcong soldiers who had defected to the other side and worked with the American and South Vietnamese forces. Because of their knowledge of the enemy, they were highly prized counterparts for the Americans.
Korean military	Three large units, comprising nearly 49,000 South Korean soldiers, served in Vietnam as allies of the Americans from 1964 until 1973. They were reported to be courageous fighters, much feared by the Vietcong.
Yokota Air Force Base	Located 20 miles west of Tokyo, Yokota has been the main American refueling base for aircrafts serving the Far East since the late 1940s.
Weapons	The M16 was the standard American infantryman weapon during the war, just as the Russian-built AK-47 was used by the Vietcong and North Vietnamese. The two weapons made distinctly different sounds during combat, making it possible for a veteran to recognize one or the other instantly. In addition to the M16, American units also carried M60 machine guns and M79 grenade launchers into combat.

CPSIA information can be obtained at www.ICGtesting.com
Printed in the USA
LVOW13s1515241013

358456LV00017B/945/P